THE SHADOW KNIGHT

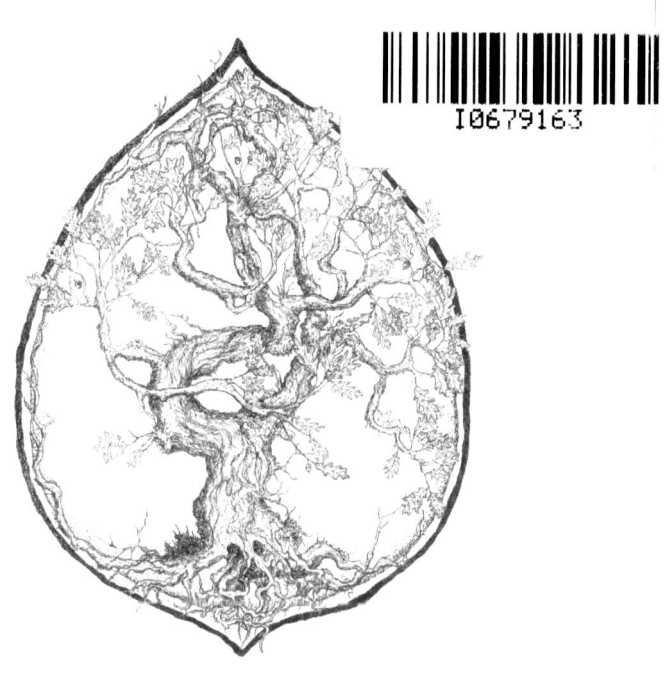

I0679163

A SHADOW KNIGHT NOVEL, BOOK ONE

A Twiin Entertainment Book
Books by Jason L. McWhirter

Cavalier Trilogy
The Cavalier
The Rise of Malbeck
Glimmer in the Shadow

The Steel Lord Series
BannerFall
Banner Lord

Non-Fantasy
The Life of Ely

Published by Twiin Entertainment
www.twiinentertainment.com
Copyright © Jason L. McWhirter
Library of Congress
All rights reserved
Cover Art by Mario Teodosio
Inside cover art by Kathryn Bronstad
Map by Jason L. McWhirter

AUTHOR'S NOTE

This is a work of fiction. Names, characters, places, and incidents are the product of the author's imagination or are used fictitiously, and any resemblance to actual persons, living or dead, business establishments, events, or locales is entirely coincidental.

Dedication

I would like to dedicate this book to my little furry boy, Macalan, who passed away this year from an enlarged heart. He was only three years old and he meant the world to my wife and me. We will miss his daily greetings at the door with his toy, his evening sprint to our backyard tree, and nightly cuddling as he wiggles his little body under the sheets. He was a great dog, and my constant friend and companion. He will be missed. RIP little buddy!

Author's Note

My plan for the Shadow Knight novels is for them all to be stand-alone stories about Jonas as Shyann's Shadow Knight, and potentially including in those stories some of the old characters from the Cavalier Trilogy. With that in mind, I think it still makes sense to read them in order, as they are written. I hope you enjoy them.

PROLOGUE

The odor of damp leaves and dirt occupied Jonas's senses as he watched the group of men below. He loved the smell. It reminded him of the earth and its beauty, corroborating why he did what he did, protecting the lands from anything that threatened to destroy such magnificence. He laid on his stomach in the bushes, nestled amongst the leaves and branches looking through a small hole, probably an animal trail. He had a direct line of sight to the men's camp. Tulari was crouched next to him, her thick fur now a blend of browns, oranges, and greens. She was presently at her diminutive size, which meant she looked like a big wolf rather than a night wolf the size of a bull cow in its prime. She was virtually invisible.

The clearing was expansive and open, surrounded by sparse tall trees, bare of branches except for the upper third that now swayed gently in the cool morning breeze. Several big rocks were scattered across the leaf strewn glade. It was early in the morning and the band of men was preparing their breakfast over a small fire. There were four men, and what looked like two younger boys, perhaps sixteen and fourteen.

Jonas had been tracking them for four days. Well, technically Tulari had, leading him further and further west of the Tundrens. They had moved through the city of Onett, and on the road west Tulari had received a calling, leading Jonas south. He spent a day in a small roadside village and learned that several farms had been raided, the brigands killing the occupants and taking anything of value. Word had been sent to Onett requesting the king's men, but that was a day ago, and the villagers did not expect help for at least three to four days. Tulari had found their scent, moving southwest.

That day they had found a burnt out wagon, two men dead, and Jonas knew he was on the right track. And now, watching the thieves, he was sure they were the brigands responsible for the recent criminal acts. The men wore mismatched pieces of armor and carried swords, crossbows lying close by as they drank from a wineskin. It was early, and to be drinking wine at such an hour told Jonas much. Two mules were tied off to a tree and Jonas could easily see the tack and harness, likely the animals taken from the destroyed wagon. There were five other horses nearby as well, along with a cart, the bed filled high and covered with a canvas cloth. It was likely filled with stolen merchandise.

Jonas watched them for nearly an hour, trying to discern who their leader was and to determine their level of discipline. Were they ex-soldiers or just farmers or traders fallen on hard times? As they ate and drank, Jonas noticed that the two young boys were quiet and not participating, simply sitting beside a bigger man, who routinely took his share of the wine. At one point, the smaller boy ladled some soup from the pot into his bowl, spilling some. The big bearded man got angry and slapped him, knocking the boy into the dirt and upturning the contents of the bowl. The older boy stood to defend him and he too was hit, but he remained standing. Jonas could see the rage in boy's eyes, but he held it in check and went to help the other boy rise from the leafy ground.

Interesting, Jonas thought. But he had seen enough. They had no discipline. They were likely thieves and murderers by trade. Silently rising, he moved away from the brush. It was time.

Jonas drifted from tree to tree, his magical cloak, given to him by Shyann, turning to colors of brown and orange to match the fall leaves. The area was open and exposed, with little to no cover to hide an approaching person. But Jonas had just spent four years traveling and training with Allindrian, the half-elf Bladesinger, and in that time he had learned to track, hide, and move silently in the forest. He had been more than proficient before in the use of bow, but now his skill was unmatched by any human that he knew of. His skill, combined with the magical properties of his garments, made him a tracker and hunter who was only seen when he allowed it. Crouching low, he drifted across the leaf strewn ground, dropping and hiding behind the boulders scattered around the clearing. The big granite rocks were the only cover he had, and he planned to use them to get as close as possible. Tulari was on the far side of the clearing, mirroring his movements, inching ever closer to the unsuspecting drunk and boisterous men.

Finally he had made his way to the closest boulder, which was less than twenty paces away from the fire. He calmly reached up and nocked an arrow to his bow. Then he narrowed his eyes and focused, dropping into the state of Ty'erm, taught to him by Kiln the swordsman. It was a mental exercise Kiln had learned from a tribal shaman over twenty years ago, taught to Jonas when he had lived with him in the mountains. In Ty'erm, Jonas's mind slowed, and he saw things more clearly, allowing him to react with speed and precision and not allowing emotion to dictate his actions. It was an invaluable skill. His mind focused, Jonas leapt gracefully atop the boulder, his bow held before him but not drawn.

"Gentlemen!" he called out, startling the thieves, "I am Jonas Kanrene and I am here to arrest you!"

Their laughter stopped suddenly as the men spun around, startled by his sudden appearance. The four men stood from their log seats at the fire, setting their bowls of food on the ground. Their startled expressions turned to smiles as they saw Jonas was alone.

The bearded man that had hit the two boys stepped away from the fire. "I'd be putting that bow down, boy," he said threateningly.

Jonas cracked a subtle smile. He knew he didn't look like much to them. He wore dark clothes and armor, his cloak now a dark gray. But everything looked nondescript and simple, certainly not warlike or threatening. The man seemed to think that he was no threat. Jonas smiled wider. I guess from his point of view he was a boy. He was twenty six years old, but he did look older, the trials of his youth aging him beyond his years. His dark brown hair was long and wavy, the top pulled back and tied behind his head. He hadn't shaved for a week and fresh stubble covered his face.

"Actually," Jonas said, "I will not. I will say it one more time. You are under arrest for murder and theft. Will you submit?"

The four men slowly spread out, leaving the two boys sitting by the fire. The younger boy's eyes looked scared, the red mark on his cheek clearly visible. The other boy's eyes were alert and tense, perhaps still filled with anger at being hit, or perhaps he was concerned with Jonas's sudden appearance. The other three brigands were your typical lot. They all looked to be about the same age, maybe ten or fifteen years older than Jonas. One looked similar to the bearded man, burly in the shoulders but smaller in height, with dirty unkempt hair and a bushy beard. Another was small in stature and thin, with a narrow face, long pointy nose, and a swarthy complexion. The last man had long straight greasy hair and his face was unremarkable as you were immediately drawn to his missing two front teeth.

"You have no authority to arrest us," the thin man said, his nasally voice irritating.

Just then the man with the missing teeth reached for a crossbow that was leaning against a log. Jonas knew it was there and had been expecting the move. In a flash, his bow was up and a blue fletched arrow slammed into the man's forehead, snapping his head back like a whip. He fell backwards to the ground. It happened so fast that the others froze, their wide eyes still trying to register the movement. "You may submit, and live, or you may not, and die. The choice is yours," he said calmly, lowering his bow once again.

Jonas was looking at the big man, figuring he was the leader. He noticed his eyes shift to something behind him. It was a subtle but noticeable glance. And two heartbeats later he heard the soft rustle of leaves. He spun quickly, dropping to his knee and nocking another arrow in the same movement. Behind him, over forty paces away near the tree line, was a fifth man, already releasing a shaft from his bow. It was a long shot, and his aim was slightly off. Seeing that the shaft was going to hit the base of the rock he was standing on, Jonas didn't flinch and his own bow twanged in response. Jonas would not miss at that distance, and as his arrow slammed into the man's chest, he leapt from the boulder, dropping his bow as he rolled gracefully across the ground, a bolt from a crossbow ricocheting off the stone he had just departed, sending sparks into the air.

Quickly assessing the attack, both of Jonas's hands reached to the knives sheathed in the bandolier at his chest, drawing and throwing them in a blink. Prior to working with Allindrian, he had not been proficient with throwing knives. But now, after years of practice with the Bladesinger, he could hit an attacker's eye at ten paces with either hand. One knife hit the shorter bearded man holding the crossbow, the magical blade burying deep in his throat. The other slammed into the small brigand's chest as he ran at Jonas with a raised sword.

The leader, seeing Jonas's skill, had decided upon a different tactic. He had run to the boys and yanked the smaller one up, holding the boy in front of him with a knife at his throat. "You move another muscle and I'll kill him."

Jonas remained still, his hands at his sides. "If you kill him then you have no leverage."

"Paaa," the boy cried, but the sound was cut short as the man squeezed his grip tighter on the kid's throat.

Jonas was disgusted as realization sank in. They were his sons. *Perhaps this was why Shyann had led me here*, he thought, to save these two boys from a life of crime and murder. Maybe it wasn't too late for them, as it clearly was for the men lying in death around him. After all, that was his new role as Shyann's Shadow Knight, to blend in, to fight evil, and to save others on the path to becoming the very thing he was sworn to destroy. If he could intercept men and woman that were walking down a road lined with shadows, then perhaps he could lead them into the light, where they could become positive members of the world, not servants of the evil constantly vying for power.

Over the man's shoulder, just up the low grade hill, Tulari sat still, crouching like a hunting cat. She had turned into her real form but even so, her massive size blended easily into the leaf strewn ground around her. The attack on Jonas had happened so fast, that by the time she was in position the men were already dead. Opting to stay back, she was now ready to intervene if need be.

Jonas said nothing, simply shaking his head from side to side but Tulari understood and hung back, her massive muscled body ready to spring forward at any moment. "You have no choice but to drop that knife, and you know it," Jonas said, staying completely still. He knew that a man, who could hit his sons and then use them as a shield, was fully capable of sliding that blade across the boy's throat if it meant he could get away. But he will also not leave this clearing alive should such a thing happen, Jonas grimly thought.

Jonas was just preparing to use his telekinetic cognivant powers, wrapping the particles around the man's hand, to freeze it in place before knocking him away from his son. But suddenly the man's eyes snapped wide and he arched his back, his hands dropping away as his son jumped to the side out of harm's way. The older son stepped around from behind the man, his eyes hard with killing rage. Stumbling, the man turned towards the older boy, a hunting knife jutting from his back. Then he fell to his knees and, with a final groan, dropped face first onto the ground.

Immediately the younger boy got up from the ground and raced to his older brother who put his arm in front of him protectively. "Who are you?" the older brother asked, warily.

"I'm Jonas. I'm here to help you. You have nothing to fear from me."

"Are you with the King's men?" he asked. He seemed very nervous. Jonas figured that he thought they were in trouble, that they would be arrested and hanged for murder and theft.

"I am not. I am a knight to Shyann. Do you know of her?"

The younger kid nodded his head. "My Ma liked her...left her bushels of corn every solstice."

"Good," Jonas said. "Let us finish eating and sit by the fire and talk. I'm not going to hurt you," he finished, reassuringly.

The older boy had seen all that Jonas had done and was still trying to process the speed and efficiency with which he had dispatched the four men. "How did you do that?" he asked, his eyes shifting to the dead bodies.

"I told you. I am a knight, trained to fight and sworn to uphold Shyann's will. Now, before we sit why don't you tell me your names?"

"I'm Bran," the younger kid said.

"Stegan," the older one added.

"Well met. Now, let's not let that soup go to waste."

Jonas had finally got the boys to calm down and trust him, or at least not view him as a threat. They ate their soup while Jonas dragged the bodies further away

11

from the fire so they didn't have to look at them. Tulari had joined them shortly, returning to her normal size and color knowing that anything else would frighten them. The boy's attitudes changed quickly as she let them pet her, even going so far as to allow them to scratch her belly and play with her like she was a normal dog. Jonas had never seen her act so meek, and he chuckled to himself watching her prance around the boys as Bran held a stick for her.

They talked and ate for nearly an hour and Jonas learned that their father was an abusive man. And when their mother died of a fever, things just got worse. He started drinking heavily and the abuse escalated. He was a mason by trade and as the drinking increased, his contracts diminished. Soon, they lost their home and were forced onto the street. It wasn't long before their father was stealing, and within half a year he had a formed a partnership with the other thieves. They traveled constantly, doing whatever they wanted with no regard for the law, property, or others' lives. They said that their father, when they arrived at any city, would make them steal, and if they didn't bring back anything of value then they would be badly beaten.

"How long has this been going on?" Jonas asked.

Stegan shrugged his shoulders. "I'm not good with time, but I'd reckon over a year."

"What are we going to do now?" Bran asked, looking at his brother.

"I can help you if you'd like," Jonas said. "I think Shyann led me here to help you."

"How do we know you serve Shyann? I have never heard of such a thing," Stegan said skeptically.

"I'm going to show you something," Jonas said. "Don't be afraid. Ready?"

They were both looking at Jonas with wary expressions, but Stegan nodded his head. Jonas willed the symbol on his black nondescript cuirass to glow, and instantly Shyann's oak tree appeared, blue light flaring brightly and reflecting off their astonished faces. Bran nearly fell off his log and Stegan jumped, startled by the sudden display of magic.

"What is that!?" Stegan said.

"Do you recognize the symbol?" Jonas asked.

Bran was nodding his head vigorously. "It's her symbol. I saw it once on a temple door."

"Our mother had a different symbol carved from wood," Stegan said, his eyes narrowing.

"Was it antlers?"

Stegan's eyes flickered with recognition. But still he seemed guarded. "It was."

"That is one of her symbols as well. But the oak tree is more common," he added, willing the light to disappear.

"Was that magic?" Bran asked. It was clear that neither one of them had ever seen anything like it.

"It was. Do you believe me now? Will you allow me to help you?"

Stegan looked at his younger brother, then back to Jonas, coming to the realization that he really had no choice. What were they going to do? They were alone. "What kind of help," he said finally.

"I will take you to Onett," Jonas added. "And once there I will book you a trip east with one of the trading caravans. I will provide you with a writ and coin to see you safely east to a city called Tarsis. Have you heard of it?" They both shook their heads.

"What's a writ?" Stegan asked.

"It's a document, signed by me and marked with the Tarsinian royal insignia. That alone should see you safely to Tarsis. The writ would mean that you are under the Tarsinian King's protection. Take the writ to any temple of Ulren and they will give you aid."

"What kind of aid?" Bran asked.

"A job for one," Jonas replied. "You will need to work, but you will be safe and fed. The city was destroyed during Malbeck's War, and they are rebuilding and in need of many workers. You will have a chance at a normal life. Do you want that?" They both nodded. "If you do not take my help, then I'm afraid you might turn out like your father, and these men. And if you do," Jonas warned, "your fate will mirror theirs. Do you understand?"

"We don't want to be anything like our father," Stegan said firmly, Bran nodding in agreement. "We hated him."

"So you will take my help?"

Stegan looked at his brother, then back to Jonas. His eyes were strong, his face set with determination. "We will."

CHAPTER ONE

Three years earlier...

"Shhhhhhh," Peron said to his two friends as they dropped to the soft grassy ground beside him. "We don't need the guards hearing us," he admonished.

Tyril, a large thick bellied boy to Peron's left, laughed softly and elbowed Peron. "You made more noise than both of us together."

Peron grimaced but said nothing, knowing Tyril was right. He knew he wasn't the athletic type, but he hated to admit it. "Fine, follow me and stay quiet."

"You sure you have the book?" Kyron asked. Kyron was thin, like Peron, but taller, with sparkling blue eyes and a mop of wavy brown hair. He looked every bit the aristocrat, and his regal pointy nose just accentuated that point.

"Of course," Peron whispered as he set off at a slow jog, moving in and out of the various gravestones. They ran through the dark night, stopping occasionally as Peron made adjustments to their route. The only thing lighting their way was the bright stars and moon. Luckily it was a clear night.

After working up a slight perspiration, Peron pulled up short before a huge mausoleum, the front door made of stone and carved into a winged dragon, each wing fanned out occupying each side of the double door. Old vines as thick as a man's wrist grew up the sides of the stone building, a mesh of thick leaves covering most of the structure. Obviously the mausoleum had been there for a long time. No one said anything as they stared up at the huge structure in awe.

"You sure this is a good idea?" Kyron asked softly, ever cautious.

"Wimp," Tyril said, nudging him in the side, nearly knocking him over. At fifteen winters, he was already large and his thick arms and legs were starting to form a respectable amount of muscle. His father was the Battle Lord and leader of the Red Guard, the elite fighting force that had been protecting the Rothar kings for five hundred years.

Peron turned to face them both. "Listen, we have been planning this for years. Don't back out on me now."

"It's a lot easier to be confident when you are the prince," Kyron said sarcastically.

Peron nodded his head in acquiescence. "Perhaps, but you have to trust me. You know you want to see the grave site." He was smiling in youthful exuberance and Tyril and Kyron both joined in, Kyron's broad smile replacing his unsure expression. "Besides, I went through a lot of trouble stealing the book and the key."

"Fine," Kyron said. "Let's just get it over with before I change my mind."

Peron nodded and turned to the door, fishing in his pocket before producing a big gold key. Looking back at his friends, he smiled before sliding the key into the steel lock embedded in the massive door. Turning the key slowly, there was an audible click, before he removed it from the locking mechanism. Then he reached out, gripped the handle, and slowly opened one side of the huge door. A gentle breeze pushed out from the crack, which brought with it the smell of musty soil and dirt. Peron stopped pushing once the opening, which was as black as a starless night, was big enough for them to squeeze through.

"Get the torches lit," Peron ordered.

Kyron removed his small pack and brought out three torches and a tinder box. Within moments he had the torches alight and they quickly slid through the opening.

"Hurry, shut the door," Peron said. "We don't want any guards seeing the light."

Tyril shut the door behind them and they all three turned to face their surroundings, the torchlight pushing back the blackness and casting ominous shadows around the large room. The stone walls on either side of them were lined with three statues, each life-size and depicting great warriors. Their workmanship was exquisite, each and every detail making it feel like they were real, standing guard over the royal family's ancestors. The floor was covered with a thick layer of dust and the stagnant musty air was damp and heavy, causing the back of their throats to itch. The wall before them was dominated by another great statue, this one even more impressive than the others, its body encased in armor and its muscled arms spread wide, each hand holding a broad sword over the two doors flanking it. The warrior's head was completely encased in a magnificent helm with curved horns jutting from each side.

"This is amazing," Tyril whispered, looking slowly around.

"I've always wanted to see this, but my father said I wasn't old enough," Peron said as he stared at the great statue in awe. It was tradition that when a Rothar prince reached the age of eighteen, that he would be allowed entry into the royal family's burial chambers, to give respect to the kings before him. Peron had three years to go.

"You sure the demon's body is even down here?" Kyron said, his voice strained as he thought about the creature of legend.

Peron flipped his backpack off and reached inside, removing a thick leather-bound book. "My grandfather has been reading me stories about Maltheil since I was a young boy. I don't know if he was just scaring me, but he told me on more than one occasion that the demon was encased in a spellbound tomb deep in my family's catacombs. As legend has it, the beast was put here so my family could watch over it to ensure it was never freed again. He said the wards that are guarding the demon were secured in a book in Master Moran's room." Master Moran was Peron's father's court wizard, his family lineage traceable to the very wizard who originally summoned the great demon thousands of years before.

"And that's the book?" Tyril asked.

Peron smiled. "Master Moran told me of the book on numerous occasions. So yes, this is the book."

Kyron looked nervous, thinking that if the book did in fact exist, that there was some truth to the stories about the ancient demon. "How did you get the book from his room?" Kyron asked.

Peron raised his eyebrows and smiled. "One can do wonders when people think very little of you. They have talked about secrets around me since I was a little boy. It took a long time, but I found out where he hid the book, and I learned how to get it."

Ever the serious one, Kyron frowned in doubt. "Come on you guys, you really think that story is true?" Everyone knew of the story of Maltheil, an ancient demon, as the stories would have it, called forth by the Rotharian court wizard. The stories suggested that they used the power of the demon to win a great war, but over time, the demon broke free from the wizard's control, killing him and enslaving the royal family. Raising an army of slaves, the demon sought power, controlling not just the Kingdom of Lanard, but moving its army east to Tur'el. Eventually the demon was killed by the Tur'ellian King, with the help of a grove of druids who protected the Lasur'een forest that separated the two kingdoms. According to the old books, this all happened thousands of years ago, and most thought of it as nothing more than a legend.

"I don't know," Peron conceded. "But this book certainly looks real." Peron held the book up so they all could see. It was made of thick leather and was plain in appearance, the old cover worn and cracked. The only thing they could make out on the ancient tome was a symbol of old Lanarian, the metal bright against the old black leather. It was somehow secured to the leather on the front of the book.

"What does that mean?" Tyril asked as he pointed to the symbol.

As the crown prince, Peron had been schooled in Old Lanarian. Being the son of a wealthy lord, Kyron had been as well. Tyril's schooling was closer to his aptitude, which meant it revolved around a shield and sword. Peron smiled mischievously as he traced the sigil with his finger. "It means *do not open*."

"Maybe this is not a good idea," Kyron said, wavering in his resolve.

But Peron was resolute. "My father can choke on a chicken egg. He can eat the dung of a slop pig for all I care. I don't care what he thinks. Don't worry about him."

If Peron was honest with himself, he was not feeling as confident as he sounded. He had never had a great relationship with his father, King Gyveel Rothar, and he had to admit that his father scared him. Peron's mother died giving birth to him, and he suspected that his father's hostility towards him was partly due to that fact. Perhaps he blamed him. He was brusque and prone to bouts of anger, all of which was more than likely fueled by the Queen's death and the fact that Peron had not turned out to be the warrior Prince as the king had hoped. Peron was tired of letting his father down, and now he was finally acting out against him.

"Peron, if we get caught we will get in serious trouble, while you get a slap on your hand," Kyron said.

Peron's anger erupted as he turned on his friend. "You see this," he snapped, pointing at his eye. "This is not just a slap on the hand." Peron's eye was healing but both could clearly see the bruising fading to shades of yellow and purple.

Kyron stepped back, ashamed of his words. They both knew the King hit Peron on more than one occasion. "I'm sorry, Peron. It's just that we could get into real trouble, and we don't have your father to back us."

Peron relaxed some. "Let's not worry about him. Besides, it's all probably just a legend. Let's go check it out. We will be back in our warm beds before you know it."

The boys shrugged and Tyril stepped forward. "Which door do we take?

One door bore the Rothar family crest, a dragon with its wings spread, its clawed paws resting on a craggy peak representing the Peaks of Annure just south of them. According to the historians the lands around the steep mountains were once ruled by the Rothar family before the Ronith tribes took them over. The other door was plain in comparison.

"I think the plain door leads to tombs occupied by the bodies of high lords. The door with my family crest must be where my ancestors are buried. If the demon is indeed hidden here, it should be there."

Tyril shrugged. "Let's go." Tyril, being the bravest of the three, reached the door with the others on his heels. It opened easily enough and a gust of wind hit them carrying the rank smell of decay and dirt. It was as if the air, long sealed in, jumped at the chance of freedom presented by the open door.

Dust covered stone steps led deeper into the ground and at the base it opened into a wide cavern with a high arched ceiling, everything expertly covered in a gray stone now marred with cracks and lichen. In some places root structures had broken through the stone tiles, dangling like spindly legs. As they slowly walked down the huge hall, they noticed that each side was filled with many shelves cut into the earth. There must have been thirty on each side and as they continued further into the hall, their footsteps echoing in the stone cavern, they noticed more and more flanking them. They stayed near the center of the walkway, avoiding the shelves as they quickly realized that each one was occupied by a set of dust covered bones. Many were encased in old rusty armor, while some seemed naked, their expensive gowns and robes long ago eaten away by time. It wasn't long before the hall opened into a large round room, the diameter easily forty paces wide. The ceiling of the room was domed, and much higher than the hall. All around the edge were ten giant columns of white marble, spanning to the ceiling. At each interval between the columns were eight sarcophaguses, each one no doubt containing the bodies of the very first Rothar Kings, Peron's ancient ancestors.

They slowly walked the edge of the room, Tyril and Kyron following Peron's lead. They each felt like they shouldn't be there, and they were looking at one another with undisguised apprehension as Peron inspected each sarcophagus, his mouth open in awe. "Look at this," he said reverently. "This is the tomb of

King Lynel Rothar, the founder of my family's kingdom."

"What's that?" Kyron said, pointing to a door made of black iron. It was inset dead center on the far wall, two columns on either side of it. They walked closer.

"Look at that," Tyril said as he pointed at an impression on the door. It was the only thing they could see along the metal surface. There wasn't even a lock. The impression was in the center of the door and it looked to be a symbol of some sort.

"It's the same symbol on the book," Peron whispered, his heart beating faster.

"You're kidding," Tyril said as they stood around Peron to get a better look at the symbol. Sure enough it was the same.

"And you said it means *do not open*, perhaps we should heed the warning," Kyron advised.

"Well I don't see a lock anyway," Tyril added, inspecting the door more closely.

Peron stepped closer to the door, a smile wide on his face.

Seeing his expression, Tyril stepped beside him. "What is it?"

"Look," Peron said, holding up the book near the impression. "The impression on the door is the same size as this symbol. Maybe the book *is* the key."

Kyron and Tyril looked closer, their unsure expressions, seeing Peron was right, were now replaced with worry. "You sure about this?" Tyril asked, voicing Kyron's concern for the first time.

"Are you kidding me?! Yes, we need to do this. Obviously there was something to the story. We have to see what's beyond this door."

"I don't know, Peron. I think we should leave," Kyron said, stepping away from the door.

"No! We are going." Peron was adamant. "Even if the demon is buried here, the thing is dead. There is nothing to worry about."

Peron lifted the book to the door as the other two unconsciously moved back a step, or perhaps it was conscious, as both boys were visibly concerned. The symbol fit perfectly into the door but nothing happened.

"Maybe you need to turn it," Tyril suggested, regretting it immediately as Kyron glared at him.

"Don't encourage him," Kyron snapped as he hit Tyril in the arm.

Peron smiled. "I feel like I'm with a couple of little girls." Then he turned the book and his smile widened as the locking mechanism spun slowly until the book had turned ninety degrees. Then there was a loud click and some grinding noise, followed by a bright flash all along the seam of the door.

Everyone stepped back, including Peron, who withdrew the book from the lock. Slowly, the door swung open revealing only blackness.

"Now what?" Kyron asked, clearly concerned.

"We go in," Peron said as he raised his torch and walked into the room. Reluctantly, the others followed slowly.

They entered a square room that was roughly double the size of most sleeping chambers. But there was no bed, fireplace, shelving, or washbasin, just a sarcophagus that sat directly in the middle of the room. But it was unlike any sarcophagus any of them had ever laid eyes upon. It was three times larger than the biggest they had ever seen. But the unique aspect of it was that it was made of steel and the entire surface was covered in blades, embedded in the steel and facing outward like a giant pin cushion. The blades were of all different sizes but they seemed to be sharp, and amazingly, they were all shining like they were recently forged and polished, none of the steel showing any signs of wear that would be normal for metal sitting in a damp cold place for several thousand years. It was the most magnificent and ominous thing any of them had ever looked upon.

No one said anything for a few moments as they gazed at the sarcophagus, staying just clear of the sharp points jutting out from the structure. Finally Tyril broke the silence. "Now what?"

Peron shrugged. "I guess we open the book." Standing at the foot of the magnificent coffin, Peron opened the book. Just as he did so the book slipped from his hands. Reacting instinctively, he reached for the falling book just as it struck one of the sharp points, slicing his hand in the process. "Ow!" he snapped, pulling his hand back as the book fell to the ground.

"You okay?" Kyron asked.

Peron picked the book up with his other hand as he stood, inspecting the cut. "Yeah," he said. The cut was on the back of his hand and it looked to be about an inch long. It wasn't terribly deep, but there was a trail of crimson dripping down the side of his hand nonetheless. He wiped it on the edge of his wool cloak. "I'll be fine. Now, let's see what this book says."

Slowly, and almost reverently, he opened the book to the first page as Kyron and Tyril looked over his shoulder. There were a few lines of words written in Old Lanarian.

"What does it say," Tyril whispered.

"It says," Peron said slowly, "This tome is a seal, the spell woven by me, Atticus Belthar, to bind it that shall not be woken. But beware, for it works tirelessly to break free from its prison, and the blood of Kings is the key."

"Whoa," Kyron said softly. "It's true then. Atticus Belthar did kill Maltheil." Atticus Belthar was an ancient druid who had helped defeat the demon and seal him away for good. "And that book was written by him, that's incredible."

"It would seem so," Tyril said. "Keep reading."

Peron flipped the page and as he did so blood from his cut dripped onto the aged paper. "Damn," he swore, wiping the blood drops from the page with the corner of his sleeve. It did nothing but smear the crimson across the yellowed paper.

Almost instantly the blood soaked into the page and disappeared in a puff of smoke that rose slowly into the dank air. Then there was a small pulse of wind in the room causing them to step back a pace.

"What was that?" Kyron asked, looking worriedly at the sarcophagus.

"It felt like it came from the coffin," Tyril said.

They were all staring at the spike covered coffin when there was a small flash of light followed by a glimmer that danced across a translucent shield that covered the coffin. They couldn't see the shield before, and it disappeared as quickly as it had appeared. It looked like the surface of a tranquil lake after a stone was thrown in, the ripple moving across the smooth surface just before the glimmer vanished.

"Peron, the book sucked in your blood," Kyron stammered, clearly frightened. "That cannot be good."

"*The blood of kings is its key*," Peron whispered, still staring at the coffin. "You don't think..."

"That *your* blood, blood of the Rothar family line, just opened the coffin." It was Kyron who interjected, vocalizing Peron's thoughts.

"It can't be," Peron said, shutting the book. Being careful not to get any more blood on it, he shoved the book back in his backpack.

"Well *something* just happened," Tyril said. Even he seemed worried.

"Look, the coffin is still shut. I think we are fine," Peron said with confidence he wasn't sure he felt. Then he faced them both. "Listen, we have to make a pact to never tell anyone what just happened. I'll get the key and book back and no one will be the wiser. Do you both agree?" They were clearly worried, but the coffin looked intact, and they nodded their heads in agreement. "Good. Now let's get out of here."

They needed no further encouragement, running to the door, eager to leave the confines of the dark room. Peron was the last to leave, shutting the heavy door behind him, his torch light descending across the sparkling steel of the sarcophagus as the door closed shut, returning the room to darkness.

In the black room there was another flash of light, followed by a second ripple across the translucent shield covering the coffin. Then it was dark again.

***

In a far off place, a void between worlds, a form floated in the nothingness. Long gangly arms tipped in sharp claws were held wide, as if suspended in water, its long snake-like tail slowly undulating to a silent song, like grass blowing back and forth in a gentle wind. It hadn't moved or opened its eyes in thousands of years, its mind as imprisoned as its body. But then it felt a pull, a slight tug from an invisible tether. Black eyelids snapped open, yellow eyes wide. It was just a knock on its prison door, but somehow a connection to the material plane had just nudged it, and maybe that was all it needed. Hope was an emotion the demon didn't have. Maybe it was desire, but the beast felt something, like a possibility to quench its anger that had been festering for thousands of years. That little nudge was a pin prick, reminding the creature of a time long ago, and just maybe the beast would once again unleash its anger on the world.

***

Present time...three years later

It was dark, the forest calm, all animals and creatures silent, hiding as the shadowed form shambled through the dense brush. With each step, the earth shrank from its presence, grass and moss turning black as one clawed foot stepped before the other. It wasn't supposed to be here, in this realm, and the land knew it. The thing had not had a corporeal form for thousands of years. Its body felt far away, its mind fragmented as it tried to take in all the senses it was now feeling. It knew it was free, as it had been striking the fracture in its prison with mental hammer blows, widening it but unable to break free. There had been a faint knock at the door, a glimmer of freedom's hope, then nothing, the door to its prison still locked. There was no concept of time in the Nethers, but long after the *knock*, the demon finally felt something again, and then the door was gone, its prison shattered in a flash. Someone had freed it. Maltheil felt it, a connection to someone, a powerful binding. But there was no calling, so the demon now walked free upon the earth.

Being sucked from a prison of nothingness, to the material plane, was disorienting at first, even for the great beast. Nearly everything felt strange, even its body. But one thing felt familiar; hate, a sense of rising anger that it knew from experience could only be quenched by blood. Stopping, it looked up through the canopy of trees, and stretching its clawed hands out wide, its long tail twitching from side to side, it roared with such magnitude that the ground shook beneath it. Then it caught the scent of something, its dog-like head snapping toward the aroma. It was man, the familiar smell rushing through its mind with exultation. It was hungry, and besides, the demon needed servants.

Not far off a wagon pulled by two oxen meandered through the forest road, ten horses with mounted warriors guarding the front and rear. Lanterns held aloft by poles at each corner of the wagon lit the road and the vigilant riders carried torches. The thick canvas of the wagon was painted with the Rothar family insignia, a dragon perched atop a mountain peak, and the warriors all wore the armor of the Red Guard, the center embossed with a black dragon, its wings spread wide, their red sashes and red capes marking them as personal guards of the king. They were the best, strong and brave, picked from the most skilled fighters, but even they didn't have a chance against the danger lurking in the shadows.

Captain Torgarrian pulled in on the reins, slowing his horse to a halt, his men doing the same behind him. He held his hand up for them to be silent. He heard, or felt, something in the night, something unfamiliar, something that didn't belong, and whatever it was left his hair standing on end. He leaned forward in the saddle and held his burning torch higher as his other hand touched the pommel of his sword. There was something before him, in the middle of the road, but he couldn't make it out. It was a shadow, but that couldn't be as it was taller than he was sitting on his giant warhorse.

Like a striking snake something shot forward from the darkness, Torgarrian's torchlight reflecting off its scaly hide just as a jet of red steam erupted from its fanged mouth. Swords rang from scabbards and men screamed, but their steel did little against the red fog as it covered them in a swath of hot air, bathing everything in its path for over twenty paces.

The men fell from their horses gagging and choking, their swords falling from their hands. Torgarrian's eyes bulged as he fought for breath, rolling on the ground and trying to stand. He could feel something inside him, growing rapidly throughout his body until he could no longer control his arms and legs. Screaming, his body arching in pain, his hands clawing into the dirt, he tried to fight off whatever was happening to him. He finally coaxed himself to his knees, still screaming. His torch was burning on the ground next to him and the orange flames shed just enough light to see his own hands. They were pale white. With what little will power he had left, he ripped his helm off and threw it aside. In the chaos of what was happening to him, he could make out his men around him in similar disarray. His head pounded in pain and he screamed loudly, his hands reaching up to his skull. Pulling them away, his hands were full of hair, and somewhere in the last vestiges of his consciousness he could feel his long dark hair falling out around him. Just then there was an itching feeling on the side of his neck, followed shortly by a burning pain as something snaked up and around his neck to the top of his skull. Looking up into the night sky he screamed again, the noises of his men around him were muffled cries through his own agony. Then something snapped in his mind and the pain was gone. But so was he, and something else stood in the darkness.

***

Peron was hustling down the castle hallway, the message to assemble in the council hall urgent. It was very early and he hadn't even had his morning meal. He was curious as to why his father had called a meeting so early, and with such urgency. One thing was for certain, he did not want to be late.

Peron had only grown a few inches, much to his frustration. He was no taller, or heavier for that matter, than a typical boy three years his younger. And for that, he was not taken very seriously. But that was nothing unusual, his size and lack of martial talent made him a disgrace in the eyes of his father's court. Combined with his lack of athleticism and his craving for academic pursuits and he had been the brunt of many jokes his entire life. And nothing had changed now that he was nearly eighteen, his birthday arriving in two days. Of course the members of his father's court didn't say anything directly to him, but he could tell, he could always tell.

He walked out the door of his family palace, the two guards flanking it taking no notice of him. He cleared the courtyard at a brisk pace, the cold morning air nipping at his skin as he pulled his thick fur lined cloak around him. It would be winter soon, the air already cold and crisp. Unconsciously his hand went to his wrist and the pink scar there. The scar itched some, but he knew it would be much worse if the royal healers had not worked their magic. A couple of days previous, in his swordsmanship class, he was accidently cut by his friend Kyron. Kyron was appalled at his actions; not just because he had hurt his friend, but also that he had accidently injured the Prince. Peron felt sorry for him, as no one ever wanted to spar with him for that very reason. Peron knew that Kyron practiced with him because he felt bad for him, and now his kindness, and Peron's lack of agility, had caused Kyron further guilt. Injury was always a possibility in sparring but, paired with his lack of skill, the odds of it happening to him went up significantly.

The double doors to the council hall were already open and under the watchful eye of two Red Guards. They nodded at him as he entered, their eyes void of emotion. But he could sense their disdain. No matter how hard they tried, he could always see it in people's expressions. It was like a slight shimmer in their eyes, and then it was gone, replaced with fake respect one must give their future king.

His father was standing beyond the conference table talking with Master Moran, his court wizard, and Peron couldn't help but notice the book that the wizard was holding in his hands. It looked all too familiar. Peron had hoped he would never see the book again, but now it was here, and his heart began to beat fast at the implication. The two seemed to be in a heated discussion, and the book was the focal point.

Sitting at the large round conference table was General Sig Moore, and next to him was Lord Inan, and opposite him were the other two members of the council, Lord Anteel, and Lord Caynon who had just entered from the north entrance and was sitting down when Peron entered and made his way to his own seat at the table. The conference room was built for the council meetings and it was spacious, with a large roaring fire on the west wall. The room was lit by a huge iron chandelier hanging by a heavy chain from the stout wood beams that crisscrossed the high ceiling. The fixture was round, like the table below it, and hanging from it were ten lanterns to match the ten chaired table. Perched atop the large stone fireplace, was a thick wood mantle, and above that a shield embossed with the Rothar standard, crisscrossed by two swords behind it.

King Gyveel Rothar glanced over and saw that everyone was there except for his brother. He cut his conversation off with Master Moran and moved to address the group. Peron thought he looked tired and stressed, more than normal. The king's hair was long with streaks of gray that shone like silver, but his immaculately trimmed beard was black as night, with no hint of fifty years, and his steel gray eyes were just as intense, despite the fact that they were red and rimmed in shadow, like smudges of smoke, that only comes from lack of sleep.

Peron looked nothing like him, more like his deceased mother, who he had never met as she had died giving birth to him. Something his father rarely let him forget. He had smooth flawless skin and green eyes that shone brightly next to his pale complexion. After all, he didn't get out much, spending more time in a book than anywhere else. And though he did share his father's thick black hair, he wore it short, trimmed above his ears and neckline.

The king of Rothar quickly glanced at each person at the table, his gaze more or less skipping over Peron as if he didn't matter. "I'm going to just get to the point, gentleman. Something seemingly impossible has happened, something that may threaten our very Kingdom." The lords glanced at one another with uncertainty, never before seeing their king speak so dire. "Somehow, Maltheil has escaped from its prison."

No one said anything for a few moments as they tried to digest words that made no sense spoken aloud. But they were spoken, and for a split second, they all hoped for them to be a joke. But the King's expression, as well as Master Moran's, silenced that thought just as quickly as it came to them. Peron's heart beat faster and he swallowed nervously, leaning back in his chair and bringing his hands under the table. He didn't want anyone to see them shake.

It was Lord Anteel who spoke first. The man was in his sixties and looked every bit his years. He wore a splendid sage green robe of cotton lined and trimmed in maroon silk. A matching belt was cinched tight and held a short sword that showed years of use. He wasn't overly built, but his hands were huge, and each finger looked like thick sausages. Peron had always liked him. He was blunt, honest, and seemed fair, and he had always treated him with respect. "I am assuming that you are not joking, which brings to mind an obvious question. How can this be true? I thought the demon was sealed away for eternity."

King Rothar glanced at Master Moran who was standing next to him. Master Moran cleared his throat. The wizard wore a dark blue jerkin lined with silver thread, and a white silk shirt underneath. A matching blue cape hung over his shoulders, the silver clasp graced with a beautiful depiction of the Rothar insignia. Master Moran's black hair was cut short near his scalp and a pointy, narrow goatee complemented his thin face nicely. If the king looked tired, Master Moran looked nervous, after all, it was his task, as it was the court wizards before him, to make sure that the demon remained sealed away. Very few knew the true story, and they were sitting in the room, all except for Peron, who was sitting in shock, the realization of his father's words hitting him like a slap in the face.

"It is true, I'm afraid," Master Moran answered. "Two guards came to us early this morning saying they were patrolling the burial grounds, which they do every other day, when they came to the royal mausoleum. The doors had been destroyed, torn asunder, and they came to us immediately to deliver the news. I inspected the tomb myself."

"But the door was magically sealed," Lord Caynon said, his voice filled with horror. Lord Caynon was younger than the other lords, not yet in his fifties, and he looked even younger. He was retired from the king's military, being an officer in the Red Guard for most of his life. The man was a warrior, and he looked it, with stern brooding eyes, and several scars visible across his hands and muscled forearms. "How did the demon get out?"

"I have some ideas," Master Moran said, glancing at Peron before returning his gaze to the others.

Peron's heart pounded in his chest. *What was that look for? Did he somehow know? Or was he just being paranoid?*

"The only way to open the door into the tomb is with this book," Master Moran continued, "and I've had it locked away safely. There are only a few people who knew of its location as well as had access to the key."

"And who had the key?" General Sig Moore asked, also glancing at Peron for a quick moment. The burly warrior had not missed the mage's quick flicker of his eyes towards the young prince. Peron never liked the General. He was gruff, and despite the fact that he was his cousin, he never showed him any respect. Perhaps it was his lack of skill with a sword, he did not know, but the man had never been kind to him. When he wasn't scowling at him, he was treating him with indifference, as if he did not exist.

"I did," the king replied.

"It stands to reason," the General added, "that someone was able to get the key and use the book, returning them with no one the wiser. Who had access to the book besides you," he asked as he addressed Master Moran, "and the key?" He finished as he looked at the king briefly, before swinging his cold gray eyes on Peron.

Peron's mind was reeling. *Did they know? Or were they just fishing, putting one and two together? Or were they picking up on his nerves?* After all, he was having a hard time hiding them. In fact, it seemed as if they were leading the discussion right to him. Thinking quickly, which was one thing he was good at, he headed them off. "Well, of course *I* had access to the key, after all I am to be the next king."

King Rothar looked at his son, seemingly confused that he had spoken, or maybe at the fact that he said he had access to the key; after all he had never explicitly shown him the location. "How do you know the location of the key and book?"

Taking the wind out of Master Moran's sails, Peron quickly spoke before the mage could interject. "Master Moran of course. Well at least he told me the location of the book, albeit indirectly. As far as the key, well you did. On more than one occasion, when I was but a boy, you checked on the location of the key, as well as your other treasures."

"The secret panel?" the king queried, remembering back. "I didn't think you were paying attention."

"Well I was. And the book, well, Master Moran was my tutor for several years. During that time he taught me languages and history, and on more than one occasion he brought up the story of Maltheil, even going as far as discussing the location of the book. He never took it out of course, but I have known of its location for quite some time now. I have thought it all just a story and legend since I was a boy. Are you telling me that the demon is real?" Peron was thinking fast on his feet, the words pouring from him as his mind tried to put the pieces together. He had no idea if what he had done three years ago was somehow connected to the demon's escape, but either way, he needed to deflect suspicion away from him.

"I'm afraid it is no mere story," the king responded, clearly despondent.

Peron was watching Master Moran carefully and again he saw a furtive glance his way. Was there something the wizard knew? Peron's quick mind was jumping all over the place. Was he just imagining things, his nerves getting the best of him? Or was his feeling that the wizard was pointing a finger at him justified?

Suddenly there was some commotion near the north entrance and everyone looked up to see Prince Dalland Rothar quickly enter, followed by two guards. He was in a sweat and looked dirty from the road.

"My Brother," he said, his eyes worried as he addressed the king. "We have found the missing patrol, or what's left of it."

"What do you mean?" the king asked, his tone on edge. A tax cart guarded by ten Red Guard soldiers was due in last night, but they had not yet arrived.

"We found the cart, and it was intact, nothing stolen," Dalland responded. "There were dead horses, several of them eaten by some animal, but no men. We could not find a single man." The prince was ten years younger than his brother, but thicker in the shoulders, with a wide square jaw that made him look more imposing than the king. There were few who could fight as well as the prince, and many whispered that the kingdom would be better off if he were to take the throne instead of Peron. But to his credit, Dalland had never spoken ill of Peron, at least not to his face, and he had always treated him fairly and with kindness. Dalland was a warrior through and through, but he seemed to have inherited all the kindness of the Rothar family, for the king rarely showed his son any such deference.

"Who would take the men but leave the gold?" Lord Anteel asked out loud.

"The demon," Master Moran whispered, setting the book on the table.

"It is said that the breath of Maltheil somehow controlled its victims, and that the beast could turn ordinary men into fighting servants, shells of their former selves." It was Peron who spoke again, and everyone turned their gaze to him in one smooth motion. It was obvious that they were surprised he had spoken, when he had just said that he thought the story just a legend.

Peron was surprised himself. He had not intended to speak, but when he knew something, anything, he rarely could hold back the desire to express his knowledge. It was a character flaw, one that earned him the reputation of a know it all. After the incident three years ago at the mausoleum, Peron made it his duty to learn as much as he could about the demon and the time of troubles associated with the beast. He read every book he could find, and a year ago he had visited the great wizard tower of Shyval as part of his studies, and there was no other place on Kraawn that had more knowledge and books than there. The visit was part of his tutelage, and he had taken every advantage of it. He read tomes that you could not find anywhere else, and he spoke with wizards and scholars, gleaning whatever he could from the vast amounts of knowledge available there. After all, that was why people with the unique talents to become a wizard went there, to learn, to investigate, and to sharpen their minds. He was sure there were very few people who had more knowledge of the demon than he.

"What do you know of the demon?" General Sig Moore asked, his tone like the snap of a whip. He realized that he sounded overly harsh, and softened his next words. "After all, you just said you thought the story a legend only."

Peron had to cover his trail. "I am an admirer of history, and as Master Moran, and my father know, am quite inquisitive." He wasn't lying there, that was for sure. "So when I went to Shyval, I wanted to find out if there was any truth to the story." It was the next part that was the lie. "Although I found lots of information that was really quite interesting, I'm afraid that most of what I found seemed to be conjecture and hearsay, and therefore I deemed the story a fine tale woven by bards and nothing more."

Master Moran looked at Peron, his skeptical expression not hidden well, perhaps seeing through his lie. But he did not challenge him. It was Lord Anteel who spoke. "What else did find out about this demon?"

King Rothar looked at the lord with a perturbed expression, almost as if he was annoyed that he was addressing his son on a matter concerning the kingdom. Peron saw the look but ignored it, taking some satisfaction in his father's annoyance. "Well, the beast is said to be from the sixth plane, as you would guess. According to the histories he was summoned from that plane by Master Moran's great ancestor. Although his intentions were altruistic, the end result was the enslavement of the entire royal family as well as a war against the Kingdom of Tur'el."

"We know all this," Master Moran snapped. "He was trying to gain help against the Ronith tribes from the south."

"Hence, altruistic," Peron shot back. Normally, confidence was not his strong suit, but when it came to knowledge and semantic wit, there were few who could best him. It was rare that he spoke at all during council meetings as most matters discussed were military, and he cared little for them.

Lord Caynon ignored the mage's tone and continued to address Peron before the mage could respond to Peron's challenging tone. "We know that the demon used some magic to enlist followers, servants if you will. Did you find anything at Shyval that shed more light onto how the beast was able to do that? It seems to me that that is our immediate concern, especially in light of what has happened to our men. We can only assume that they are now under the beast's sway."

"Actually, I don't think it's magic at all," Peron said. "Or maybe partly. The histories describe it as an inherent skill, like the great peorn bird that can stand still for hours, days even, waiting for its prey to swim below its sharp beak. It is said that Maltheil can project different breath weapons; some can burn and kill, while others allow the demon to somehow take over the minds of its victims, and yet another that turns its victims into crazed demon-spawn that drink the blood of their prey. But a demon is born from magic, so perhaps its skills are in fact magic, no one really knows. One of the accounts I read was written by a soldier who escaped such an attack, watching the entire scene play out before him while he hid in the woods. He said the men screamed and thrashed about, their bodies shaking and jerking uncontrollably. The man said that they turned pale and all their hair fell out. That was all he could see from his vantage point and therefore the account told no more. Perhaps it is magic, I do not know for sure, but either way the implication of such powers is alarming."

"How do we stop something like that?" Dalland asked softly, his warrior's mind having a hard time thinking of a way to battle a fog. They were all thinking the same thing.

"I don't know," the king said. "But the question still remains, who released the demon?"

"If the only people who had access to the key and book are in this room," Prince Dalland said, "then it seems clear to me that somehow someone else stole those tools and freed the beast."

Peron was relieved. His redirection had worked and none of the lords, except for perhaps Master Moran, thought that he had anything to do with the beast's escape. But his relief was short lived when he thought about the implications. The demon Maltheil had broken free, and the real question was...did the actions of Peron and his friends three years ago somehow help that dreadful event occur? Was he responsible? What was he going to do? If there was anything he hated, it was questions that he could not answer.

They all left the council room soon after, agreeing to tell no one and strengthen the perimeter guards around the castle. The city of Lanard was beautiful, built long ago along the edges of the north fork of the Onith River just before it dumped into Milnos Bay. The walls were tall and built of huge gray stones from the Peaks of Annure, each one the size of a wagon. The spires of the inner castle, home of the Rotharian family, were tall and round, the blue flags depicting the Rothar family crest in black, fluttering high in the clouds. The sprawling city spanned out from the inner castle, its thousands of homes and buildings wrapped protectively in its massive walls. The guards that patrolled the walls, if the sky was clear, could easily see the blue waters of Milnos Bay from their vantage point.

Peron had no intention of keeping the news to himself, and found himself quickly making his way to the north barracks. It was still early, but he had a suspicion that he would find his friend awake regardless of the early hour. The walk through the castle grounds to the barracks would not take him long, but it was enough time to mull over what he had just heard. Was the demon truly awake? And if so, what did it mean? What would the beast do? How had it happened? He needed to find answers, and he was afraid that the one person who had those answers was Master Moran. Something didn't seem right with the mage. He had never been on great terms with his father's court wizard, but they were not enemies either. Master Moran had been his teacher for over a year, and during that time they had developed a cordial relationship. He had never been overly kind, but he had shown him respect and had even admired his quick wit and intelligence. But he couldn't shake the nagging feeling that something was amiss with the wizard. One thing was for certain, Peron was nervous. Maybe Master Moran was just picking up on his nervousness. Thinking back, he remembered the book sucking up his blood, and when he had cut himself on the sarcophagus, the blades jutting from the tomb had done the same thing, drawing in his blood like it was hungry for it. He didn't know what it meant then, and he still didn't. Something about those events had his hair standing on end. Did his blood somehow bring the demon back from its prison?

As he came around the corner to the practice yard between the north barracks and the mess hall, he heard a familiar sound, and seeing who it was making it, was relieved. Tyril was standing before a thick log about five feet high, its base a steel wheel holding it in place. Two stout sticks as big around as a man's ankle were sticking out from the log at about chest height. There were several other practice dummies about but Tyril was the only soldier up this early. At eighteen years of age he was just a novice soldier, having signed up last winter. But when looking at him you wouldn't know it. He looked just like his father, tall, big in the chest and shoulders, with a thick beard and a head of curly hair that joined with the ample facial hair. His forearms were massive and they easily spun the large bladed spear with practiced precision, the short sword blade at the tip striking the dummy again and again as he expertly moved his body across the thick stone pavers. For someone so large, Peron was always amazed at how fast he moved. Tyril had a lot to live up too. His father was the Royal Battle Lord, second only to General Sig Moore, and head of the Red Guard, the elite Rotharian soldiers. At an early age Tyril had begun his career, lifting a sword before he started his schooling when he was eight. He trained harder than anyone Peron knew, hoping one day to follow in his father's footsteps. Peron knew from experience that the pressure a parent puts on their children can be overwhelming, but luckily for Tyril, thus far he had lived up to his father's desires. There were few, even amongst the veterans, who could fight as well as the young man.

"Tyril," Peron said as he quickly moved towards him.

Tyril stopped and faced his friend, wiping a bead of sweat from his forehead. The big man smiled warmly. "Peron, what are you doing up so early?"

"It's a long story," Peron said, his tone serious.

Tyril read his expression clearly. "What is it?" he asked, his concern evident.

"Are you on duty today?"

"Not until noon. I'm to go with a contingent of soldiers to meet the princess and her family at Angar."

Peron ran his hand through his hair. In all the chaos of the morning, he had forgotten about the princess. Princess Kylin Oneck, the youngest daughter to King Haten Oneck of Tur'el, was to wed his father. The arrangement had been made the previous year in the hopes that it would bring peace between the two kingdoms. It was an important event as the two Kingdoms had a long history of war, dating all the way back to the wars with the Ronith tribes and the troubles with the demon Maltheil. According to the stories, once the demon enslaved the Rothar king, the beast sent its army to destroy the kingdom of Tur'el. If the stories were accurate, which Peron doubted, then the ancient king of Tur'el, along with the druid Atticus Belthar, had somehow defeated and banished the demon. Perhaps there was some truth to the story as Peron thought back to three years ago when he had first opened the book. The writing was in Old Lanarian and written by the hand of Atticus Belthar. Peron's head was spinning. There was too much he didn't know, and he hated that.

"We have a few hours before you have to leave. Follow me."

Peron led Tyril to the Laughing Gnome, a place they frequented often, knowing it was a popular morning establishment and would be open for business. Two Red Guard soldiers followed behind them. Whenever Peron left the inner castle, which wasn't very often, he always had escorts. He hated it, as he could never blend in to his surroundings, preferring to be anonymous rather than the Prince of Lanard. Sure enough, the morning crowd was quickly filling the tavern, but once the proprietor saw Peron and his Red Guard escorts, he found a quiet table near the fireplace for them. The two soldiers stood outside flanking the door. Many people eyed them both as they sat, whispering Peron's name in quiet conversation. Peron preferred his anonymity, but he had realized a long time ago that was just not possible. He had come to terms with the fact that he could not go walking about without others knowing who he was, but that didn't mean that he was used to it. Trying to ignore the many stares, they ordered coffee and an egg pie they were famous for before Peron got right to it and told him the news.

"What!?" Tyril exclaimed, catching his tone and leaning closer to Peron, lowering his voice to a whisper. "The demon has escaped?"

"It has."

Tyril was shaking his head in disbelief. Keeping his voice low, he said, "Do you think it has anything to do with what we did?"

"I don't know."

"Does Kyron know?"

Peron shook his head. "No. I just found out myself. Is he at his estate?"

"The last I heard was he was trying to help his father secure business in Onith. He should be home in a few days." Kyron's father was once a very successful merchant whose ships traded up and down the Algard coast. His main source of income was selling weapons to the kingdom. But he had fallen on hard times since peace had been established with Tur'el nearly three years ago. The king was spending less on military equipment, and had completely dissolved his contracts with Kyron's father. He had been forced to sell all but two of his ships, trying to expand his business ventures north and south. Malbeck's War had rocked the lands, even this far west, and it seemed that conflict and war had been coming in second to diplomacy and peace. Kyron's family business had slowed to a trickle, and according to Kyron his father had become moody and depressed. It had gotten so bad that Kyron's mother had left them last year, and Kyron was now trying to pick up the pieces.

"Peron, what are we going to do?" Tyril asked, clearly worried.

Peron let out a deep sigh. "I don't know. We don't even know if it's really true. All I was told is that the sarcophagus was open and the doors leading to the crypt were broken and ripped apart."

"Who told you this?"

"Master Moran. He said he inspected the tomb himself. But something didn't seem right."

"What do you mean?"

Peron shook his head. "I'm not sure. But he seemed to be suggesting that I might have had something to do with it...almost like he knew."

"But that's impossible."

"I might have been just imagining it," Peron said. "I was pretty nervous, and perhaps he was just picking up on that."

"I can imagine."

"Oh, I forgot to tell you that one of the patrols guarding a tax cart never returned last night. Prince Dalland said they found the horses dead and the cart intact, but no bodies of the men."

Tyril looked worried. "Really? Who would leave the gold but take the men?"

"They thought it was the demon."

"If it was the demon wouldn't it just have killed the men?"

Peron shook his head. "No, according to all I've read about the beast, the demon has the power to turn men into servants. That was how it took over the kingdom and raised an army."

"How does it do this?"

"If the books are true, some sort of breathe weapon, like a sickness of some sort."

"That sounds awful," Tyril said as his hand went unconsciously to the hilt of his sword. "Peron, should we tell the king what we did?"

"No, absolutely not. Whether we did it or not doesn't change anything. If the demon has escaped, who did it is irrelevant. The important thing is finding a way to stop it."

"It's not irrelevant if someone else freed the beast," Tyril suggested.

"That's true," Peron agreed.

"What are we going to do?"

Peron frowned. "I don't know." He wasn't accustomed to that, and he didn't like the way it made him feel.

***

In the meantime, soon after the meeting was over, Master Moran was hustling down the hallway of the inner castle heading for the King's private chambers. There was a guard at the door who stepped aside and knocked on the door once he saw it was the wizard.

"Who is it?" A voice came from within.

"My King, Master Moran is here to see you," the guard said.

"Let him in."

The guard opened the door, stepping inside and allowing for the wizard to enter. Moran walked in and the guard closed the door behind him without a word.

King Gyveel Rothar was pouring himself a cup of wine at a table behind a massive cushioned couch. It was early for wine, but Moran understood. It had been a stressful morning. Not to mention the King had a lot of work to do to prepare for the coming wedding as well as the trip to Angar, and the wizard knew that work always flowed much faster with a glass of good wine, despite the early hour. The room was spacious and comfortable, with plenty of soft cushioned seats, most of which faced a roaring fire. Moran was always jealous of the fireplace. It was huge, able to fit four foot logs, and the mantle was stone, carved into muscular warriors standing, the mantle was their arms stretched wide, each holding a sword. It was beautiful. But he wasn't there to admire the workmanship.

"Would you like some wine?" the king asked.

"That would be nice, thank you. My king, I've come to discuss a few more things in private."

The king raised his eyebrows at that, handing him a cup of wine. "Please have a seat," he said as he made his way to the couch before the fire and sat down. Moran followed suit. "What would you like to say that could not have been said at the council?"

"It's about the book. I never said anything at the council as I was afraid to implicate your family. But the spell that wards the books location can only be thwarted by me, or someone with royal blood, and that means you, your brother, or your son."

King Gyveel narrowed his eyes at the mage. "You're telling me that if anyone else, even if they knew the location of the book, tried to access it, that they would have triggered the wards?"

"That's exactly what I'm telling you."

"And what would the wards have done?"

"Killed them with a shock of energy so powerful that it would have fried them to a crisp," Moran responded.

King Gyveel paused and looked into the fire, taking another long pull of wine. "So if I didn't do it, then it was either my brother, or my son."

"Yes, that is correct."

"Not entirely," the king interjected, turning to look at the mage. "It could've been you."

Master Moran looked shocked. "Technically that is true. But why would I do such a thing?"

"Why would any of us do such a thing?" the king queried. "It makes no sense."

Master Moran sighed in frustration and took a long drink. "I do not know."

King Gyveel was rubbing his chin in thought. "What if someone had access to royal blood...would they be able to use it to thwart the wards?"

Master Moran looked thoughtful. "It's possible. Frankly I never thought of that. But how would anyone get your blood?"

"I don't know," the king spat. He was clearly frustrated at not having the answers. "There must be another explanation. Keep looking," the king ordered.

"And what will we do about the beast?"

"What can we do? I have a wedding to plan. I will have more men stationed along the walls. I will order General Moore to send out more patrols, telling the men that there has been an increase in highway robbery so they do not know the real truth. I will have scouts go to Gyeen and Angar with sealed messages for the Earls informing them of the demon's escape. They too need to prepare." The king paused as he drank his wine. "Perhaps the demon will leave us alone, returning to its home plane."

"One can only hope," Moran said, sounding doubtful. "I will use all the magic at my disposal to find more answers."

"Please keep me informed," the king said, nodding towards the door.

Moran got the message. "Of course," he said, standing and setting the near empty glass on the table. Then he left, knowing that he had more questions than answers.

One week later...

Bearit stood in the back of the room where the shadows were thickest, his threadbare wool cloak wrapped tight around his muscular arms. The screaming of the people before him echoed in the underground room, a room that smelt of sewage and stale sweat. Glancing from person to person, Bearit knew he shouldn't be a part of what was happening. Their filthy clothing, scraggly hair, and gaunt features, the latter combined with their murderous howling making them look like crazed corpses recently dug from their graves. He was pretty sure he didn't belong there.

Why was he there he thought. The deep rumbling of his stomach and his bare toes breaking through his worn leather boots answered that question. Come to think of it, his appearance, minus the crazed visage, probably didn't look much better than the people around him. He was starving and had nowhere else to go, the promise of food pulling him beneath the city, through dirty and foul smelling catacombs to this very room. The hunger he felt was not the gentle rumbling one feels after a hard day of work and the promise of a warm meal soon to come. It was much deeper. It was a longing, a desire to fill a void that begged every moment to ease the pain. Over the last year, he had felt that deep emptiness often, and the desire to fill the void had finally won, beating down any resemblance of morals or common sense.

He was taller than everyone there and from his vantage point he could clearly see the four dark cloaked men torturing the man roped to the wall on the far side. There were perhaps fifteen others watching and cheering, the violence of the scene stirring them into an animalistic frenzy. Two more men, also wearing dark clothes and carrying long swords, walked amongst the onlookers, handing them loaves of bread and mugs of ale.

One man stepped toward Bearit and held a loaf of stale bread before him, a rictus grin sending a shiver down his spine. Unconsciously he reached up and gripped the rope that held his woodsman's axe in place, strapped to his broad muscled back. Of all the things he had sold and done to feed himself, he would not part with his axe, the one tool that was given to him by his father and had seen him through so much. The man's hood was off, the black wool pooling around his neck revealing pasty white skin and no hair, his skull bald and as pale as fresh milk. A black sigil snaked up his neck and swirled around his sunken eyes in an ominous pattern. His eyes were dark pits and lined in red, like he was sick. Even the gums around his teeth were crimson, not bleeding, but like they were stained from drinking too much wine. "Eat," he whispered, his voice soft but somehow audible over the yelling.

Bearit was appalled by the man, but he was hungry as well, his last meal coming three days ago. And that was no meal, but half a rotten apple and a chunk of stale cheese he managed to pull from some garbage. Reaching out, knowing he shouldn't, he took the bread and the man glided past him, his horrible smile turning to a gurgling laugh as he disappeared into the throng of men.

Pain filled screaming jerked his attention from the bread to the man on the far side of the wall. One dark robed man held a red hot length of iron as long as a sword. The prisoner was still wearing a leather tunic and some sort of black armor that looked to be made of hardened leather, steel, and chainmail. Sweat drenched his long dark brown hair that clung to his face. It was dark, the room lit by six torches as well as several burning braziers on either side of the roped man, casting ominous shadows around them. The dark cloaked man lifted the red hot steel again and slowly traced it along the man's bare arm, smoke rising from the burning flesh. Again the man screamed.

Who was this man, Bearit thought? What had he done to be the brunt of this group's entertainment? The man's arms were unusually strong; the tautness of the ropes, each held by a man that was pulling hard on the other end through a round ring embedded into the ceiling, pulled his powerful arms wide exposing massive arms and strong shoulders. Besides the new wounds being inflicted, the prisoner's flesh was marred by many old scars, the white puckered skin visible even in the dim light. One thing that really caught his eye was both his arms bore tendrils of some sigil that snaked around his biceps in an intricate pattern that looked like the branches of a tree. The mark was blue and lined in silver which sparkled occasionally as it caught the torchlight. Nothing about the prisoner seemed right to Bearit. The man was built like a warrior, and even though he was screaming in pain there was no mistaking his confident eyes as he panned the audience trying to lock gazes with the men around him. It was like he was looking for something, the pain he was enduring and his seemingly hopeless predicament an afterthought. Then the prisoner's eyes landed on his and stopped, narrowing as their intensity bore in to him. Bearit couldn't move, the strength of the man's gaze holding him still. Then there was a subtle nod of his head, as if he was communicating with him, before he screamed again, the red hot tip of the steel burning the side of his neck.

Bearit looked away but his mind was reeling. What he was witnessing was wrong, and all for a loaf of bread. Two years ago he would never have entertained such a gathering. But times had been rough on him. He was a logger through and through, trained by his father and wielding the axe since he was eight years old. He had matured early, like his father, and grew into a bear of a man, heavily muscled and toughened from the years of working long hours in the woods swinging the axe and lifting and carrying the fruits of his labor. His dark hair was curly and grew into a thick beard, and despite the fact that he was only nineteen years his mature stature made him look much older. He had never met anyone stronger, but now, as he watched the prisoner being tortured, he didn't feel so powerful. His father was killed in a logging accident three years ago and Bearit knew that if he was looking down at him now that he would be ashamed of him. Soon after his father's death the work dried up as the King of Lanard suddenly stopped purchasing the lumber for his navy. The lands were at peace, and military expenditures had decreased significantly as a result. He moved throughout Onith getting small jobs here and there, but there was never enough work, and after two years of scraping together work he found himself begging and wondering if he would freeze to death when the winter snows came. And now he was here, in this room, lured by strange men...told that he would be given food and shelter if he did a few things for them. Who were these pale and dangerous men? Who was this strange man they were torturing for their amusement? His mind elsewhere, Bearit unconsciously dropped the bread and looked back to the man on the far side of the room. By this time one of the dark clad men had given one of the onlookers in the crowd the hot poker and coaxed him into approaching the prisoner. Bearit saw that he was just a kid, perhaps fifteen years old. His clothes were disheveled and threadbare, just like his own, and his dirty skin was pulled tight to his bones. The kid looked like he hadn't eaten in weeks. Bearit couldn't hear what the dark clad man said to the boy, but it seemed pretty obvious that he was enticing the kid to burn the secured prisoner, perhaps luring him with more food and drink. The kid's eyes were wild and chunks of bread spit from his mouth as he screamed in frenzy with the others around him. They were cheering him on.

Bearit adjusted the rope around his shoulder and swung his axe free, giving little thought to what he was doing. Just as he gripped the worn wood handle of his axe, the prisoner looked right at him and smiled. Then the man rose from his knees and screamed something at the top of his lungs. Instantly his armor lit up in a brilliant blue light outlining the symbol of a glowing oak tree. It flared brightly, causing the onlookers around him to shield their eyes and back away from him. In a blink it was gone. Simultaneously he yanked hard on both the ropes. The men holding him were so surprised by the man's strength that he jerked them forward, one actually releasing the rope. Bearit watched with wide eyes as the prisoner ripped the free rope through the metal rung, and now that the tension was relieved on that end, he shot towards the other man and snapped his right foot forward, breaking the man's nose and launching him into the darkness. The ropes around his wrists were tied with slip knots, and now that the pressure was gone, he quickly loosened the knots and withdrew his hands from the nooses.

Just in time it would seem as the black cloaked men were on him in moments, their swords drawn and flashing in the dimly lit room. It was then that Bearit noticed that all the dark cloaked men looked similarly, with pale skin and bald heads, their eyes haunted and their lips curled back over red gummed teeth, snarling like animals as they attacked. The man was unarmed, but it didn't seem to matter. In a blur he spun around the attackers, avoiding their sword thrusts and attacking with lightning fast kicks and punches. Bearit watched as the man sidestepped a sword thrust, the move subtle, then gliding forward and leading with a snap punch to the man's throat, continuing his movement as he fought furiously. Several men were thrown and within four heartbeats he had disarmed one man, and was now using his sword against the others. Most of the onlookers were watching in shock, unable to register how the prisoner had reacted so quickly. But several of the black cloaked men that were in the audience had drawn their blades and moved to help their brethren.

Then a rumbling growl came to Bearit's left, towards the entrance to the room. From the darkness burst a huge wolf-like form as big as a horse, the thing's fur mottled gray and black, blending in well with the dirty stone surroundings. Bearit gripped his axe before him as the great beast launched into the stunned onlookers, knocking bodies aside with its massive head. The creature, whatever it was, was heading towards the warrior.

By this time most of the onlookers, screaming to get away from the huge beast and the attacking prisoner, had run back and out of the room. For some reason Bearit stayed behind, watching as the man spun expertly from man to man, their swords clanging loudly in the underground room. Six of the black cloaked men were down and the big wolf had another in its jaws, shaking him violently before tossing him against the stone wall like a used toy. Bearit could hear his bones break as he smashed against the rock. There was a side room that Bearit hadn't noticed in the darkness, and four more men ran from it, their swords drawn.

Seeing the men, Bearit reacted on instinct, running silently forward using the darkness against the wall as cover. He was no warrior, but he was not a stranger to violence and brawls. His father had taught him how to fight and he had bloodied his knuckles and nose more times than he cared to remember. But he had never faced a man with a blade. At the last moment one of the men in the rear caught his movement from his peripheral and spun towards him, his sword slicing for his stomach. Bearit jumped back and narrowly avoided the sword, following up with a massive two hand strike of his own. The warrior lifted his blade to block the blow but was not prepared for the strength and power of the attack. His blade struck Bearit's axe just below the heavy steel head, doing very little to hamper the blow. The sharp edge of the axe came down like it was splitting a log, cleaving the man's face in two. Bearit kicked out with his foot, the power of the kick dislodging the axe from the gruesome wound and sending the man catapulting backwards into a second warrior, nearly knocking him down in the process. Bearit leapt forward and swung his axe sideways, hoping to catch the surprised man in the stomach. But he was faster than Bearit thought and he jumped back, avoiding the axe as it struck the stone wall, sending sparks and shards of stone into the air. Reversing direction, the man came at him, his sword swinging for his chest. Bearit was out of position, the power of his strike and the weight of his axe knocking him off balance. He would not be able to bring his axe to bear to block the attack.

Suddenly the man was hit with some unseen force and knocked hard against the stone wall where he was held off the ground. Glancing to his right, Bearit saw the prisoner approach with one hand raised, the other black cloaked men dead, scattered around him. The big wolf was walking beside him, its massive shoulders reaching to the man's head. Blood drenched the wolf's maw and it was growling low, the deep rumbling sending a shiver down Bearit's spine. The man lifted the hand that held the sword and in an instant the blade zipped across the room, slamming into the man's chest who was still held against the stone wall with some unseen force. Then he casually dropped his other hand and the man fell to the ground, the last of his life leaving his body in a gurgling hiss. With a subtle flick of his wrist, the sword ripped from the man's flesh to return to his hand, crimson dripping from the silver blade.

Bearit stood before him dumbfounded. He had never seen anything like that, or witnessed such martial skill. Nor had he ever seen a beast such as the one who stood casually before him, the blood from its victims staining its fur. "Who are you?" Bearit asked, his voice stronger and more confident than he felt. Another lesson from his father...*always show confidence, men respect it, and women love it.*

The warrior stood before him, his eyes smoldering in intensity. "Jonas, Jonas Kanrene."

CHAPTER TWO

"Are you hurt?" Jonas asked as he knelt next to one of the black cloaked men.

"No." Bearit was too stunned to say anything else.

"What is your name?"

"Bearit."

Jonas was inspecting the body, looking for clues as to who these men were. They were all pale and bald, which in itself was interesting, and troublesome, as he had never encountered anything like them. Originally when Tulari led him further west, over the Tundren Mountains, he encountered servants of the Forsworn, infiltrating and destroying several of their lairs in both Onett and Mynos. He had helped a couple of boys free themselves from the tyranny of their father and his group of thieves and cutthroats. Then he was pulled further south, Tulari leading him to the trading city of Gyeen built on the shores of Fish Lake. The busy city was a hub for trade coming from Ronith, Onett, and even as far as Finarth across the Tundren Mountains. Lumber from the Lasur'een forest, fish from the lake, iron ore from the Peaks of Annure, all brought great wealth to the Kingdom of Lanard, but all of it paled in comparison to the expensive and rare fish eggs harvested from the vareeny, a rare bottom feeding fish that could only be found in Fish Lake. As a consequence, the huge lake was the home of many fisherman and sailors, all hoping to make it rich on the rare delicacy.

Jonas removed the tunic and cloak from the dead man to inspect him further. His skin was abnormally pale and blue lines like tiny veins spider webbed across his skin. The man, whoever he was, was muscular and had the body of a man who made his living from lifting a shield and sword. "Interesting," Jonas whispered to himself.

"What is? What are you looking for?" Bearit was still trying process what had just happened.

Jonas looked up. "I was expecting to find a servant of the Forsworn, but I found something different. I have never seen anything like this, and this man was a warrior, that much I know."

"What's that?" Bearit asked, pointing to his shoulder.

Jonas looked over the body at his far shoulder and saw what Bearit had noticed. There was a black sigil of a dragon head with crossed swords behind it. "I don't know. I've never seen a mark like that." Jonas drew a hunting knife from his side and moved to the opposite side of the body.

"What are you doing?"

Jonas looked up again, his eyes a bit harder. "Do you want to carry this body out of here?"

"No."

"Then be quiet for a moment." Jonas took the razor sharp edge of his knife and sliced the man's skin, cutting away the sigil in a perfectly symmetrical piece of skin. Then he sliced off a piece of the man's cloak and placed the skin in it, folding the edges around it.

Bearit was taken aback, but regardless he commented on something strange. "There be no blood."

Jonas was thinking the same thing, staring with interest at the patch of flesh now exposed. The man's flesh was pinkish, but more pale than red, and not a drop of blood dripped from the wound. "That is strange. And look at this," he added, pointing to the man's neck and head with the sharp point of his knife. "I've never seen a sigil like that either." There was a black snake-like mark that wound around the neck, stopping at the top of the skull, the end an intricate pattern of some unknown design.

"You're not going to cut off his head and take it with you are you?"

Jonas stood and smiled. "No, I think this will do," he replied as he held up the cloth protecting the piece of skin. "Thank you for coming to my aid."

Bearit smiled weakly. "It didn't seem like you needed it."

"Perhaps," Jonas said as he walked over to the area where he had been roped to the wall and went to the corner of the room. There was a pack, leather belt with two knives sheathed sideways front and back, as well as two swords sheathed on either side. Next to it was a leather bandolier holding four throwing knifes. Leaning against the wall was a black bow and a quiver of blue fletched arrows. Jonas put them all on and looked back at Bearit. "You came to my aid, and that tells me much. We need to talk. And I'm sure you have a lot of questions. Grab your axe and follow me." It wasn't a question.

Jonas didn't wait for a response. He turned with Tulari at his side and moved away into the darkness. Bearit looked about the room, and even though he knew nothing about the man who had just killed nearly ten men, he knew he didn't want to remain there, so he slung his axe over his shoulder and hastened to keep up with the mysterious warrior. One thing was for certain, he *was* full of questions.

***

"Here, drink this, it will calm your nerves," Jonas said as he slid a mug of ale across the table.

Bearit was still shaken, but he was trying hard not to show it, putting on a brave front. He had killed a man. *He had killed a man*, he thought over and over again. He could still picture the man's head split in two in an explosion of blood and brains. He had reacted on impulse, something that was not uncommon for him. He was no stranger to violence. His father was a brawler and had taught him to fight, to survive. And his size seemed to provoke other large men to want to fight him. He was raised tough and lived tough. But he had never killed anyone before and was having a hard time shaking the image from his head.

"Who ye be, then?" Bearit asked again before he downed the mug of ale hoping it would calm him. After the fight Jonas had led Bearit from the catacombs to the city above where they immediately went to an inn called the Wayward Lady. He already had a room procured and being that is was very late there were few patrons about.

"My name is Jonas."

"That I know, I did hear you the first time. That's not what I be asking though. I saw your armor glow and you killed all those men so easily. *What* are you, is my meaning," he stated again.

Tulari, now the size of a big dog, was curled up at his feet under the table. It had taken Jonas a few coins but he had eventually persuaded the owner of the establishment to allow Tulari inside. The beast seemed mellow and obedient, the complete antithesis of what she had been only an hour before.

When Jonas had been a cavalier, Tulari was his steed, given to him by Shyann, the Goddess whom he served. However, during the war with Malbeck, Jonas was captured and brutally and sadistically tortured by clerics in service to Dykreel. Though Jonas' friends did eventually find him, he was no longer the same.

During his imprisonment, the clerics had placed in his chest a barbed halo, cursed with the dark magic of Dykreel, an evil god of Kraawn, which then leeched from the talisman and into his body. The stain of Dykreel took his body over, and in order for him to survive he had to seek refuge within his own mind, protecting the part of him that made up his very essence. Elven wizards had eventually helped him, sealing off the dark magic inside the talisman, though they had to leave it embedded in his flesh. However, while they made him whole once again, he would never again be a cavalier. The magic the wizards used to seal off Dykreel's blight also broke Jonas's connection to Shyann. Nevertheless, though he would never again be her cavalier, she still had plans for him. Shyann made Jonas her Shadow Knight, a warrior capable of going places undetected - places that a cavalier could never go openly. Places such as the room he had been in tonight. To support him in his secret travels, she had also given Jonas Tulari again, but this time she was in the form of a giant and rare night wolf, a beast capable of changing its size. There were few predators as rare and deadly as night wolves.

Jonas sighed. This was always the difficult part, explaining who he was and what he was doing there. It had been six years since Malbeck's defeat, and four of those years were spent training and traveling with Allindrian, the half-elf Bladesinger. She had trained him to be silent in the woods, to merge with shadows, to become invisible unless he wanted to be seen. Jonas's skill with the bow had been more than proficient, but now it was beyond what most humans could achieve. She had taught him much in the years they had been together. She was forced to finally head home and Shyann had then called upon his service, knowing that he was now ready to take on the mantle of his new role. He was her Shadow Knight, whose job was to travel the lands and search for men and women on the verge of slipping into the black pit of evil. His job was to stop their progression towards evil and to help those, who if left alone, would eventually become the very evil he was sworn to fight.

"Bearit, listen to me. I was in that room on purpose. I let those men capture me."

"Why would you do that?"

"First, let's eat some food. My guess is that you have not eaten a full meal in a few days at least. Then we will get you a bath."

Bearit's expression was all too clear. He was embarrassed by his appearance and he was hungry, starving really, and he was not able to hide that fact. "True, I be hungry," he said slowly, as if he was ashamed. "And a bath be nice. It has been a while," he finished, looking down at the ground.

"Being hungry is nothing to be ashamed of," Jonas said as he put his forearms on the table, flinching where he had been burned. They had beaten him pretty good and despite the fact that he had already wiped the blood from his armor and face, his right eye was swollen and purple and his left cheek was scraped and red. Not to mention his lip was cut and swollen. He didn't look great to say the least. But he knew from experience that it could have been much worse.

"You look to be hurt. We should get you a salve. Some be good for burns," Bearit suggested.

"I will take care of them. Let us eat first." With that, Jonas motioned for a serving girl who was standing near the bar. There were very few patrons about and she was eager to make herself useful. She moved to the table quickly and Jonas ordered a cold meal of cured ham, cheese, and warm bread with honey and butter. She inadvertently stepped away from Bearit, wrinkling her nose in disgust but trying her best to hide her discomfort. They had already ordered ale but Jonas ordered another round. She seemed nervous, glancing at Jonas's wounds before averting her eyes. Jonas knew the severity of his injuries looked unsettling and he eased her tension by telling her that he had been mugged in an alley. He also ordered a bath for them both after dinner and she readily agreed to prepare them. She nodded to them both and left quickly with their order.

"Now, let us talk," Jonas said. "Why were you in that room? Although I have yet to determine who they were, it was clear they were agents of evil, and you were watching them torture me. Why?"

Bearit looked away, not wanting to look Jonas in the eye. He was ashamed and he didn't know what to say, so he told him the truth. "I'm starving. I have no money and I haven't eaten a good meal in months. They promised me as much food and drink as I wanted as well as shelter."

"In exchange for what?"

Bearit shook his head. "They didn't really say. They hinted at the fact that they would be taking me somewhere to meet their master. It sounded like a job."

Jonas leaned back in his chair. He wasn't sure what to make of it. He needed to learn more about who these men were. Jonas knew that the Forsworn, as well as Shyann, were not commonly worshipped this far west. In fact, many people here still worshiped the old gods.

"How did you feel watching them torture me?"

Bearit frowned. "Disgusted. That is why I helped you."

Jonas nodded. "I saw something in you, Bearit. Sometimes no one helps, too far gone in their own greed and desire to help anyone else. They often want to make someone pay for their lot in life. Other times I get three or four to help. Tonight I got one; you."

Bearit leaned back in his chair, confusion upon his face. "Sometimes you get no one? You've done this before then?"

Jonas nodded. "Yes."

Bearit shook his head, dumbfounded. "Why?"

"It is what I do. I was a cavalier once, warrior to Shyann. Do you know of her?"

Bearit nodded. "Yes. She be known here, but most do not worship her. My father, he said she is the goddess of the hunt." He paused, as if he heard him for the first time. "You were a cavalier?"

"I was."

"I have never met a cavalier before. Is that where you learned to fight?"

"Partly," Jonas said. "During Malbeck's War, I was captured and tortured, and the injuries I sustained were severe enough to make it impossible to be a cavalier any longer." Jonas saw Bearit's confused expression. "It's a long story," he added, "for another time. But needless to say Shyann did not abandon me. I am now her Shadow Knight, blessed to wear her armor and carry her weapons, upholding the righteous and her will. It was her symbol that you saw flare brightly from my armor when I attacked."

"It looked like a glowing tree."

"It was."

Bearit looked at his biceps. "What are those marks?"

Jonas's God Mark had grown over the last few years, expanding over his shoulders and down his arms, the branches wrapping around his biceps. "That is part of my God Mark," and before Bearit could ask more, Jonas cut him off, "also a story for another time."

Just then the food and drink arrived and they paused their conversation until their bellies were full of food and warm from the ale. Bearit was starving, and the first few moments were occupied with him shoving food down his throat, drinking quickly to wash it down so he could shovel more into his mouth. Once most of the food was gone, he slowed some, glancing sheepishly at Jonas. "I'm sorry. It's really good. It has been a long time since I've eaten well."

"It is alright."

"So," he said curiously. "What is a Shadow Knight? There be others like you? And what kind of beast is this?" he asked, nodding towards Tulari. "The creature was as big as a horse and now it looks to be a dog." Tulari lifted her head from the floor and growled.

Jonas smiled as he reached down and patted the side of her neck. She returned her big head to the floor, seemingly ignoring them. "As far as I know I am the first," he said, taking a drink of ale. "As a cavalier I was a beacon of hope and a symbol of all that is good. My very presence instilled in others a desire to be good, but with all that power came its limitations. I could not go anywhere without being noticed, without being seen for who I was. Now, I can pass for anyone."

"Is that how you got taken?"

"Yes. And the beast at my feet is a night wolf, very rare and powerful. Her name is Tulari and she too was given to me by Shyann, to replace my cavalier steed."

"So cavaliers really do get their mounts from their gods?"

"They do," Jonas answered, continuing with his story. "I came into town four days ago and it didn't take me long to find out what was happening."

"And what was that?"

"I went to questionable establishments and dark alleys. In the first night alone I witnessed two drunken men taken from shadowed and stinking alleys. On the second night I followed a man as he stumbled from a bar and made his way to the lake's edge. There he was accosted and dragged away by three men in black. On the third night I watched two black clothed men talk with a young boy in an alley, luring him away with the promise of bread and ale."

"That is what happened to me," Bearit said. "I was freezing and hungry, sitting under the edge of a roof in a dirty alley. Two men found me there. They promised me food if I would work for them. I knew something wasn't right, but - I was starving," Bearit stumbled, trying to find the words to justify his actions.

Jonas interrupted his thoughts. "Bearit, it's not your fault. That's how they work. They prey on people who have nothing left. What matters is that you came to my aid when the others did not. You recognized the evil and did not succumb to it."

Bearit smiled wanly. "Perhaps."

"It was simple enough to be lured away last night. I think they recognized me as a warrior. Maybe they thought I had deserted, I do not know. I think they wanted to make an example of me, or perhaps just have some fun and entertain the others, luring them into their evil ways. It's not uncommon for followers of the Forsworn to resort to such tactics to slowly mold their disciples to their will...to slide them down the path of evil so to speak."

"Didn't turn out so well for them." This time Bearit's smile wasn't forced.

Jonas shrugged and drank from his ale, his mood serious. "I do have another question. Do you know magic as well?"

Jonas looked up from his cup. "Are you referring to my sword flying through the air?"

"I am. I have not seen anything like that. He was held against the wall and your sword flew through the air to impale him, there is no doubt. That must be magic."

"Not really," Jonas said. "I am a cognivant, are you familiar with that term?"

"No."

"The elves refer to someone with my skill as an Ishmian. It is a very rare inherent ability. Sometimes it manifests as being able to read minds, but in my case I can mentally move things. I am able to see all things that make up our world, and I can control them."

"I do not understand," Bearit said.

Jonas smiled knowingly. "Not to worry, I'm not sure if I do either. The best way I can explain it is when I focus on this ability, that I see the world differently. Everything that makes up who we are, what this table is, or this chair, is the same thing. It's like they are made up of small particles, and to some degree I can reach out and touch them with my mind, even if they are far away."

"I've never heard of this before," Bearit exclaimed in surprise.

"It is very rare. And it has its limitations. If I overuse the power it can bring debilitating headaches. I must be sparing in its use."

Bearit ate some more food as he let Jonas's words sink in. Then he looked up. "Now what will you do?"

Jonas ripped off a piece of bread and dipped it into the bowl of honey, popping it into his mouth. "I'm going to find out what is happening here. Who these black clad pale men are and why they are taking people away. Something evil is happening and I'm going to find out what it is. Shyann led me here for a reason."

Bearit placed his massive forearms on the edge of the table and leaned in, his dark eyes serious. "Let me help you." Before Jonas could respond he continued. "I am strong and I be a hard worker. I can help you." Jonas looked at him, his own eyes just as serious, contemplating his request. "Please," Bearit said. "Don't save me this night to leave me to face another alone. Give me work. I can help," he said adamantly.

Jonas leaned back in his chair. There was something about the young man. He wasn't sure what it was but he had seen it before, in men and women he had known throughout his life. The young man's eyes reflected strength, a need to correct wrongs, a core of humanity supported with an iron resolve. His friend Fil had it, as well Allindrian, the half-elf Bladesinger, and his mentor and friend, Kiln. His mind drifted to images of his friend, Hagar, the ogrillian who had given his life defending the gates of Finarth because it was the right thing to do. Kromm's stern visage danced in his mind's eye as the battle king of Tarsis fought the dragon at Finarth. He had never met a man who embodied an indomitable will and charisma like King Kromm. And he could never forget Taleen. She had come to his rescue and helped him and Kiln kill the Greever, a powerful demon that would've likely killed him if not for her aid. She had taught him what it meant to be a cavalier and the pain of her death still weighed on his heart like a stone. These men and women, who it was his honor to have served with, had strength of heart that could not be subdued, and he now saw that same strength in the young man before him. If he could do something to make sure that that strength would not be crushed by the evil they fought, then he had to do it.

Jonas reached for his mug of ale as Bearit watched him intently. He took a long gulp, finishing the drink, before setting the cup back down. "I will need to teach you how to use that axe."

Bearit smiled as he released the breath he hadn't realized he had been holding.

***

They both slept in later than usual, the fight, along with the late supper and bath wearing them out. After rousing themselves, Jonas left Bearit downstairs with breakfast and plenty of coffee, instructing him to stay there while he went out to get some healing supplies. He found an apothecary easy enough and bought some salves, herbs, and as luck would have it, two healing draughts the proprietor had hidden away for those who knew to ask. Jonas was aware they were hard to come by, the healing properties and magic required were beyond most people's skill. They were very expensive, but luckily for Jonas, one of the many gifts Shyann gave him was a coin purse that was never empty. It made sense, after all, if he was to be her sword and uphold her principles of honor, courage, and most importantly, altruism, then he would need coin to do so, as proven by this very situation.

He made it back to the Wayward Lady, downing one potion along the way. By the time he arrived, his burn wounds were reduced to pink scars, and his eye and lip were no longer swollen. Bearit still sat at the table eating a second meal of warm oats and honey. Jonas paid the bill and motioned for Bearit to follow him.

"Thank you for the food," Bearit said, keeping pace with Jonas and Tulari.

Jonas nodded. "You'll need the energy."

"What are we doing then," Bearit asked, somewhat warily.

"Starting your training. But first," Jonas continued, "tell me what happened to your family."

As they made their way through the throng of people, many of them workers, traders, or locals going about their business as usual, Bearit gave Jonas an abridged version of his story. "I did not know my mother, she left when I was young. My father, he did work in the woods. A logger north of the lake. He died not long ago in a logging accident." Bearit shrugged. "After that, work slowed. I am but eighteen summers and no one wanted to give me contracts. Once I could not pay taxes, the King's men took my father's land. I've been on the road since, only finding work here and there. Not long after I ended up where you found me." Bearit finished with a despairing look on his face.

Jonas's face was passive. It was a typical story, not that much different from his own. He felt sorry for the young man, but he had heard worse. "And that axe," Jonas said, turning a questioning gaze towards the tool, "it was your father's?"

"No. He gave it to me. It be the only thing I have left from him."

"I see. The problem is that axe is not intended to be a weapon. The balance and weight is made to cut logs, not to fight."

Bearit narrowed his eyes at the implication. "I will not get rid of it."

"You don't have to," Jonas said. "But we need to get you an axe fit for a warrior." Just then he glanced up and saw the sign he was looking for. "Follow me."

Jonas entered a door on his right. Bearit glanced up and saw that the sign above read *Lowle's Armor and Blades*.

Once inside Jonas looked around with purpose. The room was nearly as large as the Wayward Lady's hearth room. The wall facing him was occupied by a counter that spanned the entire distance, another door behind the counter was the only other exit. That door was expertly made of thick boards interlaced with black steel. The lock was a heavy iron deadbolt. The door was clearly made to keep people out. The countertop was made of glass as well as the front of the counter that faced the customers. Inside, neatly placed on soft crimson fabric, were many smaller bladed weapons. The other walls were lined with weapons of various design, as well as suits of armor of different make, from leather to full plate mail. There were weapon racks placed throughout that made small walkways between them on the left and right, keeping the line of sight from the door to the counter unobstructed. Whoever Mr. Lowle was, he kept a tidy shop, and appeared to be doing quite well.

Bearit joined him as Jonas made his way to the counter where a burly man waited, watching them approach. "I have no money," Bearit whispered. Jonas just smiled as he approached the counter, Tulari obediently as his side.

The man was polishing the glass and Jonas couldn't help but notice his bare muscular arms. He must have been past fifty but still looked like he could wield any of the weapons he sold. And by the many scars across his arms, as well as a nasty one down the side of his face and neck, Jonas figured he had at one time used many of the weapons, and, perhaps, still did. His eyes were blue-gray and his enormous bald head made him look every bit the warrior. He seemed so stern looking that his wide bright smile threw Jonas off guard.

"Good evening gentleman, my name is Lowle and I am at your service. What can I do for you?" Then he noticed Tulari and his smile slipped somewhat, taking on a subtle worried expression. "Not to be rude, as your dog looks to be a fine specimen, but if any other customers come in and seem nervous, I will have to ask you to leave *him*," he requested, "outside."

"Her," Jonas corrected. "And that is fair."

"Ah, very good." Lowle's smile sprang back quickly. "Now what can I do for you?"

"I need to outfit my friend here. We will need an axe suitable for his size as well as armor. We do not have time to have anything custom fit or made for him, so I assume chainmail will be all you have."

Lowle eyed Bearit appraisingly, and even with his height, he still had to look up at the young woodsman. "You assumed correctly. But I do have a well-made set of chainmail that I think will fit him, although it might be tight in the arms."

"Very well," Jonas replied, a business-like tone to his voice. "Can we see your axes?"

"Of course," Lowle said, walking through the gap in the counter towards the wall on his right. There were eight different war axes hanging on various pegs.

Jonas stopped him quickly. "Not those weapons," he said. "*Those* weapons," he added, his eyes looking at the stout door behind the counter.

Lowle stopped and raised his eyes to match Jonas' gaze. "And you can afford *those* weapons?"

"I can. And if your steel is good I will happily pay a fair price. I would also like you to store his axe, a contract seal written up of course, with proper compensation."

Lowle glanced at the wood axe strapped around Bearit's chest. He was visibly confused why he would want to spend money to store such a simple tool, but he didn't argue. It was easy money. "Suit yourself. Please, follow me."

They entered through the door into another room, this one much smaller but no less impressive. There was another man polishing weapons, and he looked up when they entered. Jonas guessed he was in his late twenties, close to his own age, and the spitting image of his father, except he had a wavy mop of dark brown hair, the top pulled into a topknot.

"Cayden, go watch the store while I see to these customers," Lowle said.

71

Cayden rehung the sword he was polishing, glanced at Jonas and Bearit as if he was skeptical they could afford the weapons in the room, and walked out the door.

Jonas immediately went to a rack along one of the walls. There were four magnificent axes, all of various shapes and designs. Only two of them looked to be the right size and configuration for someone Bearit's stature. He picked up a double bladed axe and turned to face Bearit. The twin blades were wide and polished silver, the center ending in a long spike. The handle was thick and strong, the wood stained black. The lower handle was wrapped in black leather. The center of the wood handle was encased in steel and Jonas quickly understood the purpose. If one were skilled enough and so inclined, he could hold the axe two handed, one hand under the blades, the other at the base, and use it like a staff, blocking blades along the steel wrapped around the center of the shaft. The handle ended in a metal ball as big as a fist with two smaller curved blades jutting out in either direction, allowing damage to be done from all angles and ends of the axe. Despite Jonas's strength, it was much too heavy for him to wield properly, although the balance felt good. On each wide blade were etched intricate flowing designs to give the axe an artistic flare. It was a beautiful weapon.

"You have good taste," Lowle said. "That axe was forged by the best weapon smith this side of the Tundrens. He designed it for a lord in Osrigard but the man died before he could claim the weapon. It's too big for most warriors, so it has sat here for some time."

Jonas handed the axe to Bearit who held it before him, testing the weight. "I thought it would be heavier," he said.

Jonas raised his eyebrows at that. It seemed quite heavy to him. There were few who looked as strong as the young man standing before him. Graggis, the famous axe man from Finarth, had no match, besides maybe the dwarves, in axe fighting. And his strength was legendary. Jonas didn't think anyone could match the power of Graggis...that was until he had met King Kromm from Tarsis. The warrior king was a giant, and more fierce and powerful in battle than anyone Jonas had yet witnessed. Bearit looked as if he could easily wield the axe, perhaps in time even matching the ability and power of those great warriors. "It is a well-balanced weapon, so despite its weight, it won't feel too heavy." Then he looked at Lowle. "How much for the axe?"

Lowle rubbed his chin as if thinking of a price, though Jonas knew full well the price was in his head and he was just engaged in barter. "I can let you have it for fifty gold pieces."

"And the chainmail?'

"Another thirty."

"I'll give you seventy for both, and that will include the first year of storage for his wood axe, or until he retrieves it."

It was a fair price and Lowle knew it. "Deal. I will draw up the contract for storing the axe and get the chainmail so he can try it on. Do you have the coin with you?"

"I do not. I will need a money lender."

"You're in luck, there is one two stores down."

The magical properties of Jonas's coin purse was limited, allowing him to draw coins daily, but not enough to match the agreed upon price. It mattered little to him, however. One of the perks of being a friend to Kiln, the Lord of Finarth, the famous swordsman and commander, was that he was given a writ of purchase, allowing him to draw coins from the royal coffers in Finarth from any money lender east or west of the mountains. It would just be a matter of showing the writ, signing for the coins, and bringing the gold back to Lowle. Of course his signet ring would have to match the stamp on the writ, but Jonas knew that it did.

"I'll be back before the midday meal," Jonas said, nodding to Bearit for them to leave.

Bearit was standing there wide eyed, his mouth agape. He had never even had that much money let alone spent it on an axe and armor. Just the thought of spending that kind of coin shocked him. "I cannot let you buy those for me."

"The deal's done," Jonas said amiably, looking back at Lowle. "While you draw up the contract, I would like to purchase new clothes for my friend. Could you recommend someone?"

Lowle nodded. "It's a bit more expensive, but worth it. Jarl is honest and his product is of the highest quality. Just go down the street and turn right at the first alley. His shop is there on the right. You can't miss it."

Jonas reached out and shook Lowle's hand in the warrior's grip, hand to forearm. "I will be back soon."

Lowle nodded and led them from the room.

After outfitting Bearit, collecting the coins and purchasing the axe and armor, they ate a quick meal at a local tavern before Jonas led him out of town. They left the city gates walking at a brisk pace.

"I do thank you again," Bearit said for a third time. "I know not what more to say. Everything be so nice." He was now wearing his chainmail over a new set of cotton underclothes. His feet bore supple leather boots laced up tight over gray wool trousers, well made for comfort as well as adverse weather. A forest green cotton tunic covered most of the chainmail and was cinched tight around his waist by a leather belt, a well-made hunting knife strapped to his side. To top off the ensemble, he wore a matching hooded gray cloak that draped his shoulders and was big enough to be pulled tight around his body in cold or rainy weather. His new axe rode easily upon his back, a nice leather strap securing it around his torso.

"You are welcome," Jonas said again, with a slight smile.

They went about a half mile out of town before Jonas stopped in a clearing off the side of the main road. It looked as if it was a common campsite for travelers visiting the city. It was empty now and the flat grass and dirt would be perfect. Jonas stopped and faced Bearit, drawing both of his blades.

Bearit unconsciously stepped away from him, while unslinging his new axe at the same time. "Now," Jonas began. "I cannot train you to be a competent warrior in just a day. But we can work on the basics, giving you things to practice on your own, which you must if you don't want to die the first time you face a skilled adversary. Do you understand?"

"I do."

"Good. One more thing before we begin." Jonas's tone turned serious, and he looked grave. Bearit picked up on it, his own reflection matching Jonas's tone. "I have given you these weapons in good faith, but they do not come free." Bearit shifted uncomfortably, not sure where he was going. "You must agree to uphold all that is good, to be an image of honor, kindness, and courage, as long as you use these weapons. Do you agree?"

Bearit nodded. "I do."

"Good, now hold the handle of the axe with one arm and extend the weapon."

Bearit gripped the lower handle with his right hand and extended the long weapon. He held the axe perpendicular, his strong forearms flexing as he fought against the weight of the twin blades. Jonas was impressed with his strength.

"Good, now slowly swing the weapon back and forth to get a feel for the weight."

Bearit did as he was told. "It is much heavier than any axe I've ever used."

"Yes it is, which is why it will do severe damage to an enemy. But the weight will be something you will have to get used to," Jonas continued. "Now, grip the shaft with both hands and hold the weapon before you." Bearit did as instructed. "When you use a wood axe, you swing with all your might to split the log. You will have to correct this habit if you want to survive."

"You mean I shouldn't use all my strength?"

"Partially," Jonas continued. "You must learn to recognize when to use it, and when to withhold. You have great strength, and if you learn to harness it correctly, you may become a powerful warrior. One of the most dangerous axe men I know is strong like you, but what makes him so deadly is his ability to control the weapon that is so unwieldy for most people. You see, your strength, when used at the right moments, will make you a deadly adversary. Do you remember what happened when you swung your axe at that man that nearly killed you?"

"I do," Bearit said, thinking back. "He dodged my swing and me axe hit the rock wall. It did knock me off balance."

"That's right. If you had controlled that swing, and missed, you would have been able to adjust and get your weapon back in time to block his next swing. And it's not just adjusting your strength, but also your movements and body position."

"I understand."

"We'll see," Jonas said with a smile, holding both his blades out wide. "Now, swing the axe with both hands back and forth before you, stopping your swing just as the blade nears the tip of my swords. Start slow."

Bearit braced his legs and swung the axe. Before the blade traveled a hand-span, Jonas snapped his foot forward, striking Bearit in the chest so hard that it knocked him to the ground. Bearit got up quickly, embarrassed and a little angry.

"What did you do wrong?" Jonas asked calmly.

Bearit thought for a moment, controlling his anger. "I was off balance."

"Why?"

"My legs?"

"Yes. Never stand flat footed with your legs side by side. Always stand with your body sideways, on your toes, with your feet front to back. You can adjust to attacks and counters much faster." Jonas showed him and Bearit followed his lead. "Good, now try again."

He swung the axe slowly as instructed, stopping the weapon at one sword tip before reversing direction and moving towards the other. He did it maybe ten times before Jonas said, "Now faster." Bearit picked up the speed. "Remember, the faster you go, the more strength you will need to stop the momentum and reverse the direction. You will need to build up your core strength significantly." They continued for quite some time, with Jonas lowering his sword tips and bringing them high, at head level, forcing Bearit to adjust his swings and increase the speed. Jonas was impressed with his strength and stamina. Clearly he was used to swinging an axe and working long hours. But he hadn't swung an axe that heavy before and it wasn't long before he was sweating and his movements began to slow. Finally Jonas stopped and stepped back. "You are strong, Bearit, there is no doubt. But work on your stamina. Practice those movements daily and you will be surprised how much your speed and endurance increases."

"I will do as you say."

Jonas smiled. "We are not done yet." Bearit gritted his teeth and adjusted his grip on the deadly axe. Jonas liked his determination. "Now, what is the best way to block an attack?"

Bearit took a moment as he inspected the axe. "Well, the shaft looks like it be made to do just that. And I would think the flat of the blade would work in a bind."

"Good," Jonas said. "And don't forget that you can use the edge of the blades where they join the shaft and the spike at the front. If you look at the angle of the blade, you can catch a sword strike there, spinning it and pinning the blade against the spike," he said, pointing to the thick steel where it joined the shaft. "Then you can use the edge of the blades to redirect the attack, or even spin it away from you where you can then deliver a deadly blow. Let's try it."

Bearit looked at the axe in his hand in a new light, inspecting the front of the weapon and the points of the blades jutting forward from the shaft. Jonas lifted his blades. "I will start slowly, attacking you at various locations and levels. Use the weapon to block, and as you do so, always be thinking of attacking maneuvers." Bearit nodded his head as he held the heavy axe before him in both hands. Jonas started off slow, his swords coming in level and at a moderate pace. Bearit blocked the first few strokes with the middle of the shaft, the steel covering the wood making a ringing sound. The axe was of good design, the steel covering the middle of the shaft, in between the handles near the axe head and the base, flared up at the ends, allowing a sword stroke to slide across the steel and miss the axe wielder's fingers. Jonas reversed direction and came at Bearit with a downward stroke. Bearit hesitated for a moment before lifting the axe head up and blocking his attack on the edge of the front of the blades. "Good," Jonas said. "Remember, the other end of the axe is made to inflict damage as well. You can block with the front, then pivot your body and swing the end of the axe up and attack with the two blades there."

"Attack me again from above," Bearit said. Jonas did so, his sword coming down, this time a little faster. Bearit shot the head of his axe forward, and as the blade struck the edge of the steel, he pivoted to the side, using the points of the axe blades to knock Jonas's sword out of the way, while adjusting forward and swinging the rear of his axe up and towards Jonas's torso. Jonas pivoted away easily but smiled at his effort.

"That's the idea," Jonas said.

"Let's keep practicing," Bearit said, enjoying the work.

And practice they did. For most of the day they continued their work, stopping only for a late lunch of dried ham, cheese, and bread that Jonas had procured in the morning, drinking large amounts of water to wash it down and quench their thirst. They practiced a few more hours and as the sun began its daily descent they decided to head back into the city. Jonas walked with a purpose and that piqued Bearit's interest.

"Where we be going?" Bearit asked as he kept pace next to him. Tulari had run off during the day to hunt, returning midday and now trotting next to Jonas, and although she was in dog form, her shoulders were still at his waist.

"We need to see the Earl," Jonas said. "I need to find out if he is familiar with the sigil I cut from that man. Something tells me the mark is important. I also need to tell him what I have found so far."

"And how will you gain audience with the Earl?"

Jonas glanced up at Bearit, smiling. "I can be quite persuasive."

They made their way through the streets of Gyeen. Many people were out and the shops were still a bustle of activity, selling local goods as well as commodities from Ronith and Onett. Most of the homes, shops, and buildings were constructed of wood from the Lasur'een Forest, floated across the lake to the busy docks. Iron ore, silver, gold, and precious stones were mined from the Sarhast Mountains that lined the southern edges of the forest and shipped down river to the lake front town. Accordingly, there was quite a growing trade in jewelry as well as silver and gold ware. The craftsmen from Lanard were some of the best, their goods procuring a hefty price.

"Where be the Earl's keep?" Bearit asked.

"East side of town, overlooking the lake," Jonas answered. "When I came into town last week I saw it near the docks. If we time it right we should catch him before his evening meal."

It didn't take them long to make their way to the docks. Once there, it was easy enough to see the Earl's keep, its stone walls rising from the edge of the lake, four towers gracing each corner, the blue flags of Lanard fluttering in the wind. Gyeen was part of the Kingdom of Lanard and the Earl was appointed by the King to rule in his name. They made their way through the wharf, the street running along the edge of the docks filled with traders, sailors, and dock workers moving crates on and off various boats lashed to the docks that spanned out into the calm waters of the massive lake. They were working hard, eager to finish for the day to go home to a warm meal and a soft bed. The strong smell of fish and sweat assaulted them as they made their way through the docks. Jonas had to admit that it was beautiful there, the tall peaks of the Sarhast Mountains far off in the distance, an evening fog drifting off the calm waters of the lake.

The gate into the keep was open but the portcullis was down, two guards standing before it. Jonas looked up and saw armored men walking the wall, long bows held easily in hand. As they neared, the two guards stepped towards them, their spears held before them.

"Good evening," Jonas said casually, his hand touching the soft fur of Tulari. "I request to see the Earl."

"The Earl is not holding audience today." The guard frowned. "You must not be from around here. Earl Magnar's audience day is Saturday. Besides, it is late and he will be at supper soon."

Saturday was two days away and Jonas couldn't wait that long. "I regret to say I cannot wait that long. The Earl is the servant of the people and I have information that pertains to the safety of those people."

The guard looked at his comrade, looking for guidance. All he got was a shrug of his shoulders. Looking back at Jonas, he said, "Who are you?"

"I am Jonas Kanrene. This is my apprentice, Bearit." Bearit wasn't really his apprentice of course, but he did not know how else to explain the young man's presence. He figured it would do.

"Apprentice of what?"

"I am a knight."

The guard laughed, looking Jonas up and down. "Knight for whom?" he asked mockingly.

"Shyann, Goddess of the Hunt." His look was dead calm, and the guards shifted uncomfortably under his steady gaze. Jonas didn't blame the guards. After all, he looked like no knight they had ever seen. He wore a gray cloak over black armor of a unique design. The center, protecting his chest, was an unadorned charcoal-gray steel plate. The seams of the armor were made from black chainmail allowing for protection similar to plate but movement like he was wearing chainmail. His pauldrons were black leather covered in gray steel. His clothes looked average and even his sword hilts were black and unadorned. The bow on his back looked like the simple bow of a huntsman. His knives too were plain and simple, as unassuming in appearance as everything else. To the guards before him he probably looked like the average armed trader. But that estimation couldn't be further from the truth. Nearly everything he wore or carried was enchanted, given to him by Shyann herself, designed to allow him to blend in but giving him the power similar to a cavalier. His boots gave him extra speed, his clothes allowed him to blend into his surrounding, and his gloves gave him the dexterity of an elf.

The guards smile disappeared. "Do not jest of such things. Shyann is not common in these parts, but I know of her, and I'm sure she would not wish you to mock her name."

"I do not jest," Jonas answered calmly. "Perhaps if you give this to the Earl he will see me," Jonas continued as he reached into a pouch at his belt. He removed a ring and handed it to the guard, who inspected it carefully.

The ring was of unique design, expertly made by a master silversmith. On the top, etched into the silver, was the Finarthian crest, and underneath, also etched in silver, was the Tarsinian crest. The ring was the signet ring of both kingdoms. After Malbeck's War, King Kromm of Tarsis returned to his lands with his son, Prince Riker, and together, along with the queen, they began the slow process of rebuilding. Tarsis had been destroyed by Malbeck and his army before they moved south to Finarth for the final stand. The Finarthian royal family was all killed during the conflict, King Baylin Gavinsteal's death at the hands of the blood dragon ending the royal lineage. At least that's what they all thought. It was discovered that Prince Riker's mother could trace her ancestry back to a long dead Finarthian King, and that meant that the young prince had the blood of both royal families. The two kingdoms were now united in a way that no one could have predicted. Finarth was now ruled by a temporary council of lords, Kiln, the famous general and swordsman, leading that council. With Finarth's help, they were rebuilding Tarsis, and once complete, the two kingdoms would eventually be ruled by Prince Riker's descendants.

"What is this?" the guard asked.

"That is the signet ring of both Tarsis and Finarth. I am a Knight of Shyann, and an emissary of both kingdoms. I speak in her name, as well as theirs. I suggest you move quickly. I'd like to see him before supper."

This time the guard looked at his comrade, his early bravado replaced by uncertainty. He looked back at Jonas. "Wait here."

The guard was gone for a quarter hour before he returned with three more soldiers. All except one wore blue tunics with the Rothar family sigil of a winged dragon holding a sword in its talons over their chainmail.

One man, the only one wearing a silver cuirass embossed with the same sigil, stepped forward. He looked Jonas up and down before flicking his gaze to Bearit and Tulari. "I am Captain Taddick," he said, his voice stern. "This is your ring?" He held up the signet ring.

"It is. I am Jonas Kanrene." Jonas saw the man's eyes flash in recognition, his stern gaze replaced with something else, perhaps uncertainty, or admiration, Jonas could not tell.

Captain Taddick was tall, his black hair streaked with gray. His mustache grew into a sharp, neatly trimmed beard, both of which also had strokes of silver. "I know who you are. Your exploits during Malbeck's War are known this far west, at least to some," he said, ending his last words with a stern look at the two guards. The guards looked away from the warrior, but Jonas saw them glance back in his direction. Neither of them knew who he was, but based on the Captain's reverence, he was clearly someone important. "I'm sorry for the delay," Captain Taddick continued. "The Earl has just finished up some business. He is ready to see you."

"Very good," Jonas said as he took the ring back from the Captain.

The Captain nodded. "Please, follow me."

They made their way into a courtyard before moving through a massive set of oak doors. As they walked through a long hallway, the Captain addressed Jonas. "Your dog seems quite tame."

"She is a good dog," Jonas said, smiling and patting Tulari on the side of her head. "Her name is Tulari." Tulari growled in acknowledgement.

Captain Taddick took note of the large dog and the deep powerful growl. "Is she safe? I mean no disrespect but the Earl's safety is my utmost concern."

"There is nothing to fear from Tulari. You have my word."

The Captain seemed content with that answer. He led them into a spacious room with a raised dais on one side. On the dais was a throne and seated upon the stout wood chair was Earl Magnar. He was talking with a tall man in a blue robe when they entered. Four other guards were there, two on each side of the dais. The room was simple, with large windows on either side close to where the tall walls met with the roof, shedding the last remaining light across the stone floor. Four huge metal braziers were at each corner of the room, large fires burning brightly casting their light throughout. Behind the raised dais was a single door and above it, spanning the length of the wall, was a massive blue tapestry, the Rothar sigil expertly woven into the thick cloth. Jonas noticed a door on either wall flanking them. Once they moved before the Earl, the man in the blue robe stepped aside and stood behind and to the side of the throne. Jonas guessed he was an advisor, or perhaps a wizard. He had that look.

"Good evening Earl Magnar, I appreciate the audience on such short notice," Jonas said, standing before him.

The Earl was a big man, heavy in the shoulders and neck and thick across the chest, most of it soft, flabby flesh, a clear reflection that food was never too far out of reach. He wore a richly adorned maroon robe not succeeding at hiding his thick arms and belly, the expensive material edged with gold lacing and lined with white fur. His long hair was brown and gray, pulled back and held in place by a silver crown, the center baring the Rothar family crest. He waved away Jonas's words casually. "It is not a problem," he said with a smile. "My Captain said you are Jonas Kanrene. Is that true?"

"It is."

"I had heard you were a cavalier."

"I was," Jonas said, not skipping a beat.

Once it was obvious that Jonas was not going to elaborate, the Earl continued. "What can I do for you? Captain Taddick mentioned something about the safety of my people."

Jonas nodded and reached into a pouch at his side withdrawing the cloth that held the patch of skin. "I have been led here by Shyann and have found something strange, witnessing a handful of abductions by black cloaked men. Have you had reports of missing people?"

The Earl looked at the blue robed man next to him, his face showing his worry. "We have. Jonas, this is Galright, my advisor and court wizard," the Earl said, looking towards the man.

Jonas nodded at the wizard. "Well met."

Galright nodded his head deeper in respect. "Likewise, Jonas Kanrene. The Earl and I were just talking about such matters before you entered. It seems we have had four missing person reports in the last four days." Jonas suspected more, but many of the people the pale bald men preyed upon probably had no family or anyone who had cared enough to report them missing.

"I think that will end, at least for now," Jonas said. Galright raised his eyebrows questionably and Jonas continued. "I found a hidden safe house last night beneath the city. There were men there, wearing all black, and pale as snow, and they had many others with them. They looked to be vagrants and homeless. It seemed as if the black cloaked men were somehow recruiting them."

The Earl leaned forward in his chair, clearly interested. "For what?"

Jonas frowned. "I do not know. But I'd like you to look at something," he said, lifting the black cloth and approaching the throne. As he neared he unbound the cloth from the skin and held it before the Earl, who looked at the piece of skin with uncertainty.

"That is skin?"

"It is, but look..." Jonas didn't finish his sentence before the Earl cut him off.

"That mark is the mark of the Red Guard," he said, looking closer, his eyes wide with recognition.

Even Galright seemed shocked as he stepped closer. Jonas handed it to him to inspect. "What is this Red Guard?" Jonas asked.

"They are the personal guard of the king taken from our best warriors," the Earl answered. "Where did you get this?"

"I cut it off one of the men I was telling you about. They were pale, with no hair, and they did not bleed."

Galright looked up from the skin in his hand. "What happened to these men?"

"I killed them," Jonas said matter-of-factly.

"You killed members of the Red Guard," the Earl said incredulously.

"They were the Red Guard no longer," Jonas quickly added. "I told you. They were capturing and luring men for reasons unknown. But they were evil, there was no doubt."

The Earl sat back in his chair, thinking. Then he looked at Galright. "Do you think these men that Jonas killed could be the missing guards?"

"I was thinking the same thing," Galright agreed.

"What missing guards?"

The Earl sighed. "Jonas, we have much to discuss. We received an urgent message from the King two days ago. Something has happened." The Earl stopped, thinking if this was the time and place to discuss the message. He decided it wasn't. "Have you eaten yet? This message would best be discussed over wine and warm food."

"We have not."

"Good. I suggest we dine together. I have some rather troubling news to share with you."

Jonas was just about to respond when Tulari growled deeply, her body suddenly going rigid. *Danger... windows....evil.* Her words drifted in Jonas's mind as her body grew to its full size. Earl Magnar's eyes widened in fright as Tulari grew into a ferocious wolf as big a young bull. Jolting backwards he nearly fell from the throne just as Captain Taddick drew his blade and jumped before his Earl, thinking that Tulari was a threat, and rightfully so as he could not hear her warning.

Jonas drew both his blades in a flash. "Danger is upon us! At the windows!" he yelled. "Tulari is no danger to you!"

Captain Taddick and the other guards seemed to know that Jonas was referring to the huge beast at his side, but they had little time to ponder what had just happened as the windows around them shattered inward, raining glass down upon them. The roaring fires were bright, but their orange glow barely reached the upper portion of the ceiling where the windows were located. But it was enough.

Pale naked forms crawled through the openings like spiders, their clawed hands and feet gripping the stone like a cat running up a tree. They were human in form, with longer arms and legs, their heads bald with slightly protruding jaws, their mouths wide and filled with teeth. Their ears were pointy and their white eyes were centered with glowing red orbs. But there was little time to register what they were seeing before the beasts leapt down to the floor, landing on all fours like cats. More came from the windows, scurrying forth like ants crawling from their holes.

Jonas glanced around him quickly trying to take in the threat. He immediately noticed something. "They are blocking the doors!" he yelled. "We cannot run! Prepare to fight!"

Unconsciously they had all backed closer together, their weapons held before them. Even the Earl had a sword, his guards standing protectively around him with drawn steel. Then ten of the creatures converged on them while others blocked the exits. It was eerie as the only noise they made was the sound of their sharp claws cutting through the stone as they shot towards them.

Jonas dropped into the state of Ty'erm, becoming one with the energy around him and shutting out everything from his mind other than what he needed to survive. Of all the things that Kiln had taught him, the state of meditation had been the most important to his survival. All movements slowed and his senses were heightened. It allowed him to focus his energy, to concentrate on what he needed to do to live rather than let his base emotions of fight or flight take over.

Reaching out with his right sword he drew in the particles around him and shot them forward with a huge amount of force, striking one beast in the head and catapulting it backwards, its body tumbling head over end until it crashed against the far wall, the thing's neck twisted and broken.

Two more were on him and his swords danced left and right, the edges of the blades glowing blue as they cut into pale flesh. He brought forth Shyann's light, the glowing blue tree flaring brightly, forcing the attacking beasts to pause momentarily as they covered their eyes from the stinging pain. Bearit was next to him but he had no time to help him, the enemy numbers quickly making it impossible. One beast hissed through the light and shot forward incredibly fast, but Jonas, in his meditative state, saw it coming. Ripping one blade from the chest of a beast, he ducked low under the other attack, pushing up with his strong legs and back, using the creature's own momentum to throw it high and backwards. Hopefully the thing wouldn't crash into any of the other men behind him, but he couldn't worry about that as another slashed its claws across his leg. The steel plate on his thigh flared blue as the thing's claws struck it. His armor was blessed by Shyann and anything of pure evil would be repelled by it. The beast hissed and retracted its clawed hand just as fast as it had attacked. Jonas followed up with a snap kick to the thing's face, knocking its head back forcefully as he brought his other sword across the stunned creature's neck.

Bearit's mouth felt like cotton and his heart pounded in his chest, the creatures closing on him faster than he thought possible. He was a big powerful man, and the first thing that he did was a natural reaction to keep something as awful as the creatures before him away. He snapped his big foot forward, his new boot cracking the lead beast in the face as it paused from Jonas's light, the strike stopping it in its tracks. Another slashed at him, the thing's claws scraping across his chainmail shirt that hung below his hip. And yet a third leapt at him from over the creature he kicked. He had no time to think, he just reacted. With his left hand he spun his big axe down and to the side, cutting the arm off of the beast there. That move alone was a testament of his strength, wielding the heavy axe with one hand in a controlled maneuver. Simultaneously, he lunged forward with his right fist, slamming his huge hand into the leaping beast's throat. He was lucky actually, as he had aimed for the thing's head. If his aim had been true, he could have broken his fist on the beast's thick skull. Luckily, the creature tried to turn away from the strike, exposing its neck in the process. Something gave way under the tremendous impact and the howling beast fell to the side.

There was a bright flash to Bearit's left and he glanced over as Galright shot a bolt of lightning from his raised fist. The bolt forked and struck two creatures, knocking them off their feet. The odor of burnt flesh filled his nostrils. There was fighting and screaming all around him but he had no time to look and see how anyone else was faring. He was tired from his earlier practice but it mattered little as massive amounts of adrenaline shot through his body. He screamed and fought like a berserker, the twin blades of his axe flashing up and down, left and right, cutting into pale flesh as they got close. It wasn't pretty, but effective, the big sharp blades of the axe swung with his strength were delivering heavy damage.

Bearit felt danger on his left side and he turned to see Galright go down under three pales bodies, their long arms flashing up and down as their claws ripped into him. Blood splashed across the pavers as the wizard screamed horribly. Now that his flank was exposed, two more creatures attacked him, their red eyes boring into him. He tried to turn to face them, but another creature was before him. He cut the beast down with a vicious sideways chop, and just as he was expecting to feel the enemy claws slice into him, he heard a tremendous roar and saw Tulari slam into them, her mouth wrapped around the body of one while her huge paw pressed the other to the ground, her claws ripping through its flesh as she shook the other in her mouth. Flesh tore and bones snapped before she tossed the thing to the floor, the pale and broken body skittering across the stones.

Jonas fought furiously, creating a quick reprieve as he cut two more creatures down. Thinking quickly, he drew on his cognivant powers again, wrapping energy around him and running to the base of the stairs. Once he reached the first step, he leapt high, using the energy to propel him much higher than a man could typically jump. He landed gracefully on the throne, simultaneously sheathing his blades and spinning his bow off his shoulders. One creature blocked the door behind the throne and faster than a blink, Jonas reached back, gripped an arrow, nocked it, and shot it into the beast's forehead. Spinning on his foot to face the main battle, he jumped up on the chair's arm rests, braced his legs, and fired arrow after arrow into the remaining attackers from his elevated position. Allindrian, the half-elf Bladesinger, had taught him many things, but he was most thankful for her tireless lessons on the use of the bow. He could now nock an arrow, aim, and fire one shaft for every heartbeat, hitting nearly any target.

And he quickly passed the value of those lessons on to the vile creatures in front of him. He killed four more, the last one nearly making it to him before he shot it point blank through the open mouth. Finally having a few moments free from attack, Jonas surveyed the scene. Three of the guards were down as well as the wizard. Bearit and Taddick were fighting side by side and the Earl was behind them, a sword held in his bloody hand. It looked as if he was slashed several times on his arms. But luckily for him the fourth guard next to him was a skilled swordsman, his blade killing one beast and keeping another at bay.

Jonas whipped his arm back and dispatched that creature with two arrows to its back. As he did so he heard Bearit scream. Glancing quickly towards him he saw the big man slip on a blood soaked paver. To his horror three beasts leapt on top of him as he fell.

Bearit felt several claws find his flesh on his arms and legs as he fought furiously, his armor protecting his torso. But it would only be moments before their sharp claws found his throat, and then it would all be over. He was suddenly furious, so angry that his body instantly flushed with more adrenaline. There was no way he was going to die like this. He had just been saved from his own weakness the day before, given armor and a weapon fit for a king, as well as a second chance at a life. He would not be killed the very next day, not even by creatures of his nightmares. He roared like an enraged bear, lifting up with his powerful legs and grabbing one beast in his huge arms, bringing the other two up with him. As he lifted the flailing creature over his head, the beast's sharp claws dug channels of red up his arms before he tossed the creature far and high. He was too preoccupied with the other two creatures on him to witness Jonas's skill as he hit the flying beast twice with arrows before it hit the floor. Bearit rammed his elbow into another creature, knocking the snapping teeth away from his throat and giving him some space to punch the creature in the face three times. Then he felt sharp claws wrap around his thick neck and knew that the third beast was just getting ready to rip out his throat. As he punched the stunned creature before him, he expected to feel his blood spray from his neck, but he felt nothing of the sort. Instead the clawed hand released him, scratching him badly in the process but not inflicting a killing blow. Bearit spun around and saw the creature on its back, an arrow jutting from its eye. Looking up the stairs, he saw Jonas standing on the arms of the chair holding his bow in his hand, an arrow nocked and aimed. In a flash it thudded into the beast Bearit had punched, stopping it from ripping open his leg with its fanged mouth. Spinning around, Bearit saw that all the attackers were now dead. Suddenly weary, his arms and legs feeling like lead, he dropped to his knees next to his bloody axe. Captain Taddick was next to him panting heavily, his crimson stained sword held in his right hand. He dripped blood from several cuts, but none of them looked life threatening.

Earl Magnar was sitting on the ground surrounded by bodies, most of which were killed by Jonas's arrows. He was bleeding from several deep cuts on his arms and legs. The one remaining guard was kneeling next to him, his forehead bleeding badly from a deep cut. It looked as if they would each make it.

Jonas leaped from the chair and bounded down the steps, moving quickly to Bearit's side. "Where are you hurt?"

Bearit looked at him, his face smeared with his own blood. "I'm not sure. I'm so tired."

"That's normal. The adrenaline is leaving your body. Let me look at you." Jonas looked him over quickly and didn't see any wound that would kill him. His right fist was cut and perhaps broken. He was bleeding badly from several deep slashes on his arms and legs, but once cleaned and bound and given ample rest he should be okay.

"Am I going to live?" Bearit asked, his voice faint as the loss of blood began to take its toll.

"You'll be fine," Jonas said. "Help will be coming soon enough. Take this," Jonas said as he fished out the other healing draught from a pouch at his belt. Handing it to Bearit, the big man downed it without question. "That should at least seal your wounds and bring back some energy."

"Thank you," Bearit said wearily, feeling better quickly.

As if on cue, guards erupted from the doors and ran into the room with weapons drawn. Jonas went to the Earl as they secured the room.

"How bad are you hurt?"

Earl Magnar smiled weakly. "Not as bad as I would be if you had not been here. Worry not, my healers should be here soon. Thank you."

Jonas nodded. "We still need to talk."

The Earl's smile disappeared. "Now more than ever."

CHAPTER THREE

It was late in the evening by the time the bodies of the creatures had been removed and the Earl was healed by his clerics, servants of Toolm. Of course Jonas knew Toolm as Ulren, the High One, the god's more common title in the east. It looked as if the Earl at least was not a follower of the old gods, as were many in these parts. Jonas's understanding of the Kingdom of Lanard was that they had relaxed laws on religion, allowing all to follow whom they wished.

Earl Magnar made sure that his healers took care of Captain Taddick and the lone surviving guard, as well as Bearit, who didn't need much assistance after he had taken the healing draught. The bodies of the soldiers, as well as Galright, were removed for proper burial. After making sure to bolster the keep's defenses, they retired to the Earl's private dining room, eager to leave the bloody council hall while workers cleaned up the blood. Captain Taddick was there along with Jonas and Bearit, and joining them was the Earl's wife, whom Jonas learned was Elena, a middle aged aristocratic looking woman from Lanard. Despite her stoic personality, she was clearly concerned for her husband.

Jonas had taken the time to investigate the bodies while the clerics did their healing. They looked to be human once, but clearly something had morphed them into nightmarish beasts. They did not bleed like a man, and they seemed smaller, like shrunken abominations of their former selves, whoever that might be. Their faces and heads were distorted, no longer recognizable as human. They were naked and pale white, with no evidence of whether they were male or female. Jonas wasn't sure they were ever human. He had never seen anything quite like them.

Trays of sliced meats, bread and butter, and stewed vegetables were placed all around the long table. Goblets of wine were poured and everyone, following the Earl's lead, dove right in, dispensing with the pleasantries of court. They were tired and hungry, postponing the inevitable conversation until their bellies were full and their minds somewhat relaxed.

The Earl spoke first. "Jonas, thank you again for saving us. I fear we would have perished without your warning and skill."

"We are in your debt," Elena added, her voice soft and calm, like she was used to people listening to her every word.

Jonas nodded. "I'm glad I was here to help, and I'm sorry about Galright and your men."

"Thank you," Earl Magnar replied. "They were good men."

"Before the attack you said that you had something to tell me." Jonas was eager to get to the bottom of these mysterious assailants.

The Earl sighed and drank from his wine. "Three days ago a messenger came from the king with a sealed parchment," the Earl began. "The news he brought was dire indeed." The Earl continued to tell them all about Maltheil's escape and the disappearance of the Red Guard troops. He took some time to tell Jonas and Bearit the history of the demon and what had happened so very long ago. Bearit of course knew of Maltheil's tale, but he, like many others, thought they were just that, tall tales told by bards. He was shocked to learn that the demon was, in fact, real.

Jonas leaned back in his chair. "So, if the men I killed were in fact the missing Red Guard soldiers, then somehow this demon you speak of has the power to control others, to turn them into something beyond what they used to be."

The Earl nodded. "That is true it would seem. Legend has it that Maltheil turned the royal family into its servants, and in doing so raised an army to sweep across Lanard and into Onett. But he was stopped, thankfully."

"What I fought in the catacombs of the city was different than what attacked us tonight," Jonas mused.

"Perhaps," Taddick added, "this demon's capabilities allow it some flexibility in how in changes its victims."

"If these things that attacked you were once human, then they came from somewhere. Has there been any reports to quantify this many missing people?" Elena asked. "My guess is Maltheil will take advantage of the small settlements between here and Lanard, taking slaves and turning its victims into servants."

Earl Magnar nodded solemnly. "We have had missing person's reports from the city, but no word from any outlining settlements."

"My guess is word will be arriving soon," Jonas said. "Which reminds me. It would be wise to send a message to Lanard about what has happened and to warn the king that such an attack could, if it hasn't already, happen there."

The Earl nodded in agreement, pointing to a guard near the door. "Turgar, please bring my scribe and runner to me immediately." The guard nodded and briskly walked from the room.

Captain Taddick looked to the Earl as if he just remembered something. "My Earl, what about the king's wedding?"

Elena looked at the Earl, her stoic face shifting to one of concern. The Earl too looked worried. "I had forgotten about that in all the chaos," Earl Magnar said.

"What wedding?" Jonas asked.

"King Rothar is soon to wed Kylin Oneck, the youngest Princess of Tur'el," the Earl said. "The arrangement has been long in the making with the hopes that it would end the violence between our kingdoms."

"When is this to take place?" Jonas asked.

"Two weeks from now," the Earl said. "As we speak an emissary force is en-route to Angar, a border town between our kingdoms. Once the treaty is signed, the procession will make its way to Lanard to prepare for the big event."

Jonas didn't like it. "And I can only assume the royal family of Tur'el will be with this procession."

"You are correct," Elena said. "We will all be at the wedding witnessing the historic event."

"Sounds like a perfect time for an attack," Jonas said. It was evident by everyone's expressions that they were thinking the same thing. "I need to find this demon." Tulari agreed, growling deeply next to Jonas

"How will you do this?" Captain Taddick asked.

"Shyann will guide me, have no doubt."

***

The next morning Jonas and Bearit departed at sunrise, Tulari, in dog form, leading the way at a brisk pace. The Earl had been kind enough to offer rooms for them both, as well as horses and provisions for a week, along with a detailed map of the Kingdom of Lanard. Jonas didn't know exactly where they would be going, their destination many possibilities as Tulari guided them further north towards Lanard.

Bearit had very little experience riding and he was failing miserably at hiding his discomfort. "I be thinkin' I'd rather walk," the logger said with a grimace as he tried adjusting his back side in the saddle.

Jonas smiled, looking sidelong at him. "Don't fight against the horse's movements. Work with him. You will get sore, there is no doubt. But once you get the hang of it you will not agree with your previous sentiment."

"I hope you be right."

They rode quietly for an hour, Jonas and Bearit side by side on the well-traveled road, Tulari in the lead. The environment around them was forested, with pockets of rolling grasslands, the gentle hills occasionally peppered with massive jutting rock formations bursting from the ground tripling the height of any tree. It was beautiful country.

"You think those creatures were demons?" Bearit asked, filling the silence as they both were lost in their own thoughts.

Jonas shrugged. "They looked it, and they avoided Shyann's light, which means something."

"As of several days ago I did not believe that demon's existed."

"I wish they didn't." Jonas looked at Bearit. "You did well in that fight. Most would have frozen with fear. You have strong nerves."

Bearit gave Jonas a forced smile. "I was afraid."

"Good," Jonas added. "You should've been. Many people think that being afraid somehow makes you less of a man. It is not true. Being courageous is when one conquers their fears, and then acts. There is no courage without fear, and when one boasts they fear nothing, then they are liars, and generally the first to run when presented with real danger."

"Do you get afraid?"

Jonas thought about it for a moment. "Yes, but not to die. I fear for those close to me. I fear to fail in helping others."

"I'm be afraid to die," Bearit offered.

Jonas smiled. "Most are, my friend. One thing I've learned is that the more times you escape death, the more you stop worrying about it. It will find us all, no matter how much we try to hide from it. Besides, worrying about death in battle will manifest that very thing to happen."

Bearit narrowed his eyes in thought, his look inquisitive. "What do you mean?"

"When you fight, you need to concentrate on everything around you. You need to focus, and thoughts of death will cause your mind to wander from that focus. And that is when you miss the strike that kills you." Jonas looked at Bearit, his eyes intense. "The deadliest warriors I know have an iron will. Their minds are as strong as their bodies. There is no give in them."

"How do I strengthen my mind?"

"Your will is already strong, Bearit. And it will get stronger with time. Experience builds it and practice strengthens it. Your mind is like a muscle, the more you work it and train it, the stronger it will become. In time your mind will be as strong as your body."

"I shall work on this," Bearit said. They continued on, both deep in their own thoughts.

Jonas was thinking, trying to come to terms with what they might be up against. His mind went to memories that he wished he could forget; his battle with the Greever, a demon summoned my Malbeck and sent to kill him, a mission the creature almost accomplished after killing many young men at Finarth, all knight apprentices. The hunter would have likely killed Kiln and Jonas both if Taleen hadn't come to their rescue. He thought of Taleen often, and it frustrated him that all of his memories of her were shadowed by violence. It was the nature of a cavalier's existence, but he wished he had something else to hold onto, some memory not splattered with blood and death. He missed her dearly and thought of her often. Not to mention he could use her sword, and her council right now, but if he were honest with himself he had wanted more from her. He had had feelings for her, and part of his anger and frustration at her death was that he was never able to say anything. He was so confident in battle, but when it came to women he acted like a novice who had never held a sword. His only intimate encounter with a female was the night Myrell joined him in his room at Cuthaine. He was embarrassed to admit that again he had no part in setting up that arrangement. She had come to him, and despite the amazing night he still felt just as insecure with the opposite gender. Not to mention she had been killed the next day, just like Taleen, and Jonas blamed himself. Death seemed to follow him. Then there was Allindrian. They had a complicated relationship, one born from war and violence, accentuated by the fact that they were from very different worlds. She was a half-elf Bladesinger who had already lived six times longer than he. They both lived lives filled with constant travel, the road slick with blood as they protected the weak and battled to keep the darkness at bay. Neither of their paths was conducive for love, and despite the fact that Jonas had recently spent four years with her; he never once voiced his feelings. They had grown close, closer than any other relationship. But neither had voiced how they felt. He could face a demon dragon in combat, but telling Allindrian how he felt, that he truly cared for her, was out of the question. Risking rejection, or worse, doing something to cause a rift in their relationship, was out of the question. He just didn't have the courage to tell her how he truly felt.

"Who taught you to use the bow?" Bearit asked, snapping Jonas from his thoughts. "I have never seen such skill. You be fast, there is no doubt."

"You should see Allindrian," Jonas said, eager to drag his mind from his morose thoughts.

"Was it she who taught you?"

"I've had several teachers. But it was she who showed me what I'm truly capable of."

"Who is she? I know of no female warriors."

"She is a half-elf, and a Bladesinger...and no equal with a blade."

Bearit raised his eyes at that. "You cannot beat her?"

"No, I would be hard pressed. I'm not even sure Kiln could defeat her in a duel."

Bearit had a hard time believing any female could beat Jonas based on what he had seen so far, let alone Kiln, the legendary swordsman from Finarth. But then again he had never met a female warrior, or a Bladesinger, or an elf for that matter. His entire life was spent in the woods, alone, swinging an axe and dragging lumber. He did not know much of the world around him. Bearit had a lot of questions for Jonas, knowing very little about the world, they seemed to be boiling to the surface. "Have you fought demons before?"

Jonas looked at Bearit, his face grim. "I have. Malbeck sent one to kill as many cavaliers as possible, paving the way for his army."

"But you killed it?"

Jonas nodded. "Yes, but with help from Kiln and another cavalier. Her name was Taleen."

Bearit looked at Jonas, seeing the pain there. His use of the word *was* had not gone unnoticed. "She did not survive?"

"She did that battle, only to die in another." But Jonas said no more.

Bearit looked down the road, his mind wandering to all that he had seen and heard over the last few days. "My world has suddenly changed," he said, filling the silence. "Before I had not known of demons, or seen magic, or met a warrior such as you...and now, I see that what I thought of the world was a lie. I think I preferred not knowing."

Jonas smiled. "It's called ignorance. And I know what you mean. At one point in my life I had felt the same as you."

"You ever wish fer de quiet life once again?"

Jonas thought for a moment. "I do," he affirmed.

"Then you should live it."

Jonas shook his head. "I have the skill to help the world. Not using it would in a sense be aiding the evil in our world, something I could never do. Bearit said nothing as he thought of Jonas's words. There was a less traveled road up ahead and Tulari stopped for a moment, sniffing the air, before turning west onto it. The trees were thick and their leafy branches grew out over the road creating a canopy of green, the sun's rays broken up by the web of branches and casting patches of light onto the shadowed dirt path.

Jonas was looking at the map. "The map says there is a small town a quarter day ahead."

"You think Tulari be leading us there?"

Jonas shrugged. "Perhaps. If she is, be prepared for the worst."

Jonas's warning was sound. They saw the smoke first, and once they rode out of the thick forest and into a large field, they saw the destroyed village before them, the backdrop a massive stone formation rising tall behind the scattered homes. The houses were made of stout logs and thatched roofs, handfuls of which were still burning, the gray smoke rising high into the evening air. Jonas nocked an arrow and held the bow with one hand while he used the other to lead his horse. Bearit followed his lead and unslung his axe from around his back and laid it across his lap, holding it in place with one hand. Tulari growled and her body grew, her massive shoulders the height of Jonas's saddle. She swung her massive head towards Jonas, her yellow eyes blinking before trotting forward into the village to investigate.

As they entered the village Jonas saw several bodies, but there was signs of fighting everywhere they looked. The road in town as well as the paths that snaked around the houses were churned up, dirt and mud torn up from many feet. The few bodies he saw were men who held weapons in their bloody hands. Jonas slowed and dismounted, moving towards a couple of bodies for a closer look. One was slashed across the face with what looked like claws, while yet another had been stabbed in the back with a bladed weapon.

"Where is everyone?" Bearit asked, riding next to Jonas.

Jonas stood up from a body, his face grim. "My guess is they were taken. These men probably tried to fight off whatever attacked them, their actions resulting in their deaths. The others were taken. This man," Jonas said, indicating an older red headed man lying on his stomach, "was killed by a sword. While this man," he continued, pointing at a younger man to his left, "was killed by claws."

"You think the beasts that attacked us last night also attacked this town?"

"Perhaps," Jonas agreed. "I'm wondering if Taddick was correct in his estimate. Those creatures that attacked us could also be in league with men like the ones we killed in the catacombs. This would mean that demon has the ability to create different demon-spawn."

"This attack looks to be recent."

Jonas nodded his head in agreement. "I would say it happened last night, just as we were attacked."

"Do you think we be findin' more villages like this?"

Jonas looked bleak. "I'm afraid so."

A noise to his left ripped his attention from Bearit to a log house ten paces away, his bow coming up in a blur, the blue feather fletching gently caressing the side of his face, his black bow at full draw. A man pushed aside the broken door and stepped into the clearing. He wore a dark gray cloak dirty from the road and carried a long sword in his right hand, crimson staining the tarnished surface. His dark beard was long and unruly and his eyes were hard, like he was used to using the weapon he held. Behind him emerged another man, similarly outfitted with nondescript clothes dirty and worn from travel. This man was younger, with a shorter brown beard and a shaved head, a prominent scar crisscrossing up his head behind his ear. He carried a loaded crossbow pointed at them and there was a short sword at his belt. Two more men emerged from another house on the other side of the street. One was tall and thin and he carried a spear, while the other was his complete antithesis. He was short and stocky and held a hand axe in one hand and a long dagger in the other. His front teeth were badly chipped making his smile more ominous than anything.

Jonas didn't release the arrow, holding the difficult position easy enough. "Let me guess," Jonas said passively. "You saw the smoke and came to prey on what happened here."

The bearded man with the sword shrugged his shoulders casually. "Something like that. Now hold that arrow. You are outnumbered two to one and I have a crossbow aimed at you."

Jonas said nothing, turning slightly towards the bald man with the crossbow. The movement was subtle, like a gentle breath of air to extinguish the flame of a candle. Releasing his thumb and forefinger, Jonas's arrow hammered into the crossbowman's forehead, snapping his head back. Before the brigand's eyes crossed in death, he had another arrow nocked and aimed at the leader. The crossbowman fell to the ground. "Not anymore."

The three men looked on with shock, not fully comprehending that their friend was dead and the speed in which he had been dispatched. Bearit too looked equally surprised, his grip tightening on his axe. He hated being on the horse, having no idea how to fight from it.

The leader shifted his feet nervously and held his sword protectively before him. His eyes were wide, now more nervous than confident as he looked at Jonas. "Now take it easy. There is plenty of loot for us all. Whatever happened here the assailants took nothing with them."

Jonas kept his face calm but he was boiling with anger. One of the things he hated the most was people who preyed on the misfortune of others. Brigands and thieves were just as bad as murderers in his book, and the former usually became the latter. The older he got and the more horrible things he saw, the harder and more rigid he had become. "We are not thieves. I am a knight to Shyann and you picked the wrong man to rob."

The man's eyes narrowed, knowing he could not manipulate Jonas. Then he looked at the brigand with the spear. "Lyrus, kill him," he ordered, quickly moving towards cover.

That was all Jonas needed. His first arrow took the leader in the neck before he found cover, catapulting him backwards into the damaged door. Spinning to the right, his hand flashing back to his quiver impossibly fast, a second arrow covered the distance to the spearman in half a heartbeat, hitting him in the center of his chest. But not before he got off a clumsy throw. The man was no warrior and Jonas quickly spun a full circle to his left, easily avoiding the spear, and drawing his third arrow in the process. Dropping to his knee, he narrowly avoided the axe that flew over his head. Seeing he had no other option, the stocky man that threw the axe turned and ran down the road. He made it three paces before Jonas's arrow slammed into his back, launching him from his feet to sprawl face first in the churned up mud. They were dead before Bearit could even dismount.

Bearit was shocked at the speed and ruthlessness. "You shot him in the back," he said as he moved next to Jonas, his axe held in both hands. He didn't mean to, but he sounded accusatory, and he winced as soon as he said it.

Tulari ran from around a corner and slid in the churned up dirt. Clearly she had heard the commotion and came running. But she was no longer needed.

Jonas looked at him and felt sad for the young man, seeing in him what he too would have said just years ago. He used to be naive, but not anymore, his youthful ignorance crushed by years of violence and blood. "You are correct. What would you have done?"

"I don't know. Let him go I guess. He was running away and no longer a danger to us."

"Perhaps," Jonas agreed. "The leader had fresh blood on his sword. They had probably just finished off the survivors when we arrived. But if I had let him go then I would be responsible for all the harm and hardship he would have caused for the rest of his life.

There is a small chance that he would have found redemption for his crimes, but it is unlikely. He would have continued to steal, rape, kill, and pillage. And I would be responsible for that. Not to mention he could have run off and brought back reinforcements, becoming a danger to us once again." Then he looked up at the sky, the sun already behind the massive mountain of stone before them. "It will be dark soon. Let's burn these bodies and rest here for the night. We leave at first light."

***

Maltheil stood tall before its prisoners; its long arms spread wide, red eyes slowly swiveling across the men and women. He was standing at the opening of a huge cave, the entrance a slab of stone that spanned out into a field of grass. Water poured from various places above the huge rock face, cascading around the beast and forming rivulets that poured into the tranquil pool to the left of the opening, the water then flowing over huge rocks and boulders, the stream meandering further east and eventually dumping into the North Fork of the Onith River that flowed out of the northern section of Fish Lake.

It would have been a beautiful oasis, except now the grass was dead, blackened as if a fire had burned the entire clearing. The trees surrounding the clearing were also dead, their blackened and gnarly limbs reaching into the clearing like bony arms of the dead. The entire clearing was surrounded by Maltheil's servants, men and women who now had no recollection of their former lives. Over half were pale skinned, bald, with snaking black sigils running around their necks and up to their heads. Their eyes were lined in red and sunken in shadow. Most of them wore dark cloaks of green, brown, and black, carrying various weapons confiscated from the villages they had raided. They now stood guard around the forty humans they had corralled around their master, taken from various villages. The other half, nearly thirty in number, looked far less human. They were hiding in the shadows, many of them clinging to the dead trees, their pales bodies visible against the blackened trunks. Long claws dug into the wood, their bony heads and red eyes gazing into the clearing like cats in the night. Teeth filled maws opened, saliva dripping as they stared at the humans standing before their master, their fragmented minds thinking only of blood and the desire to serve.

Maltheil stood five heads taller than the biggest man and the beast radiated a sense of fear that was nearly overwhelming for the men and women before it. They huddled together and cried, their bodies shaking, barely able to contain the desire to flee, which they would have if they were not surrounded by dark cloaked men holding sharp blades. The demon's huge wolf-like head stopped and stared at one big man, its red eyes pulsing bright. Then the demon reached out and pointed a long clawed finger at him. "Come before me," Maltheil hissed, his voice soft, like a whisper from the dead.

The man shook his head but stepped from the throng of people anyway, his body moving forward even while his mind was saying no. On trembling legs, the man walked the ten paces it took to bring him before the great beast. Maltheil stood up taller, like it was breathing deeply, then the demon launched its head forward, a gout of black steam shooting from its open mouth to envelope the poor villager. The man screamed and the crowd watching did the same, huddling together and screaming as they heard the piercing shrieks of the dying man. The black cloud spun around the man like a vortex, keeping him within its magical embrace. Moments later the man stopped screaming and Maltheil cut off its breath. When the black smoke dissipated all that remained of the man was a blackened husk, his flesh burned down to the bones. The demon stepped toward the body as the men and women in the crowd huddled closer together. Reaching out with its right clawed hand, red energy began to coalesce around its long fingers. Then ropes of magical energy snaked down and wrapped around the body, causing the black flesh to turn red and burn away into dust leaving behind just the bones. Then Maltheil stepped back and raised its hand further, the magical ropes of energy lifting the man's bones into the air where they spun around each other, turning red and glowing brightly. Then there was a flash of light, causing the men and women watching to scream and shift backwards, the swords of the black cloaked men stopping them like a solid wall.

When the bright light was gone, floating in the air, still wrapped in tendrils of red energy, was a long bone staff, and jutting from one end was a disfigured ball of hard bone, spikes of white jutting from the club-like head forming a dangerous looking weapon. On the other end, the staff narrowed to a sharp point. With a flick of its fingers the bone staff shot into the demon's hand, the red energy disappearing as the beast held the weapon high.

"Bring me the males," Maltheil hissed. Quickly, the black cloaked men went to work dividing the men from the women. Once done, they pushed the men and boys at sword point towards the demon. There were nineteen of them and they looked up at the demon like frightened deer. But the fear they were feeling was immobilizing them, causing them to shake violently before the beast. Even if they could work up the courage to run, they were incapable of breaking free from the manacles of fear. And if somehow they could miraculously break free from the spell and run, the demon spawn in the trees would rip them apart and feed on their blood. Without skipping a beat, Maltheil brought his great head back, and breathed upon them all. This time the smoke was red, and as it coated the men before it, they all fell to the ground, writhing and screaming as Maltheil's breath entered their bodies, hunting down what made them human, and killing it, replacing it with the demon's will. After a few minutes the screaming ended, and rising from the blacked ground were nineteen pale bodies, their sunken eyes staring at their master, waiting for orders.

"Bring me the females," the demon hissed. If Maltheil could smile, it would have. The beast was hungry, and there was nothing like the blood of a scared woman. Not to mention, turning them into his demon spawn was always so satisfying, like filling an empty stomach with blood from its victims.

***

Peron was in his sanctuary, the one place he felt at home. Even in their magnificent castle, with countless luxurious rooms, he never really felt welcome. Everywhere he went he was under constant watch, either for his protection, or under the looming visage of his father, or the disapproving stares of the men and women at court. Maybe it was more his imagination than anything. He had thought of that. He knew he was insecure, and being a learned young man he knew that perhaps he was imagining much of the negativity. Either way, he had a hard time shaking the feeling that he was not the prince that everyone wanted. Or maybe, if he were to be brutally honest with himself, he wasn't the prince that *he* wanted to be.

One thing was certain, his insecurities did not carry over to one thing; his ability to tinker, to create, to solve problems. And he had been working on one such problem the last week, ever since he had heard about Maltheil's escape, and even more so when a runner had arrived the other day carrying word about the attack at Gyeen. Luckily, the Earl had survived the attack. Now the castle guards had doubled, and he had four Red Guard soldiers accompanying him everywhere he went. The officers were under constant guard while the king and his brother were away with the procession to escort King Rothar's new bride. The two sides still had a treaty to work out once they met at Angar, so it was likely they would not return for another week. Tyril was with that procession and it worried Peron. What if the demon attacked them on the road? Peron was still trying to figure out if what they did three years ago had somehow freed the beast. It didn't make any sense. If they had done something to free the creature, why would it just now have broken from its prison? And if they hadn't accidently freed the demon three years ago, then who did? Was there an enemy in the ranks? The heavy questions had been nagging at him the entire week.

Peron coped with stressful situations by spending time in his sanctuary, as he had come to call it. The room was an old barrack located near the castle gardens just inside the castle walls. At one point the gardeners used it for storage and a work station, but the king agreed to retrofit it for Peron for his tenth birthday. Even then Peron was a thinker, and he wanted a space to do his thinking away from everyone. There were a few windows but Peron had long ago had carpenters build thick wood shutters to keep out prying eyes. A big open stone fire pit was in the middle of the room, the smoke rising to a covered opening in the vaulted wood ceiling. The walls were lined with shelves covered with everything from books to tools and other equipment and supplies. He even had a small forge and the necessary equipment to work with iron, leather, and wood. Peron was no blacksmith, but he had spent a year working with Dynin, the king's armorer, volunteering his time to learn the basics of the trade. With no light coming in from the windows, Peron had to rely on oil lanterns placed all around the large room. It was his favorite place in the entire castle.

Holding up the light leather hood Peron inspected his work. The leather was soft and supple and stitched well, the seams smeared with a malleable wax. Stitched to the mouth opening was something that looked like a muzzle of a dog or wolf, the entire thing made of the same leather. The end of it had ten holes punched into it, and inside it, and sealed where it touched the mouth, was another piece of leather that had similar holes. Inside the muzzle was densely packed fibrous cotton. Peron had no idea if it would work, but he hoped that the packed cotton would act as a filter, allowing clean air in but keeping unwanted contaminates out. If the demon was really alive, which based on the missing person reports and the attack on the Earl, it seemed that that was a real possibility, then Peron wanted some sort of protection from the beast's breath, if indeed all the reports he had read were true. He had no idea if his mask would protect the wearer from the demon's breath, and even if it did, for how long. Perhaps it would give the wearer just enough time to get away before being consumed by the demon's power. Maybe it would do nothing. But he had to do something. The eyes of the mask had been the most difficult. Glass was the only substance that was clear enough to see through and yet not permeable. But attaching the glass lens to the leather had been very difficult. He had a local glass blower help him by melting lead to the edge of the lenses with many holes running the perimeter. Then he stitched them into the leather, covering the seams with the same malleable wax. It was hard to see well when the hood was on, but it would do. The final problem was how to seal it around the neck. After many different tests, he ended up going with a draw string configuration. The problem was how to seal it, so little or no air would enter. Stitching in a draw string at the base of the hood would create small gaps at the seal, even when the string was pulled and tied tight. Not to mention it was very uncomfortable on the neck. Finally he came up with what he hoped was a solution. At the very bottom edge of the mask he stitched in a soft flap of leather. He filled it with cotton and folded it over itself and then stitched it on the inside of the mask, forming a thick soft lip all the way around the circumference of the opening. Then he stitched in the draw string above that line. When pulled tight and tied off, the soft edge of the inside lip, which he smeared with thick grease used for wagon wheels, was pulled tight against the skin, hopefully forming a tight seal. It was the best he could come up with, and hopefully he would never have the opportunity to test the seal, or the cotton filter covering the mouth. Looking at the mask, Peron had to admit that it looked a little ominous, which he thought ironic as it was made to protect the wearer from a demon. He had two hoods completed and he was just about to start the work on a third when there was a knock at his door.

The guards outside knew not to disturb him so he was a little annoyed. "What is it?"

"My Prince," the guard said through the door. "Master Kyron is here to see you."

Peron smiled at that. He friend had been gone all week, away on business with his father, hopefully securing contracts to get his father's business back on its feet. Kyron did not know about the demon and Peron was eager to talk with him. "Let him in," Peron said.

The door opened and Kyron entered. The young man was tall and lanky, like his father, with shoulder length hair, dazzling blue eyes, and a short pointy beard. Peron and Tyril had made fun of him for it as he had worked nearly six months trying to grow the small patch of hair on his chin. He couldn't grow a full beard yet so he made it seem as if the little goat-like growth was his end game. But Peron had stopped with the jests once he realized that he was trying to look older as he was taking over more and more of his father's business, or at least what there was left of it. As usual, Kyron was wearing immaculate and opulent clothing, a soft cotton shirt the color of gold edged in silver stitching, intricate designs of silver leaves stitched across the front. Smooth brown leggings tucked into soft brown boots lined with fur finished his ensemble, along with a long matching coat of soft spun wool. They were a merchants traveling clothes, but of the highest quality. Kyron looked tired, but he gave Peron a welcoming smile nonetheless.

"How was your trip? Any luck finding any contracts?" Peron asked as they shook hands.

Peron's smile disappeared but he attempted to quickly replace it with something short of casual indifference. "One small contract with a merchant from Onith. Seems he needs more weapons for his caravan guards."

Peron knew that that would do little to help with their financial burden. "How is your father?"

"Not well," he said as he sat at a stool next to Peron's work table. But he offered no more. Peron had done some research on his own and found out that Kyron's father had turned into a recluse after his wife left him and his business began falling apart. At one point he was one of the wealthiest merchants in Lanard, trading weapons and textiles up and down the Algard coast. Once Kyron's mother left his father, and he had lost the king's contract for weapons and clothing for his army, he began to fall apart. He drank often and it wasn't long before he lost more contracts, a self-fulfilling result of depression. His family's wealth was nearly gone and Kyron was doing all he could to keep the business afloat. Peron knew that it had been hard for

Kyron. Not only had his mother left them, but his once opulent lifestyle had diminished considerably. Their recent business trip was the result of Kyron finally convincing his father to leave his study and his drunken morose haze. But by the sound of it they were unsuccessful. Peron worried for Kyron's father, and in turn for his friend.

"Kyron, I have some grave news to discuss with you," Peron said, changing the subject as he sat opposite his friend.

"Does it have something to do with that awful hood you are holding?"

"It does." Peron had no idea where to start so he thought he would just be frank. "Kyron, Maltheil has escaped."

Kyron didn't saying anything for a moment and a flurry of emotions raced across his face. He went from shock, to worry, to denial, to fright, all in a matter of moments. Once he realized that Peron wasn't saying anything else he decided to speak. "You're not joking?" Kyron looked nervous and scared, a fitting reaction for such disturbing news.

Peron shook his head. "It happened last week. The tomb was torn open and the doors to the mausoleum broken and smashed."

"How did this happen? You don't think it was..."

"I don't know," Peron interjected. "It's been three years since we entered that tomb and the beast happens to escape now. That doesn't make any sense. I don't think it had anything to do with what we did."

"How can you be sure?" Kyron asked nervously. "Did you tell anyone about what we did? Does Tyril know?

"I'm not sure. And no, I have told no one. And yes, Tyril knows. He is away right now with the procession escorting the young princess from Tur'el."

"Has anyone seen the demon?"

"We have not and there have been no reported sightings. But a platoon of Red Guard soldiers went missing and several small villages have been attacked, most of the people taken away. And two nights ago Earl Magnar was attacked by some creatures he described as demon-like."

"You think this is all connected to Maltheil?"

"I do. Which is why I made this hood. The demon can turn its victims into servants using its breath, like a dragon breathes fire. I'm hoping this will protect us from that attack."

Kyron knew that Peron had become obsessed with Maltheil after their incident three years ago. If anyone knew about the demon it would be him. "What are we going to do?"

"I don't know," Peron answered honestly. "My father has brought in the reserves to strengthen the army and we are on high alert."

"I was wondering why there were so many soldiers by the docks when we came in. Do you think the demon will attack us here?"

Peron looked concerned. "I think Maltheil is raising an army using the missing villagers. The attack on the Earl was just a precursor to something bigger."

"How will we stop this creature?"

"I don't know." And once again, Peron was tired of saying that.

***

Tyril hated the pomp and circumstance when traveling with the royal family, let alone two. They had arrived at Angar, the border city between Lanard and Tur'el, the previous day. For hundreds of years the two kingdoms had fought over land, and Angar, over the last five hundred years, had been part of both kingdoms as they battled along the border. For the last hundred years the Lanard Kingdom had occupied Angar, taken in battle by King Gyveel Rothar's grandfather. The royal family of Tur'el had arrived later the next day with one hundred soldiers and nearly thirty retainers as well as several important lords and their families. There was a great feast that night as King Haten Oneck, his wife, Queen Lorel Oneck, their daughter, the Princess Kylin Oneck, dined with King Gyveel Rothar. The Rothar king also brought with him several lords and their families as customary for a peaceful meeting such as this. With King Oneck was his court wizard, Carvathian, who was in his fifties but looked older, with long gray hair pulled back into a single braid. There was food, wine, and dancing, and despite the tension between the longtime enemies, conversation flowed casually between the esteemed guests as soldiers guarded their liege lords with vigilance. As agreed upon, King Rothar had also been escorted by one hundred soldiers, twenty of which were members of the Red Guard, including the young Tyril and his father, the Battle Lord of Lanard, Baylock Reen, and his brother, Prince Dalland Rothar. Of course he too had his court wizard in attendance, leaving behind General Sig Moore and the other council members to run the kingdom while he was away.

Tyril hated interacting with aristocrats, even though he technically was one. As the son of the Battle Lord, he was expected to occasionally rub elbows with other lords and ladies, some already at the pinnacle of power, and others jockeying their way higher up the ladder to gobble up whatever piece of the power pie they could get. And this evening was no different. At the main table were the three members of the Tur'el royal family, General Hyrim Galstar, leader of the Tur'el army, Carvathian the wizard, as well as King Rothar, his brother, Prince Dalland Rothar, Earl Gallinor, the governor of Angar, Tyril's father, Master Moran, and of course, himself. He never felt comfortable at events such as these, preferring to wrap his big hand around the hilt of a sword rather than a dainty salad fork. But he was raised to play the part if need be, and he was performing his role admirably, staying out of the main conversation unless directly spoken to.

He looked up from his salad and made eye contact with Kylin Oneck, the young princess arranged to marry King Rothar. He looked away quickly; his eyes fluttering back momentarily to see her still staring at him. A slight smile broke through her somber expression. She was a beautiful girl, with long hair the color of sparkling gold and blue eyes that held his own for a brief moment before he looked away a second time. Her skin was pale white, like freshly fallen snow, her thin but strong lips a light shade of pink in stark contrast. Ever since they had sat down and introductions were made, she seemed sad, like a melancholy cloud was hanging over her. She was polite and soft spoken, but it seemed to Tyril that she would rather be any place but there. He could definitely relate to that sentiment. He assumed that she did not want to marry his king. King Rothar was a handsome man, but he was over twice her age, and although arranged marriages such as this were quite common amongst the royal families, it was rare that love was ever involved. On top of that she was going to live in a far off land, a land of strangers that had been enemies of her family for as long as anyone could remember. Tyril felt for her.

He looked up as he saw her lean forward. "I can see that you are just as excited as I to be here," she whispered. She was smiling sarcastically.

Tyril looked to his left and saw that the others were in a heated conversation, surely talking about treaty stipulations tied to the upcoming marriage. Once both parties came to an agreement, their scribes would write up the documents and both parties would sign, all of this happening before the marriage in several weeks. He shrugged. "Dinners such as this are not..."

"Your thing?" she interjected.

Tyril smiled. "No, they are not."

"So what is your thing, young Tyril Reen, son of the famous Rothar Battle Lord?"

Tyril didn't need to think about that question. "Fighting, like my father."

"Are you as skilled as he?"

He was not as skilled as his father, at least not yet. He was still young and had much to learn. "I can hold my own but there is much I do not know."

"Modest, I like that." The princess took a sip of her wine, her sparkling blue eyes appraising him, her mouth posed in a slight smile.

He felt uncomfortable under her gaze so he broke the silent moment. "So what is your thing?"

Her smile went away. "It doesn't matter. I am to wed my enemy's king. My life will be as he sees fit."

"I hope we will be enemies no more," Tyril said. Looking over to make sure they were all still occupied in conversation, he leaned closer to her across the table. "Besides, King Rothar will give you all you need. You will have a good life in Lanard."

She looked up from her plate, a gentle smile returning. She didn't miss the fact that his response was diplomatic and vague. But she said nothing about it. "I am just being selfish, forget I said anything. Besides, peace between our kingdoms is what is important." Her vulnerability had disappeared and was replaced with the diplomacy one would expect from her position. Tyril had to admit that he preferred the other side of her more.

They all continued to talk over the rest of the meal, later drinking a rare sweet wine and watching musicians and dancers. After the entertainment, they said their good nights and all the guests were escorted back to their quarters. The city of Angar was a fairly large city for a border town, and the keep was in the middle of the city, its sturdy stone walls protecting a twenty room castle housing two hundred Lanard soldiers. But they had not dined with Earl Gallinor at the keep, knowing full well that the Tur'el contingent would not agree to such terms before a full treaty could be agreed upon. There was still a lot of distrust between the two kingdoms. Each side had erected tents for their men in the grassy field outside the city gate, the royal families setting up massive tent quarters nearly as opulent as their own back at home. Earl Gallinor had previously built a beautiful dining tent, the cook's quarters alongside it with cooking stations ready to go. The structure was big enough to house tables to feed the royal families as well their dignitaries, and also provide space for musicians and entertainment. The entire area was lit up by hundreds of long burning torches stuck into the ground. The next day would be spent hammering out the peace treaty, both sides knowing that the wedding would not continue if they could not come to an amicable agreement. King Rothar did not bring the subject of the demon up during their dinner, feeling it was best to discuss the matter the next day during the treaty discussions.

Tyril's shift was over and he made his way through the lit paths created by the many tents to his own sleeping quarters. Despite the fact that he was a noble, and the son of the Battle Lord, he was still in his first year of service and required to sleep with the other men until he made rank of Captain in two years. Then he would have his own sleeping tent, but tonight he was sharing a tent with two other men, both older than he. They both had the night shift, guarding the perimeter, and once he laid his sword next to him, resting his head on his warm blankets, he was quickly asleep. He kept his armor and clothes on, something his father taught him when out on the road. At first it was uncomfortable, but he was now used to it, and it bothered him little as dreams quickly found him.

CHAPTER FOUR

Atticus Belthar lay in the shallow warm water, his naked body sucking in the warmth from the natural warm spring while the cool evening air licked at his exposed skin. He loved the dual sensations, both reminding him of the strength and wonder of the natural world. But he wasn't just relaxing in the water; he was pulling energy from the earth. The natural spring spilled water from deep underground, forming several shallow pools among various strewn rocks and boulders. The water carried with it energy from the earth, and Atticus spent many hours soaking in the waters, pulling energy into him maintaining his youth and vitality. The water cascaded over the rocks of the pool he was in, running through a small river of worn stones to pour into another smaller pool, before dumping into a creek twenty yards further. The clearing was beautiful, one end dominated by a rock face twice as tall as a man, the water dumping over the rocky edge. Surrounding the grass and rock strewn clearing were massive trees, forming a protective ring around the oasis. Intermittent throughout the green grass were purple and white flowers which would soon hide their beauty as winter arrived. It was Atticus's favorite spot in the Lasur'een Forest.

Lying next to him in a bed of soft grass was a colossal cat, its black, fur covered body, stretched long and its huge head resting on its muscled forelegs, ending in clawed paws each as big as a man's head. It was a shadow cat, big predators that hunted the prevalent game all throughout the Lasur'een forest. Its name was Korum and Atticus had rescued him when he was just a kitten, his mother killed by a rock bear, the only animal in the forest that was more dangerous. Korum had been his companion for the last twenty years and there wasn't anything they didn't do together.

After an hour or so he slowly stood from the pool, warm water dripping off his lean muscular body. Korum looked up from his slumber, but quickly lowered his head back to the ground, closing his eyes once again. Atticus felt revitalized and strong, like he could run up the side of the Sarhast Mountains without breaking a sweat. His brown-blonde hair was shoulder length and he shook it out, spraying water into the cool air. Scars of various sizes and shapes covered his body, but despite the look of wear and tear the scares gave him, he looked no older than forty. No one would believe he was nearly two thousand years old. As far as he knew, he was the last druid west of the Tundren Mountains, and he had spent the last 1898 years protecting the Lasur'een Forest. For that protection, the earth gave back, sustaining him and giving him the power to protect the land. He had looked the same over the many years, gaining power and skill but seemingly not aging.

He was a legend throughout Tur'el and Lanard, told in stories as the man who defeated the demon Maltheil. Most thought him dead, long ago his name forgotten except when whispered in stories and sang in songs. He preferred it that way, known now by many names, preferring to stay a recluse as he patrolled the borders of the forest. He had four different cabins located throughout the vast forest, and when interacting with the people of Tur'el or Lanard, he used the names Torgeen, Embry, or sometimes Solum. No one had called him Atticus for over a thousand years.

He stretched his muscles and walked to the clothes draped over a nearby rock. After putting on his huntsman's clothes, all various shades of greens and browns, and donning his mithril steel chainmail shirt under his forest green tunic, he buckled on his sword belt and picked up his long bow, slinging the quiver of arrows over his shoulder. Just as he was about to leave a pulse of energy erupted from the ground at his feet, nearly knocking him over. Druids called the earth energy *Sanga*, and the Sanga was reaching out to him. Few people even knew about the energy of the earth, let alone had the ability to harness it, to understand it. Druids could of course, but there were not many left. They had either been killed in battle, or hunted down by defenders of the new gods, seeing them as heretics and followers of the old ways. But the Sanga was not a god, or even an entity, it was what made everything *something*. It was what caused the sun to rise and set and the oceans to rise and recede every day.

It pulsed again and images rocked his mind. Korum lifted his head and rose quickly to his feet, sensing something wrong with Atticus. The cat growled and looked around the clearing, ready for any danger and prepared to protect his master. For a minute Atticus stood in shock, not fully comprehending what he had just seen in his mind. The Sanga was warning him that something was threatening the forest, and that something was familiar to him. Again the Sanga pulsed through him, the image of a black skinned demon flashing in his mind. Atticus's heart pounded in his chest and his hand went unconsciously to his sword, Korum growling louder at his movement. Maltheil was back, and the dark beast's black presence had just touched the western border of the forest...his forest.

Atticus looked at his companion, his face intense. "We must go." And then he was off, disappearing quickly into the woods, the big cat leaping ahead.

***

Jonas and Bearit had been riding north for half a day when Tulari emerged from the undergrowth. Her mottled gray and black coat was now shades of green and brown making her nearly invisible as she appeared from the bushes. Having the ability to change her size as well as her color made her an extremely dangerous hunter. She had been scouting the forest around them, checking back often to make sure they were still heading in the right direction. They were following the road to Lanard and there had been no turn offs as yet.

We followed Tulari said in Jonas's mind. Her ability to form mental words was linked to her vocabulary, which was minimal, so she communicated with simple phrases and sometimes pictures, sending Jonas mental flashes or garbled words.

Jonas had heard or felt nothing, which worried him as his skill as a tracker and woodsman had improved considerably under Allindrian's tutelage. "What follows us?" He did not have the skill to talk to her with his mind, as she did to him.

Animals. Several, she added.

That was odd. But perhaps that was why he did not detect anything. There is not much that can move more quietly in the forest than the animals that lived there.

"Who be followin' us?" Bearit asked.

"I'm not sure," Jonas answered, his eyes narrowed and his lips pursed in worry. "Tulari says it's some type of animal, more than one."

"Can't she tell you what it is?"

"It doesn't work that way. She does not have the words as we do. If she recognizes the creature, than she can typically verbalize it, but if not, then I may only get images, or nothing specific." Jonas knew that if she could not send a mental image of the pursuer than that meant she had not seen it, only detected it. And that worried Jonas. There were few animals that could avoid the eyes of a night wolf, and none of them were anything you wanted following you.

Tulari led them further and at a faster rate, and within the hour they turned east off the main road following a wagon trail, which according to the map would lead them over the North Fork of the Onith River to the Lasur'een forest. They were now moving away from Lanard. The troubling part was what they found at the intersection. The ground had been torn up and disturbed, like a crowd of people had been moved from the direction of Lanard onto the side road that Tulari had indicated. Jonas dismounted to inspect the tracks.

"What do you make of it?" Bearit asked, looking down at the many tracks and smudges leading from Lanard to the east.

"A group of people, maybe twenty. But the strange part is there are tracks that I do not recognize, and a few animal tracks as well."

"What kind of animals?"

"Several look to belong to a big cat, or maybe a bear," Jonas responded as he carefully inspected the ground. "The group was tired, corralled and moved against their will."

Bearit frowned, unsure how he could see that. And he voiced his disbelief. "How can you see that by looking at tracks? And what type of group be travelin' with bears and cats? "

Jonas didn't bother looking up, inspecting the ground further. "Many were dragging their legs, not lifting them properly, a sure sign of exhaustion. The interior tracks are smaller, probably from women and children, like they were being protected. And I have no idea why there were big animals with them. It's definitely strange."

"Protected from what?"

This time Jonas looked up. "From whatever was herding them." He moved to his horse and leapt into the saddle. "My bet is that whatever is following us is somehow linked to this group. The tracks are a day old. Tulari is leading us in their direction. Be vigilant." Then he urged his steed forward with Bearit following, his eyes scanning every shadow for a threat.

Tulari continued to disappear into the forest, appearing often and letting Jonas know that they were still being followed. Jonas didn't like it. Something was following them while at the same time a group of people ahead of them were being coerced against their will. Neither of the prospects was welcoming.

It wasn't long before they approached a large stone bridge that spanned over the North Fork of the Onith River. It was late evening by this time and soon they would need a place to camp. Jonas didn't like the idea of sleeping in the open while something was stalking them. He pulled up short of the bridge to think.

"What is it?" Bearit asked.

"You tell me," Jonas replied, ending with a question of his own. "What am I worried about?"

Bearit thought for a moment, looking at the bridge, the road over it made of slabs of stone and wide enough for a wagon or cart. Looking up he measured the sun's position. "We will need to camp soon. We are being followed by somethin' unknown. The question is, where do we camp?"

"Good," Jonas responded. "And where would you suggest?"

"A defendable position in case what follows us be a threat," Bearit said, thinking out loud. He was missing something. Jonas had pulled up short of the bridge for a reason. Then it came to him. "You want to camp on the bridge."

Jonas nodded. "Good. Why?"

"Well, the bridge be narrow and the only way we could be approached is from either end. Our sides would be protected," Bearit added. "If we set up camp in the woods, attack could come from anywhere and we would never see it coming. This way, we can see what be approachin', their attack comin' from two directions only."

This time Jonas smiled. "Well done. It will be less than comfortable, but I agree with your reasoning."

Bearit shrugged. "It wouldn't be the first time I've slept on hard ground...beats a sword in the gut in the middle of the night."

Jonas dismounted. "I don't think it's a sword we will have to worry about. Whatever follows us is not a man."

Bearit dismounted as well, eager to get off the horse. His backside was still sore, but he was getting more used to the animal, adjusting better with its movements and causing less pain to himself in the process. "What will we do with the animals?"

"We can tether them here where they can graze on the grass and moss," Jonas replied as he looked around for a suitable spot. He found one easily enough and after they watered the horses and tied them off, they removed their packs from the saddles and walked together across the bridge. There was a stone wall built up on either side of the bridge about waist high and they both looked down to the fast flowing water below. It was a fifteen pace drop to the clear water and just down river looked to be a violent set of rapids, the fast moving water crashing into huge boulders, the roaring white water disappearing in a violent cascade beyond where they could see.

As they neared the middle of the bridge, their horses whinnied loudly behind them. Both of them turned and saw Tulari running towards them at full speed, her coat now shades of black and gray. She was at her full size which alerted Jonas right away that something was wrong.

Danger...ready to fight! It was like she was yelling in Jonas's mind. Jonas dropped his pack and swung his bow up, nocking an arrow quickly, his vigilant eyes scanning the growing shadows beyond the bridge. Bearit sensed the danger and stood defensively, his axe held before him in both hands. Tulari skidded before them and turned in the direction she had come from. They were still as statues; the only thing heard was the panting of their breath as adrenaline raced through them.

After what seemed like forever, Bearit spoke up. "What be out there?" His voice was a whisper, but Jonas heard the nervous strain.

Just then Jonas heard something on the opposite side of the bridge and he spun quickly, his arrow drawn back tightly. The others did the same. At the far end of the bridge, nearly thirty paces away, was a huge cat nearly as big as Tulari. The creature stood perfectly still, its yellow eyes sparkling in the evening shadows. Obviously this was the animal that had been following them. Or perhaps there were more than one as Jonas had no idea how it got on the other side of the river. But there was something about it that didn't seem right. Its yellow eyes dripped a mucous-like substance, and its coat was matted and tangled, like it hadn't bathed itself in years. Even its musculature was wrong. It seemed ganglier, almost unhealthy, and there were spots along its body devoid of hair, exposing a matte black skin.

"That be lookin like a shadow cat," Bearit whispered.

"There is something wrong with it," Jonas said softly, his arrow still held at the side of his head. Just as he spoke dark forms materialized from the shadowed brush. There were ten men wearing different shades of

130

dark clothing and carrying various weapons. They carried swords and axes and even a few held spears and wore armor. But he had seen their like before, in the catacombs below Gyeen. They were completely bald and pale as milk, their eyes sunken and surrounded in hues of red and black. Even in the dim evening light he could clearly see the black mark snaking up their necks and around their bald heads. Another animal appeared but this one was a rock bear, and it was gigantic, as big as Tulari but thicker in the shoulders. Its gray coat was in complete disarray, and combined with its red and sunken eyes looked as if it had come back from the dead.

One of the men, who was clad in a dark green cloak worn over chainmail, stepped forward, a long sword held at his side. He opened his mouth and what came next surprised even Jonas.

The man spoke, but he did not move his lips. The sound seemed to emanate from him. "I sense... something," the man hissed, "about you. Who are you?" The voice was soft but carried the weight of power.

Jonas heard something behind them and glanced back to see another ten men span out across the other bridge entrance. Another big cat was with them and the agile beast leapt up to stand gracefully on the bridge wall. The creature looked as the other, mangled and dirty, with sunken yellow eyes, long teeth dripping with saliva. They were surrounded. How did Jonas miss them? They must have been watching silently in the woods, not moving, waiting for them to walk onto the bridge where they could surround them. The cat behind them must have been the creature that Tulari had detected.

"I am Jonas. What matter of creature are you and what have you done to these men?"

"I am the destroyer of kingdoms and the enslaver of men. These," the man said, indicating the animals and men around him, "are my slaves."

Bearit's hands were sweating on the handle of his axe and Tulari was growling deeply next to him. He glanced at Jonas hoping to gain some of his confidence.

Jonas still held the bow at full draw. "Are you Maltheil?"

"I am known by that name, and many others. Why are you following my servants?"

Jonas knew that the man before him was not Maltheil. The demon must be controlling them and somehow talking through the man. "I am Shyann's servant. And I have come to end you and free these men. I bring her light to stamp out your darkness."

The man before him laughed. It was a low rumble and it seemed to emanate from the ground. "Young warrior, there cannot be light without darkness," the man said. "I thought your stench was familiar. I have known *Her* smell. You will all make fine servants. Perhaps you will lead my army."

Bearit glanced back and forth, nervously adjusting his hands on his axe. "Jonas, we can't fight them all." Bearit glanced over the side of the bridge and stepped closer to the edge.

"Don't," Jonas whispered. His voice was hard and sharp. "You will die in the water if you jump."

The man laughed again, clearly hearing them despite the distance. "You will die either way."

Just then Jonas heard an eerie clicking sound and moments later pale human-like forms scurried like spiders from under the bridge and over the wall on both sides. They were the same creatures that had attacked them at Gyeen. Sure enough, handfuls of the creatures climbed over the wall behind them as well, their sharp claws clicking on the stone as they climbed up the rock façade like lizards. They must have scurried under the bridge from both sides only to pop up less than five paces away.

They were boxed in and outnumbered. "We cannot fight them all," Bearit said, his voice rising with nervous energy. He had almost no experience in combat, and now he was faced with a threat that would surely see their end. He was always confident in his abilities, but now they seemed inadequate to see them through their predicament alive.

"We can," Jonas said confidently, his jaw set. "And we will." Then he looked at Bearit, his eyes intense and filled with a rising controlled rage. "Prepare yourself. We will survive." His jaw was set and his eyes were as hard as steel. In a flash he returned his gaze to the man, releasing his arrow at the same time.

The arrow struck the man in the forehead, knocking him backwards where he stumbled and fell to the pavers. Then the scene erupted in chaos as the two groups converged on them. Men ran at them, the demon creatures scurried on all fours, and the animals leapt and jumped, their claws splayed and their roars deafening.

"Get behind me!" Jonas yelled as he ran forward towards the group before them. Bearit had no idea what to do against such odds so he did as instructed, running behind Jonas with Tulari at his side. He couldn't believe what they were doing. They were charging a huge cat, a colossal bear, and over fifteen men and demon-spawn, with another group close to that size on their heels.

Jonas reached deep within his conscious and called upon his cognivant powers, pulling a large amount of energy from everything around him. In his mind's eye he could see the particles of energy that made up the stone of the bridge and that spun in the air around them, and he drew it into him, and just before they collided with the advancing force he flung it forward in a sharp wedge, the point of the energy plowing aside bodies just as an axe splits wood. Even the rock bear was knocked aside, its massive form crashing into the bridge wall. They busted through the line with men and demon-spawn alike cast aside by the invisible wall, their claws and swords angling clumsily for them as they tumbled to the ground or even over the side of the bridge. The shadow cat had leapt high, hoping to land on them, but it struck the side of the invisible wall and was knocked over the side of the bridge, its angry roar extinguished when it hit the water. No blade or sharp claw could penetrate the translucent shield as the trio busted through to the other side.

Once free from them, Jonas spun around, releasing the energy quickly and bringing his bow back up. He had used a large amount of cognitive energy and his head, near the base of his neck, was developing a slow ache. But the pressing situation allowed him to forget it easily enough. Now they were facing all of them, no longer forced to fight them from both sides. On top of that advantage, four of the enemy had been launched over the side of the bridge, along with one of the cats, and handfuls of others lay scattered on the bridge. But still the odds were overwhelmingly against them.

Jonas went to work, releasing arrow after arrow, every sharp point, each one blessed by Shyann, finding their mark. Enemy bodies tumbled backwards or over the bridge, pierced by his deadly arrows. Bearit and Tulari flanked Jonas, and it was a good thing, as moments later pale forms crawled over the railing from the underside of the bridge on either side of them, their thin but strong legs propelling the demon-spawn from the wall directly at them.

Bearit howled and swung his axe to meet the first body, the heavy blade cutting through the creature's head and into its torso. The logger stood like a thick oak, the impact of the beast minimal. Bearit stepped back a few steps to lessen the impact, tossing the dead body to the side with incredible strength. Two more came at him, one leaping at his right flank while the other met his reverse swing, the sharp blade of his axe cutting into its torso and flinging it over the bridge railing into the darkness below. Feeling sharp claws rip into his leg Bearit screamed in pain. Remembering the sharp blade on the other end of the axe, Bearit brought the handle end down hard on the creature's head just as it bit into his thigh below his chainmail, the blade punching through the creature's skull. Striking it with his knee, Bearit knocked the dead creature into another attacking demon-spawn. More came at him and he swung his axe with all his strength and speed, barely keeping the enemy from ripping into his flesh.

Tulari was using her huge head and claws to swat the beasts away, cutting through flesh and launching several over the railing to the water below. Using her massive size and speed, she kept all the assailants off her and protected Jonas's right flank as he killed more with his deadly bow.

The overwhelming assailants were just about to reach Jonas when he dropped his bow and drew his blades, the blue glow of Shyann's power flaring along the sharp edges and lighting up the shadowy evening. The rock bear barreled through the pale men, and lowering its head in a thunderous roar, came straight at Jonas. Even if Jonas skewered the beast with his sword, the momentum of the charge would crush him. Having only seconds to think, Jonas drew forth his cognitive powers again and wrapped his body in energy as he leapt impossibly high into the air. The combined power of his enchanted boots and the energy around his body sent him well over the bear. The snarling beast ran underneath him as Jonas landed in a throng of pale men, their rictus grins leering at him as their swords sought his flesh. One blade nicked his arm scoring a shallow cut near his elbow. Spinning like a top, his dual blades followed his trajectory, slicing into their flesh. Stopping his momentum, his swords flashed high and low, left and right, creating a wall of steel they could not penetrate. Several possessed men fell but Jonas had no time for the others as the bear had skidded to a stop and turned, its red eyes intense with anger. Roaring defiantly, the bear charged again. It seemed that Maltheil had the ability to possess animals as well as men, for clearly the forest creatures attacking them were not under their own bidding. And they had changed, becoming a demon-like version of their former selves.

Jonas was not sure what to do, sensing the sharp steel of the attackers behind him and seeing the huge bear charge. Bearit was bleeding and struggling to keep the attacking demon-spawn off him, but despite the blood on his flank his huge axe flashed back and forth impressively fast for such a heavy weapon.

A massive roar from Tulari shook the bridge and she spun to face the bear, her huge body knocking three demon-spawn over the edge, while she shot forward off her strong hind legs, catapulting into the charging bear. The impact was incredible and Jonas heard bones break as the two huge forms rolled in a flurry of claws and snarls only to tumble off the side of the bridge.

"No!" Jonas screamed as he turned on his heel to block two blades descending for his neck. A third blade reached past his swords, deflecting off his thigh guard and inflicting a shallow cut on the side of his leg. Fury, like white hot fire, roared through his body as his blades darted and flicked, slicing flesh and turning aside sharp steel. He had no time to do anything other than to block and kill, and hope that Tulari survived the fall and that Bearit was still alive and covering his flank. Bodies piled up around him as he danced across the stone pavers, his body ducking and turning as his twin swords blurred like the wings of a humming bird. He had to dig deep for everything Kiln and Allindrian had taught him to keep the enemy from striking him down.

A cat's roar broke through the din of battle and just before him two men turned aside as a huge black cat flew over them. The beast must have leaped from behind them, its huge paws were splayed wide, dagger-like claws curved like an eagles and ready to rip his flesh. Having no other choice, Jonas pointed his right sword towards the cat and drew in more cognitive energy. Pulling it from everything around him, he screamed defiantly as he shot the invisible force forward from the tip of his sword, concentrating all of the power on the cat's open mouth. There was a loud crack and it looked like the cat was punched in the face by a frost giant. Snapping hard to the left the cat's neck broke, the power of the invisible punch knocking the cat away from him where it spun in the air, careening off the edge of the bridge rail to the river below.

Suddenly the bridge shook and Jonas looked over his attackers, most of whom turned to see what was causing the shaking. His head pounded and he was thankful for the quick distraction. A column of mounted warriors rode across the bridge, striking the rear of the assailants. The men wore armor and red sashes around their waists, and each man held a shield and cavalry sword. Their horses pushed through the attackers like stalks of corn, their swords cutting into them and killing anything that was not knocked over the bridge. Within moments the attackers were dead or scattered and twenty warriors on barded horses stood before them.

Jonas was holding his glowing swords to either side and was panting heavily, the back of his head pounding from over-using his Cognitive powers. There was a pile of fifteen dead bodies around him. Glancing back, Jonas was relieved to see Bearit on one knee, blood dripping from his leg and several cuts on his arms. Over eight demon-spawn were dead on the bridge and more than likely at least a handful had been knocked over the railing. Using the bloody end of his axe, Bearit pushed his body to his feet. Standing tall, he held his bloody axe before him. Jonas was impressed. He was badly hurt and tired, but still he would not show weakness before these men.

Then he heard a low growl and saw Tulari slowly walk towards him from the other side. She was dripping wet and Jonas saw her limping and coddling her right leg, the fur around her mouth drenched in blood. Other than her injured leg, she seemed fine. He was relieved to see her, but Tulari's presence did not get the same reaction from the mounted men.

"Behind you!" the lead warrior yelled as he gripped his reins ready to heel his steed and attack.

"Wait!" Jonas yelled, running back to stand before Tulari. She lowered her head and Jonas put his arm around her thick neck. "She is with me! Hold your attack!"

The same lead warrior stayed his horse but looked ready to launch forward at any moment. The man next to him, wearing a full chest plate, pauldrons, helm, and holding a long curved sword, lifted his visor. Jonas noticed that the man's helm had a red plume, figuring it marked his higher rank. "Who are you?" He asked, his appraising eyes scanning the carnage, lingering on the demon spawn, their pale disfigured bodies all too clear. It seemed pretty clear that the warrior had never seen such a beast.

"I am Jonas Kanrene, Shyann's knight. This is my apprentice Bearit and my companion Tulari."

The man who spoke had a full beard of dark hair but even in the dimming light Jonas could see his lightning blue eyes. They were piercing, the contrast against his dark beard startling. They reminded Jonas of Kiln's intense gaze. "What manner of beast is that?"

"She is a night wolf. And she bears you no harm."

He looked skeptical, but he nodded nonetheless. "I know of you. We passed a messenger coming from Gyeen a day ago. He told us what happened there and that a knight saved the magistrate. I assume that is you." Before Jonas could answer he spoke again. "My name is Korrin and I'm a Captain of the Red Guard. We were tracking some captured villagers when we found you."

"And a good thing. Thank you for coming to our aid."

The captain nodded again. "Your man is hurt. It will be dark soon. Let's set up camp where we can see to your wounds. Then we can eat and talk."

***

They set up a camp on the far side of the bridge, their tents and fires built with precision typical of well-trained soldiers. There wasn't much room along the road's edge so most of the tents were erected on the road itself. Cook fires had been set and the hardy men sat around three different fires eating bowls of beans with salted ham and big chunks of bread.

One of the warriors saw to Bearit's wounds, cleaning the cuts and smearing them with a green salve that tingled before wrapping them in clean bandages. The bite on his leg was the worst. There was a row of deep punctures and the soldier, who was a trained healer, was worried about infection.

"Bites are the worst," the man said as he massaged the salve into the oozing holes. His name was Tamoran and he had been a Red Guard soldier for over ten years. He was lean and tall, with jet black hair cut short over his ears. "How does it feel?"

"Stings some," Bearit answered, not cringing in the least bit.

"The tingling is good...means the salve is doing its job. You should heal nicely, but keep an eye on it."

"Thank you."

The man nodded as he moved to Jonas. His wounds were shallow, the bleeding already stopped, and all that were needed were a salve and a clean bandage. Soon after, Jonas sat down as a soldier brought two steaming bowls of food. He handed one to Bearit who stayed standing and gave the other to Jonas. "Thank you," he said to the warrior, who nodded. "Does it hurt to sit?" he asked Bearit.

"Some," Bearit admitted.

"Hopefully the bite will scab up and stop bleeding," Tamoran added as he accepted a bowl of beans from Captain Korrin.

Tulari was now the size of a big dog and curled up next to Jonas, the fire's flames warming her wet fur. Most of the men seemed leery of her, keeping their distance. Jonas knew that she would heal herself with time, and that likely her injured leg would be good as new by tomorrow morning. He wasn't sure if her ability to heal was part of being a night wolf, or perhaps Shyann's doing, or maybe it was a combination of the two. He was just happy that she could heal herself, as he no longer had that ability. It was one of the hardest powers to lose, being able to heal the needy and his friends. He hated seeing people suffer and no longer being able to do anything about it.

"So how long have you been tracking your people?" Jonas asked as he dipped his bread into the salted beans.

"Since yesterday," Korrin replied. "We have stepped up our patrols on the king's orders. We found their destroyed and mostly empty village yesterday morning. The carnage looked to be a day old. We tracked them all day until we found you."

"We just came across their tracks ourselves," Jonas added. "I don't think they are more than a half day ahead of us."

Korrin nodded his head, eating his beans. "We will free them tomorrow." He was firm and matter-of-fact. Jonas liked that. He looked up from his bowl, his expression serious. "We did not expect to fight the manner of creatures we found on the bridge. What were those things?"

Jonas looked up confused. "What did you think you were following?"

Korrin shrugged. "Brigands...maybe slavers. We were told they were about and to step up our patrols."

"Who told you this?"

"General Moore, our commander."

Jonas was shaking his head. "Looks like they were trying to keep the news quiet."

"What news?" Korrin asked. The other soldiers around the fire were eating quietly, listening intently. Each one was just as concerned as Korrin. They had never seen a rock bear or shadow cat act as they did on the bridge, or fought against demon-spawn such as they saw.

"The demon Maltheil has escaped from its prison. What you fought on the bridge were its servants, enslaved by the creature's magic. They were once human. I believe that the group you follow are being herded to the beast so that it may turn them just as it has to hundreds already."

No one said anything, each man frozen in shock. Korrin set his bowl down, looking into the fire. Then he looked back at Jonas. "You are sure of this?"

"I am. I thwarted an attack on the Earl at Gyeen just yesterday. We were attacked by the same creatures. The Earl knew of the demon's escape."

"Why would the king keep this news from us?" Korrin asked.

"Perhaps he didn't want to create hysteria. My guess is you would have been informed eventually," Jonas added.

"We need to get our people back," Korrin said, his voice more grave than before. He was obviously thinking the same thing as everyone else...that they would eventually be turned into the creatures they just fought. They couldn't let that happen.

"The force guarding them may be considerable," Jonas said.

Korrin nodded. "They are our people." He said nothing more as if that was reason enough. After a few more spoonfuls of beans, he looked back at Jonas. "Is it true that you are one of the heroes of Malbeck's War? I heard a song a few years back by a traveling bard. He sung of Kiln the swordsman, and King Baylin Gavinsteal dying to protect his people. I remember the words describing a great demon dragon, an elven Bladesinger, and an ogrillion with a mace as big as a tree. He sung about a twin bladed swordsman who was once a cavalier." Korrin glanced at Jonas's blades at either hip. "Are you that man?"

There were five other men sitting around the fire talking softly and eating, but once the Captain had spoken about Malbeck's War they stopped and listened. It seemed they were all curious about Jonas's identity. It didn't go unnoticed that when they found him on the bridge he was surrounded by fifteen dead enemies and had barely a scratch on him.

"I am that man, but I am no hero," Jonas said softly. "The heroes are all the men and women that fell defending Finarth." But he did not elaborate, opting to eat his warm beans.

If he were looking around the fire he would have seen nothing but respect in the faces of the men. They were soldiers as well, and dying defending your land was the ultimate sacrifice. "And you were a cavalier to Shyann?" Korrin asked.

Jonas nodded his head. "I was."

"Will you tell us what happened?"

Jonas glanced at Korrin and saw that he seemed sincere. Warrior to warrior he seemed genuinely interested in what happened. Then he looked at the men sitting around the fire, some his age and younger, and a few in their forties and fifties, the orange glow painting their inquisitive faces. Looking back at him were expressions of curiosity, awe, and admiration. They too wanted to know how a man could be a cavalier once, and now sit before them looking as an equal. Jonas didn't like to talk about what had happened to him, but these men were warriors, and if anyone could understand, it was them.

Sensing his uneasiness, Korrin spoke again. "You do not have..."

"It's fine," Jonas interjected. "I will tell you the story." He collected his thoughts, trying to figure out where to start. "I was sent into the mountains by Shyann to find King Kromm and his family. He was needed at Finarth if we were to defeat the Dark One."

"Is he really as fierce as they say?" a young round faced warrior interjected. Every warrior in Kraawn knew who King Kromm was, even this far west, and now more

143

than ever as the stories and songs of the Malbeck's War circulated throughout the lands.

Jonas smiled. "He is. King Kromm is the largest, strongest, most fierce warrior I have ever seen on the battlefield. He has a sense about him; a drive to win that is unparalleled. And his men love him, ready to die beside him if necessary. We eventually found them deep in the Tundrens running from Malbeck's minions who had taken Tarsis and were now hunting him down. We barely made it out of the mountains alive, and some of us did not." Jonas paused as he thought back to Taleen. He didn't want to dwell on her death, afraid he might not be able to finish the tale. So he quickly continued the story. "To save the queen and prince, the king's wizard took his family away with a magic portal, separating them by hundreds of unknown miles. Not knowing exactly where they were, we headed towards Cuthaine, thinking that perhaps they would go there. We were still being hunted and the king insisted we get there as quickly as possible, so we took the Hallows Road, a road our adversaries could not travel."

"The Hallows are real?" This time it was Tamoran who spoke. The look on his face was that of a young boy who was just told that the monster under his bed did in fact exist. The Hallows were so synonymous with dark scary things that there was even a nursery rhyme about the place.

Hark the Hallows, dark and creepy

Be aware, when you get sleepy

Creepy crawly, monster follows

Dream pleasant thoughts, not the Hallows

"They are. It is a world between worlds where time is different. A few days in the Hallows can be hours here."

"How did you know how to get there?"

"Allindrian the Bladesinger was fighting with us," Jonas said. "She led the way."

A couple of the men shifted, adjusting their positions so they could lean closer. A Bladesinger was as rare as a cavalier, and even though most warriors knew of them by deed and skill, few had ever seen one, let alone fought with one. "What was she like?" Korrin asked.

"Deadly," Jonas answered. "I have seen no equal with a blade or bow. Luckily she was with us, as the Hallows was a terrible place...a place I hope to never see again. It is a place of nightmares." Jonas shuddered as he thought of the trysts, the soul worm that ate into their companion's brain and fed off his energy, and the deadly trees that nearly killed them all. "We lost a lot of good men in that dark place. But we made it through and arrived at Cuthaine just a day after Kromm's wife and son."

"How old were you when this all happened?" Bearit asked, speaking up for the first time. "You can't be more than twenty seven winters now."

Jonas nodded his head. "I was twenty." The men nodded around the fire, giving respect for such accomplishments for one so young. Jonas continued. "Once there, Malbeck's Black Hearts found us, and together they coordinated an attack. We escaped once again but I was separated as I defended an underground tunnel from an army of undead while my companions escaped."

"Undead?" An older warrior with a grey beard and grey streaked black hair asked. His nose was huge, looking as if it had been broken several times. His name was Ulngarro.

"Yes. There were dark clerics of Dykreel in the catacombs," Jonas replied. At the mention of the dark god's name the warriors leaned away uneasily, each one mumbling words or prayers of protection depending on the gods they worshiped. "They captured me and brought me back to an underground temple."

"Why didn't Shyann help you?" Tamoran asked.

At first Jonas had asked that same question, wondering if he had done something to anger her, causing his goddess to abandon him. But he had later learned that was not the case. "She was always there for me, and still is now. But the temple was shielded by Dykreel himself, and she could not find me. They tortured me," Jonas paused as he thought back to the painful memories. Perhaps it was good he was talking about it. Despite it being a time he wished he could forget, it was also a defining moment for him. It was an event that changed his life, which led him down the road he was now walking. Not only that, it was also a time where he lost loved ones, and remembering what happened to him brought back those memories. It was important that he didn't forget Myrell and all the others that died then. The men waited for him, several looking at each other knowing that the memories he was recalling must have been difficult. They seemed uncomfortable and Korrin was just about to speak when Jonas continued. "Dykreel's clerics broke both of my knees first," Jonas continued. "The pain went on for what seemed like an eternity, but the worst part was when they cut open my chest and placed a cursed barbed halo under my skin." The men around the fire were stark still, staring at Jonas, their expressions a mixture of horror, sorrow, and respect. "The symbol was cursed by Dykreel himself and the metal wrapped around my bones, his dark magic entering my body and seeking out my spirit. It was the same way they created the Banthras, by capturing cavaliers and turning them into servants of the Forsworn."

"Banthras were once cavaliers?" Korrin asked incredulously. "I did not know that."

Jonas nodded gravely, his mind still thinking of that dark day. "Most do not. They sealed up my chest as the dark magic flooded through my body."

Bearit leaned closer to Jonas. "How did you fight that off?"

"Kiln taught me a mental exercise to help with concentration during battle. I used it to center my very being. It's hard to explain, but imagine you are in a dream that you can partially control. That's what it felt like. In my mind's eye I formed a circle of my *self*, and I protected it against the darkness that sought to stamp it out."

"You fought inside your mind?" Bearit asked, stating what the others were thinking.

"Yes. I floated above my *self*, a ball of light that if destroyed would be my end. Then Dykreel would control my body and I would be dead. I fought to protect that light, knowing it was all that was left of me."

"What did you fight?" Ulngarro asked, enthralled in the story.

"The darkness took whatever shape it wanted, coming at me as black winged demons, giant worms with huge teeth filled maws...anything you can imagine from your darkest nightmares." The men around the fire shivered as they each pictured their own demons. "I fought and fought, having no sense of time. Then suddenly the demons went away and I was left alone, hiding in my own consciousness."

"What happened?" Korrin asked, his voice tense.

Jonas shrugged. "My friends had found me. But when they did, I was no longer myself. I do not remember any of it but I was told I was fighting in some arena, standing on broken and shattered legs, supported by Dykreel's magic, and killing anyone they put in the ring against me. When my friends found me, I even fought them. They had to tackle and subdue me, and once they got me back to the surface, they covered me with a shroud blessed by Ulren. That's when the darkness inside me retreated into the talisman embedded in my chest, retreating from Ulren's magic that seemed to keep me in some type of suspension. I was alive, but did not move, nor did I require any food or sustenance. Ulren's clerics tried everything, but they could not rouse me from my slumber nor could they defeat the magic in the talisman. So they took me back to Finarth with them, hoping that someone there would have an idea of what to do. There were three Ekahals there who arrived to help fight against Malbeck, and luckily for me they were able to help. I was lost within myself, so they had to send help to find me; all the while cutting into my chest and placing a stone of great power there to block the talisman's magic."

"Wait a minute," Bearit said, trying to get his bearings around what Jonas had just said. "People went inside your mind to rescue you...to be bringin' you back?"

"Yes, the elven wizards were very powerful. Allindrian, Fil, and Kiln went in after me. They brought me back from the dark world that was dangerously close to taking over my mind. As they did so, the Ekahals somehow embedded this stone in my chest, and its magic sealed away Dykreel's magic forever. But that same magic that keeps the dark god's power restrained, also blocks Shyann's magic. She could not find me or feel my presence any longer. And she still cannot."

"So you were a cavalier no more," Korrin whispered as he stared into the fire. He looked back at Jonas, his expression one of pain and respect. "I'm sorry this happened to you, Jonas." Then he nodded in respect. "You honor us with your deeds, your presence here now, as well as this story."

The men around him mumbled similar words. But Tamoran was still thinking about what Jonas had said. "So the cursed halo and magical stone are still embedded in your chest?"

Jonas looked up from the fire. "Yes."

"May we see it?" Tamoran asked.

"Tamoran, you speak out of place!" Korrin snapped at him.

"I'm sorry," Tamoran back peddled. "You are correct. It was my curiosity that spoke, not my manners."

Jonas looked at the men and he could see that they were all curious, but none of them said a thing. "It's fine, Korrin. I have not talked about these events for a very long time. I think perhaps that it is good to remember. What happened to me is part of me, literally, and I should not shy away from it. I will show you." Jonas stood and unbuckled his cloak, laying it beside him. Then he unbuckled his black armor and pauldrons, setting them in a neat pile. Finally he lifted off his tunic and undershirt, exposing his scarred and muscled torso. The firelight flickered and crackled, and the orange glow reflected off of Jonas's silver and blue God Mark. The mark covered his entire torso, Shyann's tree now snaking down his arms and even wrapping around his back. White scars in the shape of an X could be seen in the center of his chest, slightly marring the beauty of the mark. Dead center was a stone set in silver, its center swirling colors of blue and white, Jonas's flesh jutting against the silver encasement as if it was part of his body. The men around the fire had never seen such a thing, and they leaned forward, their expressions reflecting that very sentiment.

"That is amazing," Korrin whispered.

"It's beautiful," Bearit said.

"I got the mark when I was fourteen and a cripple. Shyann healed me one night while I slept and I woke with the mark."

"How did that happen?" Tamoran asked.

Jonas smiled. "That is perhaps a story for another time." Jonas put his clothes and armor back on while the others talked quietly. Once he sat back down Korrin looked over at him.

"So you are a cavalier no longer, but Shyann has not forsaken you?"

"No, quite the opposite. She has made me her Shadow Knight. My clothes, my weapons, and my armor, are blessed by her, given to me by her just as a cavalier receives their weapons. Tulari, once my steed, is still my companion, as you can see." Tulari lifted her head from the ground and growled softly in acknowledgment. "She is my connection to Shyann."

"Do you have the power of a cavalier?"

Jonas shook his head. "No, I do not. My ability to heal and bring forth God Light and Fire came from my connection to her. I am no longer capable of those skills. But I can bring forth her power from the tools she gave me at will." Just then Jonas brought forth the light from his armor. Blue silver light flared brightly from the tree symbol on the chest plate. The startled men jumped and Jonas stopped the light, Shyann's magic receding back into the chest plate, returning it to its normal ordinary look.

"Does that light have power?" Korrin asked.

"It can repel great evil, but it does not have the full power of a cavalier's God Light."

"Why do your weapons be lookin' so..." Bearit was looking for the right word. "Plain?" he asked.

Jonas smiled. "When I was a cavalier I could not go anywhere without being noticed for what I was. My armor, my weapons, everything about me screamed *cavalier*, which is the point I guess. Cavaliers, besides defeating evil, are supposed to illicit a sense of honor and courage in others. That is their purpose."

"I think I am beginning to understand your new role," Tamoran said. "As a Shadow Knight, you can do much that a cavalier could not."

"That is correct. My purpose is the same as a cavalier, and that is to say I am here to defeat evil, but I have another goal. I can now go where a cavalier could not. I can infiltrate the root of evil and destroy it. The Forsworn look for people who are struggling, and they slowly convert them, molding them into their servants. I can find these men and women, and I can help them find the light once again."

"And if they are too far gone?" Bearit asked, looking into the fire. He was clearly thinking about his own plight. How much longer would it have been before his heart had turned black and become a servant of the Forsworn. He could easily say that he would have never let that happen. But just months earlier he would have said that he never would have been found in a dark lair watching a man get tortured for a loaf of bread. It might have taken a long while, but perhaps they would have turned him. He shuddered thinking about what could have happened to him. Glancing over, he looked at Jonas, his eyes thanking him.

Jonas's expression was hard. "I kill them."

Chapter Five

"What!?" King Oneck stormed as he stood up from the negotiating table. "We have spent the majority of the day hammering out the treaty and you decide to tell me *now* that the demon has escaped!"

His retainers, including his general, Hyrim Galstar, and court wizard, Carvathian, were also sitting at the table. They scooted their chairs back but did not stand, waiting to see what their king would do.

King Rothar was calm, his intense gaze unwavering as he waited for the Tur'el king to release his anger. Sitting to his right was Baylock Reen, the Battle Lord, wearing full armor, his blue cape clasped around his neck. The Battle Lord's brown hair was wavy and long, a leather band holding it back from his eyes. His face showed two day stubble and his gray green eyes narrowed at the king's outburst. He rested his massive forearms on the table so the other general could see he was not grasping his weapon. The last thing they wanted now was to undo the treaty they had made by provoking one another to violence.

"I felt that the treaty was more important," King Rothar said slowly, waiting to see if the Tur'el king was finished. It turned out he was not.

"More important!" King Haten yelled, looking back at King Rothar. The Tur'el king was in his early fifties but looked much younger. He was tall with wide shoulders and looked every bit the battle king in his silver cuirass and gold lined green cape. Despite his age, his hair was jet black, with no hints of gray. His dark eyes were boiling with rage. "My daughter, your soon to be wife, is out on a ride! Perhaps if I knew of the danger

I would not have allowed her to go traipsing around the forest."

King Rothar shifted uncomfortably in his seat. He had not known that Princess Kylin left the camp. "Was she escorted?" He regretted the question as soon as he said it.

King Haten spun on his heal and slammed his fist on the table. "Of course she was escorted! But what can ten men do against a demon!"

This time it was Baylock who spoke. "I'm sure she is safe. But as an apology I would like to personally go find her and bring her safely back."

King Rothar narrowed his eyes at that. Clearly he was not happy that his Battle Lord had just apologized for him. But he said nothing, knowing it was not the time and place. Besides, Baylock was right. The gesture was likely unnecessary, but having the Battle Lord personally volunteer was a smart diplomatic move.

King Oneck's anger seemed to dissipate as he thought about the Battle Lord's suggestion. It looked as if something else briefly occupied his mind, but he tucked it away quickly and looked directly at King Rothar. "Very well," he agreed. "But if anything has happened to her than this treaty is off." King Rothar stood slowly, his eyes never leaving the Tur'el king. "That will not be necessary," he said softly. "We will find your daughter."

It wasn't long before twenty mounted Red Guard soldiers, along with Tyril, were mounted and galloping into the dense forest. There was a main road that went north to Mynos and another that went east into Tur'el, and off those main roads were other paths that led to various villages. Baylock Reen made sure to take their best tracker, a young man in his late twenties with long dirty blonde hair pulled back into one braid, the sides shaved short. His name was Torg and he rode in the lead, looking for fresh horse tracks. They didn't go far into Tur'el lands before Torg led them south along a narrow path heading deeper into the Lasur'een Forest. Normally of course, they would not venture into Tur'el lands, but this time was different. They had the king's permission. The tracks they followed were consistent with fresh horse tracks of a party of ten or so, which was the number the king said escorted his daughter.

They rode for an hour into the forest, the massive trees growing densely all around them, their branches spanning over the road in a canopy of shades of green. The sun was shining, but its golden rays did little to warm the cold brisk fall air, the branches blocking most of the light. As they came around a bend in the path, they pulled up short. Before them were eleven horses leashed to various trees, and standing guard were two Tur'el soldiers. When they saw the Red Guard warriors ride up to them they seemed nervous, their hands resting on the pommels of their swords. When they recognized Baylock Reen, their eyes widened in surprise, but they did not draw their swords.

Tyril pulled in next to his father, his steed stopping four paces away from the men and horses. *Where were the princess and the others?* he wondered.

He was wearing a silver cuirass his father had given him when he turned eighteen and was accepted into the Red Guard ranks. It was unheard of for one so young to pass the tests necessary to be a member of the Red Guard, and as a way to show his pride, his father gave him the armor as well as his sword, all crafted by the king's armorer himself. With the set came matching pauldrons and greaves. One could be a soldier their entire life and never have weapons of their quality. Tyril was very proud of them, polishing the armor and sword daily.

"I am Baylock Reen of the Red Guard," Baylock announced, "here on order of your king. We are looking for Princess Kylin to escort her back to Angar."

Clearly the two soldiers knew of Baylock Reen. One was older and he spoke. "She went into the woods a few hours ago with the other eight escorts. We are watching the horses and waiting for her return."

"Why did they take her into the forest?" Baylock's voice was deep and accusatory and the two soldiers felt it.

"Sir, she wanted to go. She is hunting."

Baylock swore under his breath and dismounted. "Tyril, come with me," he said. He ordered ten more soldiers to follow him, leaving the other ten to stay with the horses and the two Tur'el guards in case the princess returned before guards found her. The Battle Lord took Torg with him as well hoping that he could follow their tracks easily enough and bring her safely back to the horses. They could not risk anything happening to her. The soldiers strapped their cavalry shields to their backs and followed their Battle Lord into the dark woods.

***

Jonas and Bearit woke early with the soldiers. They ate a cold meal and everyone was mounted and traveling before the sun had time to warm the ground. It was decided that they would help the soldiers get the townsfolk back. Jonas and Bearit both agreed that they could not allow those people to be turned into demon-spawn. Besides, they seemed to be traveling the same direction that Tulari was heading. Perhaps their goals were one and the same. Either way, they were now moving deeper into the Lasur'een Forest, heading now northeast.

It was mid-day when Tulari returned. She had been scouting ahead as usual hoping to find the group before they found them. Her muzzle and fur around her neck was splattered with blood but she looked unharmed. Korrin, seeing the blood, looked at Jonas with a worried expression.

Found scout...dead...we close, Tulari announced in Jonas's mind. "Well done, Tulari," Jonas said, looking over at Korrin. "Tulari killed their scout. She said we are close." The men around him heard him and passed the word back to the others. There was the sound of armor being adjusted as the men murmured their anticipation, eager to kill the enemy and save their people.

***

Sorrin pulled his son closer to him, afraid that they would be separated, or worse, that his son would be left behind. They had been walking now for nearly two days with no food or water and his son, who was fourteen, was exhausted. The boy looked up at his father, his face streaked with mud and dirt from the road, his eyes pleading. "When will we stop?"

"I told you," he whispered. "I do not know." He didn't know what else to say and he was too tired to make something up. He was the village blacksmith and even his strong muscles earned from hard work were starting to give out. If they were not at least given water soon then they would not be able to continue much further. There were nearly thirty men and women around him, slogging through the dirt and mud, dragging their feet as they concentrated on keeping one foot in front of the other. They had just learned what would happen if they could not keep up. A village woman named Bel who had an injured leg from when they were attacked two days ago fell behind. She could walk no longer, and in front of everyone so all could see, the pale skinned demon-spawn ripped her apart with their claws and fed on her blood. It was the most horrible thing any of them had ever seen. Sorrin had thought about running, but knew that he would never make it, nor would his son. There were near twenty paled skinned bald men brandishing various weapons as well as an additional fifteen demon-like creatures that he had never seen before. They crawled on clawed hands and feet and their big heads were dominated by wide, teeth filled mouths. Some had streaks of filthy, greasy hair that still clung in patches across their misshapen heads. Perhaps they were human at one time, Sorrin could not tell.

Suddenly the rumbling of horse hooves brought Sorrin from his morose thoughts to the road behind them. He was tall and he stood up straight, looking back on the road they had just traveled. What he saw gave him hope. Riding towards them was a group of Red Guard soldiers, their silver swords angling down and their shields held before them. Sorrin's heart soared with the real possibility that they would be rescued, after all the Red Guard was the king's elite soldiers. If anyone could defeat this force, it was them.

The bald men quickly formed a defensive wall facing the soldiers while the demon-spawn scurried into the forest. *What were they doing?* Sorrin thought. There was no way they were running. More than likely they would flank the soldiers from the cover of the forest as the Red Guard were forced to fight the bald men before them. But that meant that they were now unguarded, and glancing back the way they were headed proved that to be true. They were no longer surrounded. No one was there. If they could at least distance themselves from the enemy, maybe they could escape and survive.

"Let's go!" Sorrin yelled as he dragged his son away from the fight. Everyone was so tired that they barely heard him. But they followed, stumbling and moving as fast as they could as the Red Guard soldier's crashed into the enemy.

Jonas and Bearit and five other men, all archers, emerged from the undergrowth just before Sorrin as he was picking up a man who had fallen, guiding them away from the fight.

"Keep them going!" Jonas yelled, happy to see that at least someone was thinking clearly. They needed to get the villagers away from the fight, and this man was doing just that. As planned, they fanned out on the edge of the road, nocking arrows in the process. The cavalry charge had been brutal, the heavily armed warhorses and soldiers smashing into the enemy and killing many in the first few moments. But then the demon-spawn shot from the forest, leaping from trees onto the horsed men, dragging some down from their horses. Others were blocked with shields and sword thrusts, but the flanking maneuver was successful and it had stopped the power of the charge. Now they were surrounded. This is where Jonas and his archers would perform their part of the plan.

Shooting into the flanks so as not to hit any of the warriors, the five archers, with Bearit watching beside them, shot arrow after arrow into the enemy, dropping many to the ground. But it only took a few heartbeats before some of the demon-spawn changed tactics, coming at the archers at great speed, some even angling for the retreating villagers. Tulari broke from the undergrowth and barreled into two of them, killing them quickly with claws and teeth. Several more dropped from Jonas's arrows, but three made it through the barrage and one leaped from the ground towards Bearit, its back legs launching it towards his chest.

Bearit was ready for it though, the swing of his axe already in motion. He remembered Jonas teaching him that there were times to use the full strength of a swing, and other times it was not smart to do so, and Bearit reasoned that this was one of those times to use the latter. Stepping into the swing, Bearit brought his axe over his head with all his strength, the heavy blade coming down and striking the creature in mid-air. The demon-spawn didn't stand a chance. The power of the attack stopped its momentum and split the creature from the top of its head near its belly button, killing it instantly. Bearit kept his momentum moving forward and spun, yanking his axe from the creature with a powerful jerk and coming at another who broke away from the main fight with a sideways attack. The creature hissed and tried to move under the swing, but was too slow. The axe blade struck it right in the eyes and cut the top of its head off. Bearit stopped his momentum and brought his axe in close, thinking that more of them would be attacking him.

A scream spun him on his heels and he saw the two that maneuvered around him attack the villagers. Jonas's arrow took one in the side, knocking it off its path and into the brush. The second leapt towards a man who was standing protectively before a young boy and the other townsfolk, holding a stick he must have grabbed from the ground. Bearit roared and his powerful legs closed the distance quickly just as the demon took the man's stick on the side of its head. The impressive swing was well aimed, but the demon shook it off and landed on top of the man, the young boy behind him screaming for help. Bearit was afraid to use his axe as the man was flailing wildly trying to dislodge the creature. He didn't want to accidently cut off his hand, or worse, slice into his leg. So he dropped his weapon to the ground and grabbed the creature by the back of the neck and its spindly leg, and lifted with all his might, yanking the creature from the villager. Roaring with fury he tossed the creature into a nearby tree, his prodigious strength sending the beast the full ten paces where it struck the stout trunk with its back. There was a crack and the beast dropped to the forest floor. Slowly it rose from the brush, clearly wounded, when a blue feathered arrow hammered into its head, knocking it back into the tree once again where it slumped to the ground unmoving. Bearit turned towards the main fight, but all he saw were horsed soldiers, the dirty road littered with dead bodies. The fight was over.

"Well done," Jonas said from the road as he stepped towards Captain Korrin who had dismounted and was checking on his men.

The captain turned when he saw him. "The plan worked as well as one could've hoped," he said.

Jonas nodded and looked around the carnage. "Did you lose anyone?"

Korrin's look was straight faced, but Jonas could see the pain behind his eyes. "We lost five." Then he quickly changed the subject. "Let's drag these bodies away and see what we can do for the survivors."

Bearit knelt next to the man who had struck the creature with the stick. His shoulders were bloody along with one leg, but the wounds appeared to be shallow cuts. It looked as if Bearit got to the demon-spawn before he had done serious damage. "How badly are you hurt?" Bearit asked, helping him stand, the young boy holding his other arm.

"I'll live," he said, wincing from the cuts. "Thanks to you."

Bearit nodded. "The soldiers have some knowledge of healing. I'll get some help."

The man nodded. "Thank you."

***

Two hours later, Torg the tracker found the princess. They had just killed a small deer when they came across them, startling them in the process. Several of the royal guards turned crossbows on Baylock and the others as they approached; slowly lowering them once they realized who they were. The princess was standing over the deer holding an unloaded crossbow as a man dressed the animal. She looked over and frowned when she saw the Battle Lord and his men.

"Princess Kylin, I'm sorry to disturb your hunt but your father has requested that you return to camp immediately," Baylock said.

She looked perturbed. "And he sent the Battle Lord of Lanard to retrieve me? Seems excessive doesn't it?"

Tyril was standing next to his father and he enjoyed watching her challenge him. He was pretty sure few had talked to him in such a tone. She glanced at Tyril and he swore he saw a subtle smile behind her mask of annoyance.

"I requested the honor myself," Baylock answered, his tone a bit more sharp.

She sensed it and changed her own tone. "I see. And what dangers lurk in my own lands that require the presence of Baylock Reen?"

"That is not for me to say. Please, I must return you safely before the treaty is to be signed."

She deflated somewhat at that, knowing the importance of the treaty. "Very well," she added, turning to the guard that was dressing the deer. "Take the choicest cuts and leave the rest. We depart promptly."

On the way back to Angar, Princess Kylin rode next to Tyril, who was just back in line from his father. She rode next to him for a while, the silence palpable. Finally Tyril spoke after giving her a few furtive glances. "Did you kill the deer on your own?"

She looked over at him. "Yes...does that surprise you?"

Tyril shrugged. "Maybe a little."

"The crossbow is not so hard to use. My father's weapon smith made it for me," she added, looking down at the weapon that hung from a hook on her saddle. "It's really quite impressive. He designed it with a series of gears to make it easier for me to crank and load."

Tyril looked more closely at the weapon. Sure enough, there were some gears along its shaft that were not typically found on a crossbow. "I have a friend who would like to look at that weapon," Tyril added, thinking of Peron. "He thinks of himself as quite a tinkerer."

"And is he?"

"He is," Tyril agreed. "He is the smartest person I know."

"In that case I would like to meet him."

Tyril smiled at that. "I think that will happen sooner than you think."

"What do you mean?" she queried. "And what is so funny?"

Tyril looked at her sheepishly. "Well my friend is the Prince of Lanard and next in line for the throne."

"Peron Rothar you mean?"

"I do."

"I am to be his step mother," she spat. "We are the same age I would guess."

"That is true, but when you marry his father you will be his step mother nonetheless."

She said nothing as she looked off into the forest, her mind elsewhere. After a mile or so she looked back at Tyril. "Do you respect your father?"

It was a blunt question, and one she had to whisper as Baylock was no more than four horses ahead of them. It took Tyril off guard. "Yes, I do. He has raised me well. My father is honorable and I am proud to be his son." She looked at him seriously, and seeing he meant what he said she looked away. Tyril followed her question with one of his own. "What about you? Do you respect your father?"

She looked back at him and her dark expression said it all. "No, I do not. He is a snake and wants nothing more than power and wealth. He includes me in nothing. I have no idea why he does what he does. Case in point, why would he send your father to fetch me? I can only assume that he has some ulterior motive."

"I see," Tyril said lamely. "I'm sorry." He didn't know what else to say. And he could think of no other motive as to why her father wanted the Battle Lord to find his daughter. After all, it was Tyril's father's suggestion to begin with.

"Perhaps," she added, looking off into the dark forest, "my life will be better with King Rothar in Lanard."

"I'm sure that it will," he added, trying to make her feel better.

They were still another hour from camp when they came upon a group of mounted soldiers, all bearing the Tur'el colors. Baylock Reen pulled up short of them, keeping nearly ten horse lengths between them. Tyril stopped his mount next to his father.

"Something isn't right," the Battle Lord whispered to Tyril.

Just as he did so one of the Tur'el soldiers nudged his horse closer. He lifted his visor to speak. "Baylock Reen, we have come to escort our princess back to Angar."

"We were given permission by King Oneck to do just that. As you can see," he added, "we have the princess and are escorting her back to camp. We need no further assistance, however, if you would like to join us than feel free to do so."

The man was wearing a full beard and the distance was too great to see his facial expression, but Tyril got the feeling that the man was smiling.

Torg the tracker nudged his horse closer to the Battle Lord. "My Lord," he whispered, "there are men in the brush flanking us."

Baylock Reen said nothing in return, but he nodded in understanding, glancing over at Tyril. "Son, if you can, take the princess and run. Watch your flanks."

Tyril looked at him, his expression one of worry. "But Father..."

Baylock Reen drew his blade, and the Red Guard soldiers behind him, sensing their commander's tension, followed suit. The ten Tur'el soldiers who were behind the princess looked confused, glancing at one another as if the other knew what was happening. But none of them did. "If your assassins in the woods attack us!" he shouted, "then you will be starting a war!"

This time Tyril could see the man's expression. He was smiling broadly, his white teeth visible through his black beard. "That is exactly the point! Attack!"

Just then everything exploded into motion. Men in black broke through the underbrush and came at the Red Guard soldiers. The mounted warriors before them churned up the dirt on the road as they charged.

Frantically, Baylock Reen looked at his son, his eyes wide with battle fury. "Go!" he shouted, as he smacked Tyril's horse on its flank with the flat of his blade.

Tyril's horse jumped and he pulled on the reins, spinning the well-trained horse around. Princess Kylin's face was one of shock, her eyes wide with fright and confusion. It was clear she had no idea why her father's troops were attacking them. Without saying a word, Tyril grabbed the reins from her and pulled her horse next to his, nudging his steed through the other mounted warriors around him. They bolted back the way they had come, blasting through the stunned Tur'el guards, his powerful warhorse bashing one black clad assassin to the side as he made his escape. All he could hear was the sound of battle behind him and their horses' heavy breathing as they ran for their lives.

Baylock Reen pivoted his horse to the left and swung his blade down and through the neck of an attacking assassin. He killed several more with brilliant precision as did his men around him, their skill and elevated positions giving them a massive advantage. But he knew the cavalry charge would be on them in just moments, so he turned his warhorse back towards the charge, several of his men joining him on the road. They had no time to gain any speed as the Tur'el soldier's crashed into them. But they were Red Guard cavalry and it wasn't just they who were the most trained and skilled soldiers west of the Tundrens, but their steeds were as well. Bred from the best stock and trained since youth, the Red Guard warhorses held their ground, pivoting expertly to either side of the charging animals, giving their riders the space and position to best use their shields and swords. The Tur'el horses pushed through the throng of Red Guard warriors. Swords crashed against shields as the Red Guard cavalry danced around the enemy, their silver swords cutting into the Tur'el flanks, dropping many to the forest floor.

But the assassins continued to attack from the brush. Several Red Guard fighters went down, and others were forced to turn towards the enemy that was flanking them. More Red Guard soldiers fell as they tried to keep the assassins at bay, their backs now exposed to the Tur'el cavalry. There were just too many of the enemy and they were being attacked on all sides.

Baylock Reen fought with all the savagery and skill he could muster. Enemy swords clanged against his shield as he maneuvered his sword with expert speed and precision, the razor sharp steel cutting the enemy down in staggering numbers. Bodies piled up around him as he spun his horse back and forth, churning up dirt as his shield and sword found flesh and steel alike. No one could touch him, and any who got too close felt the cold edge of his steel. Eventually, several swords found the flesh on his legs, cutting into him, and others found gaps in his horse's barding, slicing the animal's flesh. Soon blood was splattering through the air, both rider and steed fighting for their lives.

Then suddenly there was no one attacking him. Panting heavily, his sword dripping with blood, he saw that all his men were dead, over forty enemy bodies scattered across the road and forest edge. There were at least ten Tur'el riders before him and another five behind him, as well as a handful of black clad assassins standing at the ready near the edge of the forest undergrowth, their short swords held before them. Glancing back, there was no sign of Tyril and the princess. He hoped they had made it.

Turning back to the remaining men on the road he found the same man who spoke to him earlier. He had hoped the man had been killed. But that was not the case. "What are you waiting for?" he spat, sitting up straight in his saddle. He was bleeding from several wounds, as was his horse, but both stood tall and impassive, like a mountain before a winter storm.

"We have our orders to keep you alive if possible," the man said after lifting up his visor once again. "And don't worry. We will catch your son and the princess. Go find them?" he yelled to the men behind the Battle Lord.

"I will not submit," Baylock spoke. "You will not take me alive."

The Tur'el commander smiled but said nothing as a rider moved forward from the rear. He was wearing a dark gray robe and hood, his face shadowed under the cowl. The dark stranger stopped next to the commander and removed his hood. It was Carvathian, the court wizard to King Oneck. "I'm afraid you are partly right, for we will take you, but not really alive. I want you to meet someone...well, I guess it's more of an *it*." The wizard than whispered some words that Baylock could barely hear let alone understand. It sounded like a spell.

The trees to his right began to shake and sticks cracked as something large moved through the forest. As it neared, Baylock Reen could make out its shadowy form as it pushed its way through the dense brush. It was large, and the Battle Lord noticed that the forest seemed to shrink away from the creature, as if it didn't want to touch it. Branches turned black and shrubs shriveled to sticks, their green foliage dying like it was winter well on its way. Just as the thing broke through the shadows of the forest, Baylock felt a wave of fear crash into him.

Maltheil's massive form stepped from the edge of the forest and stood on the side of the road. The demon was several heads taller than Baylock Reen who was sitting on a huge warhorse. Baylock felt an intense fear rush through him. But he fought it down, and to his horse's credit, his steed did as well, somehow gaining confidence from its rider. The black clad assassins moved away from the demon, not wanting to be anywhere near the creature. Even the Tur'el cavalry turned their horses and retreated over twenty paces away, leaving Carvathian and Baylock Reen the closest to the creature.

"I'm impressed," Carvathian said. "Most cannot withstand Maltheil's fear."

The demon turned its red eyes on the wizard and Baylock could not miss the thing's hatred. But then the glowing eyes pivoted to him and he nearly fell off his horse, the fear almost grasping his resolve and crushing it for good. But he held onto his courage and beat down the fear that was all around him. The demon looked at the bodies piled around the Battle Lord. "You will make a fine general," the demon said to him, stepping onto the road, its huge clawed feet digging into the dirt.

"It was you that freed the demon?" Baylock asked.

Carvathian dismounted, knowing that his horse would not get any closer to the beast, and walked forward to stand next to Maltheil. The demon was twice his size and it looked to Baylock that the creature was fighting through an overwhelming desire to crush the little human. But for some reason he could not. "Sort of," the wizard responded. "I control the demon, but let's just say I had help."

Maltheil turned its clawed hands into fists as its red eyes looked down at the wizard. "You will make a mistake," the thing hissed. "They always do. And when that happens, I will drink your blood and feed your flesh to my servants."

Carvathian ignored the demon. "Turn him," he ordered. "Then bring your army to the wood line. We have a king to kill and a city to take." Then he turned away and went back to his horse. The assassins drifted away into the forest, eager to get as far away as possible. They knew what was about to happen.

Maltheil stepped closer to Baylock Reen. "Ready to serve me?"

Baylock Reen's heart was pounding in his chest, and somehow he dug deep for more courage, and he found it. "Never," he screamed as he raised his sword, nudging his horse in the side. Together they shot towards the demon just as Maltheil took a deep breath, spewing forth a large cloud of red steam that covered the entire road.

Baylock hit the fog and it felt like he hit a wall of pure evil. If evil had a physical embodiment, it was the dense red fog swirling all around him. He fell from his horse and barely felt the impact as the evil swarmed through his body. Gripping the dirt he screamed into the fog, his consciousness slowly disappearing. Something pulsed up the side of his neck and somewhere in his consciousness he felt his hair dropping to the ground. His last thoughts as he continued to scream were of his son. And then there was nothing.

The red fog drifted away revealing Baylock Reen standing tall, his sunken eyes staring at Maltheil. His hair was gone and a black snake-like sigil ran up his neck to the top of his bald head.

"Welcome General," the demon growled.

***

Tyril was leaning forward in his saddle urging his horse to run faster than she ever had. Princess Kylin was riding just behind him and luckily for them both she was a good rider and her horse was a strong breed. His heart was pounding and all he could think of was that he left his father and the rest of the Red Guard to die. *But he was ordered to do it*, he told himself. He growled under his breath and tried to clear his mind. He couldn't fix what had already happened. All he could do was try to survive. He knew they would be close on their tail, riding them down with greater numbers. Eventually they would catch them.

Coming to a decision he sat up and pulled hard on the reins, urging his horse to slow. Kylin shot past him but did the same, slowing and turning her horse around to see why he had stopped. Her hair was windblown and her wild eyes portrayed her fright.

"What are you doing? What are we doing? What in Toolm's name just happened?" Her questions came flowing out of her like a broken dam.

"I don't know. But they clearly wanted us dead, which could only mean one thing...the treaty was never going to happen, nor was your marriage. It was just a ruse to get the king in your father's grasp." He dismounted and moved towards her with purpose, grabbing her arm and literally pulling her from the saddle.

"What are you doing?" she screamed. "Let go of me."

He stood tall over her and held her in his iron grip. "Tell me you had nothing to do with this," he hissed, his voice like iron.

She looked aghast. "Of course I didn't!" she stormed. "My father never includes me in anything. I told you, I hate him."

"Well, it's not your head they want," he said, releasing her. "But I cannot have you returning to them and telling them where I've gone. So you're coming with me."

"I told you," she said firmly. "I am not part of this plan. My father likely cares little for what has happened to me."

Tyril relaxed some. She seemed to be telling the truth, or she was an incredibly good actor. "It matters not. You are coming with me."

"Where?"

"We need to get to Lanard. If we stay on the road they will soon catch us. We need to send the horses away and travel on foot. If we stay in the forest we will be much harder to track. Hopefully they will ride past us and not realize we have left the horses. You ready?"

"Yes," she said, her tone still angry. "Let me get my crossbow."

She grabbed the weapon and returned. Tyril noticed that she already wore a belt that contained a quiver of bolts as well as a hunting knife. He hoped she could use both, and that neither would be necessary.

Tyril slapped his horse's rear and sent the animal down the road. Kylin did the same and followed him into the dark woods.

They ran west toward Lanard, Tyril leading the way. There were animal trails through the undergrowth, but at times Tyril had to use his sword to cut through the foliage. He hated doing that, knowing it would leave an obvious trail for a tracker, but it was the only way to make good time. He had to hope they stayed on their horses' trail. If not, than they would catch up to them, sooner rather than later.

"How do you even know where you're going?" Kylin asked, her exhaustion evident as she followed Tyril through the thick brush.

"I know we were heading west when we left the main road," Tyril answered, ducking under a low lying branch. "I can only hope our direction has held true."

They had been moving through the forest for over an hour, and Tyril was worried that he indeed had no idea the direction he was going. What worried him the most was the trail they were leaving. Any tracker worth his salt could follow it.

Suddenly he heard something to his right. He turned towards the noise just as an arrow slammed into a tree beside him. "Get down!" he yelled. And just as he

171

did two men charged him from the brush. They must have been flanking them, waiting for their opportunity. A body came catapulting through the brush before him, a sword thrust for his gut. Spinning his sword across his body Tyril blocked the attack as he pivoted to the man's flank, his own blade continuing around incredibly fast and slicing across the man's back as he ran by. The Tur'el soldier wore armor but his blade still cut into the top of his unprotected shoulder as well as his buttocks as it sliced across the man's back. Another man came from around a tree to Tyril's left and he dropped just in time as his sword flashed above his head. Tyril kicked the man in the back and knocked him into the brush as he brought his sword back around to take the injured man in the neck. Another arrow whizzed by his head and out of his peripheral vision he saw Kylin ducking low and loading her crossbow. He didn't know where the archer was and he had no time to worry about it as three more men emerged from the brush, their swords held low. Kylin had jumped behind a tree, but it mattered little, the men were clearly after him.

Tyril had never killed before, or fought a real enemy to the death. But he had been trained since birth and it was the one thing he was confident in. Few were faster, stronger, and more capable with a sword than he. Even at his age, he could best nearly every Red Guard soldier. Trained by his father and waking every morning over the last ten years with a sword in his hand had morphed him into a deadly warrior.

Two men charged and their glinting swords came at him. He had no time to think. Reacting on instinct and hours of practice, Tyril parried their strikes, keeping their blades away as he danced around them, taking advantage of the cover the trees offered by ducking behind them. Enemy steel struck the trees as they tried to cut him down. One man's blade became lodged in the wood and Tyril spun around the trunk, his fist, the same one holding his sword, connecting solidly with the man's elbow, snapping it at the joint. Continuing its momentum, he sliced the blade across the man's bicep as he brought it across his body to deflect the other man's thrust aimed at his chest. His block was true, but not fast enough, and the tip of the man's blade sliced across his leg as it swung by, opening up a shallow gash. Grunting, Tyril kicked the man in the groin, knocking him back into the brush.

Tyril had a quick reprieve and that's when he noticed Kylin struggling with the third soldier. She brought her crossbow to bear and shot it point blank into the man's stomach. The man grunted in pain and fell to his back. At the same time, the man that fell into the brush regained his balance at charged Tyril again. But before he got two steps an arrow slammed into his neck, his body careening into the brush. The man with the broken arm finally freed his sword from the tree and was raising the weapon above his head with his good arm when a black cat nearly as big as a horse slammed into him, launching him five paces and disappearing into the thick bushes. The man screamed and thrashed about, but in moments he was silent, the big animal emerging from the foliage, stopping three paces from Tyril and Kylin, both of whom were staring at the cat in shock.

"He won't hurt you, but just to be sure I'd lower your sword."

Tyril glanced to his left and a man emerged from the forest like a mist carrying a bow, a sword dangling from his hip. He was tall and moved with the grace of a warrior. "Who are you?" Tyril asked, not lowering his sword.

The man smiled. "That is a good question, and if I told you, you probably wouldn't believe me. You may call me Embry. The shadow cat's name is Korum."

The big cat growled in acknowledgment and sat on his haunches, licking the blood from his clawed forepaws.

Tyril lowered his blade some and Kylin ran to his side. "There is an archer in the woods," he said, stepping protectively in front of Kylin.

"Not anymore," Embry said, moving closer to them. "I gave you my name, now it's your turn to give me yours. And do not lie to me Red Guard soldier, for I will know."

There was something about the man that reinforced his threat. He looked younger than his father, but there was something about him that carried the weight of age, or wisdom, or maybe it was power, or perhaps all three. All Tyril knew was that he didn't want to lie to him. "I am Tyril Reen and this is Princess Kylin Oneck."

Embry looked at the dead soldier with the crossbow bolt in his gut. "Why would the princess of Tur'el kill her own soldier?"

It was a good question, and one that Kylin struggled with. "I...I don't know. I didn't know what else to do. They were trying to kill Tyril and take me with them."

"Did you both come from Angar?" Embry asked.

"Yes," Tyril said, still looking at the big cat cleaning the blood from his fur. "How do you control the cat?"

"Korum is my friend. I am a druid."

"Druid? I thought they were all dead," Tyril said.

"Most are."

Kylin stepped closer to Embry. "Are you the one we call Solum, protector of the forest?"

Embry gave her a subtle bow. "I go by that name as well." Then he looked at Tyril. "You may know me as

Atticus Belthar." The Kingdom of Lanard was further from the Lasur'een Forest, hence most of its inhabitants were not as familiar with Atticus's other names. But the Kingdom of Tur'el bordered the forest, so most of its people knew of the strange druid that protected the land.

Tyril stepped back in shock. "You cannot be him," he stammered. "You look younger than my father."

"I told you, I am a druid. I protect the land around us and in return the land grants me power, some of which is used to maintain my youth and vitality."

"It was you, then, that helped defeat Maltheil thousands of years ago," Tyril said, thinking back to the druid's words in the book.

"It was, although I had help. The earth helped me seal away the beast, and it was your kingdom's job to protect the tomb and book and make sure that the demon never rose again. But someone freed it. I've been tracking the creature and that is when I found you."

"What are we going to do?" Kylin asked, looking at both men.

"I need to go to Angar and see what's amiss." Atticus looked at the bodies around him. "Let's get further away from these bodies and set up camp. From there I will leave you to go to Angar."

Tyril looked up through the canopy of trees to try and judge the sun's location. It was hard to see but based on when they entered the forest he had a pretty good idea that night was fast approaching. "Angar is several hours away. I don't think you'll make it before dark."

Atticus smiled. "Do not worry about that. Come, follow me. We can talk more once we distance ourselves from these bodies."

Korum leapt into the brush and disappeared into the shadows as Atticus headed northwest. He kept his pace at a slow jog hoping that the two would be able to keep up. Tyril was glad that Kylin was wearing hunting breaches and well-made boots as the dress she wore the other night at dinner would have posed a serious problem in the dense brush. It turned out that the princess was not foreign to running, and she was able to keep up with them just fine. They crossed the original road they were on and ran for another hour before Atticus stopped in the middle of a grassy clearing. The glade was small; maybe five paces in diameter, and huge trees surrounded it, each one as big around as ten people standing shoulder to shoulder in a tight circle. Their branches spanned out over them, nearly blocking their view of the sky. Soft grass and moss grew all around them, the green carpet climbing the trees as well.

"This is a good spot," Atticus said as he unslung his pack from his shoulders. "The sun will set soon. Let's make a fire and rest."

"Fire? The enemy will see it," Tyril warned.

"They will not. I will place a shielding around us." Atticus sat down on the soft ground and placed his hands on the grass. Tyril and Kylin stood and watched as he sat still, his eyes closed, his mouth moving as foreign words caught their ear. After a few moments he opened them. "It is done."

"What did you do?" Kylin asked as she leaned her crossbow against a tree.

"A shielding is when I ask the surroundings to hide us. If anyone were to walk by, they would see only forest. They will not hear, see, or smell us. We are safe."

Tyril didn't look so confident. He was ignorant about most magic, and therefore had no confidence in it. "How do we even know you are who you say you are?"

"Good question," Atticus said as he stood. "Perhaps you would like to ask..." and then he disappeared in a flash and standing in his place was a deer. In both their minds they heard the word *me*, before the deer disappeared and turned back into the druid. "I can do more if you'd like," the druid said, smiling mischievously.

Tyril's eyes were wide. "No, I think I am convinced."

"Good. I'll make a fire and prepare some food. Then we can talk."

Kylin and Tyril helped Atticus gather some wood and soon the druid had a big warm fire built. Then he dug around in his pack and produced a water skin and three bars of some unknown food. He gave one to each of them and started to eat his own. The bars were slightly sticky and looked like a mixture of grain, fruits, and nuts.

"What are these?" Kylin asked.

"I make them myself. They are mostly made of fruit, nuts, grains, and honey, but I have a few secret ingredients as well. They are full of energy. One bar can get you through an entire day. Try it, you'll like it."

She shrugged and bit into the bar. She was hungry and he was right, it was very good. It was crunchy and chewy and slightly sweet. Tyril followed her lead and it wasn't long before the bars were gone. Both were famished and their bodies needed the energy.

It was then that Atticus noticed the cut on the inside of Tyril's leg. "You are hurt."

Tyril nodded, angling his leg so they could see. "Sword cut. Luckily it's shallow. I should clean it."

"Won't be necessary," Atticus said as he moved next to Tyril. Keeping one hand on the ground, he touched the inside of Tyril's leg just below the wound. "Don't worry," he said when he saw Tyril's discomfort. "I will not harm you." Then he closed his eyes and whispered several words. Within five heartbeats a slight glow emanated from his hand on Tyril's leg, and in even less time the small cut sealed up. The only evidence of the wound was the blood that was still soaked into his leggings. "See, nothing to worry about," he said as he moved away.

Tyril looked impressed, and a little in awe. "Thank you. The pain is gone."

Atticus nodded. "Now, tell me what happened?"

"My King and Kylin's father, King Oneck, had spent the day negotiating the peace treaty when King Rothar told him of the demon's escape," Tyril began. "When he heard the news he was furious as he had let Kylin hunt in the forest for the day. So my father, the Battle Lord, as an apology, requested that he take twenty Red Guard soldiers into the forest to bring her back, which we did. But before we made it back to Angar we were attacked by Tur'el troops. My father sent me away while they fought. I do not know what has happened to them. All I know is we rode hard to distance ourselves from them. Then we ditched the horses and went on foot, thinking it would be harder for them to find us. But they did, and that's when you arrived."

"I see," Atticus said, thinking.

"It seems that King Oneck never meant to uphold the treaty," Tyril continued, thinking out loud. "I'm afraid for my king and the people of Angar."

Atticus looked directly at Kylin. "And you knew nothing of this betrayal?"

She was still angry from Tyril's earlier accusation so it didn't take much to have it boil over again. "No!" she said. "I do not get along with my father!" She was adamant. "I assumed he was marrying me off, not just for peace, but to get rid of me. I hate the man! And now you see why! I will say it one more time, so do not question me again. I had nothing to do with my father's betrayal!"

Atticus sighed and Tyril was silent. He wanted to believe her, and she definitely seemed sincere. The question now was...what were they going to do with her? They could send her back. But maybe she didn't want to go back. He could bring her back to Lanard with him, but then what?

"Perhaps King Oneck had capitalized on the situation when the Battle Lord had suggested finding you on his own," Atticus mused, glancing at Kylin. "After all, if he had no intention of signing the treaty, than he may have seen his chance at taking out the Rothar Battle Lord." Atticus looked at Tyril. "I'm sorry, Tyril, but I'm afraid you should expect the worst. But there is always a chance, and I need to go see what has happened at Angar before we make any decisions." Atticus stood. "Stay here. I will be back soon."

Tyril was looking into the fire, his eyes heavy and sad. Then he looked up, his expression shifting to doubt. "How are you going to travel through the forest at night?"

Atticus smiled, and suddenly he was no longer there, and flapping its wings in his place was a small black raven. *Like this* he said in their minds. And then he flew up into the branches, disappearing into the night.

"Well that's a first," Tyril said as he threw another log onto the fire. They didn't say anything for a while, both staring into the flames. Finally Tyril broke the silence. "So, what do you want to do?"

Kylin looked up, her eyes sad. "What do you mean?"

"Do you want to go back home, or come to Lanard?"

"I don't know. I won't be welcome in Lanard, especially if my father is leading an army there. But I don't want to go back home either. I hate it there. Believe it or not, despite my hesitation at marrying a man so much older than I, I was looking forward to a new adventure, anything to get out of my own existence."

"Was it really that bad?"

It took her a moment before she answered. "I guess one would say it couldn't have been that bad, after all I lived in an opulent castle and I had anything I wanted or needed." Her sad eyes looked up at Tyril again. "But that was all I had. My father did not love me, his attention saved for his son. And even then he was incapable of showing any sort of affection. My mother is weak and does whatever my father says. To be honest, she is afraid of him. He would hit her on occasion, and me as well. I rarely left the castle, I had no friends...my life was..." she struggled for the words. "Loveless...boring, and I had no means to change it. Would you want to go home to that?"

"I guess not."

"I could just run away," she reasoned.

"Why don't you come back to Lanard with me," Tyril suggested. "At least there we can help you. If you still want to run away, then you can. But you are not prepared for such a task now."

"Perhaps," she whispered, looking into the flickering flames. "Tell me about Peron Rothar?" she asked, changing the subject.

Tyril smiled. "You would like him. He is the smartest person I know, witty, and can make anything he wants. He thinks of himself as an inventor...a tinkerer."

"Is he a warrior like you as well?"

Tyril's smile disappeared. "No, he is not."

"And why does that sadden you?"

"It saddens him," he said, "not me. I feel for him as his father is a battle king like his father before him. But Peron is not, and his father never misses an opportunity to show him his displeasure. I think Peron feels he is not fit to be king."

Kylin threw a twig into the fire. "I think we need more kings who can use their heads, not their steel. Perhaps we would not be killing each other over dirt, water, and trees. Peron might be the very king this land needs." Tyril frowned, saying nothing. She looked at him. "You don't agree?"

"It's not that. Perhaps you are right. But I am a soldier, it is all I know. It's hard for me to imagine living in a world where my sword is no longer needed."

"Would you feel...unnecessary?"

"What would I do?" he countered.

"Farm, raise a family, anything would be better than shedding blood."

"Perhaps," he whispered.

She smiled and nudged him with her foot. "Fear not, my warrior. I do not think your sword will ever become...unnecessary. But dreaming of a world with that possibility is not a bad thing, don't you think?"

This time he smiled as well. "It is a nice dream."

They talked longer into the evening and just before they were going to build up the fire and sleep for the night, Atticus stepped from the darkness into the firelight. He startled them and Tyril nearly drew his sword.

"It's just me, my friend," the druid said as he sat next to the fire. His expression looked grim.

"What did you find?" Tyril asked.

"The camp outside of Angar was destroyed and the city has been taken." He looked up from the fire.

"Maltheil was there with thousands of servants, and the beast, once it had destroyed the city gates, was turning more into his demon-spawn." His expression grew even more serious, the orange firelight reflecting of his face adding to the graveness. "I saw the head of King Rothar, as well as Prince Dalland. They are both dead."

Kylin looked at Tyril, who said nothing, staring into the fire. She looked back at the druid. "And my father's army was there?"

Atticus nodded. "It was, and working side by side with the demon."

Finally Tyril looked up from the fire. "Did you see if my father was alive?"

"I'm sorry, I did not. The scene was chaotic and it was dark."

Tyril sighed heavily. "What are we going to do?"

"If the demon is working with them, then that means that someone, likely your father's," he said, looking at Kylin, "wizard worked out a way to free the beast. But it's only a matter of time before the demon will break the magical bond that holds it to the wizard."

"What do you mean?"

"It's the same thing that happened thousands of years ago. It was the Rotharian king's wizard who summoned the demon originally, and used Maltheil's power to defeat the Ronith tribes raiding from the south. After that, they used the demon's power to march on Tur'el. But over time the link between the wizard and the demon weakened, and before they could defeat Tur'el, Maltheil broke free from the spell, and destroyed everyone and anyone in its way. The same thing will happen again."

"But you defeated the beast, surely you can do it again," Kylin said.

"I did not defeat the beast on my own. I had help from my grove, and the king of Oneck was a great battle king, and together we defeated it. But I have no grove, nor do I have a powerful battle king."

"There must be a way," Tyril said.

"All I know is that once Angar is secure, the Tur'el army, led by Maltheil and his minions, will march on Lanard." Atticus put another stick on the fire. "The one thing that bothers me was how the demon was freed. The only way to use the book was to have the blood of the Rothar royal bloodline. And I know the book was kept in a chest, sealed by lock and spell, and if anyone without Rotharian royal blood attempted to retrieve it they would be fried on the spot. How did a wizard from Tur'el manage to do all that?"

Tyril was worried. Should he tell him what they did three years ago? Maybe he would have some insight. But he was worried that by voicing their deed that it would incriminate them. Being responsible for freeing the demon was something he wasn't sure he could handle. But they didn't do much besides open the book and spill some of Peron's blood. Could that have been enough? If anyone knew the answer to that question it would be the man who wrote the book. Tyril decided he had to say something.

"I need to tell you something," he began. Atticus looked at him and saw that he was mulling over something quite serious. He didn't say anything, but nodded for him to continue. Clearing his voice, he did. "Three years ago I entered the vault that held the demon with Prince Peron and our friend Kyron." Atticus sat back from the fire and Kylin put her hand to her mouth. "Peron had taken the book from its location in Master Moran's room." Once he started, he wanted to end it quickly, so it poured out of him as fast as he could get it out. "We just wanted to see the demon's prison. We were just kids. We didn't even know that Maltheil was real." Tyril stopped and looked at Atticus. "The demon broke from its prison over a week ago. It couldn't have been us, right?"

"Tell me exactly what you did," Atticus said, his voice low, a hint of rising anger beneath the whisper.

"Peron used the sigil on the front of the book to open the steel door to Maltheil's prison. Once inside, he opened the book and it fell. When he tried to catch it he cut himself on one of the blades jutting from the sarcophagus. He only read the words on the first page. But when he dripped blood on the page, it disappeared, like it was sucked in, and smoke rose from the spot. There was something like a flash, or ripple, that moved over the sarcophagus. That was it. We were so scared we ran from the tomb. And now, three years later, the demon breaks free. It makes no sense."

"Are you sure you didn't read any further in the book?"

"I'm sure. Peron returned the key and the book to their hiding spots and we have never told anyone, until now that is."

Atticus took a deep breath. "The spell that was used to seal the demon away was a banishing spell. For the spell to work, to have the power to dispel the demon to the nethers, we needed powerful blood to bind it. Royal blood of the Rothar line was used. Unfortunately it is the same blood necessary to unlock the demon's prison, which is what I wrote on the first page of the book. But if you didn't read any further, then there was no way the spell was unwound. Peron's blood was probably like a knock on the demon's door, but nothing more."

"So, someone with royal blood, if they read the entire book, could free the creature?" Kylin asked.

"Technically, the blood is just the key. Blood needs to be spilt on the book before it will reveal the words. If someone had royal blood, and they were powerful enough to read the spell and control the demon, then yes, they could've unlocked Maltheil's prison."

"What do you mean, powerful enough?"

"Freeing the demon, and controlling the demon, are not the same thing. For instance, if Peron would have used his blood on each page, and continued reading the book, the spell would've got harder and harder to read the further he went. The magic in a binding spell such as was used requires great concentration and mental willpower. He would never have been able to complete it. The words would have blurred and he would have got dizzy or fainted. And even if he could have finished the spell, once the demon was free, he would not have been able to control it. Maltheil would've killed you all, or worse, turned you."

"But a powerful wizard, if they had access to the book and royal blood, could've completed the spell and controlled the demon?" Kylin asked.

"Yes, it is possible. My guess is that Carvathian was able to accomplish such a task. He is quite powerful."

"You know of him?" Kylin asked.

"Of course," Atticus responded. "I know many things. I make it my business to know the powerful players in the lands that surround my forest."

"So we didn't free the demon?"

"No, what you did was incredibly stupid. But you did not free the beast. But if it was Carvathian, he needed help to get the book and the blood. I'm afraid you have a traitor at court."

"They will face judgment for their deeds, rest assured," Tyril replied, his voice hard like iron.

"We must stop them," Kylin said adamantly.

"Yes," Atticus said, "we must. If Lanard is destroyed, then once Maltheil breaks from his magical bond, he will unleash his army throughout the neighboring lands. He will destroy and plunder everything around us. We...I, cannot let that happen."

"What happens when Maltheil turns a soldier?" Tyril asked, thinking about the implications of turning all the soldiers at Angar to his will.

"They are his servants, mind and body. They tend to have similar abilities as they had in life, although slightly less so as they have lost their ability to think as they once did. But a talented swordsman will still be formidable once turned."

"So by turning an army of soldiers, Maltheil will have a trained military force at his disposal?" Tyril asked, already worried about the answer.

"For the most part, yes."

"And if Maltheil is killed?" Kylin asked.

"Then his servants die as well."

"Then we need to kill the demon," Tyril said adamantly.

Atticus nodded his head, staring again into the fire, knowing that that task would be no easy feat.

CHAPTER SIX

The smell of roasting horse meat filled the roadside camp. It was only midday but the people they had rescued were far too tired to do anything other than rest. They needed food and water, and the Red Guard did not have enough rations to feed that many people, so they opted on cooking one of the dead horses. The villagers ate the cooked flesh ravenously, washing it down with cold water from a nearby stream. It was going to be a cold night so the soldiers spent the rest of the day collecting wood so they could build large fires on the road to keep the townsfolk warm at night. In the morning, they would march them back to their village, at least what was left of it.

Jonas walked among the townsfolk looking for the man that had directed the villagers away from the fighting during the battle. He had some questions for him. He found him sitting by a fire with a young boy roasting several juicy chunks of horse meat. The fire was roaring and putting off lots of heat. Nearly ten other villagers were around warming their tired and cold bodies. Jonas appraised the man quickly, noticing his thick muscular arms. The man had stood up to a demon-spawn with nothing more than a stick. Jonas was impressed. The man's eyes were tired and his face was smeared with dirt. White bandages were wrapped around both shoulders as well as his thigh, but other than that he just looked worn out. He looked up and nodded as Jonas approached, gesturing for him to join them.

They had propped some logs over big stones to form some makeshift benches. Jonas sat on the log next to him. "How are you feeling?" he asked.

"Tired, but alive, thanks to you and the soldiers. Especially that man with the axe. I'm afraid my boy and I would be dead if it weren't for him."

Jonas nodded in acknowledgement. "It was luck we came across your tracks. My companion and I were hunting something else." The man looked curiously at Jonas as he turned the meat around to cook it fully from all directions. But he said nothing, pressing him no further. "The Red Guard was tracking you when we met them on the road. We decided to help."

"We are thankful for it," the man said. "I am Sorrin and this is my son, Erlan."

Jonas nodded. "Well met. I am Jonas. I wanted to ask you a few questions. I'm hunting the evil that did this to you, and I was hoping you could tell me what happened to your town."

Sorrin glanced at Jonas, his eyes quickly appraising him, glancing over his armor, knives, swords, and clothing, seemingly trying to figure out who he was and why he would be on such a daunting hunt. He shrugged, figuring it was none of his business. "There was no warning," he began. "The men you killed came from the forest around our town and attacked, while the pale creatures swarmed our homes. Anyone who fought back was killed. I was at my forge, my son helping me, when they came." He glanced at Jonas. "I would have fought, but my first thought was to protect my son. The pale men said that we would be spared if we offered no resistance. They gathered us up and marched us away. That was two days ago. I have no idea where they were taking us."

Jonas sighed, figuring that the story was typical. He bet that many villages around Lanard had suffered the same treatment. "Count yourself lucky we came across you," Jonas said. "There is a great evil about, and I'm afraid you were being taken as its slaves."

"Evil...what do you mean?" Erlan asked. He was curious, as all young boys were.

"Let's just say that the men and creatures that attacked you were once townsfolk just like you. They too were captured." Jonas's meaning was obvious.

"You mean we would have been turned into those things?" he asked, his eyes wide with fear, and disgust.

"It was likely," Jonas said.

"Who are you?" Sorrin asked. "I see a warrior, there is no doubt. But you say you are seeking out this great evil by yourself?"

"I am a knight to Shyann. I am here to destroy the demon that is doing this."

Sorrin took in his words, looking at him in a different light. "I know of Shyann. Some villagers worship her here, but not many. Are you a cavalier? I've heard tales of them, but never seen one."

"I was once, but am no longer." Jonas didn't say anything else and Sorrin didn't press further.

Erlan was looking at Jonas with eyes filled with wonder, and a little confusion. "You don't look like a knight," he said.

Jonas smiled. "I've been getting that a lot. Rest assured young Erlan, looks can be deceiving."

"Are your swords magical?" he asked with the wonder of youth.

"They are. Would you like to see?"

"Can I father?" he asked excitedly.

Sorrin nodded. It was obvious that he wanted to see as well. "Of course."

Jonas drew one of the blades and laid it across his lap. Then he wished it to glow, and instantly the edge glowed blue, and the elven sigil along the dark steel lit up in the evening shadows.

Sorrin and Erlan's eyes grew wide, never before seeing a magical blade. "What does it say?" Sorrin asked, indicating the glowing writing.

"*Redemption*," Jonas answered. "The other says *Retribution*."

"That's incredible," Erlan said excitedly. "Do you think someday I could have a sword like that?"

Jonas smiled at the boy and stood up from the fire, sheathing the blade. "You never know. Be strong and good, and help those in need. You don't need a sword like this to accomplish those goals. But if the sword does find you, wield it with honor, and respect what it can do." Jonas patted the young boy on the shoulder. "I will leave you to your meal. Thank you for the information. Good luck and safe travels."

"Same to you, Jonas," Sorrin said. "Thank you again for your aid, and I wish you luck against this evil."

Jonas nodded and walked away.

Once he was gone, Erlan looked at his father. "Was he really a knight?"

Sorrin shrugged, "I don't know, as you said, he didn't look like a knight," he answered, looking over his shoulder as Jonas disappeared into the night. He looked back into the roaring fire, his mind pondering. "But he was definitely *something*."

Jonas and Bearit left the group at first light, following Tulari further into the Lasur'een Forest. They had only gone a few hours before Tulari stopped and turned north facing the dense woods. *This way*, she said in his mind.

"You want us to leave the horses?" Jonas asked. She said *yes* and Jonas turned to Bearit who was looking at him expectantly. "Looks like we are going on foot," Jonas said.

Bearit actually smiled. "That is the best news I've heard in a while."

"Your backside still hurting?" Jonas asked as he dismounted.

"It's better, but yes, it does. I'll be happy to stand on my own two feet. Where do you think she is leading us?" he asked as he dismounted.

Jonas was taking a few supplies from the saddle bags and loading them in his pack. They only had a few days of rations left, but luckily they were able to get a little more food from the soldiers, and he made sure it was packed away securely. Bearit was doing the same. "Hard to say," Jonas responded. "She could be leading us directly to the demon, or perhaps to an important location. Whatever she is doing will help us fulfill our mission, have no doubt." He hefted his pack over his shoulders, along with his quiver, and grabbed his bow from the saddle. He glanced over at Bearit as he too swung his pack over his huge shoulders. Bearit was carrying most of the food and water and yet it looked as if the pack weighed nothing to him. "Well done saving that man and his son. That was quite a throw."

Bearit shrugged his shoulders. "I wasn't sure what else to do."

"Well it worked, although you should always hold onto your weapon. Never relinquish it unless absolutely necessary."

"I was afraid I might hurt the man if I attacked the demon with my axe."

Jonas tilted his head in acquiescence. "Which was why I didn't use my bow, but rest assured if you were not there, I would have risked it. I think you should've done the same. What if more demons had rushed you and your axe was on the ground?"

"I see your point."

"Good," Jonas said as he adjusted his pack one more time. Then he looked sidelong at Bearit, his eyes serious. "You know you can leave me at any time. I do not want you to feel obligated to stay with me," he added, seeing Bearit's hurt expression. "The supplies and weapons were given with an open heart, with the idea that you will live on and be an example for others. That does not have to be done by my side."

"I understand, and I thank you. But this is where I want to be."

"Death follows me," Jonas said softly. "Are you sure?"

"I am," Bearit said firmly. "Drought follows a farmer, beetle blight follows a logger...it is the way of the world. If one chooses to fight against evil, then death will follow them as sure as old age. I've made my choice."

Jonas nodded. "Well spoken." Then he nodded towards his wounded leg. "How is your hip?"

Bearit lifted his leg and moved it around. "Hurts some," he said honestly. "But I'll be fine. How's your arm?"

Jonas glanced at the bandage wrapped around his elbow. "Nothing to worry about." He pulled his straps tighter on his pack. "Ready?" Bearit nodded. "Tulari, lead on." Tulari leapt into the undergrowth and Jonas and Bearit followed, quickly disappearing into the thick brush.

***

The next morning King Haten Oneck sat on his warhorse, his twenty five year old son mounted beside him. Prince Bannic Oneck was the mirror image of his father, tall, with broad shoulders, dressed immaculately in shining armor. Combine his physique with a regal nose, sharp features and a strong chin, along with glossy black hair, and you have an iconic image of a ruling aristocrat. On the King's other side was General Hyrim Galstar, dressed in full armor and ready to march.

Around them were the scattered remains of the camp, the city of Angar in the background, smoke rising from various places within. Two days before, unbeknownst to the Rothar contingent, Prince Bannic had led the Tur'el army to Angar and had waited for orders from his father, all the while King Oneck was going through the motions of working on the treaty and arranging the marriage with King Gyveel Rothar. His army hid in the forests around Angar, and when the word was given, stormed the camp.

His daughter's departure into the woods had worked well in his favor. When Baylock Reen had agreed to personally find her, his actions had removed the finest fighter from the camp as well as twenty Red Guard warriors. It had provided the perfect opportunity for Carvathian to use the demon to turn the Battle Lord, and while gone in the forest, to secretly attack Angar with his hidden army. The risk to his daughter was necessary. If he could get her back, he would, but if not, the Tur'el Kingdom would survive. Her death would matter little in the scheme of things.

Once they destroyed the Lanard contingent camped in the field, they then stormed the city. Reluctantly, under the control of Carvathian, Maltheil had helped them, sending his army of five hundred men and women, now demon-spawn, over the walls of Angar. It didn't take the demon-spawn long to get the gate open, and soon after, the Rothar Soldiers, who were unprepared for such an attack, were quickly overwhelmed. It was a slaughter.

"You sure about this, Father?" Prince Bannic asked.

The King of Tur'el looked at his son, his eyes hard. "Of course I'm sure. I have been waiting for this opportunity for many years, as my father had before me." He looked back at the city. "That city was seized from my grandfather, and now I have taken it back. And I'm not stopping here. Finally the Lanard lands will be ours." The king looked ahead of him and smiled. There were four long poles stuck into the ground, and impaled on each one was a head, blood dripping down the wood shafts. The shocked and bloody visages of King Gyveel Rothar, Master Moran, Prince Dalland, and Earl Gallinor stared back at them. They had put up a good fight, especially Prince Dalland, who was one of the finest swordsmen next to the Battle Lord, Baylock Reen. But in the end the Tur'el numbers overwhelmed them, and now their heads were stuck on poles. As they marched by, he wanted every one of his soldiers to see the dead Lanard king and his brother. Behind them, spanning out across the clearing before the city were six thousand Tur'el soldiers, nearly a thousand were cavalry, the silver points of their lances glittering in the morning sun. It was cold as winter was fast approaching, and the steaming breath of the soldiers made them look like dragons ready for battle.

"I meant are you sure about the demon," Bannic added. To their left stood Maltheil, the beast's giant form surrounded by its demon-spawn, Baylock Reen to Maltheil's right, his pale bald head now covered by his black plumed helm. Near the beast, but not too close, was Carvathian. None of them could get near the demon without feeling an overwhelming sense of fear, so they stayed clear. The only one who seemed impervious to the demon's magic was Carvathian, and the wizard himself looked exhausted. His skin was more pale than normal, his bloodshot eyes surrounded in shadow. "I worry that Carvathian is not strong enough to control the beast."

"He says that he is," the king said, looking towards the demon. Maltheil stood frozen, its huge wolf like head staring right at him, red glowing eyes boring into his courage. If he didn't know better he would swear the beast was smiling. "We need the demon to take the city walls. After that we will banish the creature."

"What of the young prince?" Bannic asked.

King Haten laughed. "Peron Rothar? He will pose no problem. Besides, if the demon does its job, the prince will be dead before we arrive."

"What about my sister?"

"Carvathian is taking care of it," the king said. Then he shrugged nonchalantly. "If we can get her back alive, we will." Then he looked at his son, his eyes hard again. "Your sister should be of no concern to you. Do not let thoughts of her well-being distract you from our task at hand."

Bannic nodded. He was raised by his father, and hence felt very little for much of anything. He had spent little time with Kylin and didn't really know her. It wasn't terribly difficult to dismiss her. "And what if Carvathian fails in his task?"

"Look behind you," King Haten said. "We have an army. If we have to, we will kill the demon, just as my great ancestor did thousands of years ago." Looking forward, he raised his sword in the air. Thousands of soldiers behind him screamed and shouted, banging swords on shields and shaking lances in the cold morning air. Then he lowered the sword and the army moved forward, the glaring dead visages of the Rothar dignitaries staring at them as they marched by.

Once the army passed, Carvathian rode before Maltheil. The demon hadn't moved, which was eerie enough, but the fear that emanated from the beast nearly broke through the wizard's defenses. Baylock stood like a statue beside the great beast, his haunting eyes looking at the wizard through the slits in his helm.

"I feel you getting weaker," Maltheil hissed, his malevolent voice eager for blood.

Carvathian sat up taller in his saddle, knowing full well that showing any sign of weakness could mean his end. "I am strong," he said loudly. "We only need you for one more task."

"And what is that?"

"To take the city of Lanard."

Maltheil laughed. "Something I had planned to do anyway. Your king is a fool. His hunger for power will kill him, and you."

"Killing us will not be so easy."

Maltheil laughed again, the sound like fluid in his throat. "Killing is always easy. What do you want, *wizard*?" he said, spitting out the last word.

"The king wants his daughter back, alive if possible. I want you to send servants to get her."

"And?"

"Send assassins to kill the young Rothar Prince. My king wants him dead before we arrive. You will then follow us with your army. Any villages along the way you may destroy, turning who you like. Once we arrive at Lanard, you will climb the walls and kill any resistance."

Suddenly a wave of mental energy struck Carvathian and he nearly fell from his saddle. Digging deep, he protected his mind, focusing all of his energy on keeping the demon out of his head. He was a powerful wizard, with vast amounts of mental strength, but even he felt a stab of panic. Quickly dismissing it, he focused his mind on the mental barrier he had created between them. Sweat dripped down his back and his head throbbed as Maltheil struck his mental wall several more times. Then it was gone. Carvathian was left sweating, his head hurting, but he sat up straight, ignoring the pain and exhaustion, knowing that any sign of fatigue might instigate the demon to attack again.

"I'm impressed, *human*, you are strong," Maltheil said. "But you can't withstand me forever." Then the beast turned and walked away towards the woods, its long muscular legs taller than Baylock and the other servants who followed. The demon's long arms hung low, its clawed gangly fingers nearly reaching its knees, one holding its massive bone club. The thing's broad back was covered in tangled black hair that rose to the base of its neck. Carvathian had to admit that the creature was impressive, and glad that it was gone.

Maltheil and his army of servants didn't have to walk long before the demon found what it was looking for. Stopping near a rock face, a small clearing of grass surrounding him, he reached out and felt the waypoint. His army of four hundred servants were scattered around him, the forest broken and trampled as they carved a path through the dense brush.

Closing his eyes Maltheil could feel the weakness in the energy around him. Waypoints were scattered all across the lands, but few knew where to look for them or had the ability to use them. A waypoint was a natural door, a means to access the other planes of existence. If one had the ability, they could travel through the waypoints to other planes. As a demon of great power, Maltheil could travel to the sixth plane, his home, if he so wished. But once there, he would not be able to return to the material plane. That is unless some powerful wizard was dumb enough to summon him. So he had no intention of returning home just yet. There was plenty of blood to spill first. He had another reason for opening the gate to the sixth plane.

Maltheil began to chant. Within moments the air before the rock wall began to swirl counter clockwise. Maltheil continued to chant, the beast's long arms lifted before it, and moments later the swirling flashed to a black hole, a gate to his world. Beyond the dark breach black rocks jutted from a gray landscape, fire and smoke rising from the ground. Off in the distance you could see a castle of black towers built high on a jagged peak. It was Maltheil's home, probably now overrun with lesser demons, something the beast would have to rectify once it returned to the burning plane. Maltheil turned its hands towards its chest, as if motioning for something to come, and just beyond the door several big shapes moved. Several minutes later clawed hands reached through the opening and Maltheil stepped back, its guttural voice still chanting, rising in volume as more forms shifted near the door. Then the demon clapped its hands and the door flashed brightly, receding quickly to reveal four smoking forms standing before the rock face, the door no longer there.

The four beasts were different in appearance, but each terrifying in shape and form. Two of the creatures looked very similar, both at least two heads taller than a large orc, but looked much bulkier as their bodies were so heavily muscled. The creatures had no fingers, just three thick digits, each one capped with claws that looked more like curved horns. Dense black fur covered their torso, but their arms and legs looked to be covered in scales. The creature's heads, although slightly different, were large and dragon-like, with horns and fangs as big as its claws. Their mouths were so full of large teeth that they could not talk; they simply stood there, their eyes flickering with red and orange fire, steam drifting from their mouths as they breathed deeply.

The other two were smaller in stature, nearly human-like, with giant bat-like wings. Each creature had long sinewy arms and legs, every joint jutting with black spikes. Even their clawed hands had bony spikes sticking from their knuckles, capable of causing great damage. Their tails whipped around excitedly, spikes like knives protruding all over the appendage. They were hairless, with gray slimy skin, and their heads were human in shape, but with longer skulls, big white eyes, and teeth filled mouths twice as big as any man's.

"Welcome my hordlings, it's been far too long."

They growled deeply in response, flexing their fingers, the long black claws clicking together in an ominous sound.

***

Jonas and Bearit followed Tulari through the woods for most of the day when they came to another road. Jonas stopped and pulled out his map.

"I think Tulari has turned us more west, and this road looks like it could be the main road to Lanard," he said as he looked over the map.

"You think she is taking us to the capital?"

"Possibly."

"Should we just take the road then?" Bearit asked.

"We go where she goes," Jonas responded. As if on cue, Tulari emerged from the brush, shook her head in a follow me way, and disappeared again into the brush. "Looks like we are staying in the woods."

They continued on for several hours before stopping briefly for dried rations and water. The forest was dense and in several spots they had to cut their way through. Jonas wasn't worried about anyone following them. Normally he would be scouting ahead and behind, but with Tulari in the woods there was no need. She could cover their perimeter easy enough, and her nose and ears would pick up any threat. It was nearing dark when Tulari emerged from the brush. *Found,* she communicated, *people, come.* She had been leading them to someone.

***

Atticus led Tyril and Kylin along the edge of a small stream, the water long ago digging a rut through the stone around them. The clearing was open, the ground littered with huge stones blanketed with green grass. Giant trees surrounded them and even bigger rock faces peppered the clearing all around. They had decided to head to Lanard to warn them of the Tur'el betrayal. Once there they would need to devise a plan to defeat not only the approaching army, but Maltheil himself.

Korum was typically out scouting, but the big cat had come back to drink from the stream and walk with the group. They were nearing the forest edge when Korum, now at Atticus's side, lifted his huge head, growling towards a rock face to their right.

Atticus spun in a blur, his arm reaching back and nocking an arrow, his bow at full draw. Standing at the edge of the rock face was Jonas, his bow in a similar position, his keen eye looking down his black arrow. Bearit walked into view, his powerful arms holding his battle axe, his worried expression looking from one archer to another. A deep growl matched Korums, and Tulari, at full size, stepped to Jonas's other side, her huge shoulders at head height.

"What do we have here?" Atticus said, keeping his bow at full draw. He looked at Korum and the beast stopped growling, sitting on his haunches. Then he slowly lowered his bow.

Friend, Tulari said in Jonas's mind. Jonas lowered his bow as well, looking over the group more closely. "I'm Jonas, this is my friend, Bearit, and my companion Tulari."

A young bearded warrior, dressed in the armor and clothes of a Red Guard soldier, stood at the ready with his sword in hand, and next to him was a young girl, perhaps eighteen or nineteen, holding a crossbow at the ready. But the man with the bow drew Jonas's interest the most. Next to him was a huge cat that looked just like the animals he had been forced to fight on the bridge. Bearit had said it was called a shadow cat. But this cat looked normal, untainted by Maltheil's poison. The man was clearly a skilled archer. He had drawn and nocked the arrow nearly as fast as Jonas. He wore the clothes of a woodsman and carried a sword at his hip. He looked middle aged, but there was something about his eyes that suggested wisdom beyond those years.

"I am Atticus and this is Korum, my friend. Beside me is Tyril and Kylin," Atticus said, being vague with their identities. "Tulari is a night wolf," he said questioning, clearly wondering how Jonas could befriend such a beast. "I would like to hear this tale."

Jonas was taken aback at that. How did he know Tulari's name? And Tulari responded to him by making a shallow growl. It was what she did when she liked someone. But he didn't voice his surprise, figuring he would have his answers soon enough. "And you have a shadow cat."

Atticus smiled. "It seems we both have a tale to tell."

"Tulari led me to you. I am hunting a great evil, and it seems that are destinies are somehow entwined."

Atticus stopped smiling, suddenly more interested than before. "In that case, it will be dark soon. Let us camp here and talk. It seems we have much to discuss."

The soft ground and water from the stream provided a perfect location for a camp. Atticus started to collect wood and stack it near the rock face and Jonas looked at him with concern. "What are you doing?" he asked.

"A fire would be nice, don't you think?"

"I do, but it is not a good idea. We can go without."

"Do not worry, friend Jonas. I will cast a shielding. I am a druid you see."

Jonas had heard of druids, but never met one. They were very rare; in fact he was told there were no groves left east of the Tundrens, although he could not confirm that. "Tell me about this shielding."

"To put it in words that are easy to understand I simply ask the forest to hide us. No enemy will see us, or smell the smoke, or hear us. We will be completely shielded from them."

"What if they walk into us?" Bearit asked, clearly interested.

"The earth will shift what they see and guide them around. It is impossible."

"He did the same thing last night," Tyril said, shrugging his shoulders as if he was unsure if it really had worked.

They set up camp and everyone laid out their rations, sharing their food and drinking water next to the warm fire. Tulari had shifted to her smaller size and lay between Jonas and Atticus, her big head touching the druid's leg. Atticus noticed Jonas's stare, who was not masking his surprise. Tulari never nuzzled next to anyone except for him. "It's normal, Jonas. I am a druid. I have a natural affinity to all animals." Korum, who was sprawled out on the other side of Atticus, purred deeply, confirming his statement. "Now, why don't you tell me who you are? I sense magic all around you."

Jonas gave the druid an abridged version, explaining how he was once a cavalier and how he was now Shyann's Shadow Knight. The three new companions listened intently, very much interested in his story. After all, it was quite unbelievable.

"I have heard of you," Tyril explained. He seemed to be in awe, appraising Jonas in a new light. "You fought with Kiln the swordsman and King Kromm against Malbeck."

"I did."

"I know of you as well," Atticus said. "And Tulari was once your cavalier steed...that is fascinating. So, you were guided here by Shyann, through Tulari, to kill Maltheil?"

"I assume that is my goal."

"And you found Bearit here, starving and desperate, and took him under your wing so to speak?"

"Yes, he was in need of help," Jonas answered. Bearit said nothing, his dark eyes looking into the fire. "Now, who are you?"

Atticus laughed. "Well, I am Atticus Belthar. I am famous, just as you."

"I have not heard of you," Jonas said simply.

"I have," Bearit said, looking up from the flickering flames. "My father used to tell me tales of Maltheil, the demon, when I was a kid. According to him the beast was slain by a wizard named Atticus Belthar."

"Wizard!" Atticus laughed again. "They always get that wrong. I am no wizard, although I can wield power in a similar way."

"But that would make you over two thousand years old," Bearit reasoned.

"That's the part I couldn't believe," Kylin said, speaking up for the first time. She had been so enthralled in Jonas's story that she didn't want to interrupt him with her many questions.

"Don't ask him to prove it," Tyril said. "It's a bit strange when he turns into animals."

Atticus waved him off. "I protect the forest around us, and in return she grants me power, which I use for many things...case in point, to keep me young and full of energy so that I may continue to be her guardian."

Jonas leaned closer to the fire, putting his hands out to warm them. "Did you really kill the demon thousands of years ago?"

"Yes, and no," Atticus said. "I was not alone. I had help from my grove as well as from the Tur'el king and his army."

"Tybolt Oneck," Kylin said, "my ancestor."

"That's correct. He was a great battle king, and together we were able to banish the beast to the nethers."

"What are the nethers?" Tyril asked.

"Think of the nethers as the place between worlds. It is nothing...it is emptiness, a simple bridge to another plane. There, the beast could do no more harm. He was in limbo. If we had banished the demon to its own plane of existence, it's possible that he would be summoned once again."

"Then how was he summoned from the nethers?" Jonas asked.

"I am still trying to figure that out. I used the Rothar family blood to strengthen the spell, containing its power in a book. The book was to be protected by the Rothar royal family, the tomb of Maltheil located in the royal mausoleum."

"Why use a book?" Bearit asked. He knew nothing of magic, and he was struggling to understand just what had happened.

"For a spell of that kind of power, I could not wield the magic myself...it would destroy me. The earth's power was given to me, and to form a lock, I needed to weave the energy into something physical, a conduit so to speak. The words of power given to me by the *Sanga*, which is what we druids call the earth's power, were used in the book to bind the demon to the nethers. The book acts at the key."

"When you say Sanga, is that the same as what the elves call the Ru'ach?" Jonas asked, very much interested.

"No, it is not the same, but similar. Think of it this way. If the Ru'ach is an ocean, the Sanga is a large river. This river flows all around us, and is linked to the Ru'ach, just as a river is connected to an ocean."

"So the stream of power is all the same?" Jonas asked.

Atticus nodded, and then shrugged his shoulders, like he was not quite sure. "I believe it is. Now," he said, changing the subject, "let's get back to the matter at hand."

Tyril agreed, wanting to talk about something he could actually understand. "So someone stole the book, used it to open the tomb and free the demon?"

"That seems to be the case, however, only someone of great mental strength could do so," Atticus added. "Anyone else would not be able to read the words of power, or control the demon once it was free."

Kylin said nothing, her furtive gaze flicking to Tyril and back to the fire. Jonas noticed it. She seemed concerned.

"What are you hiding?" Jonas asked her.

She looked up and Atticus nodded to her to tell him. "My full name is Kylin Oneck, I am the Tur'el princess."

Jonas was not privy to what had happened at Angar, and his expression showed it. "I thought you were to marry King Gyveel Rothar," he said, remembering what Earl Magnar had told him.

Atticus sighed. There was a lot still to tell them. "It seems our story is not quite done," he said. And then he told Jonas and Bearit about the betrayal, the Tur'el attack on Angar, and the death of the Rothar King, as well as the attack on Tyril and the Red Guard troops while bringing the princess back to camp.

"So your father, besides betraying the treaty, has left you alone with the enemy?" Jonas asked incredulously. He did not mean for it to sound so harsh, and when he heard the words leave his mouth he wished he hadn't said them.

She looked away, seemingly embarrassed. But then she looked back at him, her eyes smoldering with fury. "I hate him," she spat. "He has never cared for anything other than power. I do not know if he has left me for dead, and if he has, I do not care. His betrayal to me cannot hurt me, because I care nothing for him. All he cares about is gaining power so my brother can eventually wield it and expand the Tur'el kingdom."

"Let me get this straight," Jonas said, linking everything together. "As we sit at this fire, a Tur'el army, joined with Maltheil and the beast's army of demon-spawn, are marching on Lanard. The demon is probably controlled by the Tur'el court wizard, although we still have no idea how the wizard was able to get a book that was locked away, protected by a spell that can only be thwarted by someone with Rothar blood. And," he continued. "Maltheil will likely break the binding spell, and kill everyone and anyone in its path while creating an army of demon-spawn in the process."

Despondent, Tyril looked up from the flames. "That sounds about right."

"Don't forget," Atticus added, "that there must be a traitor at Lanard, someone who helped Carvathian get the book and replace it."

"Is there anyone else with Rothar royal blood?"

Kylin looked at Tyril. The young warrior shook his head in frustration. "Yes, the king has a younger son, my friend, Prince Peron. But he had nothing to do with helping Carvathian."

"Would you bet your life on it?" Jonas asked.

"I would," Tyril said, his eyes hard. "Without hesitation."

Suddenly Atticus swayed a little, both of his hands coming to his head as he closed his eyes. Everyone looked at him, the movement strange and out of place.

"Are you well?" Jonas asked.

Then the druid's eyes flew open. They were wide and alert. "The *Sanga* just warned me…something that doesn't belong, is here, in the forest, and it is near."

"Belong? You mean belong in the forest?" Kylin asked.

"No," he said. He was now as serious as a general facing an enemy charge, his typical good humored flare gone. "Something that doesn't belong on the material plane. Ready your weapons."

Everyone stood and did so. "Won't this *shielding* hide us?" Tyril asked, who was now holding his sword before him, his eyes scanning the darkness.

"The shielding will hide us, but if it's a creature from the burning planes, then they, or it, will be able to see the shield. They will know magic is in use."

They had built the fire against a big rock face, and they now stood against the stone, their backs protected, looking out into the darkness, the firelight reaching pitifully into the black night.

Then they saw them. Red burning eyes looked at them from the cover of night. Korum and Tulari, who was now full size, growled deeply, but they both stood beside their masters, unsure as to what they were facing.

Bearit gripped his mighty axe nervously. "Do they see us?"

"I don't think so," Atticus said. "But they sense the shield. They know something is here."

The two sets of eyes were at least ten paces apart and much taller than a man. It wasn't long before they found out why. They heard a crunching and snapping of brush as the two eyes moved towards them, red and orange fire flaring from them. With each pace, they got closer, and as they neared, the moon's light slowly revealed what they were. Two massive muscle-bound forms stopped ten paces from them, each set of eyes staring directly at them, but seemingly not seeing them.

"In Toolm's name," Kylin said nervously, her hands trembling as she leveled her crossbow at the creatures. Their dragon-like heads were covered in horns, and their gaping jaws were so stuffed with long teeth that they were forever open, saliva dripping freely as steam hissed from the cracks.

"Demons," Jonas said, his tone hard and ready for battle. "They can only be harmed by enchanted weapons."

Tyril looked at him nervously. "Are you serious?" The thought of his sword having no effect on the creatures was unnerving. He hated being powerless.

Atticus drew his blade. "Jonas is right. Tyril, use this," he said, tossing the weapon to the swordsman. Tyril caught it easily and leaned his against the rock. Then the druid nocked an arrow to his bow.

Jonas had already done so, and holding the bow with one hand he drew one of his swords. "Bearit, take one of my swords. Your axe will do nothing."

Bearit dropped his axe and grabbed the blade. It was long and slender, and looked quite small in the logger's big hand. "I don't know how to use a sword."

"Then learn quickly," Atticus snapped, all brevity gone.

"Why aren't they attacking us?" Tyril said, his voice strained.

The demons were looking around the clearing, walking around the edge of the glade but moving quickly back to their location, sniffing the air with their big open nostrils. "They are trying to figure out what they are detecting," Jonas said.

"We have the element of surprise," Atticus said. "I'm going to lower the shield, and at the same time I'm going to make this fire really bright. They can see in the dark, but we cannot. We'll need the light. When I do so, leap away and attack the beasts with all you've got. Jonas and I will hit them both with our arrows. You two," the druid said, looking at Bearit and Tyril, "will attack the other. Kylin stay back, your crossbow will only make the beast's mad. Korum and Tulari will join where they think best." Everyone nodded in response.

Jonas looked at Bearit, and despite the logger's firm stance, there was no mistaking his wide frightened eyes. The beasts were demons, and they exuded a strong sense of foreboding, one that would have a very shattering effect on anyone who was not trained to fight them. And Bearit certainly was not. Tyril didn't look much better, and Kylin was nearly frozen with shock. Jonas reached out and touched Bearit's shaking arm. "Calm yourself. Breathe deeply, and fight back the demon's fear. You can do this."

"And watch out for their breath. I have a suspicion that they can breathe fire," Atticus warned. "Ready?" He knew they weren't, but they needed a countdown. Atticus closed his eyes and the others heard him whisper a few words, then without warning the fire exploded upward in a massive flame, and whether they wanted to or not, everyone was forced to leap into motion. The *shielding* was gone and the firelight exploded outward.

Instantly the two hordlings crouched low, their red eyes zoning in on them as they could suddenly see their targets. Then they charged.

Atticus ran to the right, his bow up and two arrows slammed into one of the creatures before it even made it three steps. The shafts, all enchanted by the *Sanga*, slammed into the demon. The beast roared but didn't stop, its massive bulk charging Atticus, both hands, each the size of the druid's head, reaching for him, long curved horn-like claws ready to rip into him.

Jonas leapt atop a small boulder several paces away from the roaring fire, his arm flashing three times as he drew his black shafted arrows, nocking and firing, each as fast as a blink. Jonas willed his armor to glow, and instantly Shyann's symbol burst with a bluish light. The charging beast shielded its eyes as Jonas's arrows struck, just moments after Atticus's, and again the demon roared, barely faltering.

Despite the blinding light, the demon's huge clawed hands were nearly upon the druid when massive roots shot from the ground, quickly wrapping around the demon's ankles like powerful snakes, holding the beast in place. The demon roared and shook its huge scaly legs, trying to break free. Atticus shot the beast directly in its mouth, snapping its huge head back. But this time the demon changed tactics, and shooting its head forward, shot a cone of red fire from its gaping mouth, incinerating the arrow in the process. Atticus dove away, but the fire burned his side as it fried the grassy ground where he had been. Rolling, he came to his feet, searing pain shooting through his hip.

Tyril moved to his left and nearly dropped his sword and ran when he saw the massive creature bearing down on him. He sensed Bearit was beside him, and knowing that gave him strength. The demon planted its feet firmly and swung a massive clawed hand towards them both. Tyril knew that if he tried to block it that it would simply crush him. So he angled his sword up with both hands and dove under the demon's attack, slicing the magical sword through its fury forearm, narrowly avoiding the powerful limb. There was a flash of light and the druid's blade bit deep into the creature's flesh.

Bearit was behind Tyril and jumped back just in time as the fist swung by him. Then, faster than the creature's bulk belied, the demon brought both clawed fists together above its head, and stepping towards Bearit brought them both down to crush him in a powerful downward stroke. Bearit knew he was going to die, there was no way he could avoid the devastating attack, and he certainly couldn't block it. But it never came as Tulari had leapt from the rock face and crashed into the demon's face, knocking it off balance and causing it to stumble backwards. No normal weapon could harm the demon, and Korum's claws would do little damage, but Tulari was no normal night wolf, she was a creature born of Shyann's will, and that gave her abilities far beyond her breed. Her front claws dug into the demon's shoulders as she tried to hang on, her snapping jaws ripping into the thing's face and neck, her back claws raking across its belly, digging deep rivulets in its flesh. But the damage was momentary as the demon grabbed her heavy body with its three pronged hands, their long claws digging deep into her flesh, and with a powerful heave threw her into the night. Tulari howled in pain and landed hard, skidding sidelong across the grassy ground to crash into a nearby tree.

Bearit pushed away the fear, realizing that Tulari had just saved him, and hoping to capitalize on that. As the demon stumbled backwards with Tulari ripping into it, the big logger ran forward and rammed Jonas's sword into the distracted creature's stomach. There were few stronger than him, and Jonas's sword, blessed by Shyann herself, sank all the way to the hilt. The demon howled in pain. There was a flash of light and steam burst from the wound just as Tulari was thrown through the air. Bearit ripped the sword free and sliced it across the demon's side as he dove away, knowing full well the speed and ferocity of the creature's attacks and not wanting to be anywhere near the demon. And luckily he did as a huge leg swooshed through the air where he had been, barely missing him.

Tyril was up and he swung his silver sword across the leg that had narrowly missed Bearit. The demon roared in pain again but did not stop, snapping its head forward and launching a cone of fire from its giant mouth. Tyril saw the fire coming, and was readying his body to jump out of the way, but he knew he wasn't going to be fast enough. Just then Bearit smashed into him, knocking him away from the demon's fire. But the flames licked across the logger's legs as they both tumbled across the grassy ground.

Atticus worked his bow with miraculous speed, and at point blank range as the beast tried to break away from his entangle spell. Two arrows struck the creature in the neck just as it snapped the roots holding it in place. Clawed fists swung toward the druid and the agile warrior dodged them easily, ducking and turning, nocking another arrow in the process, drawing and shooting as he spun under another attack. The arrow slammed into the demon's chin so hard that it rocked its head back. This time it didn't regroup so quickly, stumbling backwards the beast roared and fire shot from its mouth into the air as it futilely tried to rip the magical shaft from under its chin.

Jonas glanced at the other creature and saw that Bearit and Tyril were in trouble. It looked like Atticus was faring better so he jumped off the rock, firing an arrow into the back of the demon that was now stepping towards the men, both of whom were tangled on the ground, smoke rising from the grass where it had been burned by the demon's fire. The demon arched its back in agony as his blessed arrow hammered deep into its fury flesh. Growling in pain, the demon swung to meet the charge

Jonas, Shyann's mark still glowing from his chest plate, was moving fast and had quickly decided on his course of action. He had been working on a cognitive defense that he was eager to try, and now seemed to be the perfect opportunity. Striding towards the great beast, Jonas quickly focused on the energy around him. Drawing the particles in, he formed them into a translucent shield that was tethered to his bow arm, just like a normal military shield. He had practiced this many times with Allindrian, and had yet to use the tactic, his twin blades seeing him through his past conflicts.

The benefit of the cognitive shield was that the swarming particles formed a wall of energy that redirected any power that struck it. Normally, if something as big and strong as the demon before him struck a metal shield, it would destroy it, breaking the arm holding it in the process, or worse yet, killing the wearer. But the cognitive shield, although it was difficult to maintain for long, acted no differently than if there was a stone wall between him and the attacker. He might feel a slight thud, but the energy of the attack would be dispersed across the particles and released harmlessly to the side. At least that was what he hoped.

His body was a blur as he brought up his shield, stopping the beast's closed fist as it swung from high up to crush him. The beast's fiery eyes flared in confusion as its fist struck the shield and stopped it in its tracks. Without pausing, Jonas spun past the massive arm, ducking under it and slicing his magical blade across the beast's side, opening a large gash. The creature stepped back, still trying vainly to shield its eyes from Shyann's light and attack at the same time, swinging its other arm around. But Jonas agilely avoided it by ducking extremely low, and using the strength of his legs he launched up and rammed his sword into the demon's exposed armpit. The blade sunk in deep and the demon's roared in pain, stumbling back.

Jonas was relentless, stepping forward and blocking a desperate attack by huge claws as the monster tried to distance itself from the dangerous warrior, all the while futilely trying to avoid the glare of Shyann's light. His blade followed the block, the edge flaring blue as it sliced across the demon's exposed belly. Finally succumbing to its wounds, the demon fell to its knees, and Jonas reversed his swing, the razor edge of his sword slicing deep across its muscled neck. Gurgling black blood, the demon swayed, its eyes flashing and turning black before it fell sidelong onto the grass.

His adrenaline was roaring through his body, and he spun quickly to check on the other demon. Atticus was walking towards him, his face strained but his lips tight with the energy of battle. Korum was walking beside him. Atticus had kept the big cat out of the battle, knowing that its claws and teeth would do little damage. If it wasn't necessary, he did not want to risk his longtime friend. "Well done," he said as he approached Jonas. Jonas saw the body of the other demon lying on the ground behind him.

"You too," Jonas countered, letting Shyann's light disappear, returning his chest plate to its normal plain appearance, and releasing the energy of the shield. His head hurt, but he would live. He hadn't held the shield for long and soon the ache at the base of his skull would fade. Quickly, he turned to check on the others. Tyril was standing and helping Bearit do the same. Tulari was slowly ambling towards him, her side drenched in blood. Running to her, he put his hands on the side of her massive head. "Are you okay?"

Hurt bad, she said, nudging his face, *claws deep. Need rest.*

"Let me help her," Atticus said as he knelt beside her, one hand touching her body while the other dug into the soft grass. Closing his eyes, the druid whispered a series of incoherent words, and within moments blue light grew around the hand that was touching her. Jonas could see the deep punctures on her side close and feel her demeanor change as the druid's magic moved through her.

*Feel good...better...*she said.

"Thank you," Jonas said sincerely.

Atticus stood and ruffled the fur on her massive neck. "Of course. Now let us see to these two," the druid said.

"Your side is burnt," Jonas stated, looking at Atticus, noticing the burn along his hip.

"That is true," Atticus replied. "I will look at it once I see to them."

By this time Kylin was next to Tyril helping Bearit stand. Jonas went to him to inspect his wounds. "Where are you hurt?" he asked.

215

Bearit cringed in pain but stood tall with the help of Kylin and Tyril. "My legs were burnt." Jonas looked down and was shocked at the damage. It was bad. The demon's fire had disintegrated his leggings, exposing blackened flesh from the back of his thigh to just above his high boot.

"He saved my life," Tyril said. "That demon's fire would've killed me."

"He will be fine," Atticus said firmly, stepping before Bearit. "Sorry, but you need to lie back down. I want you as close to the earth as possible."

Bearit didn't complain, but when he tried to bend his legs to lie down, he moaned in pain, the burn on the back of his legs cracking. Trying to speed up the process, he simply dropped to the ground, arching his back painfully and swearing through the agony. Once he gained control of the pain, he opened his eyes and looked up at them. "That really hurt."

"Burns are very painful," Jonas said, kneeling beside him. He didn't have to reach far into his memory to bring forth the terrible pain when his face had been burnt by Prince Nelstrom during Malbeck's War, Kiln's son who had been raised by King Gavinsteal of Finarth as his own flesh and blood. The young prince had been corrupted by the Forsworn, becoming something of great evil, a demon that had killed his adopted father in his sleep and had nearly killed Jonas. But Jonas had survived, killing the prince during their battle. But he nearly died in the fight, his face burnt and destroyed, a sword through his gut nearly killing him. Shyann had saved him that night, healing his physical wounds. But he would never forget the pain.

Atticus knelt on the other side. He placed one hand on the thick grass and the other on Bearit's chest. "Don't worry, it will soon be just a memory." Just as he did with Tulari, he closed his eyes and drew power from the earth. His hand lit up with blue light, and as it did, Bearit's eyes grew wide with astonishment. Then his painful grimace slowly turned into one of contentment. "Feeling better?" Atticus asked as he withdrew his hand.

Bearit slowly stood, looking behind him to inspect his legs. The skin was pink, no longer black and charred. "That was amazing. And the wound on my hip is healed as well. Thank you."

Atticus nodded. "The skin will be pink and tender for a day or two. But you will suffer no more pain."

Suddenly the light from the flaring fire began to slowly recede, shadows growing around them. "What's happening to the fire?" Tyril asked.

"The spell is wearing off," Atticus answered. "Let's add some wood and return to it. I don't think we are in any further danger tonight."

"What about those demons?" Kylin said, indicating the two bodies that were now hid in darkness. Her expression was clear. She didn't want to be anywhere near those things.

"Too heavy to move," Jonas answered. "Out of sight, out of mind. I agree with Atticus. We need some rest after that fight. Let's come up with a plan and get some sleep. I'm afraid we have a lot to do in the morning."

Atticus reset his shielding and they talked a bit longer into the night. But the exertion of the fight finally got the best of them, and soon they were all sleeping next to the roaring flames.

The morning came quickly; their restless dreams keeping them from a well needed sleep. They ate a cold meal of dried horsemeat, hard stale bread, and lots of water. They were all eager to be on their way. Lanard was in danger, and they wanted to get there as soon as possible. That night they had worked out a plan, and once they repacked their supplies and slung their packs, they were well on their way.

Atticus stepped towards Jonas. "I'll see you soon," he said, shaking his hand in the warrior's grip.

They had agreed that Atticus, who could turn into a bird, should leave on his own to warn the castle, and especially Prince Peron, who was now the last member of the Rothar royal family. After looking at the map, they reasoned they were a good four days from Lanard. Atticus would get there in a day.

Jonas nodded, gripping the druid's hand firmly. "We need a plan to kill this demon."

"I'm working on it," Atticus said. "I'll see you in four days." He said his farewells to the others, and in a flash turned into a giant black raven, flying high and disappearing through the thick canopy of trees.

CHAPTER SEVEN

Kyron was helping Peron position the strange wood contraption near the far window facing the main door to his sleeping chambers. "What is this again?" his friend asked, clearly bewildered by it.

"I'll show you in a moment," Peron said, turning the covered contraption towards the front door. The wood structure was about his height and maybe a pace wide. A gray piece of cloth covered it. Peron smiled and gripped the edge of the material. "You ready to see my greatest invention yet?"

Kyron hurried him on. "Of course," he said. "Now show me. I have to get going. I'm meeting with General Moore in less than an hour."

Peron was happy for his friend. Ever since his father had ordered the reserves in, business had picked up for Kyron and his father. They needed armor, weapons, and even clothing for the thousand or more reserves that were being brought in from the fields and farms. No one really knew what was happening, but King Rothar preferred to be safe rather than sorry, and before he left to Angar he had reinforced the army.

Peron pulled the cloth off the structure with an artistic flourish, his smile as wide as can be. He revealed a wood structure, the face of it flat and rectangular, like a small table turned on end, with holes drilled into the surface. Behind the wood face was the mechanics. There was a stout wood wheel, and gears, many gears, all of which seemed to be connected to various worm gears, which in turn were connected to what looked like five powerful crossbows. When one cranked the wheel, it turned the gears, which turned the worm gear, which slowly pulled the tight string back on each bow arm at the same time. But the bows were not a normal design. They were longer, the strings, when pulled back by the gears, drew three bolts back, each one lined in tubes that ran through the holes in the front. A lever on the side was the trigger, and when pulled down, released all five strings simultaneously, launching a total of fifteen bolts at one time. It was slow to load, and even slower to draw the bolts back, but once done would unleash devastating power.

"What is that?" Kyron asked, stepping closer.

"I call it the Stopper, as it will stop anything," Peron said excitedly. "I've been working on it for months, and with all this fuss about the demon I thought it a good time to complete it. Look here," he said to Kyron as he directed his friend to the back of the weapon. "When I crank this wheel, it draws all five arms back. When the lever is pressed on the side it fires fifteen bolts."

"I can see why you call it the Stopper," Kyron said. "But why is it in your room?"

"After the attack on the Earl at Gyeen I thought it wise to protect myself. If anyone comes through that room they will be in trouble."

Kyron smiled and shook his head. "They will definitely be *stopped*," he said, hinting at the last word.

"Exactly!"

"But how will you pull the lever if you are in bed?"

"I'm going to rig up a rope system that hangs by the bed," Peron added, already having a solution to that problem. "And look here," he said, guiding Kyron to the door that led out onto his veranda. Being in the royal wing of the palace meant they were three stories up. Peron's chambers consisted of a large sitting room filled with shelves of books, and warm soft chairs, all facing a massive fireplace. From there was a door that led into his sleeping chamber. This room also had a fireplace, which was necessary in all castles to chase away the damp cold. The veranda was small and looked out to a courtyard below, the castle wall thirty paces away. He could sit at his veranda and watch soldiers patrol the wall, the height to the top of the wall just a few paces below his vantage point. On the edge of the Veranda was another wood contraption. It looked like a giant crossbow mounted on a wood base, bringing the weapon to just over the height of the railing.

"Looks like a big crossbow," Kyron said as they moved to the weapon.

"It is, but it doesn't shoot your typical bolts," Peron added.

Once Kyron got closer he could see that the bolt was bigger and of a heavier design, the steel tip adorned with three barbs each as thick as a finger. At the end of the long bolt, attached behind the fletching to a steel eye loop, was a rope coiled up at the base of the weapon, the end already tied to the strong stone railing that wrapped around the veranda. "Don't tell me that is designed to shoot to the far wall," Kyron asked incredulously, gauging the distance.

Peron smiled. "It is. I've already tested it and it works. If I hit over the battlements correctly, when pulled back the barbs dig into the stone edge."

"Okay," Kyron said slowly, trying to figure it out. "Then what?"

"I can tie it off and use this piece of leather to slide down the rope to the wall and make my escape." Peron lifted a leather belt off the weapon and showed it to Kyron. It was about half as long as a typical belt, but each end had loops for your hands.

"Why not just drop a rope to the ground?"

Peron lifted his eyebrows and replied with a mischievous smile. "That would be no fun. Besides, whoever was attacking me could just follow. They would think twice about trying to follow me to the wall."

"That's because it's dangerous. Have you tested this," Kyron asked skeptically.

"Not yet. Figured it would only be worth the risk if I was desperate."

"Well let's hope you will never have to find out if it works. Do you really think you are in danger?"

Peron shrugged. "I don't know. But I'd rather be ready. I have one more thing to show you. Come here," he added as he walked back inside and went to the dresser near his bed. On it was a small crossbow. "Take a look at this," Peron said as he lifted it up for Kyron to see.

"You built a small crossbow?"

"I did, but the design gives it far more power than a typical bow of its size. And, I've reworked the draw with these gears to counter the power of the bow, making it easier and faster to crank back but still maintaining the power. Look here," he said, lifting up a bolt from the bed. Then he grabbed the small handle on the side near the grip and turned it quickly. The gears cranked and the worm gear quickly drew the string back, locking it into place. Then he placed the bolt into the slide. It only took him a few moments to do both.

Kyron looked closer at the bolt. "What is that on the bolt's tip?"

Peron's face lit up with excitement. "That is a special surprise. I had Master Moran make me an oil of sharpness." Peron saw that Kyron did not know what that was. Few did, as most did not have a powerful court wizard on hand to make them magical things. It was one of the many things that Peron learned about while studying at Shyval. "It's enchanted oil, that when rubbed on a blade or point, adds a magical quality to it. You see how shiny the head is?"

Kyron looked more closely. "It looks like the steel tip has been polished."

"Exactly. The oil has been liberally applied and polished into the steel points. This bolt will penetrate pretty much any armor. I have it on the Stopper bolts as well as my sword," Peron added as he nodded towards his rapier hanging on a peg near the door. It was a well-made sword forged just for him. It was light and not too long, making it much easier for him to wield.

"What about a demon?" Kyron asked sarcastically.

But Peron was dead serious. "I think so, but as you said, let's hope I don't have to find out."

"Well you sure have been busy," Kyron said, shaking his head in bewilderment. He was always so impressed with Peron's inventions and schemes and was amazed at what he could accomplish when he set his mind to it. "Have you heard from your father's contingent yet?"

"No," he said. "The treaty might take a day or two to hash out, not to mention it's a week back from Angar. He said he would send runners ahead of him so we could prepare for the Arrival of Princess Kylin."

"They've been gone now for over a week, right?"

"Nine days. We should see the advance vanguard soon."

Kyron nodded. "Well I better get moving. I don't want to make the General wait," Kyron said as he walked to the door.

"Congratulations on the contract," Peron added as he saw his friend to the door.

"It's a start," Kyron added, smiling as he opened the door. Nodding to the arrow contraption on the far wall he added, "Don't shoot yourself with that thing."

Peron smiled. "I won't. Talk to you soon." And he shut the door behind him.

***

The foursome traveled hard through the thick forest, and at the end of the first day they came to a well-traveled road that led north and south.

Tyril indicated north. "This is the main road from Gyveel to Lanard. It's north we go."

Jonas figured it was the same road that he and Tulari had traveled before she had led them west, over the bridge, and deeper into the Lasur'een Forest to find Atticus, Tyril, and Kylin. But now they were much further north. "How long to Lanard?" he asked.

Tyril pursed his lips in thought. "My guess is we will reach the city in two days."

Jonas looked at Tulari who stood facing north. "Which way girl?" She looked back at him and barked softly, then she moved north down the road. "Good," Jonas said keeping pace behind her. "I'm tired of cutting through that forest." The others vocally agreed and followed their lead. They all had various scratches, testament to the thick brush they were forced to travel through as they followed Tulari.

Another two hours later Tyril walked next to Bearit, the big logger keeping pace just behind Jonas. At times Jonas would scout the forest, or run ahead with Tulari, but always he would come back appearing suddenly and without a sound. At this time he was nearly thirty paces ahead, taking point with Tulari.

Tyril looked sidelong at Bearit. "Thank you for saving my life the other night." He felt bad that he had been burned so severely in knocking him out of the way of the demon's breath. He had thanked him already, several times, but felt the need to do so again.

"I just reacted."

"Maybe so," Tyril said. "But not everyone would have reacted similarly."

"Well you're welcome...again." The corner of Bearit's lip lifted in a light smile. Tyril nodded. "That's a magnificent axe. Have you had much experience with it?"

Bearit shook his head. "No, not much at all. Jonas has been training me, but we've had little time."

"How did you come to travel with him?" Jonas had mentioned briefly how they had met nearly a week ago, but his telling had been vague.

"It's a long story," Bearit replied.

Tyril smiled. "Nothing better than a good story to kill a traveler's time."

Bearit shrugged his huge shoulders agreeing. "Three years ago my dad was killed in a logging accident. After that the contracts dried up. No one wanted to work with a sixteen year old."

Tyril looked at him sideling. "You're only nineteen?"

"Not quite yet."

"I would never have guessed," Tyril added. "I would have assumed you were three to four years my senior, at least."

"I get that a lot. After that I couldn't pay the taxes on my father's land. The king's men took my home and I roamed the land looking for work. I found it occasionally, but mostly I went to sleep cold and hungry."

"You lived for years like this?" Tyril asked incredulously. It was hard for him to imagine. His father was the Battle Lord, hence he always had what he wanted and needed. The idea of having no home or food was hard for him to grasp.

Bearit glanced at him. "You're a lord aren't you?" He didn't say it with any scorn. It was just a simple acknowledgement of the obvious.

"Yes," Tyril replied. "My father is the Battle Lord, although I don't know if he is still alive."

"I'm sorry. Was he at Angar when the Tur'el king ambushed them?" They had briefly talked of the event the day before, but with all that had been discussed Bearit was having a hard time remembering it all.

Tyril nodded. "Actually, he was with me when we were ambushed. He ordered me to run with the princess while he and the rest of the men held off the assassins."

Bearit looked at the young warrior and saw the pain. So he decided to change the subject and continue his story. "Not long ago some men found me cold and starving in an alleyway, and lured me to the catacombs beneath Gyeen. They promised me food and work, so I followed. There were perhaps ten to fifteen others there, just like me, of various ages."

"Did they give you food and work?"

Bearit looked ashamed. "They gave me food and ale, but they were torturing Jonas."

"Who were these men?"

"Your warriors," he said directly. "They were the Red Guard warriors that Maltheil had turned when he escaped. They were planning on luring us to him."

Tyril looked ahead, his thoughts going to the missing men. He wondered if he knew any of them. It made him sick to think of what Maltheil had done to them. "And Jonas killed them?"

Bearit nodded. "He was tied with ropes and they were burning him. I was...sickened, but I did nothing at first." Tyril looked at him questionably, but said nothing. It was obvious that the logger was wrestling with his own demons, likely feeling guilty for being there in the first place. "It was like he was waiting," he said slowly, thinking back to that dark room.

Tyril crinkled his brow. "Waiting for what?"

"Me," Bearit said without hesitation. "He was waiting for someone to show courage, to stand up to what was happening, despite the draw of hunger."

"So you did help him?"

Bearit nodded. "His armor flared brightly, like it did when we fought the demons. And he killed them all. I killed one with my woodsman's axe, but would have been slain if he hadn't saved me."

"And you've been with him since?"

"I have. He promised to train me, at least until I can wield *this*," he added, looking over his shoulder to the silver axe, "properly."

"Where did you get that axe? It looks like a king's weapon."

"Jonas bought me everything that you see."

"Wonderful gifts." Tyril said nothing more for a few moments as they continued down the road. A gust of wind blew towards them, shaking the branches around them, scattering leaves into the air. It was cold, and the wind sought out his skin, sending a shiver down his spine. Reaching up he wrapped his cloak more tightly around his shoulders. "I've never seen anyone fight like him. What did he have on his arm when he killed that demon?"

"You mean that translucent shield?"

By this time Kylin had woken from her trance and come closer, interested in their conversation as she picked up the tail end of Bearit's story. She had been morose and silent the last few days, speaking little and keeping her head down. She was worried what would become of her, and the stress of the unknown had occupied her mind. "I was wondering the same," she added. "Can he wield magic?"

Bearit looked at her as she stepped closer. "I don't think so. I'm not sure what that was but he did tell me that he had a special gift...somethin' to do with mental powers, although I didn't fully understand it."

Kylin's eyes were wide. "He is an Ishmian?"

Bearit nodded, thinking back to their conversation the night he had met Jonas. "I believe so. If I recall correctly Jonas had mentioned that he was an...Ish..?"

"...mian," Tyril finished for him, seeing that Bearit was struggling with the pronunciation. "It's the elven name for a cognivant," Tyril added. They both had been educated and were aware of the rare talent. Although neither of them had ever met a cognivant.

"Then yes, he is an Ishmian," Bearit reasoned.

"That's incredible," she added. "They are extremely rare."

"So you think that shield he formed was somehow connected to his cognivant ability?" Tyril asked, a bit skeptical. "Did you see that demon's fist? It hit his shield and it might as well have hit the wall surrounding Lanard. It did nothing to the shield or to Jonas. I've never seen anything like it."

Kylin shrugged unknowingly. "I know that some cognivants can move things with their minds. Maybe Jonas can form this shield with his mind. I do not know. My teacher knew very little of their abilities."

They walked together for a little longer before Tyril spoke again. "You know, Bearit, we could use men like you in the Red Guard. I think you could pass the tests with a little more training. Have you ridden a horse before?"

Bearit grimaced. "Just once, and I hated it."

Tyril smiled. "Well you will have to learn to ride. But I can help you with that, if you'd like. I would vouch for you, and that would be enough to get you in the training. From there it would be up to you to pass."

Bearit lifted his eyebrows. "You would do that?"

"Of course. You have the makings to be a fine warrior. It's the least I can do for saving my life."

Bearit pressed his lips together in thought. "I shall think on it. Thank you."

***

Peron was exhausted. He had been working hard on completing a third protection mask, as well as putting the finishing touches on his other inventions. He really had no idea if he was in danger. All he knew was that monsters had attacked Earl Magnar, the demon had escaped, and that somewhere the beast roamed, likely amassing a sizable force of demon-spawn. Although he could use a sword, he was no warrior, and he had to do whatever it took to protect himself. For him that meant using his mind, and that's exactly what he had done. Whether or not his concepts would work when put to the test he did not know, and as he told Kyron, he hoped he would not need to find out.

He had worked well into the night in his shop and finally decided to head to his chambers. The castle had long ago fallen asleep, but his guards followed him to his room and two of them remained outside his door, ever vigilant. Yawning, he took off his thick wool jerkin and cotton undershirt. Both were dirty and sweaty from working in his shop and he didn't smell much better. Servants had built up the fire in the main room, and he knew from experience that the fire in his sleeping chambers would have been burning for some time now, warming the cold castle air. There was a fresh bowl of water on his wash table and he went to it, dipping the cloth beside it and washing his face and armpits. Then he walked to his dresser and opened it, taking out a clean cotton night shirt. He was just about to step out of his cotton breaches and boots when he heard a loud thud at the door, followed by another, the second powerful enough to shake the door on it hinges.

Peron turned towards the door, moving cautiously towards it. He remembered one of the soldier's names and called to him through the thick oak door. "Towin," he said, "are you okay?" There was no reply. Peron walked closer. "Is something wrong?" he asked again, this time louder. Just then he saw something move under the door, and it froze him in place. It was blood, pooling slowly under the door, and inching its way towards him. Peron's heart pounded in his chest and he froze with indecision. Should he check on the men? Were they injured? Did they need his help against the assailant? Should he run? The indecision paralyzed him.

But then the door crashed open making the decision for him. A wave of fear hit him followed by the stench of sulfur, burnt flesh, and rotting garbage. A dark grey beast ducked its head under the door frame and stepped in, its black wings unfurling as it left the confines of the hallway. The body of one of the guards was sprawled at the demon's feet, and the other could be seen further in the hall, his body leaning against the blood streaked wall. Blood dripped from its spiked tail as it twitched dangerously in the air. The creature was human-like, with long arms and legs, all covered in sharp spikes, the ones on its hands dripped crimson. Its head was longer than a human's, covered in spikes, its wide mouth filled with sharp teeth. But it was the thing's eyes that froze Peron to the floor. They were large and all white. A gurgling hiss escaped the demon's mouth and it stepped quickly towards him, its tail raised and ready to strike.

The fear emanating from the beast was nearly overwhelming, but staring death in the face snapped Peron from his frozen trance. Spinning, he ran for the door into his sleeping chambers. He heard the beast hiss louder and the unmistakable sound of claws scraping on stone followed. His heart was pounding and he ran faster than he thought possible, slamming the bedroom door shut behind him and engaging the deadbolt. Without stopping he raced to his *Stopper* by the door, quickly turning the weapon on its swivel to face the door just as it crashed open, the power of the strike ripping the deadbolt right out of the stone.

Milky white eyes found him, and leaning forward, its long clawed arms stretched toward him, the demon propelled itself across the stones with immense speed. Peron's eyes grew wide at the frightening acceleration and he had just enough time to press the lever down. There was a loud click as all five bows fired. Fifteen bolts flew at the demon, each tip coated with the magical oil of sharpness. Eight of the bolts slammed into the demon's body, hitting the creature in its thighs all the way up to its head. The others ripped through the creature's wings. The power of the strike was immense. When the bolts struck the beast the creature was launched backwards, its heavy body catapulting to the floor. Steam rose from the wounds, the fletching of the bolts the only thing exposed, the power having driven the bolts deep into the beast's flesh.

Peron didn't wait to see if the beast was dead. He rushed through the door to his balcony and ran to the edge of the railing. He wasn't sure what to do. Was there only one demon? If so, was it dead? If not, should he try his preplanned escape route? He wasn't sure if it would even work. He'd hate to die by falling to the stone ground below if the threat was over. He ran to the door, his heart pounding. The demon was still there, unmoving.

He ran back to the large crossbow, his mind reeling over his options. With little warning, he heard the whooshing of wings and a hideous screech. Looking up, he saw a large winged shadow descend on him, its clawed feet reaching for his flesh. Reacting instinctively, he gripped the handle of the crossbow and swung it high, pulling the trigger at the last moment as the second demon was nearly on him. There was a resounding twang as the powerful weapon kicked back, and the big bolt, followed by the length of rope, snapped from the weapon to hit the creature directly in the chest. The demon screeched in pain and somersaulted backwards in the air, the bolt having ripped through its chest to burst out the other side, the barbs holding the bolt in place as the creature tumbled down to hit the pavers below with a heavy thud.

Peron looked down, and with the moonlight casting its bluish glow, he was able to see the howling demon flop around, vainly trying to rip the bolt from its chest. He had not covered the bolt's tip with the oil of sharpness, and without the magical properties of the oil, the bolt would not kill the demon. But the creature was in serious pain, and it couldn't free itself from the bolt or the tangle it had created as it struggled to free itself from the weapon and the trailing rope.

Peron ran inside to his bedside and grabbed his sword belt, flinging it over his shoulder. Then he plucked his crossbow off the bedside and was about to run out the door when he saw the demon on the ground start to rise. Swearing, he ran to the railing again. Quickly he untied the rope and pulled it hand over end until it was tight, the struggling demon on the other end acting as a weight. He tied it off just as the other beast stepped onto the veranda. With incredible speed the demon launched forward, one clawed hand swinging for Peron's head. He stumbled backwards and the big crossbow saved his life. The demon's razor sharp claws struck the side of the weapon instead of his face. A dripping oozing substance splattered from the demon's arm and when it hit Peron in the neck it burned like acid. He screamed and brought his crossbow up, firing the weapon point blank into the demon's chest. The bolt flashed blue and sunk deep, causing the demon to stumble back a few steps. Knowing that he had one chance to live, he reached up and grabbed the leather strap on the side of the weapon. Dropping his crossbow, he leaned over the railing and wrapped the leather around the rope. And without a second thought, he leapt off the edge, both hands holding onto the leather strap. Just as he cleared the railing, he felt a burning pain on the back of his legs. As he fell to the courtyard floor, he looked up to see the demon leaning over the railing. The beast must have sliced the back of his legs with its claws when he fell over the railing. But he had another problem. He couldn't get a firm grip on the leather; therefore the pressure on the rope was not enough to adequately slow his decent. He was falling too fast.

Bracing for impact, he let go of the leather strap before he hit the stone floor, hoping to land as far away from the struggling demon as possible. When he landed he heard a snap, followed by a burst of pain in his right ankle. He tumbled to the side across the stone pavers, his right shoulder hitting hard. More pain shot through his arm. Fighting back the agony he crawled away from the rope, trying to distance himself from the demon. Looking back, he saw the demon finally rip the bolt from its chest, its white eyes quickly pivoting towards him.

Two Red Guard soldiers who had been walking the perimeter saw the commotion and ran to give Peron aid. They had no idea what they were getting into. At first they stared at the demon, their eyes wide with shock, and fright. But they were both elite soldiers, and they shook away the paralyzing fear and came to Peron's aid. It was then that the second beast leapt from the balcony above, its flapping wings slowing it decent to land near the soldiers. Swords flashed in and out expertly, but the steel did little damage. There was a flurry of claws and whipping spiked tails, and within moments the soldiers were down.

By this time Peron had crawled to the base of the castle wall. He was in severe pain and panting heavily from exertion. He slowly stood on one leg and drew his sword. *I guess this is it* he thought, seeing no way out of his predicament. Then he heard a *caw* and a flap of black wings directed his gaze above him. A large black bird dropped from the sky and in mid-flight transformed into a man who landed with the grace of an acrobat, rolling forward and drawing his sword in one smooth motion. The man didn't hesitate as he attacked the demons.

Atticus held three fireseeds in his left hand and with an easy flick he threw them at the demon on the left, attacking the demon on the right with his sword. He knew that fire would do little harm to the demons as they were partially immune, but it should give him time to engage one at a time. The seeds struck the demon and exploded, causing the beast to fall backwards as fire engulfed it. Atticus lifted his glowing blade as the other demon's tail flipped around towards him. Snapping the magical blade forward, he cut the tail in two, and ducking under a claw attack he rammed his blade deep into the belly of the demon, ripping it out and diving away. Slimy goo had splattered from the creature and burned the flesh on Atticus's arms and neck. He cringed but kept moving. The wound to the demon was devastating, but still the demon sought the druids flesh.

Flapping its wings, it leaped into the air, both clawed feet angling for him. Atticus roared and rolled away, his sword flashing up expertly as he narrowly avoided the dangerous claws. Gangly toes flew through the air as his sword cut through the beast's foot. Spinning his legs under him, Atticus regained his footing, and wasting no time swinging his sword across the back of the hobbling demon's neck. His blade cut through the creature's flesh and its head landed with a grotesque thud, its heavy body following.

The second demon was slowly standing. Atticus could see at least eight crossbow bolts deep in its flesh, smoke still rising from the wounds. Its grey oozing flesh was singed, but the fire didn't seem to do much damage. But it served its purpose, distracting it while he could eliminate the other beast. Now he was facing one demon, and not two at the same time. Atticus whispered the words to a spell as the demon walked towards him. All at once there was an extremely bright light shining above the beast. It looked like a bright star, the starlight effulgent, its rays raining down on the demon. The demon hissed loudly and wrapped its black wings around its head to avoid the bright starlight. Atticus knew the light would not harm the creature, simply annoy it greatly. But that was not his goal. All he needed was a distraction, and the light provided that.

Holding his sword high in the air with both hands, he whispered the words to another spell, calling on the power of the *Sanga*. Several phrases later and there was a loud clap of thunder, the sound echoing off the castle walls. The deafening sound was followed by a crack of lighting, flashing brightly from the sky above and striking the druids raised sword. Flashing again, the lightning shot from the blade and struck the demon. The lightning exploded and sent the demon flying backwards, its entire body crackling with blue-white fire. Then the crackling subsided and the demon lay still, smoke rising from the burnt creature.

Atticus walked over to Peron, standing above him with his sword held low. "Peron Rothar?"

Peron stared up at his savor, his ashen face one of shock and pain. "Yes."

"I am Atticus Belthar."

Peron was rushed to a healer, surrounded by armed Red Guard soldiers. Atticus had offered to heal the prince, but they didn't know who he was and decided the best course was to get him to the royal healer. The castle was on high alert and General Moore, along with Lord Anteel, a member of the ruling council, came to Peron's side as soon as they received word of the attack. The healer was High Priest Vollen, who had been Peron's father's religious advisor and healer for as long as he was king. The man was nearly ninety winters and he looked it. Years of service to Toolm, the High One, had taken its toll. His bald head and weathered skin, combined with a slightly hunched over frame, could be construed as feeble, but nothing could be further from the truth. The man was a powerful cleric to Toolm, and few west of the Tundren Mountains could match his clerical strength and zeal.

When soldiers had arrived on the scene just after the demon's defeat they had assumed that Atticus had been part of the attack, as they had never seen the man. After a few words from Peron however, their attitudes towards the man had changed. And then when Peron said his name, they looked at him with shock and wonder, the same reaction Peron had had when he found out his identity. Even now, lying on the soft bed in Toolm's main temple, he wondered if the man really was the famous Atticus Belthar.

"How do you feel?" General Sig Moore asked. He was wearing full battle armor and had his usual gruff manor.

"Fine now," Peron said. "Thanks to Atticus and Master Vollen."

Atticus nodded, and Maser Vollen, who was standing near the bed, laid an old wrinkled hand on Peron's shoulder. "Of course, my boy. Your ankle was crushed badly and your shoulder was dislocated. Rest assured that you will feel no long term effects from those wounds."

"How did you escape those demons?" Lord Anteel asked, genuinely concerned for Peron's welfare.

"Luck mostly," Peron responded.

"I don't think so, young Prince," Atticus said. "The wounds one demon sustained before I arrived looked as if ten men had shot it with crossbows. And the bolts were magical. Not to mention the hole in the other demon's chest was as big around as my fist. What happened?"

Everyone was equally interested in hearing Peron's entire story. So he told it, keeping nothing out. When he was finished they seemed to look at him differently. Even General Moore looked surprised, if not a little impressed.

"And you say you made these devices?" the General asked.

Peron nodded. "I did."

"Smart thinking on the magical oil," Atticus added. "Those demons cannot be harmed by normal weapons. You would likely be dead if you had not administered the oil to the bolts."

"I'm afraid those men who came to my aid found that out," Peron said sadly. Then he looked directly at Atticus. "Thank you again for saving me. But I have to admit, I'm having a hard time believing you are *thee* Atticus Belthar."

"I as well," General Moore said. "You saved our prince, and I mean no disrespect, but why are you here?"

"To save all of you," Atticus said with no hint of bravado. "I *am* Atticus Belthar, and I am here to help you." He looked around the room and saw four guards standing near the door that led into Master Vollen's private chambers. "What I have to say is for your ears only."

General Moore got the point. "Men," he said to the guards. "Wait outside."

They nodded and left without a word.

Atticus continued. "I'm afraid I have bad news," he said, looking at Peron. "Your father is dead, as well as your uncle and Master Moran, betrayed by King Oneck. As we speak he is marching an army here."

Peron's eyes widened, and he looked at General Moore and Lord Anteel, both looking just as surprised. "What?! How can this be?" Peron said.

"Are you sure?" Lord Anteel asked, his voice just a whisper as he tried to process the news.

"I am," Atticus replied. "I flew above the fields outside of Angar and saw the destruction. King Oneck betrayed you all. His army was hiding in the woods and they stormed the camp two evenings ago after they had worked on the treaty, killing everyone."

"That cannot be true," the General said, his tone despondent.

"It is," Atticus said softly. "And that is not all. Maltheil marches with the Tur'el king, a small army of servants with him. They used Maltheil's demon-spawn to climb the walls at Angar."

Lord Anteel squeezed the spot on his nose just below his eyes, as if trying to work a headache away. "How is this possible?"

"It seems," Atticus continued. "That Carvathian, the Tur'el court wizard, is controlling the demon."

"So it was he that raised the beast?" Peron said, thinking out loud. He was still trying to process all that Atticus had said. Were his father and uncle really dead? He had no strong feelings for his father, but he was still his father. And Dalland was a good man. He genuinely liked him. His death hit him much harder than his father's, and there was a part of him that felt bad for that.

"We think so," Atticus continued. "But he had help. You have a traitor in your midst. Someone helped the wizard get the book."

The General looked up from his dark thoughts. "That someone would've had to have Rothar blood to get past the wards protecting the book. And now that the king and Prince Dalland are both dead, that leaves Prince Peron." When he realized the implications of what he said, he back peddled some. "I don't mean to say it was you, my Prince. But we are running out of explanations."

Everyone looked at Peron. "I had nothing to do with it. I think the demons trying to kill me are proof of that."

"Who else would have a motive to free the demon and help Tur'el conquer Lanard?" Atticus asked.

Everyone was silent as they thought about his words. They had all been mulling over the issue of who had freed the demon for the last two weeks. But no one had yet come to any conclusions.

Finally General Moore spoke. "I do not know. But we have pressing matters at hand. We need to prepare the city for a siege. And how are we going to stop Maltheil?"

Lord Anteel looked at Prince Peron. "My King," he said, addressing Peron with the title for the first time. "What are your orders?"

General Moore looked at Anteel, his eyes narrowing briefly before looking at Peron. It was true, the young prince was now the King of Lanard, and the realization of this passed over General Moore and his hard exterior softened some. "I'm sorry, my King. Anteel is quite right. What would you have us do?"

Peron didn't know what to say. So he thought honesty the best course. "General Moore, I know you think I am not fit to be king." The General was about to protest when Peron cut him off with a raised hand. "And you may be right. If I am to be honest with you both," he said, looking to Lord Anteel and General Moore, "I do not know if I even want the responsibility. I feel inadequate. But I no more have the choice than a young boy born to poverty and abuse. I will do my best, but know that I will need your council."

Atticus smiled. "Spoken like a wise king."

"What do you all suggest we do?" Peron asked.

"More of our reserves are coming in from the fields daily. In two days, our standing army will grow from seven thousand to ten thousand."

"Do we have two days?" Peron asked Atticus.

"They will have to travel the main road," Atticus said. "My guess is they will not arrive for another four to five days."

"Good," Peron replied. "Do we have weapons and armor to outfit the extra men?"

"We do now," the General said. "I met with your friend recently, Lord Vannearon, and he and his father have stores enough to outfit two thousand men. We have the rest in reserves."

A sudden thought struck Peron, but it was so outrageous that he shook it away. But as they continued to talk it hung around his mind, nagging at his consciousness. "Good," he said. "Prepare the city for a siege. Bring in what villagers you can and collect as many stores as possible."

General Moore nodded. "Very well."

"What are we to do about Maltheil?" Lord Anteel asked.

Peron looked at Atticus. "Any ideas?"

"I'm working on some," the druid added. "One other thing I forgot to mention. Your friend, Tyril, is alive."

Peron smiled broadly, but then it disappeared as guilt overtook him. With all that had happened to him and his family, he had forgotten about his friend. "Where did you see him?"

"I met him on the road," Atticus said. "They were ambushed by Tur'el soldiers. His father ordered him to flee with the princess. They escaped."

"What happened to the Battle Lord?" Sig Moore asked.

"Likely dead, but we do not know for sure," Atticus answered.

"Tyril is with the Tur'el princess, and they are headed here?" Lord Anteel asked. His tone was clear, wondering why the princess of a kingdom that had betrayed them would be on her way to Lanard.

"According to her," Atticus began, "she had no knowledge of her father's betrayal. She hates the man. And I believe her."

"We shall see about that," General Moore said, as if he was eager to get his meaty hands on her.

"One more thing," Atticus said. "A warrior found us on the road. Or more accurately, was led to us. He is now traveling with Tyril and they should arrive tomorrow. He has come to help us defeat Maltheil."

Lord Anteel pursed his lips in confusion. "What does one warrior matter to us?"

The corner of Atticus's lips lifted into a knowing smile, like he knew something they didn't, which he did. "His name is Jonas Kanrene. He was once a cavalier to Shyann, and now he is her knight. He still servers her will and he brings with him great skill and power. With his help, we may have a chance."

Master Vollen had been silent the entire time, taking in all the news, but now he spoke, very much interested in this new turn of events. "Is this the same man who fought Malbeck in the Great War?"

"The same man who trained under Commander Kiln himself?" Peron asked.

Atticus lifted his eyebrows. "One and the same."

"That is good news," General Moore said. "If the songs and stories are true, he will indeed be of great service."

"It's late everyone," Peron said, directing his gaze to the General. "General Moore, please prepare the army. Then get some rest. We will have much to do tomorrow."

General Moore bowed, deeper than he ever had towards him while Peron's father was alive. "It will be done." Then he left the room.

Lord Anteel stepped to Peron's side and placed a callused hand on his arm. "I'm sorry about your father and uncle," he said. "Your uncle was my friend and he will be missed. Do not try to be them. You are your own man." Then he gently patted his arm. "You will be a fine king. May I give you some further advice?"

"Of course."

"Don't let on that you have no idea what you're doing." Then he smiled, and walked away.

"I like him," Atticus said when the door shut behind him.

Peron looked at Atticus, his expression like stone. "How do we defeat Maltheil?"

"As I said, young king, I'm working on it."

CHAPTER EIGHT

Peron was in the council chambers when Tyril, Jonas, Bearit, and Kylin entered. He was working with General Moore, councilmen Inan, Anteel, and Caynon, planning for the upcoming battle. He was tired; the last few days spent preparing the city for the advancing Tur'el army. There was so much to do and so many unknowns, the least of which was what they were going to do about the demon and his army of demon-spawn. The appearance of his friend and guests were a welcome distraction.

"Tyril," Peron exclaimed, getting up from the table and crossing to them as several Red Guard soldiers escorted them to the massive round table. "It is so good to see you, my friend." They shook hands while the others at the table stood from their seats.

"You too." Then he placed his arm on his friend's shoulder. "I'm sorry about your father and uncle. I guess I need to call you king now."

"I don't think I will ever get used to that," he said, smiling at his friend. The last few days had been very stressful for him, and seeing his friend gave him some needed strength, his presence alone helping him feel that he was not alone. Then he looked at the others, stepping away from Tyril. "I am Peron Rothar, and you must be Jonas Kanrene, Bearit, and Kylin Oneck. Welcome to Lanard."

Jonas nodded as they shook hands, hand to forearm. Peron was no warrior, but he knew protocol, especially when greeting one such as Jonas. Tulari was sitting next to Jonas. Peron had been briefed on her, but despite what he knew, she unnerved him. Even though she was not at full size, she radiated a sense of power. Peron smiled at her but said nothing, unsure how he should greet her. He greeted Bearit in a similar fashion, casual yet firm. Bearit shook his hand, thanking him for the welcome. Then Peron stepped towards Kylin, his smile wide.

She looked away for a moment, her nervousness at meeting him overwhelming her briefly. Regaining her composure she tried her best to portray confidence, like she had been taught at court. But it was difficult. She knew that everyone in attendance was aware of her father's betrayal, and likely looked to her with disdain, or even still thinking that she had been a part of it. And she couldn't blame them. "I..." she began, stumbling over her words.

"Do not worry," Peron said. "Atticus has informed us what happened. You are welcome here."

She smiled. "I thank you for your sanctuary. I don't know what to say. I cannot believe that my father betrayed the treaty and your kingdom. I hope you believe that I had nothing to do with it."

Peron wasn't sure what to make of her. She was beautiful yet average at the same time. She had strength about her. Perhaps it was her chin he thought. It was strong, but as he examined her narrow face and firm lips, he realized it was her eyes. They were set, determined, and despite the fact that she was nervous, there was something deeper there...a sense of competence. He reached for her hand and kissed it, as was tradition. "Princess Kylin, you are safe here," he added, smiling warmly, trying to make her at ease. "Now," he announced as he turned around. "I'm sure you are tired and in need of refreshments. We could use your council however. Would you mind eating and drinking here while we discuss our current predicament? We could use some new perspectives."

"Very well," Jonas said, his vigilant eyes continuing to scan the room. "Where is Atticus?"

"In our library," Peron answered. "I'll send a runner to him immediately. Please have a seat. Food and drink will come soon." Peron ordered food and drink from several nearby servants, then he ushered his guests to the table.

They ate and talked for the better part of the evening. Peron had told them of the attack the other night and everyone listened intently, especially Tyril, who couldn't believe that his friend had survived. They discussed the condition of their army and other preparations necessary for a siege. Jonas listened but said very little, analyzing the men around him. He knew there was a traitor somewhere in their midst, and it was likely someone high up in the nobility, or at least someone who was close to the royal family. Anyone at the table could be the man that helped the Tur'el wizard free Maltheil.

Atticus had arrived soon after their meal and greeted them with tired eyes. "You made good time," he said to Jonas and the others as he sat down to join them at the conference table. "That is good."

Jonas, speaking up for the first time in a while, cut right to the point. "We need a way to kill the demon. If not, I'm afraid the beast's demon-spawn will scale the walls at night and break through the defenses. Have you found anything?"

Everyone knew he was talking to Atticus. The councilmen had learned of the druid's identity the day before. They had spent their entire lives at court; dealing with the intrigues, petty squabbles, power struggles, rules and etiquette, but the druid's presence still had an emotional effect on them. They looked at him with wonder and awe, with respect and deference. "I have some ideas," Atticus said as he sighed, shaking his head. "But it's just a foundation. As of yet I do not have the intricacies worked out."

"The Tur'el army is two to three days out," General Moore said. "We do not have much time left."

"Can we even kill the demon?" Lord Caynon asked. As a retired Red Guard officer, his first thought was always to pragmatic military solutions, and in this case he hoped that their problem could be resolved with the blade.

"Not fully," Atticus said. "Maltheil is not of this world. If we kill its body here, then its essence will be banished back to his home on the sixth plane."

"That is good, isn't it?" Lord Caynon asked.

"Yes," Atticus answered. "But not great. It will solve our immediate problem, but," he warned, "he may find a way to come back. I believe the beast's vengeance for its imprisonment is all consuming."

"But did you not banish him to the nethers before," Jonas added. "And still he found a way to come back."

"That is true," Atticus said.

"Is there a way to permanently kill the beast?" Peron asked.

"Yes," Atticus answered quickly, looking over at the young king. "He needs to be killed at home, on his own plane."

Peron sat back in his chair, releasing a deep breath. Everyone else looked equally resigned, except for Jonas. "Can we travel to the sixth plane?"

All eyes stared at him in bewilderment. When they saw he was serious they didn't know what to say. It was Atticus who answered. "Yes, it's possible. But there are several problems with that plan." Atticus knew that Jonas was serious. The young warrior had accomplished much in his short life, and the druid reasoned there was very little that the warrior thought was beyond the realm of possibility. After all, he felt the same way.

"Several," Lord Inan balked sarcastically. "It's impossible. Fighting something that powerful here is bad enough, but trying it there...is just ludicrous. I suggest we focus on the plausible, not the impossible."

"If you *think* it's impossible, then it is," Jonas said softly, his tone serious as he rested his strong forearms on the table. "I have faced many dilemmas that seemed impossible at the time, but I am still here. Where there is courage, wisdom, and strength of arms, then anything is possible, Lord Inan."

"Let's hear the problems of the plan first, before we decide if it's possible," Lord Anteel suggested.

Lord Inan looked perturbed, glancing around the room for support. Glancing at Jonas last, he looked into his hard narrow eyes, and looked away quickly, not able to hold his intense gaze.

Atticus continued. "The first problem would be banishing him to his home and then us following. If we succeeded there, then we would have to devise a way to defeat him where he is the strongest. He would surely have minions at his disposal, which would add to the difficulty in killing him."

"Not to mention," Tyril reasoned, "that we would need a way to return home."

Atticus pursed his lips, sighing through his nose. "There is that as well."

"Can it be done?" Jonas asked again. "All of it?"

"It can," Atticus said. "The only way that we can get the demon, and a contingent of warriors, to the sixth plane, is through a portal, a gateway. I have the skill to open one here, but once there I will not be able to open another to return. My power comes from the earth, the forest around us, and there will be neither in that hellish place. I will not be able to touch the *Sanga*."

Jonas was familiar with portals, having traveled once to the Hallows, a world between worlds. He wondered if the Hallows was a similar place to the nethers, but according to Atticus's description he did not believe so, besides both of them were places that one did not go to purposefully. Portals, he knew, were located at waypoints, doors so to speak between the worlds. "How would we lead Maltheil to a waypoint?" Jonas asked.

"What is a waypoint?" Tyril asked.

"Weaknesses between the worlds," Peron answered, thinking about all he had read and studied over the years. "The elves call them sikani, or holes, as they view them as disturbances in the Ru'ach. Or holes that lead to tunnels, that, if one were so empowered, could follow to various worlds."

"That is correct," Atticus confirmed.

"So they are magical?"

"In a sense, yes," Atticus said. "Many elves can find them as they are more attuned to the Ru'ach. But very few others can locate the waypoints, let alone use them."

"So," Peron said, thinking out loud. "Let us pretend that we could trick Maltheil to enter a gateway, with a small group of select warriors, and that we can kill him once we arrive on the sixth plane. How would we get back?"

Atticus sighed, his frustration evident, as well as his exhaustion. "That is what I've been working on. I cannot reopen the gate once there as I will have no connection the *Sanga*. But I may be able to create a link to something here, and use that connection to reopen it. It is magic I have never done, but," he said softly, "I believe it is possible."

"And if not?" General Moore asked.

"Then whoever is there will die."

"What are our other options?" Peron asked.

"We could try to imprison Maltheil with a demon trap," Atticus answered. "Then I could try to banish him. Although I am stronger now than I was two thousand years ago, I am unsure if I have the strength to banish him on my own."

"I read once that wizards can link minds with others, to gain more strength," Peron said. "Is this something you can do?"

"Yes, that is exactly what I did with my grove so long ago. But the minds from which I'm linking with must be strong." Atticus saw where Peron was going and warned him. "And it is dangerous. If not mentally strong enough, Maltheil can destroy you in the process. And one more thing. My power is limited here, in the castle, with all this stone and mortar. I need the earth at my feet and the forest around me to be at my strongest. I suggest we bring the fight to them before they arrive at our gates."

"That would give us very little time," Lord Anteel said.

"And also the element of surprise," Jonas added.

"There is a gateway close," Atticus said.

"Where?" Peron asked, sitting forward again.

"Taren's Crossing."

"The bridge?" Peron asked. The bridge was built nearly five hundred years ago by one of Peron's ancestors, naming it after his son, who by all accounts became a good king.

"Yes," Atticus said. "The bridge was actually built at that location because of the gateway."

"I did not know that," Peron replied.

"That is the only way for an army to cross the river. The Tur'el army will be there in two days," General Moore said, his tone showing his concern. They did not have much time. "We do not even know if Maltheil is traveling with them. The beast and his army could be moving much faster. We need information."

Jonas knew the bridge well. It was the same bridge where he and Bearit were attacked. "The bridge is narrow," he said. "A fine spot for a trap. As far as information, I can send Tulari. There is no other who can move as fast and not be noticed."

"Do it," Peron said.

***

Tyril's sword came down fast, his silver blade striking between the blades of Bearit's axe as he lifted the heavy head to meet it. Angling down, he pushed his sword away and kicked out with his powerful leg. But Tyril spun quickly, blocking the kick with his shield, his own sword spinning by Bearit's stomach, retracting the blade at the last minute so as not to cut him.

Stepping away, Tyril smiled. "That was a nice move," he said. "If I didn't have my shield, your kick would have connected."

"And maybe I would not be dead from that last strike. You are very fast," Bearit added.

Tyril was impressed with Bearit's strength and stamina. They had been sparring for quite some time, Tyril giving pointers where he could. Although Tyril had scored several fatal blows, the big logger had held his own for some time. And Tyril was extremely strong, but he could still feel the power of Bearit's strikes in his arms. He had never fought against someone that strong, not even his father.

They had spent another hour on their make-shift plan when they all had left to prepare, and get some rest if possible. Jonas had sent Tulari away and stayed with

Atticus to discuss the matter further. Tyril had suggested to Bearit that they practice, and Bearit, eager to learn all he could, readily accepted.

"I've been training since I could lift a sword," Tyril responded. "You started a month ago. It is I who am impressed."

They moved to the water basin and ladled big gulps of water. "I'm sorry about your father," Bearit said. "Do you think he is still alive?"

Tyril wiped the sweat from his face. Resigned, he unbuckled his shield and leaned it against the basin. "I don't know. If anyone could've survived that ambush, it was him."

"He is good with a blade?"

Tyril smiled for the first time. "The best. He was so fast and strong, and utterly fearless."

Bearit shook his head and let out a deep breath. "If I am to be honest, I am afraid."

Tyril looked at him with no derision. "I as well," he agreed. "Fighting the demon is bad enough, but doing so in that place of monsters and fire...well, it is not something I'm looking forward to." Both Tyril and Bearit, along with Jonas and Atticus, had agreed to enter the gate if they could in fact get Maltheil through it. They were presently looking into getting several more Red Guard soldiers to join them, some of the best warriors, but those men had yet to be determined.

"My greatest fear not be facing the demon, but being stranded there if we actually survive," Bearit added.

Tyril thought about it for a moment. Dying in that fiery place would be bad. But Tyril had to agree that being stranded there would be worse. "You might be right there. Come, let's bathe, eat, and rest. We have a big day tomorrow."

***

Peron knocked on the large heavy wood door, an escort of ten Red Guard soldiers behind him. The door was four heads taller than he, and well built, surrounded by thick white granite walls, the second floor dominated by ornate stone balustrades, green plants growing well and hanging over the sides. It was the home of wealthy person. It was the home of Lord Vannearon, Kyron's father, located in the wealthy part of the city just inside the north wall. They had spent hours at the council table working over the plan. Peron was tired, but he was eager to speak with his friend.

The door opened and a young servant girl was just about to respond when she fully noticed who it was at the door. Stumbling, she said, "My King, I...who... what can I do for you?" Everyone knew that Peron and Kyron were childhood friends, but it had been at least a year since he had paid a visit to their home. Word had spread quickly of Peron's father's death. And even though they had yet to properly coronate Peron as the new ruler, everyone knew he was now their king. "I am hoping to speak with Master Kyron. Is he here?"

"I'm sorry, my King. He is not. He is at the warehouse with his father. But he should be back shortly for dinner."

"I will wait for him in his chambers," Peron said matter-of-factly.

"Oh, umm," she said, stumbling again over her words. "Yes, please follow me." She opened the door and Peron entered with four soldiers. The rest stood guard at the entrance.

The foyer was grand and opulent; a large chandelier covered with hanging lanterns made of expensive blown glass the center of attention. "I know the way," Peron said, walking through the foyer into the massive high ceilinged living space. Kyron's living quarters were on the main floor with the two guest and servant's rooms, while the entire upstairs was his father's quarters and office. Peron turned right down the stone hall, hanging lanterns lighting the way. The door to his room was locked and Peron looked at the servant, who was quickly following him.

"Please open it," Peron said kindly. The servant girl hesitated. It was obvious that her orders were to keep the room locked. She only opened it to light the fire in the evening, which she had already done. But it was the king that was asking, and she had no choice. Fumbling with a set of keys around her neck, she found the one she needed, and opened the door. "Very good. Will you please light the lanterns," he asked her. Then he looked at the guards. "Stay out here." They nodded, but said nothing. She went inside and lit the lanterns throughout the room. The fire was going strong but the room was still chilly. "Thank you," Peron said. "You are dismissed." She eagerly left Peron alone in the room.

Peron had spent a lot of time playing here when he was young. The room looked different now of course, matching Kyron's growth into a well-traveled young man. There were tapestries and carvings from all around Kraawn, as well as beautiful artwork and palatial furnishings. Soft chairs faced the warm fire and book shelves lined one wall entirely, a massive wood desk sitting in the middle, the shelves expertly built around it. There was a single door that went into Kyron's sleeping chambers.

Peron went to the desk and opened the drawers. He didn't know what he was looking for. There was something nagging at him, something pulling at his memories, trying to piece things together. There were files there, ledgers with account information, most of which looked like purchases and payments. He knew that Kyron had taken over much of his father's business since his mother had left, leaving Lord Vannearon to his depression and vices. Kyron had been forced to run the business or lose all that his father had worked for. Everything looked to be in order.

Then he went to the book shelf and found what he was looking for. Long ago, when Kyron was young, his father had his builders put in a secret panel for Kyron. It was more for fun, and Peron remembered fondly hiding all kinds of things behind the panel. There most prized possession was a book of drawings that showed in great detail, not only the female anatomy, but also what a man and women can do with their anatomy. Peron had stolen it from the royal library and they had hidden it in Kyron's secret panel. Peron removed the ten books by placing them on the desk. Then he placed his hand on the wood panel behind and dragged it sideways. The panel slid open easily, which told Peron that it had been used recently. Inside was a secrete shelf that was a half a pace deep.

Looking inside Peron saw a small chest. He lifted it out and was amazed at how heavy it was. He set the chest down on the desk and opened the lid. It wasn't locked. Perhaps Kyron thought the hiding place alone was significant enough. Inside was gold. Lots of it, piled to the edge of the chest.

Peron frowned, reaching in he picked up a single coin. It was then his heart stopped. The coin was stamped with the Tur'el mark.

Just then the door opened and Kyron entered, Peron's guards remaining just outside the door. Kyron's eyes narrowed momentarily, glancing at the chest, before he sighed heavily, his face going pale before moving to a jug of wine on a side table. "Would you like some wine?" he asked, pouring himself a glass. He looked nervous.

"No, thank you," Peron said calmly, trying to slow his beating heart.

Kyron lifted the glass towards Peron. "To old friends." Then he drank the entire glass. "I didn't think you would come here," he said, his voice tired.

"Why do you have a chest of gold stamped with the Tur'el mark?"

Kyron stepped closer to Peron, his expression stolid. "I think someone as smart as you can figure that out. In fact, if I know you, which I do, I bet you already have several possible answers."

Peron dropped the coin back into the chest. Absently he touched the scar on his wrist. All the loose connections he had been feeling began to assemble into a hypothesis, one that if he were honest with himself he had already thought about in his subconscious, but was unwilling to admit to it. He rubbed the scar, the same one caused by Kyron's accidental strike during their swordsmanship class over a month ago. "Was it you?" he asked incredulously.

This time Kyron's self-control faltered, his false confident gaze and posture shifting slightly under Peron's accusation. He poured another glass of wine and drank it quickly, looking at Peron now with a pleading look. It was then that Peron knew he was guilty. "I did not mean for it to escalate as it did," he said.

Peron put up his hand, his anger rising. "Just tell me!" he snapped. "Was it you that helped them free Maltheil?"

Kyron's eyes dropped and he seemed to deflate. "Yes, but you have to understand. They came to me. They offered me contracts and gold, lots of it, enough to get the business back on its feet." Kyron's voice was now beseeching, his tone shrill as he argued his defense. "You don't understand, Peron. We were going to lose everything. I would have lost the estate. I would have been thrown out on the street."

"You could have asked for help," Peron said, his anger palpable.

"They promised me that you would not be hurt," Kyron continued. "I...I would have been destitute. It was the only way."

"You're a fool," Peron snapped. "How did you get past the wards on the chest?"

"Wards?"

"If anyone outside the Rothar royal family attempted to open the chest, the magical wards would have killed them. How did you survive?"

Kyron stepped back to the wine, pouring another glass. "I...I didn't know that," Kyron said. "It must have been your blood."

Peron's hand went to his wrist again. "You cut me on purpose, didn't you?"

"Yes," he exclaimed. "But I knew you would be healed. When I helped you wrap the wound I kept the blood soaked towel. Once I transferred some into a glass, it was enough for Carvathian to use to free the demon. I had it with me when I stole the book. It must have been that which saved me." Kyron slammed another glass of wine and stumbled towards Peron. "Please Peron, you have to forgive me. I didn't think it would get this out of hand."

"You freed a demon!" Peron shouted. "What did you think was going to happen!? Your actions, based on self-preservation, may be the downfall of Lanard! Guards!" Peron shouted. The door opened and the Red Guard troops entered, hands on the hilts of their swords. "This man is under arrest for treason! Take him away!"

"Yes, my King," the lead officer said, grabbing a stunned Kyron and leading him from the room.

Kyron was yelling *I'm sorry*, his voice dying away as he was dragged from the Vannearon estate. Peron's anger subsided and turned to heartbreak. Despondent, he sat in Kyron's chair, anguish at his friend's betrayal feeling like rocks strapped to his back. He put his head in his hands, and hoped that he would have the strength to see his people through their predicament. Right now, he felt sick, empty, and wanted to fall asleep and wake up in a different world.

***

Tyril found Peron in Toolm's temple, speaking with High Priest Vollen. The young king was tired, and he looked it, the typical intelligent sparkle in eyes replaced with resignation. Kyron had been arrested two hours ago and Tyril had just found out, knowing that Peron was at the temple as a runner had come for his sword, just as they had planned earlier that day. They were standing beside Toolm's altar, which was located in the middle of the sanctuary, a large statue of Toolm looming down at them against the wall facing the pews. Lying on white translucent silk that draped over the altar were Tyril's sword, as well as Bearit's axe. If they were to face the demon, they needed their weapons to be enchanted, a process entrusted to Toolm's High Priest.

"Peron, is it true?" Tyril said, walking briskly towards him from the aisle. He was clearly despondent. High Priest Vollen raised his eyes at the young man's breach of etiquette; after all, they were childhood friends no longer. Peron was now the king, and it was obvious that the High Priest felt they should act accordingly.

The High Priest cleared his throat. "Perhaps, my *King*," he said, emphasizing the word, "you would like some privacy."

"No, no, we have much to do," Peron said. "You may stay." Peron turned to face his distraught friend. "I'm afraid it is."

Tyril was shaking his head in disbelief. "I cannot believe it! He betrayed us!? What is going to happen to him?"

Peron knew that Tyril was aware of their laws, but perhaps there was a part of him that hoped that Peron would be able to give their friend some allowance. But he knew that was not true. "He will be tried for treason. And if found guilty, executed." All crimes against the state were tried by the high council, and that meant Lord Inan, Lord Caynon, and Lord Anteel. It would be up to the tribunal to decide his fate.

Tyril ran his hands through his hair, sitting down on a nearby pew, looking utterly drained. He looked just as Peron felt when he had learned of Kyron's betrayal. The three of them had been friends for as long as they could remember. It was inconceivable that Kyron had betrayed them. "How could he do this?" Tyril mumbled.

Peron sat next to him. "I've been asking myself that very same question. The truth is...we have all grown apart over the last few years. I knew that Kyron's family business was nearly bankrupt, and that his father was more or less incapable of running the business any longer, but I did very little to help Kyron, or at least try to understand what he was going through. Kyron had a lot of strain placed upon him, and under its weight, he cracked."

Tyril looked up from his hands. "You are defending him?"

"No, just trying to rationalize why he did what he did. It was wrong, there is no doubt. He was nearly thrown out into the street. They had not paid their taxes for over a year, and it's my guess that it was his families' rank, as well as their relationship with me, that kept my father from doing so. I was angry at first, really angry. Now I'm just sad. In a moment of weakness he made a choice that will change his life forever, and perhaps our own." Peron stood and put his hand on his friend's muscled shoulder. "You need to get some sleep. We have much to accomplish tomorrow."

Tyril stood, his doleful expression accentuated by his red eyes. He nodded towards the weapons. "How goes the blessing?"

"We just started," Peron answered.

Tyril nodded. "I'll see you tomorrow." He turned and walked away.

Peron watched his friend go and sighed heavily, turning back to High Priest Vollen, who had already begun the preparations. "How long will this take?"

High Priest Vollen looked up from his task. He was brushing anointed oil upon the blades, covering every inch of the steel with slow methodical strokes, the nut brown oil slowly seeping into the steel. "For me, all night. You are not needed here, my King. Go and get some rest."

Peron could not agree more with him. "Thank you, Master Vollen, for everything." Then he turned, eager for his bed, afraid however that sleep would elude him.

***

Atticus flew through the night. He had a plan, and if successful, would increase their odds of success in the coming fight. His raven form caught the currents, and luck was with him this night as the wind was blowing strong from the west, pushing him east, his wide black wings expertly using it to his advantage. Hours later he saw the camp, his bird-keen eyes easily spotting the hundreds of fires as the army of Tur'el desecrated his forest, filling the long road for miles and miles as they camped for the night. He came in closer, flying low over the thousands of tents, looking for one in particular. He could feel the demon nearby, but knew he would not find the beast camping with the army. It was impossible. But the link between Carvathian and Maltheil was a tight leash, and the demon and his army of minions had to be close, likely nestled in the forest, ready for when Carvathian lost his strength, their very presence a blight on the land around them. When the war was over, if he survived, he would have to spend many years healing the land, asking the *Sanga* for the power to make it whole once again, to eradicate the black stain of the demon and its army.

He flew over the king's tent, spotting it easily, its wide berth literally filling the entire road, as well as occupying space to either side, likely where trees and shrubs had been hacked down to accommodate its size. But it wasn't the king's tent he was looking for. He came in low and landed gracefully on a low lying branch flanking the road, his black eyes darting back and forth, analyzing one tent in particular. It was near the king's tent, as it should be, the cloth dark blue. Two guards stood at the entrance, tall burning torches pounded into the ground on either side. The tent was spacious, but not quite as grand as the king's. Flying low, Atticus glided to the side of the structure, its edge masked in shadow, the light from the torches blocked by the corner of the tent. Quickly he took on his human form, looking from side to side to make sure no one could see him. It was pitch black, and he would only be spotted if someone walked around the tent with a torch, which was a likely possibility as part of the guard's duty. He had to hurry. Atticus grabbed a stick from the ground and held it before him. Taking a deep breath he began to chant quietly, the soft words barely discernable. Moments later the stick moved, undulating back and forth as if it was alive. Finishing the spell quickly, the stick was no longer a stick, but a small brown snake that wrapped its scaly body around his wrist and hand. Holding the snake before him, he whispered more unintelligible words. The snake's head came up and stopped just inches from his mouth, holding its writhing body still, as if it was listening. Then he laid the snake on the ground and watched it slither away, easily finding the seam on the tent flap and disappearing within its confines.

Atticus turned back into a raven and flew into the night air, moving high above the canopy and landing upon a perch overlooking the entire camp. He knew from experience that Carvathian likely had wards protecting him from attack. In fact he could feel the magical wards all around the tent, which was confirmation that Carvathian indeed slept inside. He knew the wards would protect the wizard from magical or physical attacks, but hoped they would not defend him from a natural creature such as a snake. He would find out soon enough.

Moments later he heard a scream of terror and pain from inside the tent. But it was the sound that soon followed that he was hoping to hear. A roar, loud and unworldly rocked the still night, and Atticus flapped his wings, flying higher above the forest. His sharp black eyes caught the movement easy, as it looked like the forest was undulating like prairie grass in a strong breeze. If Atticus could have smiled, he would have. The snake's poisonous bite had killed Carvathian, thus freeing Maltheil from his control. Moving through the forest at an incredible pace, fueled by anger and rage, was Maltheil and his army of demon-spawn. He could not see them in the dark night, but knew they were coming for them. The demon army did not sleep. They did not eat. He knew they lay in wait, and that they would crash into the unsuspecting Tur'el forces and unleash their fury, killing, turning, or scattering them all. He had just increased their odds considerably. If Maltheil could indeed crush the Tur'el forces, and if they could find a way to defeat the beast, then they just might have a chance. Atticus angled west and headed to Lanard. There was still much to do to get ready.

***

It was still dark when two thousand Lanard soldiers marched through the main gate, led by five hundred Red Guard cavalry. At the head of the column were King Peron, Tyril, Jonas, Bearit, Atticus, Lord Caynon, and Captain Korrin, who had been asked to follow Jonas and the others through the gate to Maltheil's home plane. According to Tyril, he was the finest swordsman in the ranks now that his father was no longer with them, and his weapon was enchanted, given to him as a gift from Peron's father for winning the yearly combat tournament to mark the summer solstice. The Captain had agreed to join them, despite the possibility that he would not survive.

They were all outfitted for war. Even Peron wore armor, made by Dynin, the royal armorer, when he had turned eighteen just a few days ago. There had been no celebration, or formal gifting of the armor. Dynin simply brought it to him, knowing that the time was coming that he may need it. It was beautifully crafted, and Peron felt unworthy of it. His sword hung from his side and his small crossbow was sheathed in a unique leather holder of his own design, buckled nicely to his thigh. A quiver of bolts, each laced with the oil of sharpness, was strapped to his other leg. He knew he would be of little help in a battle, but he also knew that he needed his men to see him lead. Peron was no battle king, and perhaps the fact that he led the army to face a demon, complete with his lack of martial skill, would instill a sense of courage within his men. He certainly didn't feel heroic. If anything, he was scared beyond belief, but the presence of his friends, Jonas, and Atticus, disseminated in him a sense of courage, and perhaps it was enough to shed some to his men.

Kylin was there as well. She would not be persuaded to stay behind, and despite Peron's misgivings at leading her to battle, he finally gave in. There was a part of him that understood her desire to be a part what was to come. Perhaps she felt she needed to prove to everyone that she had no part in her father's betrayal. Or maybe she felt she needed to help, knowing that if Maltheil were to win then there would be no stopping the beast from razing more cities to the ground. And now, after what Atticus had done, she wanted to find out what had happened to her father. Had he been killed by the enraged demon? It was likely. They would find out soon enough. But despite Peron's allowance at agreeing to her accompaniment, he made it clear that when the fighting started she was to remain at the rear of the column. She had frowned at that, but relented, knowing she was not going to win that battle.

Jonas rode next to Atticus and he glanced over at the warrior. The druid seemed preoccupied, and Jonas questioned him about it. "Are you rested?" Jonas asked. Atticus had informed them all of what he had done last night, bringing a needed boost to their morale. But while others had slept, Atticus worked throughout the night. There was much of the plan that weighed heavily on the druid, and Jonas was worried about him.

Atticus smiled wanly. "I'm fine actually. Last night, after I completed my tasks, I went into the forest and lay in the grass. The Sanga brought me strength and energy, like I have slept for a week."

"That is good," Jonas responded. "I'm afraid you will need it. What seems to be troubling you then?"

Atticus reached into a pocket on the inside of his tunic and withdrew two blue stones. "I do not know if these will work," he said. "And if they do not, then we will all perish in that evil place."

"We know the risks."

"Yes, I know. It's just that bravery should not be rewarded by a death such as that."

Jonas smiled. "I agree, but it often does. If not, then those actions would not be considered brave."

"Just the same," Atticus continued. "I wish it was just my life I was risking." Atticus had worked magic on the stones all night, drawing from the Sanga to bind the two stones together. One stone would accompany Atticus through the gate while the other remained with Peron on the other side. If successful, then once the stone on the other side was shattered, the magic contained inside would automatically open the gate, drawn to its partner stone. They would not have long, but the gate should remain open long enough for them all to enter. The druid had used the various spells before, but never in this application. He believed he bound them to the stones correctly, and they would work, but regardless, the unknown provided him much consternation.

"We have, and will, do our best," Jonas said. "It is all we can do."

Atticus pursed his lips, the edges tight with worry. His typical flippant attitude was nowhere to be seen. "Let us hope it will be enough."

Tulari found them four hours into their march. She was sweating and her fur was in tangles, branches and leaves sticking to her in a disheveled mess. She had run hard, and fast. She informed Jonas that they would reach the bridge by mid-day, well before Maltheil. From what Tulari could tell, and pass on to Jonas, Maltheil and his servants killed many Tur'el soldiers, scattering the rest. It was hard for her to know the exact size of his force, but it made sense that the demon's ranks had likely swelled. What she did not know was what had happened to the King and Prince of Tur'el. They were likely dead or turned. Jonas figured they would find out soon enough.

As it turned out Tulari's estimation of distance was accurate. Once they made it to the bridge they began the preparations with earnest, each person knowing exactly what to do. The army rested and ate a meal, their fighting role not to be fulfilled until Maltheil arrived. It was Atticus that had the most to do. Firstly, he found the location of the gateway. As luck would have it, the gateway was directly in the middle of the bridge, the door located on the stone pavers of the ancient structure. That would help them immensely. Atticus was the only one who knew that luck had had nothing to do with it location. The bridge was actually built long ago at that location precisely because of the waypoint. Doors don't always take into consideration the layout of the world around them. Sometimes they can be floating in the air, or on the bottom of a lake. This one however, was located in a position that would benefit them. Once he knew where the gateway was, he went to work creating the demon trap just behind the waypoint. If the door didn't work, then they would fall back to their secondary plan, and that was to trap the demon and banish him to his own plane. Peron's role in the creation of the demon trap was not so pleasant. For the trap to be its strongest, it needed to be created from Peron's blood.

"I'm sorry to have to do this," Atticus said. "But worry not, I will heal you when I'm done."

Peron held his arm out to the druid, looking up he glanced at Kylin, who was standing nearby. He took a deep breath and smiled weakly at her. "Get it over with."

Atticus took his knife and drew it across his flesh, opening up a shallow wound. He would need a lot of blood. Peron cringed but didn't cry out. He looked up into the sky, blinking away the pain as he tried to push it away, his mind concentrating on all that would be sacrificed that evening. His pain was paltry compared to the horrors that were likely to occur. He felt a hand on his shoulder and looked down to see Kylin next to him, her face showing her concern. Blood poured from the wound into a large gold chalice. Once the cup was full, Atticus handed the cup to Kylin, putting both hands on Peron's injured arm. Then he whispered the magical words, drawing from the *Sanga* around him. Moments later the cut sealed up, leaving behind a barely perceptible scar, smeared with blood that no longer welled up from the wound

As he worked diligently and methodically drawing the intricate trap, many others collected piles of dried leaves, scattering them all over the bridge. The idea was to hide the trap using dirt and leaves, but they couldn't very well just have leaves covering one part of the bridge. It would be too obvious that something was hidden there. So they opted to cover the entire expanse.

Peron had brought along his *Stopper*, and had it placed just behind the demon trap, loaded with bolts all soaked in the magical oil. Cavalry and footman spread out behind the bridge, filling any open areas further down the road. The bridge was narrow, and only three could fight side by side across its width. Behind the trap sat Captain Engle, with thirty of the finest Red Guard cavalry, their heavily armored horses taking up the entire span of the bridge behind the demon trap. Captain Engle had seen thirty-eight winters, and most of those were spent astride a horse with a sword in his hand. Besides Captain Korrin and Baylock Reen, there were no others in all of Lanard who were more experienced, or skilled. Peron and Lord Caynon, sitting on their horses, were behind them just off the bridge, the entire Red Guard cavalry occupying the road behind, the footman further still. Peron knew he would be of no use when the immediate fighting started, but he did not want to seem like a coward to his men. So he stayed off the bridge, but remained near the front, still visible to his soldiers. Under the direction of Lord Caynon, who was once a Red Guard officer, Peron had sent soldiers into the woods forming two perimeter lines angling towards the river bed. Luckily the river in this particular section was fast moving, deep, and filled with precarious rapids. It was unlikely that Maltheil and his demon army would be able to cross the river and flank them. But he wanted to be ready in case they found a way to do just that. Kylin was next to Peron, and as soon as violence broke out she was to ride to the rear of the column. If they succeeded in tricking Maltheil into the gateway, then it would be up to Peron and his army to fight off the demon-spawn until Maltheil was killed. The army behind them would act as a wall of steel if Maltheil's minions broke through the cavalry. They didn't know how long they could hold off the unworldly force, but since the bridge was too narrow for an all-out assault, they hoped that the Lanard military would be able to hold off Maltheil's minions until they succeeded in killing the demon.

Jonas, Bearit, Atticus, Tyril, and Korrin, stood before the trap, at the front, just behind the location of the gateway. They were silent as they waited for Maltheil to arrive. Tulari was ahead scouting and she would return with news of Maltheil's approach. The nervous tension around them was palpable. Tyril was swinging his sword from side to side, warming up his muscles. Bearit was standing tall, his fingers gripping his axe handle over and over again. Peron had given Tyril, Bearit, and Korrin, his three masks in case the demon attacked with its breath. He told them he was unsure if they would work, but they saw the wisdom in their design and accepted them with gratitude. Peron had tried to give the masks to Jonas and Atticus, knowing they were the two most valuable fighters. But they both refused. Jonas, if need be, hoped that he would be able to use his cognivant powers to protect him, and maybe the others, from Maltheil's dangerous breath. Atticus refused with admission that he had spells that should protect him.

Bearit glanced over at Tyril. The young warrior's face was set in stone, focused, and taciturn. "Do you think these will protect us?" he asked, holding the mask that Peron had given him.

"If anyone could design a mask to protect its wearer from the beast's breath, it would be Peron," Tyril said.

"If the beast breathes," Atticus said, opening his eyes from his deep meditation, "then do not stay before it for long, despite the mask. If the mask does work, it will likely only protect you for a short period of time."

"Wise advise," Jonas added.

Atticus stood up from the edge of the bridge. Looking back he saw the cavalry behind them, the big warhorses shifting their shod hooves on the stone bridge, the clacking noise the only sound. No one was talking, the seriousness of the task at hand silencing them. "Remember," Atticus said, looking at them all. "The demon hates me the most. Maltheil will want to kill me, to exact its revenge on me for its two thousand year prison. Stay behind me. When I open the gate the beast will feel the magic, but will not see it." Atticus had already cast a shielding over the gateway. "My hopes are that the beast will feel the magic, but not know its source. If we can get it to charge us, then it will fall through the gate. Then we jump in behind it."

"When you appear on the other side, you may be nauseas," Jonas warned. "You need to fight through that quickly. Your life may depend on it."

"If I'm to be honest," Korrin, the veteran Red Guard Captain, said, "it's not dying that scares me, it's being left behind in that horrible place."

"We will make it," Jonas said with steel in his voice.

"Let me go first," Atticus said. "I have the return stone. Without it, you will not be able to get back home."

Everyone nodded, too nervous to say anything, except Korrin. The dark haired warrior casually held his sword at the side, his blue eyes scanning each man. "I'm honored to fight with you all. Your courage gives me hope, and despite what happens to us, our bravery will be a blow to the darkness."

"Well said," Jonas added. Jonas's mind had been occupied with the plan for the last day and a half. And now that it was upon them, it seemed surreal, like they were trapped in a nightmare. He had fought demons before, but the idea of following one to the hellish sixth plane made even him hesitant. But what choice did they have? He glanced over at Bearit, his concern for the young man evident. He had tried to dissuade him from joining the group, but he wouldn't listen. Jonas tried to argue that it was not his fight, but the young logger flipped his argument around on him and told him that it was more his fight than Jonas's. After all, the demon was in his homeland, not Jonas's. He felt a strong desire to protect it, and although his decision seemed foolish to Jonas, he had to admit that he was proud of him. His choice in saving the young man had been justified several times now, the young logger's actions testament to backing Jonas's decision. *All we can do is our best,* Jonas thought.

Tulari suddenly appeared from the edge of the shadowy forest, her massive size startling them, snapping them from their nervous tension. She ran towards them, her massive head held low. *They come*, she said in Jonas's mind.

Jonas nocked an arrow, the movement freezing the others in place. "Prepare yourselves," Jonas said, his voice low, his unblinking gaze finding each one. "They are near."

CHAPTER NINE

They heard the demon horde before they saw it. The terrifying sounds of screeches and howls found them first, followed by the cracking and crunching of broken branches as thousands of demon-spawn moved towards them, some occupying the road, while most pushed their way through the forest. Hundreds of pale lithe bodies leapt from tree to tree, their sharp claws carrying them quickly through the canopy, branches swaying, while others, wearing armor and swords, cut their way through the dense forest below, never tiring, their only goal to serve their master.

Maltheil was easy to spot, its wolf-like head cresting the gentle hill before the road flattened out to the east side of the bridge, its colossal body following in long strides. The evening shadows veiled the tree lined road, but still the demon's dark form was somehow discernable, its evil radiating from it, impossible to miss, red eyes intense with rage. Beside it marched armored Red Guard soldiers and Tur'el warriors alike, oblivious of how just hours before their standards were at odds, but now their uniforms mattered little. They were all of one body and mind, and that was to serve Maltheil. Baylock Reen, wearing his Battle Lord helm and carrying a steel war shield, walked just behind the demon, not capable of matching the beast's huge strides.

As Maltheil neared, tree branches hanging over the road shrunk away, green leaves dying and turning to dust as the beast passed. The closer they got, the clearer Maltheil's power and size became. If Atticus got on Jonas's shoulder, the demon would still be a few heads taller. One long muscular arm hung past its knee, the other carried a sizable bone club, resting the sapling sized weapon over its shoulder.

Thousands of demon-spawn busted through the thick brush along the river's edge spanning both sides for as far as they could see. The demon spawn screeched hauntingly, the bald headed servants standing eerily still, weapons held low. They would have to cross the river to pass, impossible in the turbulent current, so now they waited on their master's call.

Maltheil stopped before the entrance of the bridge, lowering its massive club to the side. Baylock Reen stopped beside the beast as the rest of its army filled the road behind them until their numbers vanished beyond the hill.

"In Toolm's name," Bearit whispered, his steadfastness faltering.

"That's my father," Tyril said, his voice strained with grief.

"He is no longer," Atticus warned. "Focus your mind. That is just your father's shell, nothing more." His good hearted attitude was gone, replaced with a sternness backed by an indomitable will.

"Calm your nerves," Jonas said. "I've killed powerful demons before, rest assured, they can die." Jonas matched Atticus's intenseness, his own jaw set to the task at hand. Any thought of defeat was squashed, his focus on the steps necessary to achieve their victory.

"Remember," Atticus warned. "Follow my lead."

Maltheil's powerful voice suddenly rocked them back on their heels, like a focused gust of wind had struck them. But there was no wind, the demon's power propelled by its words. "Druid," Maltheil boomed. "I've been waiting a long time to make you suffer."

Back down the line the horses pranced nervously, the sound of Maltheil's voice nearly shattering their ardent will. Captain Engle had never seen anything like the demon before, and his heart pounded in his chest. He knew his men felt the same fear, and he wanted desperately to ease their angst, to lift their morale, but no words came to mind as he wrestled with the overwhelming fear evoked by the creature.

Peron looked on from the other side, his position near the edge of the bridge allowing him a decent view of the demon. "How will they kill that thing?" he said softly to himself, panic making it hard for him to breath. Kylin was next to him, her hand to her mouth in shock. She had frozen with fear when the lesser demons had attacked them the other night, but now, despite the distance from Maltheil, she felt inadequate in its presence, and that impotent feeling could not be shaken.

Atticus stepped forward, an arrow nocked to his bow. Jonas stood just to his side, the others flanking him further. He had already cast the shielding spell, and once cast, required no further concentration. The question was when to open the gate. It would not take him long, but he didn't want to complete the task too early, as it did require some concentration on his part to keep the gate open. "Maltheil!" Atticus yelled. "You do not belong here! Your very presence offends me and this land! Go back home, or die, those are your choices!"

"How can we defeat it?" Korrin whispered, shaking his head, his sword arm trembling.

Jonas's eyes narrowed intensely. "Fight it," he hissed. "You are strong enough. Dig deep, find your courage, it is there, waiting."

Bearit stepped closer to Jonas, his huge axe held effortlessly. "Like you said, it can die." And despite the subtle shake of his hands, he nodded towards Korrin. "We will kill it." His tone was sharp, and matter-of-fact, no room for reproach. Jonas was impressed with his resolve, his ability to break through the demon's innate ability to spread dread to all around it.

Korrin looked at him, and took several deep breaths, finding strength from the young man. He set his jaw, the lines around his eyes deepening as he focused on holding onto his courage. He didn't say anything in response, but nodded his head in gratitude. Jonas looked at Bearit, again feeling validated for his decision to not only save him, but to teach him.

"I smell the light of Shyann!" Maltheil continued, the demons red eyes flaring brightly. "Something I shall have to extinguish!"

This time Jonas spoke. "Your brethren have threatened that before! But I am here, and they are not!"

"Everything comes to an end! So you five are the land's best defense? Let us see if you are worthy!" And without much warning, Maltheil lifted his bone staff and pointed it at them. "Kill them!"

"Make sure to stay in front of the shielding!" Atticus yelled as he jumped forward, his bow twanging as arrows flew at the charging enemy. Jonas joined Atticus and together they assailed the charging enemy with a barrage of arrows faster and more overwhelming than anyone had ever seen. Five, ten, fifteen, shafts ripped across the clearing in a few heartbeats, hammering into flesh, many of the dead flying into others, creating a tumbled mess of bodies near the entrance of the bridge.

But still they came, swords and shields coming at them with no sense of organization. Jonas kept his bow in one hand, drawing a sword in the other. It was not the first time he fought with the bow, its magical properties making it impervious to attacks. Even the string could not be broken and the enchanted wood bow could be used to block and parry, killing with his blade. Atticus kept his bow low, drawing his sword and wielding it with one hand. Tyril leapt into the gap between them, and together they met the onslaught of bald headed warriors. All three blocked and dodged, cut and stabbed, killing and kicking the bodies away. They fought on, bodies piling up before them, but still they came.

Baylock Reen was suddenly before Tyril, his shield bristling with four arrows, his emotionless eyes barely visible beyond the slits of his black plumed helm. Down came his sword and Tyril met it with his own shield. They exchanged blow after blow, Tyril experiencing the familiar strength of his father. But something wasn't the same. He could hear him grunt and growl behind the steel helm, but he lacked the speed and technique of his father's mind. But he was still the Battle Lord, and with skill worthy of the title he flicked his wrist and rolled the tip of his sword around Tyril's block, the edge of his blade nicking his exposed bicep, drawing a bead of red. Tyril growled as he spun his shield before him, knocking his father's sword out the way and following it with a lighting quick riposte. The enemy fighters around them were pressing forward with no sense of organization, something that worked in Tyril's favor. As he attacked, enemy warriors behind Baylock shoved him forward with their shields, eager to draw the blood of their enemies. Tyril's sword found his father's chest as the Battle Lord was knocked forward by his own men, his blessed blade splitting his armor and cutting his heart in two. Just like that, he fell to the side as the enemy pushed forward. Tyril lanced another man in the gut, but a flanking attacker brought his shield down on his blade, slamming it into the stone pavers. A typical sword would have shattered, but Tyril's, now enchanted by a High Priest of Toolm, held. But he could not get the sword back in position, or his shield, to block the shield charge. Turning at the last minute, and angling his shield toward the attack, a Tur'el shield slammed into his shoulder, beating him backward. Luckily his own shield impeded the power, the attack shoving him backward but offering no serious injury other than a bruised shoulder.

Without missing a beat, Bearit glided past him, his axe already descending, splitting the man's head in two. Taking Tyril's place, Bearit went to work blocking and cutting, and along with the deadly efficiency of Jonas and Atticus beside him, killed many more. It wasn't long before the pile of bodies was so high, that the enemy had to climb over them to get at the defenders, who were forced to back up to the edge of the shielding.

On the other side of the bridge, Peron dismounted as the sounds of battle assaulted them. "Where are you going, my King?" Lord Caynon asked.

"To the front," Peron said. "I need to see what is happening."

"That is not wise," Lord Caynon warned. "We cannot lose you."

Peron wondered if he really meant that. He thought of himself as rather insignificant, and assumed that when the recent circumstances had thrown him into the mantle of king, that others felt the same way. Perhaps it was only him thinking it. It was a fleeting thought, and he smiled at his adviser. "And you won't," he said, running to the bridge and jumping onto the narrow ledge.

"Wait for me," Kylin said as she too jumped from her horse to follow him onto the railing. The bridge railings were built of heavy stone that rose to waist height, and were half that wide. It was plenty wide for Peron to safely run on. As he ran by the cavalry, the Red Guard soldiers slammed their swords to their light bucklers, chanting his name, thinking he was running toward danger.

When he got to the front, Captain Engler looked down at him from his horse. The Captain's face was tense. From their vantage point, they had a very clear view of the fighting that was taking place no more than twenty paces away. "My King, what are you doing here?"

"I cannot see," Peron said, standing tall to get a better view. His eyes grew wide as he watched the enemy crash against the seemingly impenetrable wall of steel. There were so many dead piled up before them that the ranks of enemy attackers began to slow.

"I've never seen anything like it," Captain Engler said. "Jonas and Atticus have killed more than I can count." The warrior was clearly enthralled by the dazzling display of martial skill.

Back at the fight the enemy finally stopped attacking. Jonas, Bearit, and Atticus backed up slowly, barely able to see above the pile of bodies, stopping just before the shielding. Bearit was exhausted, and Korrin took his place. Tulari hung back, waiting for her chance to take part in the battle.

"Eat the bread I gave you, quickly," Atticus whispered. They all reached into their pockets and quickly withdrew a small cake, eating it hastily. He had told them of the nourishing properties of it, and that it could sustain them through combat for many hours, even without water. Looking up, they saw the upper body of Maltheil walk towards them, the beast's huge bone staff held easily in its right hand. "Here he comes," Atticus said. "Put on your masks." Atticus didn't have to say anything to Jonas, who had already dropped into the state of Ty'erm, focusing his mind on the energy around him, pulling it in and amassing it before him, preparing the energy for immediate use.

Everyone readied themselves. Jonas and Atticus sheathed their blades, nocking an arrow to their ready bows. Korrin, Bearit, and Tyril had placed the masks over their faces, drawing the string tight. The grease along the edge of the mask had been applied liberally, and when the soft edge pressed against their necks the grease oozed out, hopefully making a tight seal. They could not see well, but it was better than becoming servants to the demon.

Maltheil stopped before the huge pile of bodies, and without pausing, swung its club back and forth before him. Bodies, two and three at a time, were tossed over the side of the bridge. Several moments later and the pile of bodies was cleared, and standing not more than ten paces from them was the massive body of Maltheil, fear rolling off it in waves.

Jonas felt the fear hit him again, this time more powerful, and fought it off, but knew that the others would be struggling. Willing Shyann's light, his cuirass lit up, brightly casting a white blue glow around them. The light did not have the strength and power of a cavalier's light, but it did have a similar effect, deadening the fear and giving those around him hope.

Korrin stepped closer to him, his sword held high. "Thank you." His voice was muffled through the mask, and Jonas had to admit that he looked quite frightening.

Maltheil's black lips curled back, exposing rows of sharp teeth. His great bone club swung threateningly before it, the weight and power so great that they could feel the displaced air. "Time to die," the beast said, its head rearing back to breathe.

As planned, Atticus ducked backwards as Tyril took his place; simultaneously Jonas pushed a wall of translucent energy before them, forming a wedge that blocked the entire width of the bridge. Red steam shot from the demon's mouth, striking the wall of energy and rolling off it to the sides, most of it harmlessly falling away over the edge of the bridge. Some however swirled around the shield, engulfing Korrin and Bearit, who were both on the edges of the bridge, before drifting harmlessly away. Nothing seemed to happen to them, and Jonas silently thanked Peron for his inventiveness.

Atticus began his chant, keeping his words low as he opened the gate behind the shielding. In the meantime, Maltheil stopped its breath and moments after Jonas dissipated the wall, drawing his bow and releasing an arrow, hoping to distract Maltheil before the beast learned what Atticus was up too. They knew that the demon could detect magic, but they hoped they could occupy its attention with relentless attacks, angering it so much that it would charge without reservation.

Jonas's arrow struck the beast in the neck, snapping its head back with a flash of blue light. Howling in rage, Maltheil stepped forward and swung its club in a deadly arc. As the club descended dangerously fast, Korrin ducked below it, the peak of its arc higher where he stood. But Tyril was not so lucky. He tried to jump back, throwing up his shield at the last moment once he realized he was not going to avoid the weapon. The edge of the spiked club struck the shield, spinning him around and catapulting him towards Jonas. But Jonas was already moving, his magical boots reacting impossibly fast. To everyone's astonishment, Jonas jumped high, above the club and Tyril, his right foot planting on the demon's wrist as it swung by. Pushing off it, he drew his blade in one smooth motion, the razor edge lit in blue light arcing across the demon's thick chest. Again Maltheil howled and stumbled back a few steps, Jonas landing softly just before it. Black blood poured from the deep cut across its muscled chest, but it seemed to have little effect. Maltheil kicked out with its huge foot, and Jonas barely avoided it, spinning away and leaping back, hoping to distance himself from the creature's attacks.

"Hey!" Atticus yelled, standing high on the edge of the bridge just to the side of the shielding. The gateway was open, a black swirling hole spanning the width of the bridge. But Maltheil couldn't see it, its swirling blackness hidden by the shielding. His bow was drawn and he released the shaft. Maltheil took the arrow in the shoulder as it turned to try and avoid the missile.

By this time Bearit, Korrin, Tyril, and Tulari, had made their way around the shielding, standing behind it. Tyril's arm hurt badly, but luckily the club just clipped his shield. If it hadn't, his arm would be broken, or likely worse. From Maltheil's viewpoint, they simply disappeared. To the demon, it looked like the bridge before it was now unoccupied, minus the row of cavalry over twenty paces away. It was an illusion of course, the druid's shielding hiding what was really there. Jonas was still standing in front of the shielding, and Atticus was on the edge, but the others had simply vanished, shielded by the spell.

But Atticus didn't want Maltheil to have time to ponder where they went. They had to anger the demon, to keep the beast busy, or their plan would not work. Following the arrow, Atticus jumped down from the ledge to stand next to Jonas. He would not do well in a fight, having to concentrate on the task at keeping the gateway open. But he could manage. He hoped it would be enough. He drew again, releasing a shaft. This time the arrow struck Maltheil in the chest, a flash of light following as it buried deep into its flesh.

The demon's red eyes flared and it charged them, its powerful weapon swinging dangerously before it. This time the demon resorted to magic as well as the physical attack, something they were not prepared for as they knew very little what the beast was capable of in that arena. The stone under Atticus's feet suddenly turned to mud, dropping him into the muck just below his knees. Frantic, he tried to evade the club, but his movements were hampered by the thick sludge clinging to him. Jonas saw the club descent and knew that Atticus was in trouble, and there was no doubt, that if that weapon hit him head on, that he would be killed.

Reaching for his powers, he hastily formed a weak shield before the druid. He did not have the time to fashion a proper defense, and the powerful club smashed through it, striking Atticus in the chest and launching him from the mud so high that he flew over the shielding to land in a heap near the others. The attack was devastating, but Jonas's hastily formed shield reduced the power of the impact, perhaps saving his life. In a flash the gateway closed.

Jonas stood alone before the beast, unsure if Atticus still lived. But he had no time to contemplate the druid's fate, as the demon was barreling forward, its club reversing and coming towards him. Rather than stay and attack the beast, Jonas wanted to keep Maltheil moving, hoping that it would stumble unknowingly into the gateway. So he turned and ran, narrowly escaping the club, the powerful weapon swooshing behind his back. Please be open, Jonas chanted in his mind as he jumped impossibly high over the shielding, Maltheil close on his heels.

Pain lanced through Atticus as he tumbled to a halt. Both his ankles were broken, snapped as he was launched from the magically induced hole. He felt pain in his side and arm, likely broken ribs and more. His mind swam and he faltered, the magic holding the gate open teetering tenuously in his mind, the gate flashing shut. Digging deep, knowing that their plan depended on it, he fought the pain away, shoving it deep below his consciousness, focusing his mind again on the task at hand. Wrestling with the pain, he fought it, finding once again the words to the spell. Looking up, he saw Jonas leap incredibly high over the shielding, the tall head of Maltheil just behind him. Three more steps and he would be on the portal. Closing his eyes he slammed the pain down, saying the words to the spell flawlessly, his agony buried below a purpose so strong that it could not win. The gate flashed open as Jonas landed beside him. Spinning around, Jonas, along with Bearit, Tyril, Korrin, and Tulari, faced the demon as the great beast stepped past the shielding, its club angling down towards them. But instead of setting its foot on stable ground, it disappeared into the black hole, throwing the creature off balance as it tumbled into the portal, its deadly club striking the edge of the breach, knocking the weapon from its grip to tumble over the side of the bridge. In a flash, the demon was gone.

"Go!" Atticus yelled through clenched teeth. He didn't know how much longer he could maintain consciousness. His wounds were so severe that pain erupted all across his body, shooting like burning lightening to all four limbs.

Without hesitation Jonas jumped into the hole, followed by Bearit and the others. As he entered, disorientation following, Jonas realized one fatal error...Atticus carried the return stone.

Peron was glued to the battle, as was everyone on the bridge who could see. When Atticus's body flew over the shielding, his heart sunk. "No," he cried, moving forward on the ledge. Then the demon pushed through the shielding and fell through the portal, and moments later the other followed. *Atticus has the stone*, he screamed in his mind.

Without thinking Peron ran forward and skidded next to Atticus's body. The shield was flashing in and out and the druid's eyes snapped open when he felt Peron beside him. "I...can't...keep it open," he stammered. Then he narrowed his eyes, his impressive will pushing through his bodies desire to find sleep, to free him from the pain. He pushed one more time, his mind focused on keeping the gate open. "Go!" he screamed.

Peron looked at the hole and the flashing stopped, the swirling blackness solidifying once again. He had no time. Without a second look back, he jumped into the hole.

Atticus finally lost the fight, the pain easing away as he lost consciousness. The gateway snapped shut and the shielding evaporated, leaving Atticus's body behind, backed by Red Guard cavalry, staring at an army of demon-spawn. The army howled, and then they charged.

CHAPTER TEN

Jonas was ejected from the portal landing on black rock, the smell of sulfur and brimstone smacking his senses immediately. Bearit, Tulari, Korrin, and Tyril followed, stumbling through the portal as they tried to orientate themselves. Jonas's head swam as he pushed away the nausea. Both Bearit and Tyril dropped to their knees, keeping themselves from falling over; their spinning minds nearly overwhelming them. Tulari stood strong, growling.

Maltheil was before them, and the great beast wasted no time in attacking, his anger so deep and powerful that it radiated from the demon like light from the sun. Stepping forward, the demon leaned forward and black gas shot from its gaping teeth filled maw.

"Look out!" Jonas shouted, bringing forth his cognitive powers. Their surroundings, however different, was still made up of the same things, particles of energy so small that even Jonas figured what he could see in his mind's eye was just a glimpse of their diminutive size. Again, he had no time to weave an adequate shield, and seeing the different color of the gas worried him greatly. A weak wall of energy formed before them, and the gas struck it, rolling around it. But some pushed through, wisps of blackness falling upon them.

Jonas and Tulari moved aside quickly, and Bearit and Tyril somehow broke through their dizziness to stumble to the side, leaving Korrin slowly standing as small clouds of the mist struck him. Instantly he screamed, the smell of burning flesh assaulting them as they all ran to the demon's flanks. Korrin, still screaming, followed, moving as fast as he could through the pain and nausea to distance himself from the deadly burning gas.

The black steam disappeared as Jonas attacked the demon, Tulari moving quickly around Maltheil, her fur now black to match the landscape. The terrain was a mixture of black dirt and rock, stone formations jutting from the ground all around them. Some were as tall as a man, others, huge, like the spines of a dragon bursting from the ground. In the distance were bigger ones still, huge ranges of black stone, the horizon shades of red and orange, accentuated by brush strokes of gray clouds. Black tree-like formations were peppered all around, their spiny branches like black bones and sharp claws hanging from the trunks. Pockets of steam rose from the ground, and occasionally pits of fire burned, giving the surroundings the look of a long ago burned and destroyed forest.

Jonas's bow thrummed and three arrows struck the beast in the chest. Roaring, Maltheil stepped towards him just as a huge sword of fire appeared in the beast's hands, the fiery blade coming for him with inhuman speed as the beast's long strides brought him quickly before Jonas.

"We must kill him quickly!" Jonas yelled, digging deep again for his cognivant ability, knowing that if he were to block the massive flame sword with his own blades, that its power would likely crush his arm, or perhaps worse. So he spun energy around his left arm, the one holding his bow, forming a blue translucent shield just as the great sword swung down. The blade hit the shield and fire erupted, and despite the size and power of the demon, it did not move Jonas's shield arm any more than it would if struck by a normal sword. Jonas attacked quickly, darting inside the demon's reach, the edge of his blade glowing blue as its edge dug deep into the flesh of the demon's legs.

Faster than Jonas thought possible, Maltheil reached under him, its long arm snapping for him.

Jonas, sensing the attack, tried to spin away and distance himself from the beast, but the demon's long clawed fingers hooked his cloak, ripping him from the ground and flinging him into the air like a rock thrown from a catapult.

As Jonas flew through the air, Tulari leaped upon the demon's back, sharp claws like daggers raking its flesh as her huge mouth clamped on the top of its shoulder. Maltheil roared in pain and reached back, grabbing Tulari by her black fur, the beast's sharp claws digging in deep, and flung her easily over its shoulder. Tulari struck a rock structure and one didn't have to be close to hear bones break.

Tyril and Bearit, now in full control of their senses, ran at Maltheil's back, their sword and axe hacking at its thighs like a logger cutting down a tree. Maltheil spun, its fire sword coming around. Tyril twisted at the last moment and the blade flashed by, the heat from the weapon burning his cheek.

Bearit saw the attack but the demon was so fast, and all he had time to do was hold his axe before him, hoping that the blade would not snap it and then cut him in half. The fire blade struck Bearit's weapon in the middle of the shaft. There was a flash of light as the blessed weapon held, but the power was enough to pitch Bearit into the air. If it wasn't for his prodigious strength, he probably would have broken his arms. Instead, he landed on the hard rock and slid five paces, scorched wrists and a few bruises his only injuries.

Back at the portal, Peron dropped through the opening and stumbled to his knees, the gateway flashing shut behind him. It took him a moment to wrestle with the nausea, the stagnant thick air doing little to help. He heard the fighting and after a few moments was able to make out the scene. Maltheil was locked in battle with Bearit and Tyril, while Korrin was nearby, trying to stand and moaning in pain. They still wore his masks, so that was good. He didn't know what to do, or how he could fit in. He knew that he would be no match for the demon, and if he were even able to work up the courage to attack, his actions might get in the way of the others. Looking around, his heart beating nervously, he hastily looked around hoping for any ideas to spring to mind. He needed to do something to help.

Jonas stood, his body bruised but nothing seemed broken. His heart was pounding with fear as he saw Tyril and Bearit engage the demon. Running with great speed, he planted his right foot on a black stone, using it as leverage he jumped to the top of another formation that was much higher. Sheathing his blade smoothly, he drew shaft after shaft, the black arrows covering the distance in a blink to pound into the demon's back. Flashes of light followed each one, and after three, the demon roared loudly in pain, spinning, its red eyes finding Jonas with murderous intent.

Tyril took advantage of the demon's distraction and rammed his blade straight into Maltheil's thigh. The blessed weapon parted scaly flesh and sunk two hand spans into its leg. Like a horse kicking its trainer, Maltheil roared and snapped that leg back and struck Tyril in his shield arm, hitting him so hard that he flew over ten paces away. He rolled and tumbled over the hard black ground, finally stopping, his arm bent at an awkward angle, the weight of the shield causing him further pain.

As they fought, Peron was sneaking through the shadows, running from one stone formation to another, heading to a small ledge of stone that overlooked the fighting. Perhaps he would get a better view and come up with a way to help. Howls in the distance froze him still, his shaking body pressed up against a black rock sticking from the earth like a dark spike. Something else was out there, and it was heading in their direction. Taking a few deep breaths, Peron moved and ran to the stone ledge. It was no more than five paces high, and the black stone offered many hand and foot holds with which to climb. The howls came again, but closer, and they ate away at his resolve. Trying his best to find his nerve, he began to climb.

Jonas got three more arrows off, all finding their marks before Maltheil was close enough to bring the fire sword to bear. The stone structure he was on put him at the demon's head height, and the massive blade came around, striking the base of the stone, shattering it in an awesome display of power. Instead of leaping away, Jonas jumped forward, and to the demon's dismay, placed his foot on the top of its head, using it to jump further still, somersaulting through the air to land on his feet behind the beast. Again his arm was up and two arrows slammed into the demon's back.

Maltheil turned to face him, and if Jonas didn't know better he thought the beast moved slower, with less power. The countless arrows and other attacks seemed to barely hamper the demon, but perhaps they were beginning to take their toll. The demon paused as howls filled the dark night, or day, one could not tell. "My servants come," Maltheil hissed. "You will pay for what you've done."

Bearit ran to stand next to Jonas, with Tulari, blood drenching her fur, doing the same. Maltheil moved to the side near a rock ledge, its fire sword held low. It looked as if the beast was using the ledge to protect it from attacks from the rear. Jonas smiled, knowing at that moment that they had indeed hurt the beast. Maltheil was taking them more seriously, but he was also stalling, waiting for his servants to arrive.

Back with Korrin, the injured Red Guard captain knelt next to Tyril. "Are you okay?"

Tyril moaned, his shattered arm sending waves of lightning pain up his side. "My arm is broken. Take off my mask, I cannot breathe well."

Korrin reached down with burned arms and slowly took off Tyril's mask. Then he helped him unbuckle the shield, trying his best to not cause him further pain. Tyril moaned in agony and gritted his teeth, doing his best to not cry out. Korrin's flesh was burned in numerous places but he pushed past the anguish and re-buckled Tyril's shield, placing his own arm through the straps. "We'll be back for you." Then he got up and ran towards the fight.

"We must kill him now," Jonas warned. "If the beast's servants arrive, we will not have a chance." As if to accentuate the point, the howls grew louder. They were nearly upon them. Korrin joined them, Tyril's shield held before him. "Does he live?" Jonas asked. They knew he was speaking of Tyril.

"Yes," Korrin responded, his voice muffled from the mask and clearly strained, his own pain nearly unbearable.

"Atticus never made it, did he?" Bearit asked.

Maltheil was not attacking, waiting for his servants to arrive, or perhaps healing itself, something they could not let happen.

"No," Jonas said. There was nothing else to say. Each of them had known the dangers when agreeing to the plan, and none of them now saw any sense in worrying about their fates. They had one task now, and that was to kill the demon.

Jonas nodded to them and brought his bow up, and together they attacked. More arrows struck the demon as they all came together. Maltheil brought the great sword across its body, aiming for Bearit and Korrin who attacked while Tulari had leapt high and Jonas hung back, his arrows continuing to hit their marks. Korrin dove forward narrowly avoiding the flaming sword, springing up under the creature and ramming his sword up into Maltheil's stomach. Bearit saw the flaming sword coming and pivoted his body, spinning by it and using the blade of his axe to push it away. The fire burned his flesh but he kept his momentum going, swinging the axe around and striking Maltheil's left leg with all the power he could muster. The sharp blade buried itself deep, stopping when it hit bone. Maltheil's cry of pain was louder than any they had ever heard, but still the demon would not relent. Bringing his hands together, he brought both fists down, including the pommel of the sword, on Korrin's head. The move was so fast, fueled by the pain from Bearit's wound, that Korrin had no time to avoid the strike. He looked up, and in a flash Maltheil's fists smashed through his head, pounding his dead and broken body into the ground. Great anger coursed through the demon's body and he brought those same fists to bear, swinging them mightily across his body towards Bearit.

Then Tulari struck the beast in the chest, knocking it back into the stone ledge, her claws ripping into it once again. This time her powerful jaw clamped onto the demon's thick neck.

Maltheil roared and flailed, dropping its sword the beast brought both hands around Tulari's strong body, its black claws ripping into her flesh. But still she held on, her mighty jaws snapping, teeth ripping and tearing at the beast's neck. Howling louder, Maltheil used its magic, and in one great burst of power, the demon's body glowed red. Then, moments later, its body erupted in fire. Tulari was propelled into the air, her fur and flesh scorched badly. Bearit too was knocked from his feet, the power of the explosion sending him through the air to land next to Jonas, who had also been blown from his feet.

They slowly got up as Maltheil leaned against the rock ledge. Arrows riddled the demon's body and black blood gushed from many devastating wounds. The worst was its ripped and torn neck. More howl's shattered the silence precluding the intense violence. Within moments they would be overrun by Maltheil's minions, and he would use his powers to heal himself. Korrin was dead, and Bearit was burned so badly that he was forced to take off his mask, the leather and cloth destroyed by the fire. Black burns covered his arms and snaked up the side of his neck, one ear a shriveled black mess. His face was tight as he wrestled with the pain, but still he stood tall, his burnt hands holding his axe. Tyril limped to them, his left arm hanging limply, his face pale even in the shadowy light. Tulari lay on her side nearby, whimpering through the pain. She struggled to rise, but could not, two of her legs burnt and blacked from the fire, her coat drenched in blood.

"You have done well," Maltheil said, the demons voice low, lacking its previous bravado and power. "But my servants will kill you, and I will heal. The end is the same. You will die."

Peron held his pitiful sword in both hands, the blade shaking as fear flooded through him. He could see Maltheil's head just above the ledge, and he crouched no more than four paces away, behind a chunk of black stone. He could not tell exactly what had happened, and nor could he see his friends from his vantage point. But the way the demon leaned against the stone, and the fact that he was not attacking, leant one to think that he was seriously injured. The howls came again, and this time Peron knew that what was out there would be upon them soon. He closed his eyes and took a deep breath, releasing the air slowly and trying his best to overcome his fear. Looking at his sword arm, the blade shook, uncontrollable nervous energy getting the best of him.

"We must attack now!" Jonas yelled, "Or the beast will heal and his servants will converge on us!"

Tyril narrowed his eyes and dug deep for the last of his strength. Bearit glanced at him, a knowing look passing between them. Then they charged.

Jonas drew back on his bow as the two injured men attacked with the last of their strength. His arrows slammed into the demon as the beast kicked out with its clawed foot. Bearit, slow from exhaustion and pain, tried to spin away, but the creature's foot clipped him in the shoulder and sent him sprawling to the hard ground.

Tyril's left arm hung useless at his side and as he ran fiery pain shot through is body. Grunting away the pain, his sword arm carried his blade down and across the demon's exposed leg, cutting deeply into its flesh. Howling, Maltheil quickly retracted its leg, its left arm snaking down simultaneously like a striking adder and grabbing Tyril around the sword arm and lifting him high, dangling him in the air like a caught rat. Tyril screamed as new pain shot through his broken arm.

Several more of Jonas's arrows struck the demon in the chest, and a third sheared off his thick skull. Maltheil's eyes glowed red in anger as the sting of Jonas's arrows took their toll. The beast brought forth its inherent magic, and instantly a globe of blackness surrounded Jonas. Then the demon turned its glowing eyes, dripping with hatred, on Tyril, who was swaying helplessly before it.

Peron's eyes widened as he saw his friend dangling dangerously in the air. Suddenly his sword arm stopped shaking, the nervous energy pounded down by something else, something primal that he had never felt before. He thought of all the sacrifices his friends have made. He thought of all the soldiers that were likely dying now, fighting on the bridge while he hid behind a rock. And that was enough. Opening his eyes, he ran from the protection of the stone, covering the four paces quickly and without a second thought he leapt from the cliff edge.

Jonas had no idea what was happening, the blackness around him thick like oil. Running and diving to his left, he quickly rolled free from the darkness, rising to his feet to an astonishing site. Jonas's breath caught in his throat when he glimpsed Peron jump off the ledge, his sword angled down towards Maltheil. He was even more amazed when he landed on Maltheil's shoulders, his rapier coming down hard, the sharp narrow blade busting through the demon's skull and burying itself hilt deep in the top of its head.

Maltheil's body went rigid and bolted upright, ejecting Peron into the air and dropping Tyril to the ground. Howls spun Jonas around, and converging on them from the darkness were human-like shapes, their pale white skin emerging from the shadows. Their legs and arms were human in appearance, but misshapen, their claws and toes capped with sharp claws. Their heads were equally misshapen, with bulging elongated skulls, red eyes, and large mouths filled with teeth. They screeched and howled, their awkward gate propelling them forward faster as they saw their prey. There were easily fifty of them, and more appeared from the darkness every moment.

Jonas ran to Peron who was getting up slowly from the ground. "Come quickly!" he yelled to the others as he helped Peron up. The young king's face was bleeding from a bad cut across his skull, but other than that he seemed intact. Jonas guided Peron to Tulari's moaning body and the others joined them. Tyril could barely move, but the presence of his friend somehow gave him the energy to stand and limp towards them. Bearit's face was ashen and his movements slow, the pain of his burns apparent as he struggled to stumble to them. "Do you have the stone!" Jonas yelled as he rose and drew his bow, firing two arrows into a few lesser demons that were getting close.

"Yes," Peron said, the advancing demons enough to shake him from the dizziness of his fall. He reached into his pocket and pulled out the stone. Bearit growled like an animal, masking the pain as he cut a reaching demon down. In moments they would be overrun. "Smash it!" Jonas roared, firing his bow again, killing three more demons as they neared.

"Wait!" Bearit yelled as he somehow managed to find more strength to run towards Korrin's body. A few of the lesser demons were already there and Bearit, despite his injuries, swung his axe with all his remaining strength, cutting left and right into the reaching demons, his defiant howls helping him wrestle with the pain. He looked like a berserker as he roared and killed three lesser demons before reaching Korrin's body.

"Bearit!" Jonas screamed, his bow firing again and again, his enchanted arrows piercing demon flesh and spinning the bodies away from Bearit.

Bearit reached down and with an incredible amount of strength, a power born from something deep within him, he lifted Korrin's body and slung it over his shoulder. His burns were exploding in agony, but he growled it away and ran back to the others, his heavy axe, wielded with one hand, cutting down a reaching demon. Jonas arrows blurred by him, taking several more down just before Bearit reached them, his eyes wild with adrenaline, his chest heaving up and down as he held Korrin's body.

Jonas looked at his friend, an understanding flashing between them. The young man was not going to leave the body in this forsaken place. More creatures came at them as Jonas looked at Peron, his bow already back in position. "Now!"

Peron grabbed a black rock and brought it down upon the blue stone. Instantly there was a flash, and energy shot from the stone, its power coalescing into a spinning vortex. Blue light from the stone continued to pour from it, disappearing into the vortex. It was that energy that had opened the portal, and that very energy was seeking the stone on the other side, and Jonas knew, that once the blue energy left the stone, that the portal would close. "Go!" he yelled. "Quickly."

Bearit, Tyril, and Peron jumped through the portal. Jonas backed up to it, his bow firing again and again. Tulari tried to stand, but she could not rise, her legs too far gone to put any weight on. *Go*, she said to Jonas.

"No!" Jonas growled and dug deep for more cognitive energy, all the while firing his bow faster than even he thought possible. He was not going to leave

Tulari to die in this place. Taking the swirling particles around him, he wrapped them around Tulari's body, his bow twanging rapidly at the same time. The mental concentration required to perform both tasks was immense, and Jonas felt the pain of a debilitating headache rush to the surface. More demons fell, and with one great heave of strength and power, he pulled Tulari towards him, the force of the pull knocking her heavy body into him, and together they tumbled through the portal just as the blue energy dissipated.

The portal flashed, and then it was gone.

Epilogue

The dining hall was clamorous, laughter and music pervading the large room. Servants bustled about, carrying trays laden with succulent fruits, cooked vegetables, roasted meats, and pitchers of ale and wine, the best that Lanard could provide. Large opulently set wood tables flanked the room, a long aisle covered in thick carpet woven in gold and red cloth running down the center. The aisle ran to the base of a set of stairs that rose to another platform, occupied by two beautifully built tables on either side. Here sat select nobles and officers. The stairs continued to rise another five paces to the top level, the center of which was occupied by the king's table. The exquisite table was accentuated by legs carved into the paws of a dragon, and the palatial setting was dominated by flowers and silver dinnerware. More vibrant flowers of red and white grew from huge stone planters placed all around the upper platform and the king's table.

Huge beams, each one honed from massive trees, lined the hall, intricate carvings snaking up their entire length to disappear in the shadows of the high ceiling. Several more, these two even larger, were on either side of the head table. Braziers were positioned before the beams, their heat warming the fifty or so occupants as they talked excitedly amongst each other, the topic of their conversation, as well as the direction of their many unveiled glances, clearly the king's table. Huge iron chandeliers hung above the tables, many lit lanterns hanging from each casting a warm glow throughout the room.

It had been a week since the battle at the bridge and Maltheil's defeat. When the group had entered the gate, Maltheil's servants had attacked the defenders of the bridge. Luckily for the Red Guard cavalry, the fight against Maltheil was not prolonged, and as soon as the demon was slain by Peron all of the beast's servants collapsed dead. The fight had been brutal however. They had lost nearly five hundred warriors on the bridge as many of the demon-spawn had scurried along its underside to attack from the flanks as well as the men beyond. Atticus's body had been moved off the bridge away from the fighting to be healed. Soon thereafter, a gate had opened next to the druid as the blue energy from the shattered stone sought his mate. Then Peron and the others followed. Most were badly injured; beaten, bruised, burned, tired, and bleeding. The healers, once done with Atticus, turned their attention to the others.

A guard stepped from the shadows behind the king's table, which was unoccupied, and raised a horn to his lips. He blew it, one long note, followed by two short, and ending with another slightly longer than the first. Instantly the crowd of dignitaries and nobles quieted as the guard stepped away. The floor was raised in such a way that no one below could view the area beyond the king's table, so all they could see was Peron walk from the shadows to stand before the table, six Red Guard soldiers silently moving to the sides to flank him. He was wearing his battle armor, recently cleaned and polished. The armor was silver, lined with gold filigree that expertly adorned every edge. A splendid red cape lined in white fur hung from his shoulder. He wore no sword; his own had been left in the head of the demon. The crown of Lanard kings rested on his head and as Peron stepped before his people he smiled warmly.

"Demon Slayer!" someone yelled in the crowd and the silence was instantly filled with the roar of applause and whistles. Peron shook his head and smiled, raising his hand to silence the boisterous crowd. He was not comfortable before them, not at all. Nor was he comfortable with his new title, *Demon Slayer*, which seemed to find his ear wherever he went since the defeat of Maltheil. Peron didn't think of himself as the hero. It was the brave men that followed the beast into the fiery pits that should be honored with that title, not him. Not to mention the soldiers that fought on the bridge that had no idea what was going to happen, fighting for their lives and hoping that Maltheil would be killed, ending the power of demon-spawn army in the process. It may have been his sword that had finally killed the demon, but it was not he that faced the creature alone in the dark, injuring it until it was weak and feeble. He had snuck up behind the injured beast and rammed his blade into the demon's head while the others had fought it face to face. *Stop it*, Peron admonished himself. *Stop second guessing yourself. You are king now, act like it, think like it. True, you did not fight the beast one on one, but you did jump through the gate, and you did act when it was required of you. Give yourself some credit.* One thing Peron learned over the last month was that he needed to fight off his insecurities if he was going to rule. His people needed him, and they needed a confident king. He was definitely going to take Lord Anteel's council and not let on when he had no idea what he was doing.

"Ladies and gentlemen, Lords and Ladies, welcome," Peron said, his voice loud and clear despite the nervousness racing through him. "We are here tonight to celebrate our victory." There was an immediate outcry of applause as the richly dressed dignitaries clapped and banged their fists on the wood tables. Peron raised his hand again and everyone went silent. "Maltheil is dead, no longer a threat to us, and the Tur'el army is scattered and defeated, our vindication of their treachery!" Again there was huge applause.

Thinking of Kylin, he glanced down at the table to his right. There sat the lords that made up the council, and their wives, as well as General Sig Moore. Next to him was Kylin, dressed in a luxurious white gown, the milky white skin of her neck adorned with sparkling diamonds on a silver chain. Her hair was pulled back and held in place with silver clips decorated with vibrant diamonds. She smiled at him. He did know not what was going to happen to her, and he felt for her, as she was now a guest in an enemy kingdom. Few knew who she really was, and they had all decided to keep it that way. Her plans were unknown to him, but for now she had agreed to stay, at least for the event.

"Maltheil caused great pain to many, and the suffering endured by that beast will not be forgotten. As we celebrate, bodies are buried, men and women who were killed by the demon and its servants. Tonight, we eat and drink to them!" This time the applause was deafening, the hoots and hollers, clapping and cheering, a cacophonous roar of excitement. Peron let it go on for a bit before raising both hands. "Let us give thanks to those who followed the beast into the fiery pits of hell," Peron continued.

"Demon Slayer!" Again the title was yelled from the crowd. Peron smiled again and lifted his hand to silence them once again. "Not me, my friends. Maltheil's death was caused by a culmination of the actions of five men, who if not for them, we would have seen our homes burned, the land turned black under Maltheil's army. Tonight we honor them. First, I would like to honor Korrin Torgard, Captain of the Red Guard, slain in combat facing Maltheil the demon."

A young man wearing the armor of a Lanard soldier stepped through the massive set of double doors at the far end of the hall. He was young, maybe twenty winters, with dark hair cut short above his ears. His face was set as he moved briskly across the hall, following the red carpet to the base of the stairs.

"To accept the kingdom's honor in his stead is Tybol Torgard, son of Korrin, member of the Lanard infantry!" The hall exploded in applause as the young warrior walked the steps, stopping on the last rise before the top, just below Peron. A Red Guard soldier stepped from the shadows and held a red stained wood box before the king, opening the lid. Peron removed a necklace, a gold medallion hanging from the end. "For your father's act of bravery, and his dedication to Lanard, I give you the King's Seal, the highest medal of honor awarded in our lands. Keep it with pride." Peron draped it around the young man's neck and handed him the beautiful wood box.

Tybol held the medal in his shaking hands. Then he looked up at Peron. He was nervous, and his expression showed it. "Thank you, my King," he said softly.

Peron winked at him. "Don't worry, I'm nervous as well," he whispered back. The young man smiled. "Now, take your seat of honor." Tybol walked around and sat on the edge of the king's table.

"Next is Bearit Foehym, one of our very own, a logger from Lanard, and now a slayer of demons and a Red Guard recruit!" The crowd roared again, the fact that Bearit was from Lanard somehow adding to the already deafening applause.

Bearit walked through the doors, following Tybol's path. He was wearing his armor, his big silver battle axe strapped to his broad back. He wore immaculate but simple clothes, a soft spun black cotton jerkin and matching leggings, contrasting nicely with two red sashes wrapped around his wrists marking him as a Red Guard recruit. Bearit walked proudly before Peron, stopping two steps from the top, his huge frame nearly blocking Peron's like an eclipsing moon.

"Bearit of Lanard!" Peron began as the guard brought another box to him. "I give you the King's Seal. Keep it with pride, and remember, we are forever in your debt!" He removed the medal and draped it over Bearit's thick neck.

Bearit smiled. "Thank you, my King." Peron nodded and motioned for him to take his seat behind him. Bearit walked to the other side, sitting on the opposite end of the table.

"Now!" Peron continued. "I want to introduce to you all my friend, son of Baylock Reen, demon slayer, and now Captain of the Red Guard, Tyril Reen!" The crowd went crazy, the vociferous applause even louder than before.

Tyril, his armor buffed and polished, walked confidently down the long aisle. The Red Guard sash was tied at his waist and a plush red cape fluttered behind him.

"Never before has there been one so young to be Captain!" Peron yelled. The crowd continued to cheer as Tyril made his way to stand before Peron. He looked up and smiled.

"Having fun?" he whispered.

"No," Peron shot back, his voice just a murmur.

"You're doing great."

Peron sighed, giving Tyril a waning smile. Then he looked up, his demeanor kingly once again. "Tyril Reen, I give you the King's Seal! Wear it with pride for your actions, and your father's, who died defending his country against overwhelming odds!" Another box was given to Peron and he hung the award around Tyril's neck as the crowd continued the rambunctious applause. Then he placed his hand on Tyril's shoulder, leaning in closely. "Thank you, my friend."

Tyril nodded, "I'm lucky to be your friend, but more importantly, I'm proud you are my king. And I owe you my thanks. I would not be standing here now if you had not found the courage to follow us into that dark place. You killed Maltheil. Never again doubt your abilities."

Peron smiled thankfully as Tyril walked away, making his way to sit beside Bearit, one seat closer to Peron's, whose large wood chair sat in the middle. "Ladies and gentleman!" Peron continued. "We have two more awards to give, and to two humble warriors who would have left without your knowledge of their deeds! I could not allow that, and they, after much kingly groveling, decided to stay for the event!" Many of the guests laughed and the energy was palpable, the story of Atticus and Jonas already told from soldiers to men and women throughout Lanard. Everyone was eager to see the two warriors. "Without their help, I'm afraid the outcome would have been dire indeed!" Peron paused as the room grew silent. "We owe them everything," Peron continued, his voice lowering as the silent anticipation built. "With the help from the men behind me, they fought and killed Maltheil. They protected our land, and the kingdoms beyond. I present to you, Atticus Belthar, Druid, Protector of the Lasur'een Forest, Demon Slayer, Champion of the Sanga's Light. And," Peron added quickly, holding up his hand for continued silence. "Jonas Kanrene, Shadow Knight to Shyann, Defender of the Righteous, Giant Killer, Destroyer of Demons, Dragon Slayer, Hero of Malbeck's Wars, and Harbinger of the Light!"

The doors swung open again and Jonas and Atticus entered, followed by an explosion of applause that set the chandeliers to shaking. Everyone stood and clapped, yelling their applause, together the noise was thunderous. There was no lessening of the praise until they ascended the steps to stand just below Peron.

Tulari walked next to Jonas and sat by his leg, looking up at Peron. People had heard rumors of Jonas's battle wolf, but now, when they looked upon her, she looked nothing like the stories had portrayed her. Her gray and white fur was clean and her dog-like size not threatening in the least bit. Jonas wore his typical black clothing and armor, all now clean of dirt, grime and blood. His clothing, all enchanted by Shyann, never looked worn out or damaged. It always looked the same, innocuous in appearance in every way. He wore his swords but kept his bow in his room, figuring it would not be needed for dinner.

Atticus wore a clean forest green jerkin lined in gold over his silver chainmail. His leggings and boots were plain and simple, the clothes of a ranger. His sword and hunting knife hung at his hip and his long wavy dirty blonde hair bounced with every step. His smile was infectious and more than one noble lady returned it with her own, blushed cheeks and giggles following.

Several soldiers came forward with two boxes, their lids open. Peron raised his hands and finally the crowd quieted. "Jonas Kanrene, Atticus Belthar, we grant you the King's Seal!" he said as he removed the medal one at a time and placed it around their necks. "Please keep it in remembrance of all that you have done! Every time you look at it, remember, there is a kingdom grateful for your actions!" The crowd roared again, the sound just as ear-splitting as before. Peron raised his hands again and reluctantly the noise dropped to a tolerable buzz. "There is one more gift I would like to honor you with!" Peron reached into pouch at his side and withdrew two rings. "I bestow upon you the king's signet ring, with all the power accompanying its seal!" And yet again, the crowd responded, cheering and clapping as Peron handed them each the ring.

Atticus smiled and winked at Peron. "Well done, my boy," he said over the noisy accolade. "Oh, and just for future reference, I've killed a dragon as well." His roguish smiled returned as he moved to the table to sit next to Korrin's son.

Jonas's smile was more subdued, but equally warm. "You will make a fine king," he said, leaning closer. "*Harbinger of Light*?" he added, his eyebrows raised with a playful smile.

Peron shrugged. "I thought it fitting," he replied, smiling back.

Jonas walked around Peron, with Tulari at his side. *Perhaps you are right,* Jonas thought, as he sat next to Bearit, smiling at the young man as Peron stood before his cheering and adoring crowd.

***

Jonas was up the next morning, the sun barely noticeable as the darkness of night still dominated the countryside. He had said his goodbyes the night before and wanted to be on the road when the sun rose. He was a loner now, his life poignantly marked with sojourn after sojourn. The crowds, the praise and conversation the night before, all feeling like a rock in his boot. He had a hard time enjoying it. He wasn't sure why. Perhaps he knew it was temporary for him, short lived, a preclude to more violence and death. Or maybe it was because he knew as he sat and ate food fit for a king that somewhere out there, was somebody who required his help...a young boy or girl that needed saving, or a man or women that needed to be prodded in the right direction or they would become the very thing he fought against. There was too much to do, too many people to help.

"I knew you would be leaving early."

Jonas turned from the main gate, the entrance just opened by the guards once they saw who he was. Bearit stood in the shadows, stepping towards him. "You been there long?" Jonas asked.

Bearit shrugged. "Like I said, I knew you would be leaving."

"It's time."

Bearit glanced at Tulari. "You have a calling?"

Tulari growled in response, coming up to lick Bearit's hand. Jonas smiled. "Yes. I will always have a calling." He sounded more melancholy than he meant to.

"I wanted to say goodbye," Bearit said, stepping closer with a raised hand. "To thank you once again for all you have done for me."

Jonas shook it in the warrior's grip, marveling again at the logger's powerful forearms. "As I said before, you are welcome. Be strong, my friend. We need those, like you, strong in mind and body, who are willing to stand up to the darkness."

"You have my word, Jonas," Bearit said. "I will become that man."

Jonas smiled and turned away from him, striding towards the gloomy dawning light beyond the gate. He stopped and looked back, his face serious. "You already are." Then he walked into the darkness, Tulari's white fur turning to gray, their forms receding into the waning shadows.

THE END

About the Author

Jason McWhirter has been a history teacher for twenty one years. He lives in Washington with his wife, Jodi, and their dog, Meadow. He is a certifiable fantasy freak who, when he wasn't playing sports, spent his childhood days immersed in books and games of fantasy. He'd tumble into bed at night with visions of heroes, dragons, and creatures of other worlds, fueling his imagination and spurring his desire to create fantasies of his own. When he isn't fly fishing the lakes and streams of the Northwest, or wine tasting and entertaining with his wife and friends, he spends his spare time sitting in front of the computer writing his next novel or screenplay.

Check out McWhirter's Steel Lord Series....

In this extraordinary new fantasy epic, Jason L McWhirter, author of the Cavalier Trilogy, leads readers into a world where the fate of a land, of a people, rests in the hands of two young men, one an untried prince, the other a scarred fighter forged from a life of violence. Can they save the lands from its new threat, a violent race far from the west, whose goal is to subjugate the people under the shadow of a new god, Heln?

Look for them on Amazon and Barnes and Noble!

Looking for something fantastic to read?

The Life of Ely is Jason L. McWhirter's first non-fantasy book. Twenty one years in the classroom as a teacher and coach has given him a unique perspective on the trials and tribulations that some students experience as they attempt to survive their adolescence. This story, although fiction, is inspired by these experiences.

Look for it on Amazon and Barnes and Noble!

www.ingramcontent.com/pod-product-compliance
Lightning Source LLC
Chambersburg PA
CBHW071110250626
47159CB00002B/680